Matthew Feldman

Falsifying Beckett

Essays on Archives, Philosophy, and Methodology in Beckett Studies

With a foreword by Erik Tonning

Matthew Feldman

FALSIFYING BECKETT

Essays on Archives, Philosophy, and Methodology in Beckett Studies

With a foreword by Erik Tonning

ibidem-Verlag
Stuttgart

Bibliografische Information der Deutschen Nationalbibliothek
Die Deutsche Nationalbibliothek verzeichnet diese Publikation in der
Deutschen Nationalbibliografie; detaillierte bibliografische Daten sind
im Internet über http://dnb.d-nb.de abrufbar.

Bibliographic information published by the Deutsche Nationalbibliothek
Die Deutsche Nationalbibliothek lists this publication in the Deutsche
Nationalbibliografie; detailed bibliographic data are available in the Internet at
http://dnb.d-nb.de.

Cover illustration: navaneethks / openclipart

∞

Gedruckt auf alterungsbeständigem, säurefreien Papier
Printed on acid-free paper

ISBN-13: 978-3-8382-0636-3

© *ibidem*-Verlag
Stuttgart 2015

Alle Rechte vorbehalten

Das Werk einschließlich aller seiner Teile ist urheberrechtlich geschützt. Jede
Verwertung außerhalb der engen Grenzen des Urheberrechtsgesetzes ist ohne
Zustimmung des Verlages unzulässig und strafbar. Dies gilt insbesondere für
Vervielfältigungen, Übersetzungen, Mikroverfilmungen und
elektronische Speicherformen sowie die Einspeicherung
und Verarbeitung in elektronischen Systemen.

All rights reserved. No part of this publication may be reproduced, stored in or introduced into a
retrieval system, or transmitted, in any form, or by any means (electronical, mechanical,
photocopying, recording or otherwise) without the prior written permission of the publisher. Any
person who does any unauthorized act in relation to this publication may be liable to criminal
prosecution and civil claims for damages.

Printed in the EU

*For Steven Matthews
mentor, mate, and
uncursed progenitor*

TABLE OF CONTENTS

Preface and Acknowledgements 9

Foreword by Professor Erik Tonning 13

Introduction 19

Part I: Methodology and Interpretation

1. "I inquired into myself": Beckett, Interpretation. Phenomenology? (2002) 39

2. Beckett and Popper, Or, "What stink of artifice": Some Notes on Methodology, Falsifiability, and Criticism in Beckett Studies (2006) 59

3. Beckett and Philosophy, 1928–1938: A Falsifiable Reappraisal (2012) 75

4. Beckett and Philosophy (2013) 89

Part II: Archives and Falsifiability

5. "Agnostic Quietism" and Samuel Beckett's Early Development (2009) 105

6. Beckett's Poss and the Dog's Dinner: An Empirical Survey of the 1930s "Psychology" and "Philosophy Notes" (2005) 129

7. Beckett and the BBC Radio Revisited (2014) 153

8. Beckett's Trilogy on the Third Programme (2014) 173

Part III: Archival Criticism and Beckett's Interwar Philosophical Note-taking

9. Samuel Beckett, Wilhelm Windelband and the interwar "Philosophy Notes" (2011) 191

10. Samuel Beckett, Wilhelm Windelband and nominalist philosophy (2011) . 211

11. A "suitable engine of destruction"? Samuel Beckett and Arnold Geulincx's *Ethics* (2009) 235

12. "But what was this pursuit of meaning, in this indifference to meaning?": Beckett, Husserl, Sartre and "Meaning Creation" (2009) 255

Bibliography 281

Index 303

PREFACE AND ACKNOWLEDGEMENTS

The friends and colleagues made in Beckett studies this century have truly been a blessing. Yet the hand that giveth over the last generation has also taken away. Julie Campbell, Suzanne Dow and Seán Lawlor, amongst others, died in recent years, and are dearly missed. They, as well as my several other Beckettians struggling with poor health of late, remain prominent in mind and heart. For happier reasons, so too my wonderful fiancé's family, who provided me the shelter, warmth and love in Oxford needed to complete this volume; and to Aristotle Kallis, Gregory Maertz and Dan Stone, whose scholarly advice and collaboration continues to be of great value for me. Mary Bryden has been a revelation, offering just the right reassurance at perfectly-placed moments. Rónán McDonald's support for my work has also been tremendous, as have his antipodean colleagues, from Mark Byron and Chris Ackerley's hospitality and friendship to the brilliant academic hosts Alex Howard, Julian Murphet, Holly Phillips, Sean Pryor and Octavian Saiu.

Closer to home, Oxford-based scholars have been made to suffer a great deal of discussion on the issues raised in this book. For their patience and suggestions regarding parts of this collection, I am grateful to Ron Bush, Anna Castriota, Tom Crook, Finn Fordham, Kevin Ireland, Henry Mead, Pablo Mukherjee, Cathryn Setz, Janet Wilson, and René Wolf. For more specific discussion of matters Beckettian, I am also grateful to speakers and participants of the decade-long *Samuel Beckett: Debts and Legacies* seminar. David Addyman has been a valued collaborator—and thankfully transplanted-Yorkshireman down South—my favourite and most didactic chapter to write in this collection was our co-authored text on Wilhelm Windelband's anti-nominalism. David Tucker's willingness to read versions of the introduction and make incisive comments helped at a critical time, as did his encouragement and comradeship more generally. This goes for Erik Tonning too, who has been the best academic partner any scholar could hope for: generous and scrupulous; full of ideas and energy; hard-working and far-sighted; but above all, always a source of insightful readings of modernism, and a major brain on Beckett's work.

Still others working on Beckett have improved this work in a variety of ways, and a name-check does no justice to the kindness these colleagues have continued to show me over the years: Verity Andrews, David Avital, Iain Bailey, Elizabeth Barry, Edward Beckett, Marco Bernini, John Bolin, Peter Boxall, Enoch Brater, Llewellyn Brown, Conor Carville, Daniela Caselli, Colleen Coalter, John Coffey, Steve Connor, Rick De-Villiers, Nicolas Doutey, Christian Egners, Matthijs Engelberts, Lotta Einarsson, Peter Fifield, Julian Garforth, Stan Gontarski, Alexander Gungov, Trish Hayes, Jonathan Heron, Jennifer Jeffers, Nicholas Johnson, Pavneet Kaur, Seán Kennedy, Rina Kim, James Knowlson, Doireann Lalor, Catherine Laws, Geert Lernout, Claire Lozier, Karim Mamdani, Alys Moody, Catherine Morley, Peter Murphy, Mark Nixon, Lois Oppenheim, Lois Overbeck, Marjorie Perloff, John Pilling, Rosemary Pountney, Bill Prosser, Jean-Michel Rabaté, Stefano Rosignoli, Laura Salisbury, Russell Smith, Paul Stewart, Ashley Taggart, Yoshiki Tajiri, Anthony Uhlmann, Pim Verhulst, Dirk van Hulle, Martin Wilson, Katherine Weiss, Shane Weller, Kathryn White, and Andy Wimbush. Anyone that has been left out can simply place the blame this upon volume's dedicant, Steven Matthews, who stirred me into this poss in the first place.

The team at ibidem-Verlag, finally, have enthusiastically supported this collection from the start, and I am especially grateful to Christian Schön, Florian Bölter, and Valerie Lange for their consistent enthusiasm and trouble-shooting, but also for their patience and understanding at various points. Without them, the hurdles facing this collection may well have been insurmountable. That goes equally for the copy-editing necessary to turn disparately formatted chapters into a book, which was undertaken professionally, efficiently and intelligently by Anna Pivovarchuk. She sweated this volume into shape and played a major role in helping to fashion a whole from various parts. However, despite her—and many others'—assistance with this project, any mistakes in the text to follow are solely my responsibility.

Oxford, England
February 2015

Both author and editor of *Falsifying Beckett* would like to express our gratitude to the following for their timely and generous permissions to re-publish the slightly revised chapters collected here:

To Koninklijke Brill for permissions to reprint chapters 1, 2, 3, and 8:

'"I inquired into myself": Beckett, Interpretation. Phenomenology?'. in *Pastiches, Parodies & Other Imitations/Pastiches, Parodies & Autres Imitations*, eds. Marius Buning, Matthijs Engelberts, and Sjef Houppermans, *Samuel Beckett Today/Aujourd'hui* 12 (2002), pp. 215–234

'Beckett and Popper, Or, "What Stink of Artifice": Some Notes on Methodology, Falsifiability, and Criticism in Beckett Studies', in *Notes diverse holo*, eds. Matthijs Engelberts and Everett Frost, with Jane Maxwell, *Samuel Beckett Today/Aujourd'hui* 16 (2006), pp. 373–391

'Beckett and Philosophy, 1928–1938: A Falsifiable Reappraisal', in *Samuel Beckett: Debts and Legacies*, eds. Erik Tonning, Matthew Feldman, Matthijs Engelberts, and Dirk Van Hulle, *Samuel Beckett Today/Aujourd'hui* 22 (2010), pp. 163–180

'Beckett's Trilogy on the Third Programme', in *Revisiting the Trilogy*, eds. David Tucker, Mark Nixon, and Dirk van Hulle, *Samuel Beckett Today/Aujourd'hui* 26 (2014), pp. 41–62

To Edinburgh University Press to reprint chapters 4 and 6:

'Beckett and Philosophy', in *The Edinburgh Companion to Samuel Beckett and the Arts*, ed. S.E. Gontarski (Edinburgh: Edinburgh University Press, 2013), pp. 333–344

'Beckett's Poss and the Dog's Dinner: An empirical survey of 1930s "Philosophy" and "Psychology Notes"', in *Beckett the European* Special Issue, ed. Dirk van Hulle, *Journal of Beckett Studies* 13/2 (2005), pp. 69–94

To Palgrave for permission to reprint chapter 5:

'"Agnostic Quietism" and Samuel Beckett's Early Development', in *Samuel Beckett: History, Memory, Archive*, eds. Seán Kennedy and Katherine Weiss (Basingstoke: Palgrave, 2009), pp. 183–200

To the Beckett International Foundation for permission to reprint chapter 7:

'Beckett and the BBC Radio Revisited', in *On in their company: Essays on Beckett, with Tributes and Sketches*, eds. Mark Nixon and John Pilling (Reading, Beckett International Foundation, 2015), pp. 163–180

To The Johns Hopkins University Press for permission to reprint chapter 9:

(co-authored with David Addyman) 'Samuel Beckett, Wilhelm Windelband and the interwar "Philosophy Notes"', copyright © 2012 The Johns Hopkins University Press. First published in 'Samuel Beckett: Out of the Archive', eds. Peter Fifield, Bryan Radley, and Lawrence Rainey, *Modernism/Modernity* 18/3–4 (2012), pp. 755–770. Reprinted with permission by Johns Hopkins University Press.

To Sofia University Press for permission to reprint chapter 10:

'Samuel Beckett, Wilhelm Windelband and nominalist philosophy', in *Beckett/Philosophy* Special Issue, eds. Matthew Feldman and Karim Mamdani, *Sofia Philosophical Review* 5/1 (2011), pp. 123–155

To Bloomsbury Academic for permission to reprint chapters 11 and 12:

'A "suitable engine of destruction"? Samuel Beckett and Arnold Geulincx's *Ethics*', in *Beckett and Ethics*, ed. Russell Smith (London: Continuum, 2009), pp. 38–56. © Matthew Feldman, reprinted by permission of Bloomsbury Publishing PLC.

'"But what was this pursuit of meaning, in this indifference to meaning?": Beckett, Husserl, Sartre and "Meaning Creation"', in *Beckett and Phenomenology*, eds. Ulrika Maude and Matthew Feldman (London: Continuum, 2009), pp. 13–38. © Matthew Feldman, reprinted by permission of Bloomsbury Publishing PLC.

FOREWORD:
Feldman 'After Feldman'

Professor Erik Tonning

In 2006, Steven Connor endorsed Matthew Feldman's first monograph *Beckett's Books: A Cultural History of Samuel Beckett's 'Interwar Notes'* in prescient terms:

> Feldman's study of Beckett is the first to take the measure of the huge hoard of unpublished notebook material that has become available to scholars in the last few years. For the first time, Beckett's voracious reading in philosophy and psychology during the crucial period of the 1930s is fully documented [....] By teaching us to read as Beckett himself read, Feldman enables us to read him anew. The effect of this work will be seismic. From now on, Beckett studies will have to be dated 'AF'—After Feldman.

Connor's playful designation 'AF' foresees a shift in the discipline of Beckett studies that has indeed occurred: it is now very difficult, given the amount of documentation in the public domain about precisely what Beckett was reading and when, for scholars to shirk the task of building any assertion about what Beckett 'must have read' (and when he read it) upon empirical evidence. Furthermore, if scholars today wish to use a particular theoretical approach as a key to Beckett's texts, they are faced with the task of trying to reconcile the assumptions of that approach with Beckett's known philosophical preferences, from the pre-Socratics to Schopenhauer and beyond. Thus Feldman's advocacy of the principle of 'theorising from a position of empirical strength', using Karl Popper's methodological principle of aiming for testable, 'falsifiable' assertions, has enforced a vital new precision in the discussion of Beckett's reading and influences. The onus is now on any scholar who disagrees with that principle to make a case for an alternative approach. In one sense, this state of affairs in Beckett studies could just as well be labelled 'AK', for it was James Knowlson's unprecedentedly detailed documentation of Beckett's life and sources in his 1996 biography *Damned to Fame* that blazed the trail for the following decades of Beckett scholarship. Nonetheless, 'AF' is a more provocative designation, for Feldman quite explicitly throws down the methodological gauntlet in arguing that the tools of responsible historiography are indispensable aids to literary criticism generally, and Beckett studies in particular. In fact, as the essay 'Beckett's Poss and the Dog's Dinner' (chapter 6 in this collection) argues, Beckett's famous obsession with scepticism, ignorance, and the failure of reason and its categories, is a dish (like Watt's 'poss') made from specific and largely traceable philosophical ingredients: for Beckett needed knowledge *in order to* write 'ignorance' and 'failure'. Accordingly, any approach that tries to come to grips with Beckett's characteristic concerns without first examining the genesis and details of his philosophical development is on Feldman's reading bound to remain several steps behind Beckett himself.

But this methodological attic clearing, however indispensable, is only one aspect of Feldman's approach to Beckett. As Connor's comment also hints, Feldman has a historian's passion for accurate dating—and a historian's rich sense of the *significance* of chronologies and the archival documentation needed to establish them. 'Dating' is in fact key to Feldman's own theorising: and it makes this new collection of mostly post-2006 essays crackle with incident and surprise. It is my privilege, as a close collaborator of Feldman's since 2005, and as an enthusiastic reader of his work, to offer some impressions of his critical approaches in this fascinating new collection.

Consider, for example, Feldman's treatment (chapter 11) of Beckett's decisive turn towards Arnold Geulincx's works (making detailed notes on the original Latin) in January 1936 as he was struggling to finish the novel *Murphy*. Here, Feldman finds not just a quarry of quotations directly incorporated into Beckett's novel, but a first encounter with lifelong themes: the virtue of Humility as *contemptus negativus sui ipsus* [negative disregard of self], and a philosophical elaboration of an attitude that Feldman elsewhere (chapter 5) fleshes out as 'agnostic quietism', involving submission to human powerlessness and ignorance. Paradoxically, as Feldman goes on to demonstrate, such 'knowledge of ignorance' becomes a crucial spur to composition for Beckett, especially from the novel *Watt* onwards.

A further significant date emerges in '"But what was this pursuit of meaning, in this indifference to meaning?": Beckett, Husserl, Sartre and "Meaning Creation"' (chapter 12), where Feldman shows how Beckett's interest in Jean-Paul Sartre—initially sparked by a reading of *La Nausée* in May 1938—was further fuelled by his subsequent reading that same year of *L'Imagination* (1936), Sartre's reworked École thesis on the founder of Phenomenology, Edmund Husserl. At this point, Feldman makes the startling (risky, falsifiable) claim that this engagement with Husserl-and-Sartre marks the endpoint of Beckett's *systematic* engagement with Western philosophy, by way of yet another angle on the 'subject-object' divide that had preoccupied him so intensely throughout the 1930s. After this, Feldman claims, he mostly returned to past notes and conceptions. It is, therefore, not the later 'existentialist' Sartre, but the 1930s 'phenomenological'

Sartre that makes a fundamental impact on Beckett's fiction—again starting from the pivotal *Watt* onwards.

Feldman's flair for the telling date is also evident in his recent exploration of another neglected archival corpus: the Beckett files in the BBC Written Archives at Caversham (see chapters 7 and 8). These files reveal a creative engagement with radio that extended well beyond even Beckett's much celebrated and discussed works for that medium. Feldman uncovers a broader interaction with the Third Programme that included multiple adaptations of *The Beckett Trilogy* of novels, *Molloy*, *Malone Meurt/Malone Dies* and *L'Innommable/The Unnamable* between late 1957 and early 1959. It was, of course, *L'Innommable* that made Beckett feel as though he had written himself into a corner—after its completion in 1949, he was unable to produce another sustained prose work until the highly 'aural' text *Comment c'est/How It Is*, begun in December 1958 and finally completed in January 1960. Feldman's suggestion, then, is that examining Beckett's return to these key earlier works through adapting them as 'radiogenic' texts sheds new light on a crucial transition in Beckett's creative development.

These examples bring us closer to the characteristic originality of a Feldman essay: its interventions are dateable, precise, provocative and consequential; its hypotheses aim for a risky falsifiability, making evidence-based assertions that are intended to be open to challenge and refinement; and it is consistently based around genuine and often extensive archival discoveries. In this way, as Connor aptly put it, Feldman teaches us to 'read as Beckett himself read'.

One surprising way in which this is true about Beckett's philosophical reading is demonstrated in the two essays on Beckett and Wilhelm Windelband (chapters 9 and 10; the former co-authored with David Addyman). A particular strength of *Beckett's Books* was Feldman's documentation of the extent to which Beckett relied on secondary literature—surveys or anthologies rather than primary texts—in his philosophical and psychological reading. One telling coup here was his demotion of the previously-unquestioned centrality of Descartes to Beckett's thought; for Beckett did not read as widely in this philosopher as had been assumed, but instead relied on the 1892 *Choix de Textes*. This hammered home the necessity of close attention to the actual editions Beckett used, and to his extant marginalia and notes. The essays on Windelband build on this strain of Feldman's previous work, now training the focus explicitly on Windelband himself as a creative influence on Beckett. After all, Beckett's corpus of notes on Windelband's two-volume *History of Philosophy* is the most extensive he ever produced.

But to 'read as Beckett read' using the evidence of these notes is no straightforward matter. To be sure, Beckett does insert the odd subjective intervention into his summaries of Windelband's text, but they are few and far between. It is, however, clear that Beckett encountered many schools and philosophers that would directly impact his work for the first time through Windelband: such as the pre-Socratics, nominalism, Arnold Geulincx, and Baruch Spinoza. In a remarkable number of cases, the allusions to these and other philosophers in Beckett's work are taken directly from Windelband's text. This is all the more significant because we know that Beckett went back to these notes much later on; for instance explaining the 'Old Greek' in *Endgame* to the director Alan Schneider with reference to his 'notes on the pre-Socratics'. But as we have seen with Geulincx, there were also cases where Beckett decided to further engage with the primary texts after a crucial first encounter through Windelband. Nor does this exhaust Windelband's impact: Feldman further argues that the very scope and sweep of Windelband's history gave Beckett a vantage-point on the whole systematic enterprise of philosophy—and thereby the tools to question and erode the edifice as a whole. But at this point, the ironies and tensions in Beckett's approach to Windelband begin to emerge. Chapter 10 focuses on Beckett's fascination with nominalism, a school that Windelband himself deplored, but that Beckett would explore further—ultimately through Fritz Mauthner's Pyrrhonian 'critique of language' that questions philosophical nomenclature as such. In the co-authored chapter 9, the analysis of this tension is carried further, through a closer examination of Beckett's implicit and explicit responses to Windelband in his notes. In appropriately Beckettian fashion, this response is mediated via notable absences, for Windelband's individual philosophical voice is often silenced or distorted by Beckett. Both these chapters are valuable for their stress on the degree of detailed and specific attention necessary to fully account for Beckett's reading practices and his creative deployment of what he read.

This present collection also shows us Feldman 'After Feldman' in a different sense: for in essays like the Sartre/Husserl (chapter 12), the Geulincx (chapter 11) and the 'agnostic quietism' (chapter 5) already mentioned, as well as in the insightful piece subtitled 'Beckett, Interpretation. Phenomenology?' (chapter 1), some of the motivating concerns behind Feldman's approach to Beckett are on clearer display than in his first monograph. For one thing, the ethical stance Feldman finds in Beckett also serves as an inspiration for Feldman's own ethics of reading Beckett. Feldman's Beckett adopts humility, agnosticism, quietism and doubt precisely as creative, paradoxical modes of *proceeding*: echoing the 'no' that inverts to an 'on' in Beckett's texts. In fact, Feldman's emphasis on the tentative, stepwise, fumbling, risky, but revelatory method of 'falsifiability' is not unrelated to such an attitude. Moreover, in chapter 1, Feldman proposes a theoretical move back to Husserlian doubt for Beckett criticism: for Husserl's 'perhaps' also hints at a tentative affirmation, and an irreducible, niggling, residual 'astonishment that the world exists'. This would be a move backward to the grandfather of both existentialism and post-structuralism, whose offspring may, on Feldman's reading, have betrayed some of Husserl's most fruitful insights. With Husserl's account of 'intentional' acts of consciousness (uncertainly straddling the 'subject-object' divide) clearly in mind, Feldman defines the 'fundamental nexus' at the heart of Beckett's writing thus:

> Acceptance of failure, submission to obligation, expressing the inexpressible; these are the unlikely tools with which Samuel Beckett whittles the square peg of sense-making into a spherical shape, not in order to neatly fit into a circular hole of reason or comprehension but precisely to demonstrate that consciousness can only take blurred snapshots of memory and experience.

Feldman's stance throughout this volume is that 'blurred snapshots' are still worth taking, worth examining closely, worth comparing, worth adding up—and worth submitting to open-ended, intersubjective, scholarly critique. His work, then, is an invitation: Beckett scholarship 'After Feldman' may still present a characteristically bleak and bare landscape, but an open horizon beckons the explorer onwards.

Bergen, Norway
November 2014

INTRODUCTION

Every refutation should be regarded as a great success.
– Karl Popper, 'Truth, Rationality and the Growth of Knowledge'

Ever tried. Ever failed. No matter. Try Again. Fail again. Fail better.
– Samuel Beckett, *Worstword Ho*[1]

§1

The articles and book chapters brought together here were originally published between 2002 and 2015. Save for the earliest, all were marked by what has been commonly referred to as the 'archival turn' in Beckett studies. Some tendencies featuring in this return to the archives, and one of the methodological approaches proposed to help make sense of it, will be discussed presently. This introduction will then survey the texts to follow, situating these dozen parts in relation to scholarly concerns and developments that, it is hoped, make for a larger whole. As the chapters here collectively stress, Samuel Beckett's elliptical, challenging work—so worthy of archival excavation to recover his 'intent of undoing',[2] in and of itself—has called forth a bewildering array of scholarly readings.

The very opacity of Beckett's work, which is a key part of its universal relevance and force, evokes a darkened horizon that, no matter how well populated, yields few interpretative black holes. In trying to narrow this horizon of interpretation, the methodology advocated across this volume, and sketched below, can be shorthanded in the proposition: *theorising from a position of empirical accuracy is advantageous*. Drawing out advantages as they relate to Beckett's work in English follows—especially focussing upon the pivotal 1930s and late 1950s/early 1960s, in chapters reading Beckett's philosophy and psychology notes against his oeuvre. Before turning to the individual chapters, then, and '[p]ending new advice', as Beckett wrote in a long-unpublished comment piece from 1938: 'Let's get on with falsifying.'[3]

Beckett was scarcely using this term in Sir Karl Popper's ideational sense, with whom it is most identified. Popper claimed to have developed this demarcation at the other end of the interwar period, in 1919–1920 (if only publishing a generation later), 'by saying that *the criterion of the scientific status of a theory is its falsifiability, or refutability, or testability*'.[4] Though not without detractors, Popper's view remains pertinent: 'The distinguishing mark of a statement belonging to science—or, more generally, an empirical statement, is, according to Popper, its *falsifiability.*' At the core of this epistemological *via negativa* is the view that 'universal statements are not verifiable'; for 'he demanded that whosoever proposed a scientific theory should answer the question: "Under what conditions would I admit that my theory is untenable?" His idea was that "*the more a theory forbids, the more it tells us.*"[5] Popper's falsifying, then, was less a theory per se than a way of sifting competing theories. At the time, his main aim was at the scientific pretensions of Marxism and psychoanalysis, leading to the general advocacy of grounded, refutable hypotheses capable of getting closer to the truth (for Popper was no essentialist). As he observed in *Conjectures and Refutations*: 'Equating rationality with the critical attitude, we look for theories which, however fallible, progress beyond their predecessors which means they can be more severely tested, and stand up to some of the new tests.'[6]

Yet what has any of this to do with the study of literature; and more specifically, with Samuel Beckett's art? Underscored by the above epigraphs by Popper and Beckett, granted, there is little doubt that failure was a valuable resource for both writers. But in terms of written output and intellectual sensibility, they were diametrically opposed. Popper's 'critical attitude' celebrated scientific progress, while Beckett's literary judo used the weight of rationality's assumptions against itself—exemplified by *Watt's* ruminations, permutations, and (often false) computations—that I have elsewhere termed 'non-Euclidean logic'.[7] Popper valorised the systematic acquisition of knowledge; yet Beckett believed his art was founded on getting 'back to ignorance'.[8] Whatever the two men's similarities and differences, more importantly, is Popper's methodology, and the scientific register generally, not unnecessary in approaching Beckett's works; or for that matter, a kind of anathema for scholarship on modern literature? If good disciplinary fences make for good neighbours, then the language of 'tests', '*refutability*', and the growth of empirical knowledge, for many literary critics, is best left to the territory of science.

The contours of Popper's 'critical attitude' may not be applicable to artists—engaging the imagination, working creatively with objects (marble, canvas, mixed media)—but does that extend to the discipline of, say, modern literature, or the subject of Beckett studies? To put the question another way, does the scientific method for generating empirical knowledge of a given subject have any place the study of literature? In response, the avowedly interdisciplinary approach taken here emphatically suggest that the best neighbours loan and borrow across boundaries. Researching literature, all are agreed, plays a fundamental role in 'increasing human knowledge'—Popper's basic epistemological criterion. As with Beckett's work, its subject matter may dismiss—even scorn—the rational acquisition of knowledge, but that is no license for literary critics to do the same. As a self-reflexive method for making better theories, this volume maintains that the practice of falsifying leads to theories with greater explanatory power, utility and relevance.

Following Popper, the use of refutable arguments founded upon empirically established facts has as much a place in literary criticism as in the natural sciences. That these go by terms like 'interpretations', 'readings', and 'criticism' in the former rather than 'hypotheses', 'experiments' and 'equations' in the latter should not diminish the heuristic value of falsification—across every scholarly discipline: 'The critical attitude, the tradition of free discussion of theories with the aim of discovering their weak spots so that they may be improved upon, is the attitude of reasonableness, of rationality.' It is this modest restraint, this emphasis upon the provisional, halting nature of knowledge acquisition that characterises, and underwrites the utility of, falsification:

> the role of logical argument, of deductive logical reasoning, remains all-important for the critical approach; not because it allows us to prove our theories, or to infer them from observation statements, but because only by purely deductive reasoning is it possible for us to discover what our theories imply, and thus to criticize them effectively.[9]

At the same time, it should be stressed that falsifying is a *method* for improving, advancing and refining interpretations—usually one's own—not some club or rite of initiation. Nor is falsifying a club for beating down contrasting approaches, for mandating how research must be undertaken. That misses the essential humility and collaborative spirit of the Popperian enterprise. Its value, instead, is in promoting methodological rigour, reflexive theorising, and the employment of various types of primary source materials—correspondence, manuscripts and drafts, memoirs and production notes, reading notes and marginalia, and all manner of useful contextualising sources like news reports or judicial records.

§2

While having much to say to literary criticism more broadly, the principle of falsification, above all, is especially pertinent for the aforementioned 'archival turn'. Despite the close reading and poststructuralist theorising still dominant in the study of modernism, *The Oxford Handbook of Modernisms* observes that 'a general "archival turn" is nonetheless altering the shape of modernist studies'. One manner in which this is evidenced is with 'archive' as metaphor;[10] and still another, rather more productive strategy, is engagement with archives as resources. This tendency in modernist criticism, contends James Knapp, 'has regrounded much scholarly debate in the archive as a corrective to ahistorical theorizing'.[11] Finn Fordham conditionally agrees, rightly adding that 'modernist studies, since its inception, has always known of scholars turning to archives, whether for editions of letters, for biographical work, or for genetic studies'. This characterisation certainly corresponds to Beckett studies; indeed, 'The Modernist Archive's advocacy is in close keeping with the falsifying methodology outlined here:

> We are not "beyond an archival turn", but within the force of its swerve, and so we shall be for some time. This is a condition we should not only get used to, but also one we should respond to by imagining, finding out, and *testing different ways of making use of it.*[12]

Anglophone Beckett studies, in many ways, presents an exemplary case study in 'The Modernist Archive'. First of all, there is a strong tradition 'of letters, for biographical work, or for genetic studies'. The University of Reading, home to the Beckett International Foundation, had been collecting materials on Beckett since shortly after his receipt of the 1969 Nobel Prize.[13] Even before then, private collectors, friends and, increasingly, academics, publishers, and even media networks (such as the BBC in Britain and RTF in France) were amassing textual materials from, or associated with, Beckett.[14] Unusually, by the time of his death in 1989—and quite beyond his exhaustive published body of work over six decades—there was a growing body of published work that might well be described as archival: a 1967 'festschrift' of memoirs and appreciations;[15] theatrical workbooks of *Krapp's Last Tape* and *Happy Days*;[16] bibliographies,[17] and catalogues of manuscript holdings;[18] volumes of critical writings about[19] and by,[20] Beckett— there was even some early genetic criticism,[21] as well as an impressively durable biography.[22]

A decisive step change in tempo occurred in the 1990s with the publication of previously unpublished works, manuscript and theatrical notebooks, as well as letters;[23] these were crowned by James Knowlson's acclaimed biography from 1996, *Damned to Fame: The Life of Samuel Beckett*. More than any single text, the latter animated the 'archival turn' in identifying an enormous cache of drafts, manuscripts and correspondence that has since become known in Beckett studies as an unpublished 'grey canon'.[24] Exemplifying the value and surprise of these materials were Beckett's previously-unknown 'German Diaries'; six notebooks compiled during Beckett's travels in Nazi Germany—ostensibly to visit paintings in German galleries, many later banned and some even destroyed—between autumn 1936 and spring 1937.[25] Also deposited at the Reading archives after Beckett's death and made available for study early this century are the 'Interwar Notes': summaries and transcriptions from subjects ranging from reading notes on St Augustine, Dante and Goethe to historical summaries of English and German literature, Dutch art and much else besides, all engaging Beckett's dwindling academic interests across the roiling 1930s.[26] Amongst these 'Interwar Notes', Beckett's reading notes on, and from, western philosophy and psychology—alongside falsifiable arguments about their subsequent relevance to his art—are given pride of place in several of the chapters to ensue.

Additionally, more recent contributions to this 'archival turn' in Beckett studies merit briefly pausing over for two reasons. First, the majority of these texts are not referred to later on: most have appeared only in recent years. At this point it is important to note that the following chapters, while hopefully cohering as a whole, were also a product of their time—and are presented as such here. For one thing, it is hardly falsifiable to go back and silently overhaul one's texts in light of new material! Save for some re-formatting and rephrasing, the parts comprising *Falsifying Beckett* are presented (with one exception[27]) as they were written. Rather than shoe-horning in newer archival research, particularly that underwriting secondary studies, this will be instead surveyed alongside individual chapters in the following section.

Second and more significant, primary source editions released in the last few years underscore just how diverse the types of approaches in Beckett studies alone are that fall within the broad church of an 'archival turn', let alone how slippery that term is—to say nothing of modernism or English studies more widely. Consider John Pilling, a trailblazing scholar on Beckett's 'grey canon' since 1976, who has thus both predated, and been an integral part of, the 'archival turn' this century.[28] His co-edited (with the much missed Seán Lawlor) *The Collected Poems of Samuel Beckett: A Critical Edition* is a comprehensive reproduction, over some 250 pages, of Beckett's poetry in the languages in which they were originally composed, alongside more than 200 pages of appended commentary. Likewise, his analysis of the prose stories forming *More Pricks Than Kicks* combined a lengthy section of traditional close reading with annotations, publishing history and even 'An Unknown Letter' relating to Beckett's collection of stories from 1934.[29] While obviously continuing his archival research into Beckett's works, the close readings and annotations comprising the latter studies mark a notable contrast (and not a conflict, it hardly needs be said) with his 2006 *A Samuel Beckett Chronology*, which reproduces literally thousands of meticulously dated events relating to Beckett's life and work.[30] Yet even there, no matter how scientific or 'objective' Pilling's account is, key elements of interpretation are still essential; for example, the necessary inclusion of some dates rather than others. In Beckett studies alone, then, different approaches to prose and poetry over several decades *by the same scholar* only serve to underscore the methodological nuances covered by the all-encompassing term 'archival turn'.

As Popper knew only too well, key terms and demarcations are vital to place under continued scrutiny—and it may be that, in doing so, it turns out the descriptor 'archival turn' is now both too broad (does the 'archive as resource' include published work *from* archives?) and too narrow (is it *only* this century?) with respect to Beckett studies. For example, would his limited use of archives exclude the most recent biography by Andrew Gibson, which places valuable emphasis on Beckett's historical context in wartime and post-war France? Does the 'archival turn' include the chronologically arranged memoirs of *Beckett Remembering/Remembering Beckett*, edited by James and Elizabeth Knowlson; or for that matter, that of book history, exemplified by the chapters comprising the edited *Publishing Samuel Beckett*?[31] Other paradigms might extend to Chris Ackerley's paperback annotations to *Watt* in 2010, building upon his earlier annotations to *Murphy* (which did not have the falsifying benefit of the six recently catalogued 'Murphy Notebooks', now held by the University of Reading's Beckett International Foundation).[32] Surely safer categories for inclusion in an 'archival turn' are Cambridge University Press's expansively referenced selection of Beckett's letters (only those 'bearing upon his work', an undertaking at present extending to three excellent volumes, covering the years 1929–1940, 1941–1956, and 1957–1965)[33]; or again, the recent publication of the long-neglected short story, 'Echo's Bones', intended as an afterpiece to *More Pricks Than Kicks*, with Mark Nixon's detailed scholarly annotations longer than the text itself.[34]

Needless to say the above publications are all, albeit in different ways, primary source engagements with Beckett's work. Whether that work is biographical or chronological; whether engaging with handwritten letters or ledgers of book sales; and whether the undertaking is what Chris Ackerley has termed '*validity in annotation*',[35] or the more intertextual approach to reading notes and commonplace notebooks taken in the bulk of chapters below, what these approaches share is an interest in linking Beckett's published texts with evidence—frequently archival, but always empirically-underpinned—beyond its covers. That is to say, in providing historical context, examining the literary compositional process, or engaging in letter- or source-based transcription—and many more besides—this approach to criticism seeks corroboration by objects and information outside the text. This entails neither a replacement nor closing down of contrasting literary-critical readings, but instead inclines toward moving back from the published text to examine the scaffolding helping to build it. This stepping backward to different types of 'blueprints', in turn, facilitates new textual understandings—raising perspectives of influence, working methods or historical context that can often lead to redoubled advances in knowledge of the 'construction' in question. While others working with primary source materials in Beckett studies and beyond may not recognise the analogy—let alone the utility of methodological demarcation and theoretical falsifying—it seems to me that this is a key aspect of what might be called archival criticism, or even 'archivalism'.

An essential ingredient separating the above, recent tendency from a much older and better-established new historicism, in modernist studies at least, is that 'the literary canon' remains an important starting point. Whereas new historicism 'is interested in history as represented and recorded in written documents' and tends toward a 'parallel study of literature and non-literary texts', archival criticism tends toward recognised, oftentimes canonical or critically-lauded, writers.[36] Sidestepping the vicissitudes of canon formation—those 'accepted' books researched by scholars or appearing on English Literature syllabi—manuscript scholars tend to gravitate toward leading modernist authors: James Joyce, Ezra Pound, Virginia Woolf, W.B. Yeats, Mina Loy, Samuel Beckett.[37] Part of the reason is obvious: known authors frequently leave behind sizeable literary estates (sometimes, as with Kafka, even against their will!), which are then acquired by research centres like Yale's Beinecke Library. The value of primary sources—ranging from newspapers to diaries—may be shared by both approaches, yet the mediation of institutions and power relations tends to be much less an object of theorising, and indeed concern, with archival criticism. New historicism may well be 'resolutely anti-establishment'; in contrast, different types of archival work cited above are to some degree predicated upon 'the establishment' for canon formation, funding for research trips, manuscript access and even scholarly collaboration (for esoteric authors rarely have multiple scholars working on them, and their Estates and/or unpublished papers are less uniformly collected into holding libraries).

If new historicism is an ill-fitting precursor and descriptor of this recent tendency, so too is the Marxist-oriented cultural materialism. The emphasis on neglected contexts and recovering alternative histories again bears some important similarities with more recent archival criticism. Yet the latter's political commitments appear less explicit, and are often accompanied by a wariness toward grand narratives—even literary grand narratives (e.g. 'Beckett was an existentialist/psychological/ deconstructive writer').[38]

A still greater contrast stresses that cultural materialism, and its offshoot, cultural studies, 'does not limit itself to "high" cultural forms' but extends to 'forms like television and popular music and fiction'. Canonical modernist authors are precisely those '"high" cultural forms' downplayed by cultural materialism which also (like its 'American counterpart', new historicism),[39] has tended to research Shakespearean or early modern subjects—rather than those since the printing revolutions of the late nineteenth century, when books and journals started to circulate widely in an age of 'mechanical reproduction'.[40] Given their emphasis upon prior theoretical and political commitments; moreover, neither cultural materialism nor new historicism appear to place Popper's falsifying, 'critical approach' at their core.

Both movements, finally, seemed to have waned over the last generation as another essential ingredient to archival criticism continues to wax exponentially: the digital revolution. Finn Fordham has recently and rightly discerned that the latter has 'combined' with a 'historical turn' over the last generation, noting that large digitisation and preservation projects are in process (e.g. 'the Beinecke at Yale has digitized the copy it has of Conrad's *Heart of Darkness* draft').[41] So too with scholarly websites devoted to everything from reproducing modernist 'little magazines' to the University of Iowa's International Dada Archive[42]—and that is but the tip of the iceberg. Thanks to digital photography and document scanning, reproduced documents can be obtained without physically visiting a holding library or archive. An emailed request for .pdf scans uploaded to Dropbox now makes it possible to consult 'archives' on an android phone or Kindle anywhere in the world. Increased emphasis on collaboration—in shared transcriptions, photographing, and other methods—also comes to the fore. At the same time, a collapsing of geographical strictures has likewise been a good thing for archival criticism: not many scholars around the world are able to physically, let alone repeatedly, get to, say, the Beinecke archives in New Haven, Connecticut, or to the Beckett International Foundation holdings in Reading, England. A digital library of unpublished materials, available mere clicks away, has doubtless been amongst the greatest impetuses in the so-called archival turn.

In Beckett studies the different features of archival criticism sketched above have been manifestly strengthened by what might, rather more falsifyingly, be called the 'digital turn'. In again but scratching the online surface representing some of archival criticism's different forms, that of 'critique génétique' ['genetic criticism'] thrives more than most in the digital age. Most prominently, Dirk van Hulle and Mark Nixon's Beckett Digital Manuscript Project series intends to publish the pre-publication compositional evolution for all of Beckett's texts in an 'electronic part and a printed component'; the first 'module' was launched in 2011, followed by a second in 2014.[43] At a more prosaic level, digitally-scanned photographs, media commentary and events notifications are provided on 'Samuel Beckett' Facebook pages and, still more google-able, on www.samuelbeckett.net—if not exactly trending on Twitter. Specifically digitised resources range from digital recordings of many prose and dramatic works—including, impressively, 'The Voice of Samuel Beckett'[44]—to the British Library's CD/MP3 re-release of Beckett's 'radiogenic' work originally from the late 1950s and 1960s; and the variable, if better-known 'Beckett on Film' project, presenting 'all 19 plays filmed for the first time in a unique project'.[45] Online catalogues for archival holdings are now *de rigeur*, and often quite detailed; in fact, the entirely pre-digital holdings at the BBC Written Archives Centre in Caversham, England posed challenges in collecting research toward chapters 7 and 8.[46] Also directly bearing upon ensuing chapters is a last, interactive example of text and images corresponding to Beckett's 'German Diaries'; specifically, his time in Hamburg between October and December 1936—with one example describing objects and the Hamburg Kunsthall as 'a whole room of quatsch'.[47] Quatsch it may well be *but it is there*, and so Beckett went (and saw the 'degenerate artist', Ernst Barlach's, memorable expressionist Great War memorial upon leaving): so too with Beckett's 'grey canon' more generally, through which, this volume contends, archival criticism can facilitate re-interpretation in a fruitful, empirically-grounded way.

§3

The falsifying approach sketched above as archival criticism clearly has a number of overlapping, often reinforcing, modus operandi. Underpinning many of the following chapters here is source-based analysis and recovering reading traces—marginalia, notes, intertextual references, and the like—which, as per the point above, in the case of primary sources is often available online via websites like www.archive.org. To a greater or lesser degree, the essays here collectively attempt to go back to the archives in order to challenge traditional interpretations of Beckett's texts. Or rather, as noted at the outset, this is the case for final 11 chapters. By contrast the first, published halfway through my doctorate in 2002, was untouched by the nascent 'archival turn' in Beckett studies. I had not yet travelled to the Beckett archives at the University Reading—fortunately for me, only a half an hour up the road from Oxford Brookes University—which was just in the process of making the 'German Diaries' and 'Interwar Notes', amongst other portions of Beckett's 'grey canon', available for scholarly consultation. Nevertheless, '"I Inquired into Myself": Beckett, Interpretation. Phenomenology?' discerned some very different philosophical readings of Beckett's work at the turn of the century. By surveying two of these influential Beckettian 'grand narratives', existential-humanism and post-structuralism, this chapter raises some of the recurring methodological challenges posed by Beckett's literary project. An overview of some principle non-fiction and prose within Beckett's oeuvre then argues that a more consistent reading of 'Beckett and philosophy' is possible by stepping back to the shared interpretative terrain of phenomenology, as first conceived by Edmund Husserl. The first chapter in this collection thus betrays an ongoing interest in methodological approaches to Beckett's art—above all, philosophical approaches—that is subsequently taken up throughout, even if a falsifying return to unpublished documents was not yet in view for me. To the extent that phenomenological readings have since been seen as fertile interpretative territory, the 2009 edited volume *Beckett and Phenomenology* contained chapters on Beckett and Martin Heidegger; Maurice Merleau-Ponty; Jean-Paul Sartre; as well as a second section devoted to exploring a number of recurrent themes in Beckett's work via phenomenological criticism.[48]

A marked development in my working methods occurred in the ensuing years, when archivists and scholars at the University of Reading introduced me to the Beckett International Foundation's holdings. Again published by one of two Beckett studies 'house journals', *Samuel Beckett Today/Aujourd'hui*, 'Popper and Beckett: or, On Falsifiability, "What stink of Artifice"' (from 2006, chapter 2 here) was the product of reflections upon how archival work in Beckett studies could both destabilise and refine existing interpretations. In addition to hosting the first deployment of Popperian falsifying in Beckett studies, in 2008 the same journal hosted a lengthy reply by Garin Dowd, entitled 'Prolegomena to a Critique of Excavatory Reason: Reply to Matthew Feldman', immediately followed by my shorter response: 'In Defense of Empirical Knowledge: Rejoinder to "A Critique of Excavatory Reason"'.[49] Readers are strongly encouraged to read all three together. In the former, Dowd's objection was more than that of an unwelcome importation of Popper into Beckett studies, but that placement of such methodological 'guardrails' were intrinsically problematic and, in any case, unnecessarily exacting. That different epistemological priorities were at play in our exchange was clear, and my response tried to draw this point out along the lines of the following three questions:

> Are attempts at historical verification worthwhile in the study of contemporary literature?
> How do we account for conflicting theories seeking to 'explain' Beckett's work?
> What makes one theory of Beckett's art better, or having greater 'explanatory power', than another?
> Is there a difference between advancing knowledge of Beckett and his works, and advancing knowledge of a 'Beckettian' modern world?

By 2010, my attempt to put a falsifying methodology into action vis-à-vis 'Beckett and philosophy' focussed on Beckett's years of autodidactic learning between the wars. One of the major empirical finds was that Beckett was usually content to read textbooks and other 'primers' for much of his knowledge of philosophy. A derivative argument was that the core of Beckett's philosophical knowledge was developed at this time, and roughly entailed three stages. The first of these was largely using philosophy for pastiche in the Joycean mode in the late 1920s and 1930s—above all exemplified in the 1930 poem *Whoroscope* on the life of Descartes—while the second was devoted to the construction of a 100,000+ word notebook on the history of western philosophy: the 'Philosophy Notes'. By the middle of the 1930s, 'Beckett and Philosophy, 1938-1938: A Falsifiable Reappraisal' argues, Beckett had moved into a third phase of transcription from primary sources that lasted until roughly the outbreak of World War Two and, shortly thereafter, the commencement of the pivotal novel *Watt*. 'Beckett and Philosophy', the fourth and final chapter in this opening section, 'Methodology and Interpretation', contends that this archival recovery is one of two dominant modes for approaching Beckett's philosophical knowledge. In addition to working *backwards* from Beckett's published texts for falsifiable traces of philosophical intertextuality or 'scaffolding' is another method seeking to be corroborated by the published text, and thus moves interpretatively *forward*. These philosophical applications have been the hallmark of Beckett criticism since his reception started to take shape in the 1950s, particularly after the unexpected success of *En Attendant Godot/Waiting for Godot*.

Less methodologically occupied, the second section opens with a 2009 chapter originally appearing in *Samuel Beckett: History, Memory, Archive*, the first volume in Palgrave's 'New Interpretations of Samuel Beckett in the 21st Century'. '"Agnostic Quietism" and Samuel Beckett's Early Development' grapples with the elusive subject of Beckett's artistic temperament. To do so, Beckett's early reading traces are marshaled to argue that Beckett was drawn, from early on, towards a stoicism and acceptance of suffering that marked his later writings. A key theme, Schopenhauer's description of a 'veil of Maya' dividing individual perception from the Kantian 'Thing-In-Itself', was subsequently developed by Ulrich Pothast in the most expansive study to date on Beckett's relationship to Arthur Schopenhauer's philosophy.[50] Also making use of the 'Interwar Notes' chapter 6, a 2005 article from the *Journal of Beckett Studies*, attempts to trace the long-term impact of these archival materials upon Beckett's art. More than anywhere else in *Falsifying Beckett*, a critical engagement with Beckett's note-taking methods and main sources of philosophical and psychological knowledge from the 1930s concerns 'Beckett's Poss and the Dog's Dinner: An empirical survey of 1930s Philosophy and Psychology Notes'. Since these texts, the 'Philosophy Notes' have been shown to have been deployed in the composition of both *More Pricks Than Kicks and* its abortive tailpiece, 'Echo's Bones'.[51]

The final two chapters in this middle section, 'Archives and Falsifiability', represent my most recent archival research into Beckett, moving from the interwar years to the late 1950s and early 1960s. Several years ago, I came across a large corpus of Beckett files and microfilm at the BBC Written Archives Centre (WAC) in Caversham, near Reading. While well-hidden in a cavernous archive not yet digitised, texts there make clear that the BBC played a central role in Beckett's Anglophone reception. Chapter 7, 'Beckett and the BBC Radio Revisited', underpins this falsifiable contention through an overview of BBC files and microfilm materials—connecting them to several current debates in Beckett studies. In addition to his 'canonical' radiogenic works between 1957 and 1964 (*All That Fall, Embers, Words and Music, Cascando* and *Rough for Radio I* and *II*; and sometimes including his Robert Pinget translation, *The Old Tune*), for example, the BBC WAC archives document fully another 9 programmes by Beckett, and another 17 about him, during these same years. Of the 9 'adaptations' of Beckett's work—ranging from *Fin de Partie* in French to *Waiting for Godot* with a narrator!—a trio of productions stand out from the late 1950s, as recounted in chapter 8, 'Beckett's Trilogy on the Third Programme'. Adapting *The Beckett Trilogy*, above all, was a collaborative effort, one involving different BBC staff, as well as musical accompaniment by his cousin, John Beckett—and a surprising amount of latitude in the BBC's framing, presentation and sometimes unsolicited cuts of the Third Programme's newfound favourite writer. Rethinking the role the radio in Beckett's wider canon at what turns out, in retrospect, to be a critical moment for his art is only just beginning; although in the spirit of moving backward in order to progress further forward, Pim Verhulst's impressive genetic study of the radio plays shows how well-integrated this radiogenic writing was in the simultaneous composition of more well-known works from the period: *Endgame/Fin de Partie, How It Is/Comment c'est, Happy Days*, and *Play*.[52]

The final section, '"Archival Criticism" and Beckett's Interwar Philosophical Note-taking', returns to the 1930s in chapter 9, with the 2011 'Samuel Beckett, Wilhelm Windelband and the interwar "Philosophy Notes"', co-written with my colleague and friend, David Addyman. Like the subsequent chapter appearing in the same year, 'Samuel Beckett, Wilhelm Windelband and nominalist philosophy', it makes the case that nominalist philosophy, as mediated by the neo-Kantian philosopher Windelband in his two-volume *A History of Philosophy* and other works, was of a crucial significance in Beckett's works. Both this doctrine and Windelband's intellectual context are recounted across both chapters, as is Beckett's extensive engagement with the subject of nominalism. Insofar as recent archive-based research has shed light on Beckett's interest in a nominalistic (or indeed, 'terministic') successor in twentieth century philosophy, linguistic skepticism—exemplified by statements in the 'German Letter' of 1937—the subject of Mauthner continues to generate interest in Beckett studies. After confessing 'that the reading experiences which have affected me most are those that were best at sending me to that elsewhere', the first influence cited by Beckett in a revealing 1954 letter—that 'he explored for Joyce'—initially was Mauthner's *Contributions to a Critique of Language*, 'which greatly impressed me. I have often wanted to re-read it. But it seems impossible to find'.[53] A still more recent, relevant example from amongst many in the ground-breaking *Samuel Beckett's Library* finds 'more than 700 marked passages' in the margins of *Beiträge zu Einer Kritik der Sprache*.[54] That Beckett seems to have not owned a copy of Mauthner in the mid-1950s—strongly suggesting that his Mauthner notes from mid-1938 were from a borrowed edition—will fuel interest in this falsifiable case of philosophical intertextuality for years to come.

The last two essays, both published in 2009 in edited collections with Continuum (now Bloomsbury Academic), analyse different philosophical aspects of Beckett's focus in the 1930s: ethics and cognition. *Falsifying Beckett's* penultimate chapter, 'A "suitable engine of destruction"? Samuel Beckett and Arnold Geulincx's *Ethics*' addresses the former via the by-now familiar methodology of archival criticism. Front and centre in this case study is the seventeenth-century occasionalist philosopher Arnold Geulincx, recently the study of a comprehensive, empirically-grounded study of Geulingian 'ignorance' and 'impotence' deployed across Beckett's works.[55] With respect to cognition, chapter 12, '"But what was this pursuit of meaning, in this indifference to meaning?": Beckett, Husserl, Sartre and "Meaning Creation"', comes full circle to the question of phenomenological approaches to perception in Beckett's art. Moving backwards to phenomenology, then, heralded in chapter 1 as one method of advancing in Beckett studies, is now approached via a falsifying methodology in the process of refinement over the intervening chapters. This archivalism poses falsifiable argument that Beckett was struggling with properly phenomenological questions. That these riddles influenced subsequent works from *Watt* on—and no less important, can assist in interpreting this and other works across the Beckett canon—is perhaps the most important of the empirically-grounded arguments here. Just how this reading will be refuted in its turn, or better, form part of a more explanatory theory in terms of 'Beckett and philosophy' must remain an open one, in keeping with the spirit of falsifying. Yet if the Popperian principle has valuable insights to offer Beckett studies, and modernist literary criticism more broadly—not least in the wake of the 'archival turn' this century—it could do worse than taking heed (if not rejecting the maddening inductive logic) of that empathetic satire on rationality, *Watt*. Recall the neglected build-up Ernest Louit's doctoral defense of *The Mathematical Intuitions of the Visicelts*:

his anticipations were of failure, rather than of success. And such a loss would be irreparable, for of the countless observations made during his tour, and of the meditations arising thence, hastily under the most adverse conditions committed to paper, he had to his great regret little to no remembrance. To the relation of these painful events, that is to say the loss of his boots, his dog, his labour, his money, his health and perhaps even the esteem of his academical superiors, Louit had nothing to add, if not that he looked forward to waiting on the committee, at their mutual convenience, with proof that his mission had not been altogether in vain.[56]

In a not dissimilar spirit, then, let's get on with falsifying.

NOTES

[1] Karl Popper, 'Truth, Rationality and the Growth of Knowledge', in *Conjectures and Refutations* (London: Routledge, 2002 [1963]), p. 329; and Samuel Beckett, *Worstword Ho*, in Beckett, *Company, Ill See Ill Said, Worstward Ho, Stirrings Still*, ed. Dirk van Hulle (London: Faber, 2009), p. 81.

[2] S.E. Gontarski, *The Intent of Undoing in Samuel Beckett's Dramatic Texts* (Bloomington: Indiana University Press, 1985). From the perspective of genetic criticism, a more recent description of this compositional process as 'work in regress' has been advanced in Dirk Van Hulle's ground-breaking *Manuscript Genetics, Joyce's Know–How, Beckett's Nohow* (Tallahassee, University of Florida Press, 2008), see esp. Part 3; his recent monograph has characterised this process as 'creative undoing', see Dirk van Hulle, *Modern Manuscripts: The Extended Mind and Creative Undoing from Darwin to Beckett and beyond* (London: Bloomsbury, 2014).

[3] Samuel Beckett, 'The Two Needs', private translation of 'Les Deux Besoins' (for further details see ch. 3, note 5), corresponding to Samuel Beckett, *Disjecta: Miscellaneous Writings and a Dramatic Fragment*, ed. Ruby Cohn (New York: Grove Press, 1984), pp. 56–57.

[4] Karl Popper, 'Science: Conjectures and Refutations', in *Conjectures and Refutations*, p. 48; italics in original.

[5] Herbert Keuth, *The Philosophy of Karl Popper* (Cambridge: Cambridge University Press, 2005), cited pp. 51 31, 30; italics in original. For one of Popper's chief detractors, see Isabelle Stenger, *Power and Invention: Situating Science*, trans. (London: University of Minnesota Press, 1997), esp. ch. 5; for further discussion see also Garin Dowd, 'Prolegomena to a Critique of Excavatory Reason: Reply to Matthew Feldman', in 'Elements and Traces', eds. Matthijs Engelberts, Danièle de Ruyter, Karine Germoni, and Helen Penet-Astbury, *Samuel Beckett Today/Aujourd'hui* 20 (2008).

[6] Karl Popper, 'Three Requirements for the Growth of Knowledge', in *Conjectures and Refutations*, p. 336. See also, for instance, Gunnar Andersson, 'Naïve and Critical Falsification', in *In Pursuit of Truth: Essays on the Philosophy of Karl Popper on the Occasion of his 80th Birthday*, ed. Paul Levinson (Brighton: Harvester, 1982); C.J. Misak, *Verificationism: Its History and Prospects* (London: Routledge, 1995); Stefan Amsterdamski, ed., *The Significance of Popper's Thought: Proceedings of the Conference Karl Popper 1902–1994: March 10–12, 1995, Graduate School for Social Research Warsaw* (Amsterdam: Rodopi, 1996); Geoffrey Stokes, *Popper: Philosophy, Politics and Scientific Method* (Cambridge: Polity, 1998); J.W. Gonzalez, 'The Many Faces of Popper's Methodological Approach to Prediction', in *Karl Popper: Critical Appraisals*, eds. Philip Catton and Graham MacDonald (London: Routledge, 2004); John Losee, *Theories on the Scrap Heap: Scientists and Philosophers on the Falsification, Rejection, and Replacement of Theories* (Pittsburgh: University of Pittsburgh Press, 2005); and William Gorton, *Karl Popper and the Social Sciences* (Albany: State University of New York Press, 2006).

[7] Matthew Feldman, *Beckett's Books: A Cultural History of Samuel Beckett's 'Interwar Notes'* (London: Bloomsbury, 2008), pp. 13–20.

[8] Anne Atik, *How it Was: A Memoir of Samuel Beckett* (London: Faber and Faber, 2001), p. 121.

[9] Popper, 'Science: Conjectures and Refutations', p. 67.

[10] Finn Fordham, 'The Modernist Archive', in *The Oxford Handbook of Modernisms*, eds. Peter Brooker, Andrzej Gąsiorek, Deborah Longworth, and Andrew Thacker (Oxford: Oxford University Press, 2010), p. 53; approaching the archive as metaphor relates to 'its structure and construction, its principles of arrangement, order, and organization, and its relation to institutions of power'.

[11] James Knapp, cited in *ibid.*, p. 47.

[12] *Ibid.*, p. 48; italics added.

[13] For further details, see James Knowlson, *Samuel Beckett: An Exhibition held at Reading University Library, May to July 1971* (London: Turret Books, 1971).

[14] A good overview of Beckett's 'willingness to donate manuscript material to institutions, charities and individual friends' has recently been provided by Mark Nixon, "Beckett's Manuscripts in the Marketplace", in "Samuel Beckett: Out of the Archive" Special Issue, *Modernism/Modernity* 18/4 (2012), p. 827.

[15] See *Beckett at 60: A Festschrift* (London: Calder & Boyars, 1967); and *As No Other Dare Fail: For Samuel Beckett on his 80th birthday* (London: Calder, 1986). This note and the following reference make no claims to comprehensiveness, and are only concerned with Anglophone texts as indicative of the diffusion of Beckett's primary source materials.

[16] James Knowlson, ed., *Samuel Beckett, Krapp's Last Tape: A Theatre Workbook* (London: Brutus Books, 1980); and James Knowlson, ed., *Happy Days: The Production Notebook of Samuel Beckett* (London: Faber and Faber, 1985).

[17] Raymond Federman and John Fletcher, *Samuel Beckett: His Work and his Critics: An Essay in Bibliography* (Berkeley, University of California Press, 1970); see also James Tanner and Don Vann, *Samuel Beckett: A Checklist of Criticism* (Kent: Kent State University Press, 1969); and Robin J. Davis, *Samuel Beckett: Checklist and Index of his Published Works, 1967–1976* (Stirling: The Compiler, 1979).

[18] Richard Admussen, *The Samuel Beckett Manuscripts: A Study* (Boston: G.K. Hall, 1979), see also *The Samuel Beckett Collection: A Catalogue* (Reading: University of Reading, 1978); Carlton Lake, *No Symbols Where None Intended: A Catalogue of Books, Manuscripts, and other Material relating to Samuel Beckett in the Collection of the Humanities Research Center* (Austin, University of Texas, 1984); and Sharon Bangert, *The Samuel Beckett Collection at Washington University Libraries: A Guide* (St Louis: The Washington University Libraries, 1986).

[19] Lawrence Graver and Raymond Federman, eds., *Samuel Beckett: The Critical Heritage* (London: Routledge & Kegan Paul, 1979).

[20] See the first edition of the oft-cited Samuel Beckett, *Disjecta*, ed. Ruby Cohn (London: John Calder, 1983).

[21] Rosemary Pountney, *Theatre of Shadows: Samuel Beckett's Drama, 1956–1976, From All That Fall to Footfalls with commentaries on the latest plays* (Gerard's Cross, Colin Smythe, 1988); see especially her appropriation of the word 'vaguen'—from a manuscript note from the 'first typescript of both acts' of *Happy Days*—to describe Beckett's wider compositional process, p. 149.

[22] Deirdre Bair, *Samuel Beckett: A Biography* (London: Cape, 1978 [1990]).

[23] See, respectively, Samuel Beckett, *Dream of Fair to Middling Women* (Dublin: Black Cat Press, 1992); Beckett, *Eleuthéria: A Play in Three Acts*, trans. Michael Brodsky (New York: Foxrock, 1995); John Pilling, ed., *Beckett's Dream Notebook* (Reading: Beckett International Foundation, 1999); James Knowlson, ed., *The Theatrical Notebooks of Samuel Beckett* [*Waiting for Godot; Krapp's Last Tape; Endgame*; and *The Shorter Plays: With*

Revised Texts for Footfalls, Come and go *and* What Where (London: Faber and Faber, 1992–1999); and Maurice Harmon, ed., *No Author Better Served: The Correspondence of Samuel Beckett & Alan Schneider* (London: Harvard University Press, 1998).

24 A brief description of these materials is described in James Knowlson, "Preface" to *Damned to Fame: The Life of Samuel Beckett* (London: Bloomsbury, 1996), pp. xix-xxi. For recent use of the term 'grey canon' in Becket studies, see Dirk van Hulle, 'Notebooks and Other Manuscripts', in *Beckett in Context*, ed. Anthony Uhlmann (Cambridge: Cambridge University Press, 2013), p. 420, with key holding libraries of Beckett materials listed on pp. 419–420.

25 See Knowlson, 'Germany: The Unknown Diaries 1936–7', in *Damned to Fame*, 230ff; and the more recent, dedicated study by Mark Nixon, *Samuel Beckett's German Diaries, 1936–1937* (London: Bloomsbury, 2011), esp. chs. 5 and 8. For further discussion of these diaries, see also Bruce Arnold, 'From Proof to Print: Anthony Cronin's *Samuel Beckett: The Last Modernist*', in *Samuel Beckett Today/Aujourd'hui* 8 (2000).

26 See the catalogue provided in *Samuel Beckett Today/Aujourd'hui* 16 (2006).

27 The exception is the most recent text of James Knowlson's Festschrift, appearing a few months before this collection. Some introductory remarks about Professor Knowlson's personal influence, in the spirit of a Festschrift, were intended for a radically different context and were not included in ch. 7. Other amendments were overwhelmingly cosmetic and organisational.

28 See John Pilling, *Samuel Beckett* (London: Routledge and Kegan Paul, 1976); and James Knowlson and John Pilling, *Frescos of the Skull: The Later Prose and Drama of Samuel Beckett* (New York: Grove Press, 1979). In 1976, Pilling was also a founding editor of the *Journal of Beckett Studies*.

29 See Samuel Beckett, *The Collected Poems of Samuel Beckett: A Critical Edition*, eds. Seán Lawlor and John Pilling (London: Faber and Faber, 2012); and John Pilling, *Samuel Beckett's 'More Pricks Than Kicks': In a Strait of Two Wills* (London: Bloomsbury, 2013), esp. ch. 5, 'Notesnatchings: Allusions, Borrowings and Self-Plagiarisms in *More Pricks Than Kicks*', and 238ff.

30 John Pilling, *A Samuel Beckett Chronology* (Basingstoke: Palgrave, 2006). See also his more discursive *Beckett Before Godot* (Cambridge: Cambridge University Press, 2004).

31 Andrew Gibson, *Samuel Beckett* (London: Reaktion, 2010); James and Elizabeth Knowlson, *Beckett Remembering/Remembering Beckett: Uncollected Interviews with Samuel Beckett and Memories of those who Knew him* (London: Bloomsbury, 2007); Mark Nixon, ed., *Publishing Samuel Beckett* (London: British Library, 2011). For further methodological considerations relating to 'the archive' in Beckett studies, see Peter Fifield, '*Samuel Beckett: Out of the Archive*, An Introduction', *Modernism/Modernity* 18/3–4 (2012).

32 C.J. Ackerley, *Obscure Locks, Simple Keys: The Annotated* Watt (Tallahassee: Journal of Beckett Studies Books, 2010 [2005]); and C.J. Ackerley, *Demented Particulars: The Annotated* Murphy (Tallahassee: Journal of Beckett Studies Books, 2004 [1998]).

33 Only half of the following chapters had available, at the time of writing, any of the hugely important *The Letters of Samuel Beckett*, 3 vols. [1929–1940; 1941–1956; and 1957–1965], eds. George Craig, Martha Dow Fehsenfeld, Dan Gunn and Lois More Overbeck (Cambridge: Cambridge University Press, 2009, 2011, and 2014, respectively).

34 Samuel Beckett, 'Echo's Bones', ed. Mark Nixon (London: Faber and Faber, 2014).

35 Chris Ackerley, 'The "Distinct Context of Relevant Knowledge": Beckett's "Yellow" and the Phenomenology of Annotation', in *Beckett and Phenomenology*, eds. Ulrika Maude and Matthew Feldman (London: Continuum, 2009), p. 195; italics in original. Ackerley continues: 'a good annotation should offer insights based on the kind of textual and contextual evidence that compels consensus, that is, agreement that *this* set of conclusions for *that* particular problem is more probable than any others that have been or might be advanced; in a word, that it is valid. Like [E.D.] Hirsch, I claim that validity does not entail 'truth' or 'certainty', but *probability*; any hypothesis (any annotation) is at best provisional, to be replaced when another of greater explanatory power or elegance is advanced.'

36 Peter Barry, 'New Historicism and Cultural Materialism', in *Beginning Theory: An Introduction to Literary and Cultural Theory* (Manchester: Manchester University Press, 2002) pp. 174–175.

37 These authors are covered (in some cases, by multiple books) in the *Historicizing Modernism* series published by Bloomsbury Academic. Albeit not representative of modernist studies as a whole, this list offers an indicative example of archivally-driven research; see the series profile, available online at www.bloomsbury.com/uk/series/historicizing-modernism/ (all websites last accessed 12/12/14).

38 See John Brannigan, *New Historicism and Cultural Materialism* (Basingstoke: Palgrave Macmillan, 1998), Part 1.

39 Barry, 'New Historicism and Cultural Materialism', pp. 183-84.

40 See, for example, Ryan Kiernan, ed., *New Historicism and Cultural Materialism: A Reader* (London: Bloomsbury, 1996), esp. chs. 7–12.

41 Fordham, 'The Modernist Archive', p. 48. I am grateful to the author for discussions on this issue, and for his helpful suggestions in the drafting of this introduction.

42 For different approaches to modernist 'little magazines', for instance, note the different databases and materials compiled in Britain (www.modernistmagazines.com) as against that in the United States (http://modjourn.org/); see also the International Dada Archive, mentioned in Fordham's 'The Modernist Archive', available online at: www.lib.uiowa.edu/dada/.

43 Cited in Dirk van Hulle, *The Making of Samuel Beckett's* Stirrings Still/Soubresauts *and* Comment dire/what is the word (Antwerp: University Press Antwerp, 2011); see also Dirk van Hulle and Shane Weller, *The Making of Samuel Beckett's* The Unnamable/L'Innomable (London: Bloomsbury, 2014), p. 19. For further details of both modules, see the Samuel Beckett Digital Manuscript Project, available online at: www.beckettarchive.org.

44 Beckett speaks for roughly 30 seconds upon receipt of the Italia Prize in 1959, then followed by *Embers*, his award winning radio drama for the BBC; available online, alongside other sound clips, at: www.ubu.com/sound/beckett.html.

45 See 'Samuel Beckett: Works for Radio' on CDs (London: British Library Publishing 2006), available online at: http://shop.bl.uk/mall/productpage.cfm/BritishLibrary/_ISBN_9780712 305303/87294/Samuel-Beckett-Works-for-Radio-(audio-CD); and "Beckett on Film" on DVDs, available online at: www.beckettonfilm.com.

46 Contrast, for example, the website of Yale's aforementioned Beinecke archives (http://beinecke.library.yale.edu) with that of the (now itself archived) BBC Written Archives Centre (www.bbc.co.uk/archive/written.shtml); for more on the latter, see Jacquie Kavanagh, 'BBC Archives at Caversham', in *Contemporary British History* 6/2 (1992).

47 Containing both Beckett's text and a corresponding image, see the 21 October 1936 'Beckett in Hamburg' entry for Samuel Beckett's 'German Diaries', available online at:

http://schaukasten.sub.uni-hamburg.de/beckett/beckett_e/index.php?okt02.php; see also Michaela Giesing, Gabby Hartel, and Carola Veit, eds., *Das Raubauge in der Stadt: Beckett liest Hamburg* (Goettingen: Wallstein Verlag, 2007).

[48] See Ulrika Maude and Matthew Feldman, 'Introduction: Beckettian Phenomenologies?', in *Beckett and Phenomenology*, eds. Ulrika Maude and Matthew Feldman (London: Continuum, 2009).

[49] See Garin Dowd, 'Prolegomena to a Critique of Excavatory Reason'; and Matthew Feldman, 'In Defence of Empirical Knowledge: Rejoinder to "A Critique of Excavatory Reason"', both in 'Elements and Traces', eds. Matthijs Engelberts, Danièle de Ruyter, Karine Germoni, and Helen Penet-Astbury, *Samuel Beckett Today/Aujourd'hui* 20 (2008).

[50] See Ulrich Pothast, *The Metaphysical Vision: Arthur Schopenhauer's Philosophy of Art and Life and Samuel Beckett's own way to make use of it* (New York: Peter Lang, 2008), pp. 69ff. For another important source in the early development of Beckett's 'agnostic quietism', namely the Bible, see the recent study by Iain Bailey, *Beckett and the Bible* (London: Bloomsbury, 2014), esp. ch. 2.

[51] See Pilling, *Samuel Beckett's 'More Pricks Than Kicks'*, p. 179; and Beckett, 'Echo's Bones', pp. 3, 55–56.

[52] Pim Verhulst, *The Making of Samuel Beckett's Radio Plays: Interpretative Implications of Reading and Writing Traces* (Unpublished PhD. Thesis: University of Antwerp, 2014).

[53] Beckett to Hans Naumann, 17 February 1954, in *The Letters of Samuel Beckett, 1941–1956: Volume 2*, eds. George Craig, Martha Dow Fehsenfeld, Dan Gunn, and Lois More Overbeck (Cambridge: Cambridge University Press, 2011), p. 465.

[54] See Dirk van Hulle and Mark Nixon, *Samuel Beckett's Library* (Cambridge: Cambridge University Press, 2013), p. 158.

[55] David Tucker, *Samuel Beckett and Arnold Geulincx: Tracing 'a literary fantasia'* (London: Bloomsbury, 2013).

[56] Samuel Beckett, *Watt* (London: Calder & Boyers, 1971), pp. 169, 172.

"I INQUIRED INTO MYSELF":
Beckett, Interpretation. Phenomenology?

§1

'All this was duly revolting to Murphy, whose experience as a physical and rational being obliged him to call sanctuary what the psychiatrists called exile and to think of the patients [in the asylum] not as banished from a system of benefits but as escaped from a colossal fiasco.'[1] So wrote Samuel Beckett in his first widely published novel about the second in a long line of ambiguous characters or voices rejecting even the basics of social convention, in favour of 'nothing but he, the unintelligible gulf and they'.[2] Not only did Beckett develop this unique form of characterisation over the course of his writing life, but in doing so, also gave impetus to a critical pattern licensing virtually every conceivable interpretation of his texts. Murphy's solipsism, rejection of society and final affinity with the Magdalene Mental Mercyseat have been variously read as a 'turn away from the social world at large to find the sanctuary of the All'[3]; 'a revolt against the rational tradition represented by Pythagoras'[4]; 'a reality which cannot be penetrated by human knowledge'[5]; and 'an unassimilable hero with characters who are caught up in a standard fiction'.[6] Thus a spectrum of readings—from the sanctuary of lunacy to alternative rationality, absurd reality or an art aspiring to truthful realism—can all be justified in *Murphy*. For example, while Murphy's success with insane patients 'meant they felt in him what they had been and he in them what he would be'[7], his preference for surds (irrational numbers), such as his typical 1.83 cups of coffee, testifies to his rejection of Pythagorean rationalism; the transgression of time and space evidenced by Miss Carridge's knocking 'timidly on the door on the outside some time after she had closed it behind her on the inside' exemplifies total absurdity,[8] despite the narrator's comment 'All the puppets in this book whinge sooner or later, except Murphy, who is not a puppet',[9] which suggests the greater realism of Murphy himself.

From these brief impressions—epitomising so much Beckettian criticism over the years—Samuel Beckett's texts appear as a fun house mirror, the perception of which shifts as a result of the placement and frame of the viewer. As illustrated above, the assessments of *Murphy* seem dependant upon critics' own view of the world: whether it is a reasonable or absurd place; whether art can faithfully imitate life; whether Truth(s) are inscrutable; whether asocial eccentricity is a legitimate response to the vicissitudes of modern life, and so on. I will argue that Beckett's writing *intentionally* reveals the ever-conflicting values held by readers more visibly than that of other modernist writers precisely because of his awareness, incorporation and presentation (rather than conclusion) of these disparities in his texts. Unsurprisingly, this is phrased more succinctly by Beckett himself: 'The definition of outer reality, or of reality short and simple, varied according to the sensibility of the definer',[10] or in the words of his reformed Pythagorean character Neary, 'Life is all rather irregular.'[11] In fact the only value judgement universally agreed upon, issued in the 12 March 1938 *Times Literary Supplement* (which Molloy was to wrap around himself in winter because 'of a never failing toughness and impermeability. Even farts made no impression on it'[12]), is that Beckett's writing offers a 'very unusual and spirited performance'.[13]

Beyond this, however, value judgements are just as susceptible to diametrical readings as scholarship. This can be glimpsed by two further contemporary reviews of *Murphy* from March 1938. The first, a disparagement by Dylan Thomas, states 'that *Murphy* is difficult, serious and wrong' on account of the fact that 'it is [not] what Mr. Beckett intended it to be' and thus 'fails in its purpose' of delineating the mental world from the physical one, and is generally too 'loosely written'; inducing Thomas to assert 'always it is Freudian blarney: Sodom and Begorrah' [sic]. A week later, citing the precise same (Cartesian) reasons which provoked Thomas' disdain, Kate O'Brien wrote that *Murphy* 'is a sweeping, bold record of an adventure in the soul; it is erudite, allusive, brilliant, impudent and rude', rewarding for anyone who is not a 'gentle skimmer' 'by the rich peace of his response to Murphy's flight from the macrocosm into the microcosm of himself and his own truth'.[14] To be sure, this confusion also extended to the forty-two initial publishing houses rejecting *Murphy* as well as the forty-third, evidenced by Beckett's 1936 *crie de coeur* to his friend George Reavey regarding the misgivings of Chatto & Windus—the eventual publisher of *Murphy*—which prompted him to write: 'Do they not understand that if the book is slightly obscure it is because it is a compression [...] And of course the narrative is hard to follow. And of course deliberately so.'[15]

As a result, we are compelled to wonder if the incompatibilities exemplified by the diverse readings of *Murphy*, viewed as the most 'straightforward' of Beckett's prose, do not consciously challenge the very word 'exegesis' meant to characterise scholarly elucidation. This poses a particularly difficult critical problem. While it can be asserted that deliberate complexity is a Beckettian trademark, the purpose of the literary critic, and the academic more generally, is to explain or clarify the meaning of things. Through his friendship with scholars like Rudmose-Brown and his own grooming for the academy, Beckett was well aware of, and had an early disdain for, the authoritative nature of university life, prompting his resignation from the Trinity lectureship in 1931.[16] Yet even earlier than this, Beckett had voiced his own misgivings about the dispassionate and constraining nature of criticism in his first published essay entitled 'Dante...Bruno.Vico..Joyce': 'Must we wring the neck of a certain system in order to stuff it into a contemporary pigeon-hole, or modify the dimensions of that pigeon-hole for the satisfaction of the analogymongers? *Literary criticism is not bookkeeping.*'[17]

The formation of this view can be largely ascribed to his early experiences with the French avant-garde and their groundbreaking ideas on the reception and evaluation of modernist art at this time, which was instituted into a dissatisfaction with criticism that was to be refined and restated throughout his life.[18] Just as importantly, this rejection of the academic ethos was repeatedly translated into ironically drawn characters and situations in Beckett's texts, such as the Polar Bear, Professor of Bullscrit and Comparative Ovoidology, Chas and the students' interactions in 'A Wet Night', Neary's rationalism in *Murphy*, and of course Lucky's infamous reference to the 'Acacacademy'.[19] Consequently, we are therefore obliged to wonder if 'crrritics!'—that most dirty of words in *Waiting for Godot*—striving all too frequently to uncover the overarching 'meaning' in Beckett's texts, are unwittingly trapped by a masterful ironist in their attempts at resolution. Surely any account of Beckett's texts must take this essential rider into account. But at the very least, it is highly likely that Beckett's own revolt against academic gnosis and 'analogymongers' encouraged some of his syntactical experimentation and enigmatic textual construction.

Further compounding the resistance to critical exegesis and intentional elusiveness that so epitomises Beckett is his notorious reticence to discuss his own texts: 'But when it comes to journalists I feel the only line is to refuse to be involved in exegesis of any kind [...] we have no elucidations to offer of mysteries of their own making.'[20] It is important to stress that this quotation is not specific to time and place. Like the chasm of scholarship distinguishing Beckett, his personal aversion to fame, self-analysis and critique of his own writing was a continuing paradigm throughout his life. These generate a powerful image of Beckett the man, Beckett the writer, Beckett the public figure, and particularly Beckett the Nobel Prize-Winning-Literary-Genius, as an extremely enigmatic nexus of roles that at their very core seem to defy cogent explication. Nor have the increased publication of biographies, letters, unpublished plays and fiction, and the outpouring of academic criticism since the author's death assuaged this inscrutability.

In this regard, the similarity of two juxtaposed quotations, the first taken from Martin Esslin in 1962, and the second from Peter Boxall in 2000, are instructive:

> his texts continually seem to pull the rug from under the feet of the philosopher by showing themselves to be conscious of the possibility of such interpretations; or, better, such interpretations seem to lag behind the text which they are trying to interpret; or, better still, such interpretations seem to lag behind their object by saying too much: something essential to Beckett's language is lost by overshooting the text and ascending into the stratosphere of metalanguage.[21]

> Beckett's drama was beyond the interpretative powers of theory or philosophy, because what it dramatised was the failure of such discourses to be able to express the depravity of contemporary conditions, which is expressible only in the desolate spaces of Beckett's stage.[22]

Significantly, though both locate Beckett's inherent indeterminability and direct challenge to interpretation as a central aspect of his writing, neither can refrain from making scholastic characterisations of the texts. It is this contradiction which seems to underlie the vast bulk of writings on Beckett. Esslin, while pioneering an extremely influential 'existential humanist' approach holding that the representation of meaninglessness and negation is not metaphysical but is instead a kind of personal sovereignty 'of the individual that matters and has precedence over any abstract concepts', nonetheless assigns a central role to critics 'as the sense organs of the main body of readers'. Esslin then uses an acquaintance with the philosophical tradition to show Beckett's rejection of that tradition, and constructs a system to demonstrate the degree to which Beckett is an anti-systematist.[23] And while Boxall's survey of Beckettian criticism is aware of this quagmire and treads more warily, it too is contradictory at the very core: if Beckett's texts are truly beyond 'the powers of theory or philosophy' how is it possible to collect 'essential criticism' while simultaneously smuggling in his own reading ('the depravity of contemporary conditions')?

A more specific substantiation of what I shall call the 'prism of interpretation' is especially evident in Beckett's later texts, which often lack the very narrative foundations that might be said to reside in the early work.[24] For example, in *Ping* the very lack of a comprehensible setting, pronouns, expected punctuation, and ambivalent contextual words—such as the thirty-four 'pings'—leads Eyal Amiran to conclude that a 'human figure…is confined in a room' [… within] 'a seemingly fixed world […] which proclaims the end of life and shows a deathly figure in a mental sarcophagus' that is paradoxically 'also near its birth point or beginning'.[25] Almost inverting this 'realistic' reading of *Ping*, David Lodge asserts that

> "Ping" seems to record the struggle of an expiring consciousness to find some meaning in a situation which offers no purchase to the mind or to sensation. The consciousness makes repeated, feeble efforts to assert the possibility of colour, movement, sound, memory, another person's presence, only to fall back hopelessly into the recognition of colourlessness, paralysis, silence, oblivion, solitude.[26]

But what foothold is offered, if any, is offered in the text itself? 'Light heat all known all white planes meeting invisible. Ping murmur only just almost never one second perhaps a meaning that much memory almost never. White feet toes joined like sewn heels together right angle ping elsewhere no sound.'[27] This representative passage seems to both confirm and belie Amiran's reading insofar as parts of the human anatomy are mentioned and the unpredictability of the syntax seems to give way to an internal logic centring on the malleability of the word 'ping', yet phrases such as 'white planes meeting invisible' and 'perhaps a meaning that much memory almost never' suggests a highly metaphorical significance centring on consciousness as the seat of language, meaning, and the very construction of reality. For exactly the opposite reasons—the intangibility of the 'known', the meeting of 'white planes', and the concrete description of murmurs, toes and heels—Lodge's reading of *Ping* is, also, simultaneously insightful and perplexing. As evidenced by the archetypes above, even the most refined critics are seemingly returned to formative questions typically decontested in other authors' texts.

But do the above problems mean that Beckett either rejects criticism outright or feels there is no mode of interpretation worth pursuing with respect to his art? As *Disjecta* clearly demonstrates, Beckett's early non-fictional writings indicate a honed critical mind that, while rejecting the analytic 'bookkeeping' of much academic scholarship, promotes an understanding of texts through the sensations and impressions created in the reader. This approach is evident in his 1931 *Proust*:

> By his impressionism I mean his non-logical statement of phenomena in the order and exactitude of their perception, before they have been distorted into intelligibility in order to be forced into a chain of cause and effect [...] It may be objected that Proust does little else but explain his characters. But his explanations are experimental and not demonstrative. He explains them in order that they may appear as they are—inexplicable.[28]

Furthermore, in a 1967 letter, Beckett sanctions the study of his texts, adding the caveat that one should not look for 'rational' relations with other authors in his work, but instead a kinship with ideas: 'I simply do not feel the presence in my writings as a whole of the Proust & Joyce situations you evoke. If I were in the unenviable position of having to study my work my points of departure would be the "Naught is more real..." and the "Ubil nihil vales..." both already in *Murphy* and neither very rational.'[29] This suggests Beckett, despite fundamentally questioning the critical assumptions of reason and comprehensibility vis-à-vis modernist art, nevertheless locates a role for textual exegesis in readings with empathy not evaluation, individual response not judgement, and most importantly, feeling not intellectualism.[30] Thus it is the *form* that criticism takes which is of importance to Beckett. As will be shown, to follow this standard is to circumvent much of the existing critical assumptions on Beckett, while at the same time hopefully remaining more faithful to underlying consistencies in his writing. Following this survey of some characteristic themes within Beckett studies, I will contend that the problem with many interpretations stem from two dilemmas: first, they often highlight negative and contradictory impulses whilst obscuring the aesthetic 'underlying affirmation' Beckett has discussed regarding his texts.[31] Second, this essential 'so-said void. The so-missaid' is built upon methodologies and theoretical ideas not yet suitably excavated.[32] I will conclude with some suggestions for a critical synthesis based upon this more formative approach, linking both Beckett's writing and interpretations of it, arguing in a typically paradoxical (but not contradictory) Beckettian fashion that to advance in this field is to step backward.

§2

Recently, post-structuralist critics provided an important alternative reading of Beckett's texts, one grounded in analyses of his communication of incommunicability. In this regard, the work of Connor, Hill, Locatelli, Tresize, Barker, Jewinski and others have signalled nothing less than an interpretative detour, placing post-structuralist criticism at the fore of Beckett studies. By substituting an analysis of language within a text for overarching signification, readers following the Beckettian post-structuralist account also posit the texts' fundamental indeterminability and dissolution of consistently tenable theoretical positions. Viewed as a more fundamental criticism, a 'closer reading' looking principally at individual words or sentences rather than passages or texts, its proponents are often scornful of Anglo-American pretensions about decoding meanings in texts. This is exemplified by Leslie Hill blandly and unconvincingly labelling the Anglo-American tradition 'bland and unconvincing' due to its misguided attempts to reveal 'intentions' in Beckett's texts where there is only 'indifferent language' and 'intentionless writing'.[33] Despite Hill's claims to have advanced the debate over Beckett's texts, it is quite difficult to see how indifference and un-intention can be forged by accident or coincidence, especially from an author as notoriously meticulous as Beckett.

Nevertheless, like existential readings of Beckett, in general, the post-structuralist approach has undoubtedly yielded valuable insights by fruitfully emphasising the problematic role of Beckett's language through the centrality and conspicuous inescapability of words, undermining of narrative, continual self-opposition and reinterpretation, fusion (or interchangeability) of subject and object, and so on. In the texts, this is effectively seen as having a self-cancelling and contradictory effect, tending toward the conflux of words, leading writing toward disintegration or lack of signification. A passage chosen nearly at random from *The Unnameable* gathers together a number of elements typically seized upon:

> I'm in words, made of words, others' words, what others [...] wherever I go I find me, go towards me, come from me, nothing ever but me, a particle of me, retrieved, lost, gone away, I'm all these words, all these strangers, this dust of words [...] fleeing one another to say, that I am they, all of them, those that merge, those that part, those that never meet, and nothing else, yes, something else, that I'm something quiet different, a quite different thing, a wordless thing in an empty place [...][34]

Interestingly, the 'wordless thing in an empty place' foreshadowing the presence in *Texts for Nothing* and *Company* always 'finds me' despite confinement 'in words'. In his analysis of *Company*, Ed Jewinski notes that philosophical scepticism pervades this novella, one that succeeds in peeling away the layers of superfluous phenomena through the 'sustained series of efforts to deprive the protagonists of attributes and possessions which are inessential to the core questions of *how* Beings imagine themselves'. By considering Jacques Derrida's deconstruction of language, 'an approach [that] is both necessary and inescapable' in *Company*, Jewinski asserts that 'contradiction is as intolerable as it is inescapable'. As a result, Jewinski is lead down a cul-de-sac of binary oppositions (such as mind/body, he/you pronouns, etc.) existent in language, all of which are held to be proof of Beckett's interests in demonstrating linguistic incomprehensibility. This is because 'the trust in the power of the voice to describe human experience fully and unequivocally is precisely what Beckett's works seem to reject'.

Like many post-structuralist scholars of Beckett, Jewinski is able to locate both cart and horse: 'When the final break with the shared world is accomplished, what is left is the speaker alone with the consciousness of himself, so alone that his consciousness is neither [linguistically] directly confirmed nor directly denied.' But by placing the cart first, it appears this arrangement proceeds nowhere: 'Man, because he is the product of language, becomes the play of language, and he is unable to extricate himself from that language [...] without any solid frame of reference either to accept or to question the insistent droning of the voice asserting Being.'[35] The deconstructive process thus asserts that the prism of interpretation in Beckett—no longer swinging by the thread of intelligible intention-reception—plummets by virtue of the disrupted link between signifier and signified. But just as postulating the conceivability for a full linguistic account of 'human experience' directly challenges Jewinski's earlier assertions about Beckett's peeling away of 'inessential' questions to 'essential' self-conception, in attempting to show the primacy and non-referentiality of language by using Beckett's nebulous late texts as proof of linguistic imprisonment, Jewinski's essay becomes generally contradictory. Although maintaining that the expressed power of imagination is Beckett's central contribution to literature, Jewinski suggests that the subversion of reading expectations (plot, character, setting, etc.) through authorial linguistic techniques actually brings about the subjugation of imagination. Hence language becomes capable of beheading consciousness through constructed tropes in language. By claiming that Beckett can be best 'understood' through linguistic bars in the cell of consciousness—with access only to the post-structuralist jailer who is of limited utility when it comes to nourishment—treachery is suspected of the critic-as-cellmate.

But does consciousness need be so inherently self-cancelling and enslaved to language? As is memorably demonstrated in *Watt*, the very power of the imagination to envision negations in an affirmative light, such as $-2 \times -2 = 4$, casts grave doubt on these assertions. In *Company*, it seems that whether or not language can obliterate itself is less important than the positing of its existence through a creative imagination: 'What visions in the shadeless dark of light and shade! Yet another still? Devising it all for company. What a further addition to company that would be! Yet another devising it all for company. Quick leave him.'[36] Indeed, this seems more like affirmative creation(s) gone mad by an interminably devising imagination rather than a negating language finally unobscured in literature. For irrespective of whether expressions of consciousness are deductively causal (such as a flying unicorn) or even rationally explicable (such as 'tears of joy' in either the literal or metaphoric sense), it would seem that their origination *in* consciousness would, by definition, make them linguistically expressive of *something*, and therefore fundamentally consistent.

Indeed, the ability of language to harness and construct paradoxical ideas and statements seems to demonstrate linguistic malleability rather than the servitude of consciousness to communication. This idea, advanced by the philosopher Heraclitus—whose epistemological concerns with flux and the limits of knowledge Beckett was much interested in—covers a range of obscure and seemingly contradictory concepts. By demonstrating the propensity of language to posit inconsistencies or instabilities in logic, such as the delimiting of moving waters as fixed 'rivers', Heraclitus was the first to systematically inquire into the struggle between the known and the unknown:

"We step and do not step into the same rivers, we are and we are not" [B 91], "Combinations—wholes and not wholes, concurring differing, concordant discordant, from all things one and from one all things" [B 10], "Those who search for gold dig over much earth and find little" [B 22], "Most people do not understand the things they meet with, nor do they know when they have learned; but they seem to themselves to do so" [B 17].[37]

With a pedigree longer than two millennia, this line of thought stands in sharp contrast to post-structuralism (and for that matter, existential humanism) due to its appreciation of paradox and inconsistency, both of which are built into its method. One critic, comparing Heraclitus and Kafka's metaphorical and arational use of language as a philosophical method and a literary path, labelled this a 'methodological paradox [...] to express problems of human oblivion [... by] saying that oblivion is an essential component of philosophical method'.[38] Shades of Beckett are immediately apparent, not only with respect to his avowed knowledge of both Kafka and Presocratic philosophers, but particularly regarding their 'share in a struggle between disclosure and obscurity that is perhaps as old as writing itself'.[39] Centring on investigations of how to locate the elusive and to express the inexpressive, this methodology offers an entirely separate explanation of linguistic mutability and arationalism by making these into an indispensable muscle of Being rather than an Achilles Heel of linguistic or experiential understanding.

Despite emphasising fundamentally different aspects of Beckett's texts, post-structuralist and existential interpretations nevertheless share the same critical inconsistency. We are therefore faced with a repetition of the dilemma described earlier: critics loosely tied by a philosophic approach and methodology applying a system (however asystematic) to Beckett's texts in order to demonstrate that system's unclassifiability. Yet asserting what is not is still an assertion, and not having an essence is still locating an essence, albeit a negating one. As long as either group of commentators apply their readings *to* Beckett, they are frequently forced into the contradictory assertion that his writing is indeterminate, or at least cannot be adequately determined by criticism. But at the same time, both approaches find that there is much to recommend their readings *in* Beckett; that is, he illustrates their readings more effectively than they can describe his writings.

One particularly striking example of Beckett's interpretative flexibility can be found in 'Lessness'. The short story consists of a small body, alone in a desolate location, surrounded by ruins. Cursing God and without the benefit of reason, this grey body seems condemned to an endless oscillation between black and white, left only with memory and imagination. An existential reading would invariably emphasise the protagonist's (and the setting's) symbolic nature, tinged with the humanism of perseverance found in the ever beating heart and willingness to go on in an unknown and inescapable environment: 'Earth sky as one all sides endlessness little body only upright. One step more one alone all alone in the sand no hold he will make it.'[40] In this sense, 'Lessness' is placed in the context of all texts (especially from *Watt* onwards), showing the inaccessibility of meaning and transcendent truth from within the sphere of an absurd and inexplicable situation, one which could just as easily be Mr Knott's house, the cylinder in 'The Lost Ones', or the stage itself in *Waiting for Godot*: 'Thus making visible the invisible essence of our existence, Beckett's works move us by their fearful starkness, for they frame the miserable emptiness and utter futility of the human condition.'[41]

Yet at the same time, the continual repetition of phrases such as 'all gone from mind' and sentences such as 'Little body ash grey locked rigid heart beating face to endlessness' suggests that instead of existential symbolism, the creation of language itself may be what we are asked to consider in 'Lessness'. Highlighting different forms of aporia in Beckett is characteristic of the post-structuralist approach, and has been particularly detailed by Steven Connor.[42] Beckett's rearrangement of sentences and phrases suggests the infinite play of meaning contained within the relatively small number of words within the text. Thus, the sentence 'Blank planes sheer white eye calm long last all gone from mind' is subsequently broken into the different fragments 'sheer white all gone from mind', 'white blank planes all gone from mind', 'light of reason all gone from mind'— each with their own significance. This eventually forms the composite 'Light refuge sheer white blank planes all gone from mind' which is the only time the word 'refuge' is used where it is not preceded by the word 'true'.[43] The sentence is finally reconstructed near the end of the text to its initial form in a paragraph containing five repeated sentences from various places earlier in the text, all of which are partially used to construct other composite sentences. The very act of showing the malleability of language in this way appears at the heart of the post-structuralist enterprise. Thus it is hardly surprising that these critics typically argue that Beckett shared many of their views regarding language and meaning, in a sense preempting and short-circuiting the activity of deconstruction by his awareness and incorporation of similar themes in his art.

An archetypal example of this is the incompatible positions taken between Georges Duthuit and Beckett in the latter's *Three Dialogues*. Duthuit wants neat answers for his formulaic questions about art, but Beckett has none to offer. For this, Duthuit admonishes Beckett in the final dialogue for his 'absurdity' and inability to make a 'connected statement'. Yet Duthuit mistakes Beckett's outline of an inexpressive art as merely defining 'a painter who does not paint, does not pretend to paint'. Here is the dilemma faced by critics trying to interpret Beckett's art: how is it possible to make a sensible assertion about something that attempts to be 'inexpressive'? One cannot say that it expresses meaning, but neither can one say that it does not express *some* meaning. However radical Beckett's project is, the very act of committing words to paper, not leaving a blank page, or in the case of Bram van Velde, a blank canvas, *is still a form of communication*. When speaking of a new medium that does not submit to the 'ultimate penury' of an art detached from its occasion, Beckett explained revealingly to Duthuit:

> I know that all that is required now, in order to bring even this horrible matter to an acceptable conclusion, is to make of this submission, this admission, this fidelity to failure, a new occasion, new term of relation, and of the act which unable to act, obliged to act, he makes, an expressive act, even if only of itself, of its impossibility, of its obligation.[44]

Acceptance of failure, submission to obligation, expressing the inexpressible: these are the unlikely tools with which Samuel Beckett whittles the square peg of sense-making into a spherical shape, not in order to neatly fit into a circular hole of reason or comprehension but precisely to demonstrate that consciousness can only take blurred snapshots of memory and experience. This methodology, at once consistent and paradoxical instead of non-sensical or incommunicable, is here contended to be a fundamental nexus at the heart of Beckett's prose writings. Like Kafka's Hunger Artist, this method of characterising flux remains at the intersection of life and death, innocence and insight, disclosure and obscurity.

§3

One of the few readings highly sensitive to the problem of critical contradiction underlying the prism of interpretation in Beckett is P.J. Murphy's indispensable *Reconstructing Beckett*. Murphy argues that Beckett, in keeping with his Parisian avant-garde milieu in the late 1920s and early 1930s, is engaged in a positive search for meaning that could found a new form of art-life integration by constructing 'new languages for being' which could establish 'solid foundations, solid signifieds'. This is a far cry from formalism and *art pour l'art*, which, at least in the case of Beckett exegesis, Murphy feels is so 'riddled with contradictions' that a new approach is necessary:

> We obviously lack clearly worked out methodologies for dealing with Beckett's art: we have used the very guiding principles of the old "New Criticism" [existential humanism] and the new "New Criticism" [post-structuralism] to describe an art that may be striving to subvert in radically new ways these very principles. [This would be an] ultimately more defensible assumption that he is trying to discover new means of integrating self and fiction, word and world, rather than being guided by the need to de-

ny the power of words to express, the so-called "art of failure" which has so fascinated so many Beckett critics.⁴⁵

What emerges is an overview of Beckett that is at once unique and overdue: an assessment that treats his texts as a coherent lifelong process toward a goal of 'accommodating author and other, language and being' finally achieved in the late prose.⁴⁶

What is most important about this study is the consistency Murphy realises is necessary to advance beyond the prism of interpretations invariably leading to inconsistent readings. *Reconstructing Beckett* views Beckett as engaged in a positive search for an artistic essence to accommodate the oscillating modern world. This does not deny that much of Beckett's subject matter is nihilism, meaninglessness, or absurdity. But Murphy contends these are necessary means, not ends, in the process of constructing a fiction that can 'accommodate the mess' of existence.⁴⁷ Although suggested throughout, Murphy does not explicitly highlight the role of paradox as a vehicle for affirmation in Beckett's life and writing. Before progressing toward the possible nature of the affirmation contained within Beckett's oeuvre, a few citations on the role of Beckettian paradox as a specifically creative force is necessary. To be sure, his interest in Early Greek philosophy and the 'identification of opposites' championed by Vico is evident as early as his essay on Joyce's *Work in Progress* entitled 'Dante...Bruno.Vico..Joyce'. Yet by the completion of *More Pricks Than Kicks* four years later, this dialectical rapport had become suffused throughout the eleven tales of Belacqua, lover and voyeur, poet and drunk, a man part ethereal and part material, part lunatic and part *animus rational*. Moreover, a passage from 'Yellow', where Belacqua fittingly dies while undergoing an operation intended to return him to health, is particularly instructive as it demonstrates the potential 'assistance' of paradox:

> At this crucial point the good God came to his assistance with a phrase from the paradox of Donne: Now among our wise men, I doubt not many would be found, who would laugh at Heraclitus weeping, none which would weep at Democritus laughing. This was a godsend and no error. Not the phrase as a judgement, but its term, the extremes of wisdom that it rendered to Belacqua.⁴⁸

Even decades later Beckett's fascination with paradox remained, and more tellingly, in a series of interviews with Charles Juliet he suggests 'you can't even talk about truth. That is part of the general distress. Paradoxically, it's through form that the artist can find a kind of solution—by giving form to what has none. It is perhaps only at that level that there may be an underlying affirmation.'⁴⁹ But an essential question remains: how is it possible to find the right language as an author to clarify this sort of 'inexpressive affirmation'?

This issue is clearly of as great and longstanding an importance to Beckett as it is currently to Beckett critics. Yet in contrast to these critics, Beckett seemed to be searching for a language capable of constructing a 'literature of the unword'. This is clearly stated in Beckett's infamous 'German Letter' of 1937:

> language is most efficiently used where it is not being misused [...] As we cannot eliminate language all at once, we should at least leave nothing undone that might contribute to its falling into disrepute. To bore one hole after another in it, until what lurks behind—be it something or nothing—begins to seep 'through; I cannot imagine a higher goal for a writer today.[50]

As this passage suggests, rather than deconstructing language in order to show its inherent insensibility and indeterminacy, Beckett is searching for an ideal language more faithful to shifting perceptions and communication. As demonstrated in *Watt*, it is the protagonist's difficulty in finding a mode of expression for his experiences which causes his first confusion in Mr Knott's house. Following the piano tuning by the Galls, Watt notes that something had happened, specifically 'a thing that was nothing had happened'. But crucially, in a point seemingly unappreciated by critics, neither Watt nor Arsene, Walter or Vincent could accept the *lack* of something happening. The very event of an absence therefore had to be understood in terms of its occurrence:

> No, he could never have spoken at all of these things, if all had continued to mean nothing, as some continued to mean nothing, that is to say, right up to the end. For the only way one can speak of nothing is to speak of it as thought it were something, just as the only way one can speak of God is to speak of him as though he were a man [...] But if Watt was sometimes unsuccessful, and sometimes successful, *as in the affair of the Galls father and son*, in foisting a meaning where no meaning appeared, he was most often neither the one, nor the other.[51]

As *Watt* reveals, even a picture of nothingness (such as the image of a black hole), is still an image of something, while *true* nothingness remains inconceivable. Significantly, the paradox of a 'nothing' actually 'happening' here creates a positive search for meaning. The first instance of this immediately follows Watt's meeting with the Galls, and centres upon the indefinability of a simple pot. Despite resembling a pot in appearance and utility, Watt cannot call the pot a pot for its essence becomes detached from its existence, a sensation subsequently extended to everything he perceives. Watt is 'more troubled perhaps than he had ever been by anything' by this loss of 'natural attitude' and accompanying inability to name things.[52] Although we are led to believe that Watt's inability to give phenomena meanings leads to his institutionalisation, he nevertheless continues to communicate with Sam through two 'independently burst' holes in their respective fences.[53] Moreover, it is Watt's ability to convey his experiences at Mr

Knott's, albeit through spliced, inverted, backward or rearranged language, that leads to the construction of the narrative by Sam, who understands Watt despite his fluctuating, tropic language.

Thus, it is possible to assert in contrast to both interpretative paradigms reviewed that, as evidenced in the case of *Watt*, the search for meaning and the search for a language to communicate that meaning is both consistent and positive even though the 'natural' modes of perception and communication are deemed insufficient. And unless Beckett reversed this position in *The Beckett Trilogy* less than a decade later, instead of searching for meaninglessness, he 'had to eliminate all the poisons [intellectual decency, knowledge, certainties] and find the right language.'[54] Nevertheless, both readings advance important, and in many cases, essential analyses of Beckett's own intertextuality, his operations on language and syntax, the desolate landscapes and often solitary voices that resonate throughout his oeuvre. But how can we use these insights in an affirmative way about a paradoxical author, while still retaining a cogent critical framework?

§4

An answer to this problem could be more closely aligned with methodology. Carla Locatelli interestingly suggests

> methodologically, Beckett could thus be compared to Husserl, whose "reductions" constitute a process, a dynamic, investigative device, well known to the analyses of descriptive Phenomenology. Obviously, Beckett's investigation develops on and through literature, and in a non-transcendental direction. Unlike Husserl, he is not looking for an irrefutable foundation of knowledge, a discovery which in itself is charged with an important cognitive significance. [55]

We have already seen that P.J. Murphy believes Beckett is looking to transcend art toward a re-integration with life, toward 'solid foundations' and 'solid signifieds'. This would indeed be fraught with 'cognitive significance'; moreover, the role of consciousness has been asserted by critics such as Katz, Weller, Kenner, Tresize and others: 'The ultimate goal of Beckett's entire literary production is to create a fictional being that can exist completely detached from the physical body, a creature that can function outside human knowledge *as a consciousness* inventing its own fictional surroundings.'[56] Yet to date no systematic study has appeared analysing Beckett's relation to the ideas of phenomenology.[57] Crucially, phenomenology, as developed by Edmund Husserl, was the methodological buttress supporting both existentialism and post-structuralism. And given the difficulty advancing consistent readings discussed above, the potential in a comparative study of Husserlian and Beckettian foundationalism is enormous.

This could avoid the difficulties encountered by Butler's important study *Samuel Beckett and the Meaning of Being*. Despite raising insightful points about Beckett's similarity with these existential thinkers, Butler compares the characteristics of each author rather than searching for an underlying unity. An example of this can be found in the case of Heidegger's *thrownness*, which Butler compares to the literal act of being thrown on stage at the commencement of *Act Without Words I*. Although many of these characteristics are quite similar, it is what fundamentally unites them that truly merits investigation. In Husserl's own words, a methodological search for essences that is constantly revised and renewed, phenomenology as 'self-acquired knowledge tending toward universality [takes philosophy in a radical direction] from naïve Objectivism to transcendental subjectivism—which, with its ever new but always inadequate attempts, seems to be striving toward some necessary final form, wherein its true sense and that of the radical transmutation itself might become disclosed'.[58] Time and again, Husserl stressed the centrality of the 'transcendental reduction' of experience to consciousness and the accompanying role of 'intentionality', which posited that a bracketed consciousness was always directed toward phenomena, irrespective of whether it was 'real' or 'imaginary'. This bracketing, or suspension of conclusions, reinforced the emphasis on experience and on the things one could actually perceive. Thus, although the jury may have been fooled by the testimony, all it had to decide upon was the evidence given in the courtroom. In this way, Husserl was able to advance on a number of Cartesian propositions which were circular in construction. There was no division between mind and body, no trickster to convince us our dreams were real; at least, if there were, we could not know it. There was also no *a priori* reliance upon science, mathematics, or God, as phenomenology strove to truly be a 'science of beginnings'.

But it was precisely this very 'perhaps' central to the methodology of phenomenological reduction by Husserl that was jettisoned by later existentialists and post-structuralists. Although they maintained the rigorous attention to experience and phenomena, the very possibility of satisfactorily affixing essences was conceded as unrealistic. Doubt, as the very basis of Husserlian epistemology, was discarded in favour of a view that *knew* it could not *know* absolute meaning or truth. This 'perhaps' about the very existence of the world and the act of world-creation by consciousness was therefore replaced by an ontology of language and existence that was elusive and essentially uncharacterisable. But more importantly, the role of Husserlian paradox in the necessary interdependence and independence of the world, mind/body co-ordination, commingling of realism and idealism, essence and uncertainty—are all removed by later existentialist and post-structuralist thinkers appropriating the original phenomenological method.

The 'astonishment that the world exists' is replaced with the uncertainties *within* the world, thus giving rise to the potential prism of interpretation of everything from 'brackets' to Beckett. Yet at the same time, the malleable but definable practice of phenomenology remained central to the practices of quite different analyses, philosophies and even disciplines: 'the literature on Husserl, and on these competing extrapolations of his views, has reached a point of near unsurveyability'.[59] It is this very unsurveyability that is currently at the heart of Beckettian criticism. Just as importantly, the emphasised role of consciousness in Husserl and Beckett, the suspension of a 'natural' attitude toward the world, and the need to create a phenomenological field *from* the void, all encourage an underlying correspondence between Beckett and phenomenology. One might say that the suspension of disbelief in existence itself is the point of departure for Husserl's philosophy of creation and Beckett's creative philosophy.

In short, focussing on the methodology Husserl undertook to analyse the acts of creation by individual consciousnesses could offer a coherent foundation from which to locate Beckett, while simultaneously offering a synthesis of the two principle readings so dominant in Beckett studies. By retracing our steps toward a foundation that would attempt to highlight Beckett's techniques rather than interpreting his meaning/lessness, new avenues could be pursued. And surely, it is this consistent phenomenal reality that is sought by epistemologists such as Husserl, his progeny, and Beckett—each of whom in their own way echoed Heraclitus' ancient mandate for those wishing to investigate rather than hide from the remarkable paradoxes of Being: 'I inquired into myself.'[60]

NOTES

[1] Samuel Beckett, *Murphy* (London: Calder & Boyers, 1969), p. 101.

[2] *Ibid.*, p. 134. The first such character, used in Beckett's abortive 1932 novel *Dream of Fair to Middling Women* and then the 1934 novel *More Pricks than Kicks* was Belacqua Shuah, a character disaffected with the life's 'kicks' in love, health, time, justice and finally death.

[3] Eyal Amiran, *Wandering and Home* (University Park: Penn State University Press, 1993), p. 97.

[4] Anthony Farrow, *Early Beckett: Art and Illusion in* More Pricks than Kicks *and* Murphy (Troy: Whitson, 1991), p. 14.

[5] Hugh Kenner, *A Reader's Guide to Samuel Beckett* (London: Thames & Hudson, 1973), p. 55.

[6] Wolfgang Iser, *The Implied Reader* (Baltimore: Johns Hopkins University Press, 1974), p. 262.

[7] Beckett, *Murphy*, p. 51.

[8] *Ibid.*, p. 43.

[9] *Ibid.*, p. 71.

[10] *Ibid.*, p. 101.

[11] *Ibid.*, p. 152.

[12] Samuel Beckett, *The Beckett Trilogy* [*Molloy, Malone Dies* and *The Unnamable*] (London: Calder, 1959), p. 29.

[13] 'Unsigned Review' of *Murphy,* reprinted in Lawrence Graver and Raymond Federman, eds., *Samuel Beckett: The Critical Heritage* (London: Routledge & Kegan Paul, 1979), p. 46.

[14] Kate O'Brien in 'Spectator', reprinted in *Ibid.*, pp. 48–9.

[15] Beckett to George Reavey, 13 November 1936, cited in Samuel Beckett, *Disjecta: Miscellaneous Writings and a Dramatic Fragment*, ed. Ruby Cohn (New York: Grove Press, 1984), p. 103.

[16] For details on Beckett's early problems with publication, see Lois Gordon, *The World of Samuel Beckett 1906–1946* (London: Yale University Press, 1996), p. 132, and on Beckett's resignation from Trinity, see Anthony Cronin, *Samuel Beckett: The Last Modernist* (London: Harper Collins, 1996), pp. 119–130; and James Knowlson *Damned to Fame* (London: Bloomsbury, 1996), ch. 6.

[17] Beckett, 'Dante…Bruno.Vico..Joyce', in *Disjecta*, p. 19.

[18] For Beckett's relationship with the avant-garde in France, see Norma Bouchard, *Céline, Gadda, Beckett: Experimental Writing of the 1930s* (Gainsville: University Press of Florida, 2000). For confirmation of Beckett's continued divergence from academic signification, see Beckett's series of interviews with Israel Shenker, Gabriel D'Aubarede, Tom Driver, and Charles Juliet, between 1956 and 1973. The first three can be found in Graver and Federman's *Samuel Beckett: The Critical Heritage*, 215ff; and the latter in Charles Juliet, *Conversations with Samuel Beckett and Bram van Velde* (Netherlands: RA Leiden, 1995).

[19] 'A Wet Night', in Samuel Beckett, *More Pricks Than Kicks* (London: Calder & Boyers, 1970), pp. 50–88; Neary is defined as a Pythagorean and makes an overt reference to Descartes in Samuel Beckett, *Murphy* (London: Calder & Boyers, 1969), pp. 6–8; and for Lucky's speech, see Samuel Beckett, *The Complete Dramatic Works* (London: Faber, 1986), p. 42.

[20] Beckett to Alan Schneider, 29 December 1957, cited in *Disjecta*, pp. 108–9.

21. Martin Esslin, *Samuel Beckett: A Collection of Critical Essays* (Englewood Cliffs: Prentice-Hall, 1965), p. 141.
22. Peter Boxall, *Samuel Beckett: A Reader's Guide to Essential Criticism* (Cambridge: Icon Books, 2000), p. 7.
23. Esslin, 'Introduction', in *Samuel Beckett*, pp. 1–15.
24. This is not to suggest, however, that Beckett's earliest work is devoid of the problematics more finely honed in the post-war literature. Although *Murphy* might be said to read like a normal 'story'—at least insofar as it contains a 'beginning', 'middle' and 'end' with plot, character development and climax—Beckett had already demonstrated in his abortive novel of 1932 many of the ambiguities characterising his later texts: 'The only unity in this story is, please God, an involuntary unity. Now it occurs to us that for the moment at least we have had more than enough of Belacqua the trinal maneen with his wombtomb and likes and dislikes and penny triumphs and failures and exclusions and general incompetence and pedincurabilities, if such a word may be said to exist.' See Samuel Beckett, *Dream of Fair to Middling Women* (London: Calder, 1993), p. 132. This point is reinforced in Gordon's *The World of Samuel Beckett*, which asserts that Beckett's early writing in the 1930s already contained many of the themes later seized upon by post-modern literature.
25. Amiran, *Wandering and Home*, pp. 173–6. Amiran further notes that, of the thirty-four 'pings', the first seven and last seven constitute a palindrome, the thirteenth through seventeenth 'pings' are reverse images of the eighteenth through twenty-second 'pings' read backwards, and the entire thirty-four 'pings' show 'an hourglass pattern that suggests the Yeatsian shape of life'. Despite these assertions, Amiran's next sentence, casting doubt on the importance of his entire point, seems to evince the type of 'literary bookkeeping' Beckett disliked: 'The pattern's irregularities, however, render its meaningfulness doubtful.' (172–3, n. 11).
26. David Lodge, cited in S.E. Gontarski, 'Introduction', in Samuel Beckett, *The Complete Short Prose, 1929–1989*, ed. S.E. Gontarski (New York: Grove Press, 1995), p. xxviii.
27. *Ibid.*, p. 194.
28. Samuel Beckett, *Proust and Three Dialogues* (London: Calder & Boyers, 1970), pp. 86–7.
29. Beckett, *Disjecta*, p. 113.
30. As to the last point, Beckett's response to D'Aubarede is instructive: 'I'm no intellectual. All I am is feeling. *Molloy* and the others came to me when I became aware of my own folly. Only then did I begin to write the things I feel.' (Graver and Federman, eds., *Samuel Beckett: The Critical Heritage*, 217).
31. Juliet, *Conversations*, p. 149.
32. Samuel Beckett, *Nohow On: Company, Ill Seen Ill Said, Worstword Ho* (London: Calder, 1989), p. 113.
33. Leslie Hill, *Samuel Beckett's Fiction in Different Worlds* (Cambridge: Cambridge University Press, 1990), p. 162.
34. Beckett, *The Unnamable*, in *The Beckett Trilogy*, pp. 355–6.
35. Ed Jewinski, '*Company*, Post-structuralism, and Mimetalogique', in Lance St John Butler, and Robin J. Davis, eds., *Rethinking Beckett* (London: Macmillan Press, 1990), pp. 141–60.
36. Samuel Beckett, *Company* (London: Calder, 1996), p. 84.
37. Jonathan Barnes, ed., *Early Greek Philosophy* (London: Penguin, 1987), pp. 100–29.
38. David Schur, *The Way of Oblivion: Heraclitus and Kafka* (London: Harvard University Press, 1998), pp. 6–9.
39. *Ibid.*, p. 3.

40 Beckett, 'Lessness', in *The Complete Short Prose*, p. 201.
41 Hannah Copeland, *Art and the Artist in the Works of Samuel Beckett* (The Hague: Mouton, 1975), p. 28.
42 See Steven Connor, *Samuel Beckett: Theory, Repetition, Text* (Oxford: Basil Blackwell, 1998), esp. ch. 1.
43 Beckett, 'Lessness', in *The Complete Short Prose*, pp. 197–201.
44 Beckett, *Proust and Three Dialogues*, pp. 121–5; italics added.
45 P.J. Murphy, *Reconstructing Beckett: Language for Being in Samuel Beckett's Fiction* (London: University of Toronto Press, 1990), pp. xiii-xv.
46 *Ibid.*, p. xv.
47 Beckett's term, used in a 1961 interview with Tom Driver, reprinted in Graver and Federman, eds., *Samuel Beckett: The Critical Heritage*, p. 219.
48 Beckett, *More Pricks than Kicks*, p. 175.
49 Juliet, *Conversations*, p. 149.
50 Beckett, *Disjecta*, pp. 171–2.
51 Samuel Beckett, *Watt* (London: Calder & Boyers, 1971), pp. 74; italics added.
52 *Ibid.*, p. 79.
53 *Ibid.*, p. 159.
54 Juliet, *Conversations*, p. 140.
55 Carla Locatelli, *Unwording the World* (Philadelphia: University of Pennsylvania Press, 1990), pp. 2–3.
56 Raymond Federman, *Journey to Chaos* (Berkeley: University of California Press, 1965), p. 76.
57 Eugene Kaelin's study does examine phenomenology and Beckett, although its chronological approach and virtual silence on phenomenological themes reads more like a reader-response theory; see *The Unhappy Consciousness: The Poetic Plight of Samuel Beckett* (Boston: Kluwer. 1981).
58 Edmund Husserl, *Cartesian Meditations*: *An Introduction to Phenomenology* (London: Kluwer, 1988), pp. 2–4.
59 David Woodruff Smith, 'Mind and Body', in Barry Smith and David Woodruff Smith, eds., *The Cambridge Companion to Husserl* (Cambridge: Cambridge University Press, 1995), p. 32.
60 Barnes, *Early Greek Philosophy*, p. 113.

BECKETT AND POPPER, OR, "WHAT STINK OF ARTIFICE":
Some Notes on Methodology, Falsifiability, and Criticism in Beckett Studies

> And while the verificationists laboured in vain to discover valid positive arguments in support of their beliefs, we for our part are satisfied that the rationality of a theory lies in the fact that we choose it because it is better than its predecessors; because it can be put to more severe tests; because it may even have passed them, if we are fortunate; and because it may, therefore, approach near to the truth.[1]

> The place where they now found themselves, where they had agreed, not without pains, that they should meet, was not properly speaking a square, but rather a small public garden at the heart of a tangle of streets and lanes [....] It had something of the maze, irksome to perambulate, difficult to egress, for one not in its secrets. Entry was of course the simplest thing in the world [....] Mercier and Camier did not know the place. Hence no doubt their choice of it for their meeting. Certain things shall never be known for sure.[2]

§1

The methodological topic of this chapter is only vaguely described by the title—with little seeming help from the epigraphs—and thus requires some justification. In doing so, this short text will also broach a matter of implied partition within that expanding library now indexed as 'Beckett studies'; indeed, boldness permitting, perhaps the entire industry of Anglophone literary criticism. In short, this chapter will look at how critics tend to look at Beckett, asserting that a fissure in theoretical approach to a shared subject is detectable and noteworthy. Rather than tracing this lineage in the development of Beckett studies, however, a shortcut will instead be mapped out here via a proper pseudo-couple, Beckett and Popper.

As we shall see, a bold assertion is a useful point of departure: Samuel Beckett never referred to Karl Popper, and Popper never referred to Beckett. Certainly neither cited the other in any extant material. My title is, then, rather misleading, for there is no Beckett and Popper beyond the one currently established here. No *first order* connection between the two exists; that is, no evidence of any sort can be found to demonstrate any correspondence whatsoever. As such, placing the two together is an association of the *second order,* indirect and, in fact, methodologically subjective. 'Beckett and Popper' stands revealed as a red herring, having no relationship besides that offered in this paragraph—paradoxically (and we are in well-charted waters here), of a non-existing relationship.

In this light, the uninitiated might wonder what Beckett studies itself holds as its guiding principles, if not the *attempt to increase general and scholarly knowledge about Samuel Beckett; and especially, his literary oeuvre.* If this is so, might not a title like the above bridle against such a remit? For my own title, if pursued along the lines of 'second order' literary exegesis, appears to have a different agenda, instead focussing on the comparison, relation, mixture, or impression of two historical figures intersecting only indirectly in time, in the mind of the critic.

Nevertheless, one can readily call to mind instances like these, whereby a third party establishes a connection between historical figures or ideas, in an attempt to evoke, relate, or synthesise, like a librarian classifying books under the headings 'old' and 'new'. In short, what I want to suggest is that this theoretical process—for that is what I shall take it to be—is methodologically distinct from another type of theorising, squeezed within the same discipline. Some have called this second approach 'literary history', others 'genetic manuscript studies', 'empirical criticism' or sometimes 'literary archaeology'. This is to distinguish it from 'critical theory', often shorthand for forms of 'post-modernism', 'deconstruction', or 'post-structuralism'. In this sense, Beckett studies may be seen as a window opening onto Anglophone literary criticism as a whole, whereby these two manners of discourse intermingle rather uncomfortably along the same shelf.

To assist in untangling these overlapping approaches to Beckett, it can be heuristically useful to *appropriate* some of Karl Popper's basic parameters for establishing a theory, in order to argue why a title like 'Beckett and Popper' is intrinsically problematic in terms of demonstrably *increasing scholarly knowledge.* That is to say, whatever their similarities, or indeed differences, we shall not consider Popper *with* Beckett at all; instead, Popper's ideas will only serve as a conceptual template, helping to demarcate critical approaches *about* Beckett in our shared discipline. In doing so, some criticism within Beckett studies will be considered, illustrating what will here be construed as (at least) two divergent methods of literary interpretation bearing upon a single subject.

§2

Sir Karl Popper, an Austrian émigré settling at Cambridge to work on the philosophy (and methodology) of science, spent much energy constructing ways by which to analyse theories; in *The Logic of Scientific Discovery* this is called a 'distinction between *empirical* and *synthetic* statements'.[3] Without doing too much violence to his groundbreaking arguments on the (frequently) implicit rules governing theories, let us review a few of Popper's points in relation to Beckett studies, especially those contained in a collection of shorter papers entitled *Conjectures and Refutations*. Here, in establishing a theory, Popper was adamant that 'falsifiability'—the possibility of refuting an argument—was the key principle in palpably advancing knowledge. At the outset of 'Truth and Content: Verisimilitude versus Probability', Popper painstakingly establishes a schism in modes of theorising (one reprised in his conclusion, partially given in the epigraph above), namely 'that falsificationists or fallibists [argue...] that what cannot (at present) in principle be overthrown by criticism is (at present) unworthy of being seriously considered [while "verificationists"....] demand that we should accept a belief *only if it can be justified by positive evidence*, that is to say, *shown* to be true, or, at least, to be highly probable'.[4]

What then of our scarecrow, 'Beckett and Popper'? Contending that there is no direct association between the two can in fact be falsified; that is, evidence—say, in the form of a letter of Popper's mentioning his reading of *Watt*, or a copy of *The Logic of Scientific Discovery* in Beckett's library—can be produced to refute my assertion. This is on account of the twin pillars buttressing Popper's theory of falsification: 'empirical corroboration' and 'relevance'.

As to the latter, Popper considers the utility of evidence as analogous to courtroom testimony, whereby 'the *whole truth*, and nothing but the truth' generally omits what the witness had for breakfast or shoe size, unless either is pertinent to the case at hand. By way of example, the earlier statement denying any direct relationship between Beckett and Popper may be falsified by a single quotation from Popper in Beckett's letters or notes; but at the same time, should our hypothetical reference to Popper (say, in Beckett's so-called '*Whoroscope* Notebook') merely refer to Popper's toes, this would be unlikely to justify an entire paper on the relationship between Beckett and Popper's feet. By failing to provide what Popper terms 'interesting content' and 'explanatory power', a study on Popper and Beckett's feet may provide new facts and comparisons—both had ten toes, Beckett had surgery on his feet in the 1930s while Popper did not, and so on—but these associations are not likely have the sufficient relevance, or utility, to 'answer a problem' or move beyond Popper's undesirable 'uninteresting assertions'. Clearly, relevance is at the centre of this endeavour, as a sifting tool distinguishing between applicable and inapplicable materials with which to construct theories. Likewise, although I contest the merit of reading Beckett through Popper, or vice versa, the latter may nevertheless prove relevant to questions of method in Beckett studies. Or in Popper's words, since it 'is always possible to produce a theory to fit any given set of explicanda [....] I can therefore gladly admit that falsificationists like myself much prefer an attempt to solve an interesting problem by a bold conjecture *even (and especially) if it soon turns out to be false*, to any recital of a sequence of irrelevant truisms'.[5]

Here the second methodological pillar, 'empirical corroboration', is central to advancing such 'bold conjecture[s]'. Popper is no essentialist, preferring terms like 'verisimilitude' and 'approximation' when suggesting ways in which theories have differing degrees of 'explanatory power'. For example, 'verisimilitude is most important in cases where we know that we have to work with theories which are at best approximations—that is to say, theories of which we know that they cannot be true. (This is often the case in the social sciences.) In these cases we can still speak of better or worse approximation to the truth'.[6] Both here and elsewhere, Popper relies upon inter-subjective facts in making this distinction. Within Beckett studies, a fitting example concerns the now-accepted date of Beckett's birth, on Good Friday, 13 April 1906. Against claims that 'Beckett deliberately created the myth that he was born on Friday the thirteenth', James Knowlson is able to offer the more explanatory theory, as well as accompanying evidence, arguing that 'a mistake was made' in registering Beckett's birth. His introduction is in keeping with the entirety of *Damned to Fame* which throughout 'sought to discover the facts', to use a telling phrase from Bruce Arnold's text on the recent Beckett biographies.[7] It is hard to disagree: Knowlson's finding of the *Irish Times* listing Beckett's name on 16 April 1906 surely refutes all other explanations, on the logically consistent grounds that had Beckett been born in May, he could not have been on any listing of births in April 1906.[8] This 'scientific method' is vital to Popper's 'empirical corroboration' (and again, perhaps a scholarly contribution): the growth of knowledge that is not synthetic and secondary must be defendable in terms of corroboration with acceptable, documentary, or logically consistent evidence.

§3

Before considering the overarching concept of falsification, let us first look more closely at Popper's supporting concepts of 'empirical corroboration' and 'relevance' with respect to Beckett studies. Regarding the former, a long running debate within Beckett studies over Fritz Mauthner, another Austrian philosopher, is particularly apt. Following Beckett's 1953–4 interviews with Richard Ellmann (in anticipation of the latter's expansive biography *James Joyce*—the first published account of Beckett's reading of Mauthner's *Beiträge zu einer Kritik der Sprache* [hereafter *Beiträge*])—placed the encounter in 1932, as an aide to James Joyce's 'Work in Progress'. Although a few noteworthy texts on the subject did appear in the interim, the scholarship of Linda Ben-Zvi between 1980 and 1986 heralded a new emphasis on Fritz Mauthner as a powerful figure in Beckett's intellectual development. Testifying to the importance of Ben-Zvi's work, consider this quotation from 'Beckett and Postfoundationalism', in a volume entitled *Beckett and Philosophy*, which shall be further examined presently. Here, Richard Begam's contribution attempts to advance 'Beckett seriously as a philosophical writer' by situating his views within twentieth century philosophy, drawing 'especially [on] Linda Ben-Zvi's illuminating work on Beckett and Mauthner [....] Certainly Mauthner's nominalism represented one of the earliest and most influential forms of postfoundationalism Beckett encountered'.[9] Yet from the perspective of 'empirical corroboration', available evidence challenges Ben-Zvi's account; instead 'Mauthner's nominalism' can be more empirically theorised as the *last* form of 'postfoundationalism'—indeed, depending on how narrowly the term is defined, the *only* form—Beckett encountered.

Looking more closely at Ben-Zvi's unquestionably valuable texts on Mauthner between 1980 and 1986, beyond Ellmann's (and Deirdre Bair's biography) bare accounting of Beckett's knowledge of Mauthner, her grounding is provided by Beckett's 1979 letter: 'Recently I came across an ancient commonplace book in which I had copied verbatim from the last section of the work [*Wissen und Worte*] beginning "*Der zeine* [sic] *und konsequente Nominalismus*"'– the first of eleven quotations from Mauthner's *Beiträge* in Beckett's '*Whoroscope* Notebook.' In this letter, Beckett also suggested that Mauthner's influence was due to drawing his attention to linguistic ineffability: 'For me it came down to: Thought words/Words inane/Thought inane/Such was my levity'. This, in turn, led Ben-Zvi to conclude in 1984: 'For over fifty years—from the composition of *Dream of Fair to Middling Women* in 1932 to the 1979 [sic] completion of *Company*—two Mauthner themes appear and reappear in Beckett's works: the impossibility of verification and the impossibility of proving this impossibility.'[10] Implied here is an inspiration for Beckett covering most of his poetry and prose, and all of his novels and plays—substantiating such an influence thus becomes understandably vital.

Yet herein rests the dilemma: in Ben-Zvi's first text she castigates Deirdre Bair for placing the date of Beckett's study of Fritz Mauthner in 1929/30 on the one hand, while on the other criticising Knowlson and John Pilling for placing such an encounter a decade later. And in her 1984 article for the *Journal of Beckett Studies,* Ben-Zvi applies a similar comment to Ellmann, whose 1932 dating of the Beckett reading of Mauthner encounter is 'offered without supporting citations, [and] is not sufficient'.[11] Yet problematically, and also 'without supporting citations', in her 1986 *Samuel Beckett* Ben-Zvi unaccountably moved back Beckett's reading of 'Fritz Mauthner, Austrian philosopher of language, whose "Critique of Language"(*Beiträge zu Einer Kritik der Sprache*) Beckett read in 1929 at the suggestion of Joyce, [which] described the impossibility of individuals coalescing parts of the ego'.[12] Justifications for locating Mauthner at the very outset of Beckett's writing career—despite contrary views considered momentarily—remains as forthcoming as Ben-Zvi's appreciation of (by now) well-documented alternative interpretations a generation later: 'The notion of using words to indict words was an idea Becket came across in 1929 when, at Joyce's behest, he read the *Beiträge*.'[13]

Quite simply, Ben-Zvi's most recent, yet fundamentally unchanged, text on this critical encounter employs a letter and interviews, the latter after more than a generation and the former after nearly fifty years, to assert that Mauthner's linguistic ideas helped to shape Beckett's earliest published essay, 'Dante…Bruno.Vico..Joyce' (and by implication, of course, all his writing thereafter). Consequently, Ben-Zvi is guilty of the unwarranted assertions others had previously made regarding Beckett's reading of Mauthner. For if we return to Popper's principle of 'empirical corroboration', Beckett's reminiscences to both Ellmann and Ben-Zvi simply require further, independent (and preferably contemporaneous) confirmation. But more difficult is the nature of her verification: One need not be a Beckett aficionado to know that memory is oftentimes an imperfect indicator of past events, nor that Beckett's letter in the late 1970's—indeed after the play containing Beckett's only reference to Mauthner was first performed as *Rough for Radio II* on 13 April 1976—needs to be corroborated by supplementary evidence to verify such a matter.[14] This is not least because of the importance of the issue at hand: did Beckett, at the start of his literary career in 1929, have a pedigree in German linguistic philosophy influencing his writing, or did such an encounter (whatever its interpretative *value*) occur later?

Archival revelations, and especially noteworthy research by Pilling and Dirk van Hulle, have combined to offer a response to the above question by exemplifying the principle of 'empirical corroboration'. Given that 1938 was the first substantial period since 1930 when Beckett and Joyce were in the same city for any length of time, Beckett was unquestionably one of those asked for help by Joyce (as was his wont), whose eyesight was notoriously bad at this final stage in the long-progressing *Work in Progress*. That Beckett read Mauthner with the latter (if not for, alongside, or indeed independent of) here is clearly demonstrated by van Hulle's research, providing complete transcriptions of Joyce's two contemporaneous notebooks in question—consisting of 66 entries in VI.B.46, and a further 49 entries in VI.B.41, both composed between December 1937 and October 1938.[15] These '*Wake* notebooks', along with other supporting material (like notes on Heinrich Zimmer), strengthen the case for a later date, not least as Beckett's own notes correspond to 1938. But if van Hulle has established an empirical link between Beckett, Joyce, and Mauthner's *Beiträge* over 1938, might this still compatible with Beckett's reading of Mauthner in 1929 nonetheless?

By way of response, Pilling's meticulous attention to detail empirically substantiates van Hulle's scholarship, and addresses precisely this issue. In the first instance, Joyce appears to have been unaware of Mauthner's work before Eugene Jolas' recommendation in Zurich—a trip most likely taken over winter 1934–5. By the time of Beckett's full reintegration into Joyce's circle around his stabbing three years later, Joyce was completing *Finnegans Wake* and needed assistance, while Beckett was free of time and desperately needed money. These circumstances aside, Pilling's immense contribution with respect to Mauthner concerns his dating of two of Beckett's texts, both particularly important in terms of Beckett's interwar development. Vitally, Pilling is able to establish that the '*Whoroscope* Notebook'—the 'ancient commonplace book' of Ben-Zvi's all-important letter—almost certainly runs in chronological order around Beckett's transcriptions from Mauthner's *Beiträge*; and furthermore, that entries both preceding and following those on Mauthner could not have possibly been recorded prior to late 1937 or January 1938. The more important of these sources, Ernst Cassirer's 1922/3 complete works of Kant—in 11 volumes[16]—makes an oblique appearance in Beckett's (probably May) 1938 French poem 'ainsi a-t-on beau', alongside similarly veiled references to Mauthner (especially 'générations de chênes' and 'les périodes glaciaires').[17] In a flurry, then, Beckett went from having no documented connection to Fritz Mauthner whatsoever—despite Beckett's brief suggestions to the contrary in the decades following, for whatever reason—to a number of notebook entries, contact with Joyce regarding the *Beiträge*, and a poem making specific reference to Kant and allusion to Mauthner in the first half of 1938. Rather than any hidden, decade-long Beckett-Mauthner connection, this scenario is much more in keeping with Beckett's scribal tendencies, in addition to a number of other relevant considerations.

First, as demonstrated by a handful of exercise books composed just before travelling around Germany between September 1936 and March 1937, Beckett's German proficiency was only good enough to manage *Faust* on the eve of his departure. Still, other notebooks from 1936 show Beckett recording German verbs, phrases and parts of speech—self-directed learning much in keeping with Beckett's labours in the 1930s. It is also worth recalling a letter of 21 November 1931 to Thomas MacGreevy, further pointing up a modest knowledge of German *after* 1929: 'I am reading German and learning a little that way.'[18] In summary, the 23-year-old Samuel Beckett simply did not have linguistic mastery over German sufficient to make use of Mauthner's *Beiträge* until nearly a decade later—let alone the philosophical background or intellectual iconoclasm painfully established over that decade. Further corroboration is found in another recent archival discovery regarding Mauthner: Beckett's verbatim transcription of pages 473–479 in Volume II of the *Beiträge*, subtitled 'Concerning Linguistics'. Vitally, these pages correspond to Mauthnerian entries in Joyce's notebook, VI.B.41, as well as to the overwhelming majority of transcriptions in Beckett's *'Whoroscope* Notebook' (featuring a dozen entries sequentially covering pages 309–715 of Volume II). The following translated and reproduced excerpt from pages 476–478 demonstrates the fascinating subject matter of these typed notes and is—in light of scholarship considered above by Ben-Zvi, van Hulle and Pilling—especially apposite:

> Kant has guided the world up to the present. He knows—admittedly only as far as the critique of language aspects are concerned—that human concepts are always attached to pictorial ideas, that *until we get to the recognition of the world of reality, the thing-in-itself, we will never make progress, because our thinking—as we can call it without any constraint—is metaphoric, anthropocentric* [....] One could on the basis of Kant's works put together an unassailable critical theory of knowledge of 'not knowing', and even more liberated one as that of the once famous "docta ignorantia"of Nicolaus Cusanus. In his negative thinking Kant is already the destroyer of everything; we bow before the intellect which in its strongest hours started the gigantic work, which in the form of the de-construction of language or of thought was necessary. But Kant's last worldview is still nevertheless only that of a period of transition; or perhaps it was especially his recognition of his gigantic power *which misled him to permit the negative act to be followed by a positive system* [....] *Kant remained standing before the gates of truth. The critique of language alone can unlock these gates and show with friendly resignation that leads from the world and thought into the void.*[19]

Ideally, the above serves as both insight into Beckett's demonstrable connection to Mauthner in 1938, in addition to a methodological caution along the lines suggested by Popper's 'empirical corroboration'. To be sure, this bare archival review nonetheless allows us to confidently assert that Beckett first read Mauthner in 1938. To be more precise, Beckett's first reading of the *Beiträge* occurred around mid-1938, perhaps even as early as late spring.[20] The ramifications are decisive: Beckett's interwar journalism and essays on aesthetics, let alone the first decade or so of creative writing, were all accomplished without recourse to Mauthner's linguistic scepticism. For the esoterically uninitiated, the equation may be made clearer: Beckett read the Fritz Mauthner's *Beiträge Zu Einer Kritik der Sprache* after the 'German Letter' of 1937, but before the outbreak of the Second World War; that is, between the writing of *Murphy* and *Watt*.[21] Moreover, the cross-checking of material, the collection and subsequent employment of all available evidence, and indeed the conscious reference to methodological principles in the interest of minimising guesswork; all these *allow for theorising with empirical accuracy*. For even the compelling evidence for Beckett's 1938 introduction to Mauthner is not yet explicitly a theory: that Beckett read Mauthner in 1938 is not the same as saying that such an event mattered, either to Beckett's development, or for that matter, to anything else.

This segues into our second point, that of 'relevance'. The fundamental reason for introducing the above point on Mauthner is quite straightforward: it is here maintained that Fritz Mauthner was notable to Beckett's literary development. That is, the empirically underpinned dating of Beckett's encounter with the *Beiträge* has *relevance* to our discipline insofar as it might contribute to a theory with more *explanatory power* than that previously advanced by Ben-Zvi. For example, a theory with more explanatory power might be: Beckett's reading of Mauthner in 1938 is a major reason for the change in presentation and content between *Murphy* and *Watt*. To date, only Jenny Skerl's 1974 essay has looked squarely at Mauthner's influence on *Watt*, surely an oversight in Beckett studies bearing further critical attention. Still, many commentators have noted the decisive change in the tone, structure and increasing linguistic emphasis in *Watt* (and of course in writings thereafter)—even the degree to which Mauthner's influence 'may be it', as Beckett put it in *Rough for Radio II*—although charting this neglected shift at this point in Beckett's oeuvre falls outside the scope of this text.[22] But another context entirely is more suitable for examples of Popper's second methodological pillar in Beckett studies.

§4

At some point during his psychotherapy with Wilfred Bion between late 1933 and late 1935—almost certainly between May 1934 and spring 1935—Beckett constructed about 20,000 words of typescript notes from various psychological texts. Beyond obvious connections to his own psychotherapy, the meticulousness of these transcriptions is unmistakable, and gestures toward the importance of Beckett's inquiry into psychology, and especially psychoanalysis. Unfortunately, only one example from these 'Psychology Notes' must suffice as positive proof of their relevance to later writings; in this case, probably the most important psychological source for Beckett: Robert Woodworth's 1931 *Contemporary Schools of Psychology*. Representing fully one-quarter of the entire corpus of psychological entries—summarised from nine books with a few additional extrapolations and handwritten underlying, emphasis, and so on—Woodworth's is the only text not specifically on psychoanalysis, comprising instead a synoptic overview of psychology. Among numerous references plucked from Woodworth by Beckett for his art (especially in *Murphy*) is the following excerpt on Wolfgang Köhler's proto-Behaviourist study of apes at Tenerife during World War I, forming the source for Murphy's initial jibe at Neary—'Back to Teneriffe and the apes?'—and the entirety of Beckett's extant notes on Köhler's work:

> Köhler's studies on apes at German arthropoid station of Teneriffe [sic] during the war. Did the apes possess <u>insight</u>? Was their learning more than a mere matter of trial & terror [sic], as concluded by Thorndike? Köhler was able to show that the apes did possess insight, provided they were allowed to see all the elements in the situation (its pattern), instead of being placed in such a blind situation as a box, maze, etc., & that they could close gaps. Thus a chimpanzee could join two sticks together to get at food beyond the reach of either, or similarly pile up boxes.
>
> Insight essential in learning: this view opposed to that of associationism, with its conception of learning as made up of linkages, native & acquired, between stimuli & responses. The brain works in large patters, closing gaps.[23]

Twenty years later, Köhler's research acts as the setting and structure for *Act Without Words I*, 'A mime with one player': 'He takes up a small cube, puts it on big one, tests their stability, gets up on them and is about to reach carafe [marked 'WATER'] when it is pulled up a little way and comes to rest beyond his reach.'[24] Revealing the intertextual reference affords a striking contrast between Köhler's apes as 'can-ers' in conceptual learning and Beckett's mime as a 'non can-er', with relief ever beyond reach.[25] Furthermore, additional examples demonstrating such correspondences between Beckett's notes on psychology and published writings merely await further documentation. Even more significantly for present purposes, given the amount of time Beckett spent composing this material, given his biographical circumstances at this time, and given the later employment of some of his notes into subsequent writings, one would be hard pressed to dismiss this psychological evidence as lacking 'relevance' or 'explanatory power'.

In contrast, a recent text by Didier Anzieu provides a representative and instructive counter-point. Anzieu's *Beckett et le Psychanalyste*, partially translated for a 1994 issue of *The Journal of Beckett Studies*, is organised by dated entries from 18 October 1990 to 14 April 1991; that is, after Beckett's death in December 1989. As J.D. O'Hara's excellent review of this monograph in the same issue of *JOBS* suggests, 'we hear in various styles about his professional work, his conversations with acquaintances, and his concerns about his writing, himself, and his relations with his parents. He shows this writing to others and reports their opinions. He contrives dialogues between author and reader'.[26] O'Hara's vital pronoun here refers to Anzieu, not Beckett. In accepting O'Hara's reading, our previous methodological question arises: how is this relevant to our understanding of Beckett? Do any of these entries have sufficient explanatory power with respect to Beckett studies? Space only permits two short examples from Anzieu's text itself:

> [Beckett and Bion] found themselves trapped by a negative transfer and countertransfer. Beckett had transferred *en masse* to his analyst hostile feelings aimed at his mother in particular and at reality in general [....]. Its because he took the initiative in breaking with Bion that he was able, afterwards, to leave his mother as well as his English language. For his part, Bion undoubtedly had trouble dealing with a patient who resembled him too much, and he unconsciously encouraged Beckett to leave.[27]

In relating this to our first consideration, no empirical evidence of Beckett and Bion's sessions is available to scholars (Bion refused to publish his case notes on Beckett). But as regards 'relevance', it is difficult to understand how any assertions can be 'undoubtedly' made about an individual's subconscious state by a third party—in this case Anzieu—who had no access to either protagonist. In short, from a methodological perspective, this approach is unlikely to demonstrably advance knowledge of our subject, Samuel Beckett, because it never leaves the subjectivism of Anzieu's impressions. Hopefully a final quotation from Anzieu's text will make this clear, an excerpt from an imagined discussion between 'Reader' and 'Analyst' on 13 December 1990:

> R: Why do you dislike *Happy Days* so much?
> A: Beckett had finished his self-analysis in 1960 and, with it, the severe demands of the soliloquy that had made it possible. The period of the internal struggle, which had such a powerful impact on me, was over. *Happy Days* has the flavor of a comedy of manners [....] The audience could go slumming at little cost to itself.[28]

All this, and especially Anzieu's final passage above, places us in a position to consider the overarching methodological principle at stake: falsification. Put simply, how can the assertion 'Beckett had finished his self-analysis in 1960' be shown as incorrect? The inability to construct a refutable explanation able to increase our scholarly knowledge is, in Popper's view at least, the cardinal sin of theorisation. Falsification is refutability, through the aegis of evidence, relevance, and explanatory power.

§5

A final, more representative, instance is in order to conclude more squarely with the problem of falsifying theoretical readings in Beckett studies. Taken from a recently edited volume entitled *Beckett and Philosophy*, Richard Lane's insightful chapter nevertheless seems to offer evidence of Popper's 'synthetic' statements. In 'Beckett and Nietzsche: The Eternal Headache', Lane's interest does not appear to be anchored to the 'growth of knowledge' in Popper's sense, but is instead directed toward evocation, and a subjective comparison of

> the relationship between Beckett and Nietzsche. Does this mean Nietzsche *in* the work of Beckett? Or Beckett *in* the work of Nietzsche (ignoring a certain chronology)? Or could this mean Beckett *as* Nietzsche or Nietzsche *as* Beckett? The former can be read or thought of in two ways: the banality of saying that Beckett was influenced by Nietzsche, or the more unusual statement that Nietzsche was influenced by Beckett; either of these two options are essentially predictable, leading me to assert the far more interesting notion that there is a Beckettian and Nietzschean textual moment found *denied* in both, yet *shared* by both.²⁹

Again, the aim here is not upon questions of insight, but those of methodology. The above statement, similar to a number of others in *Beckett and Philosophy*, cannot be refuted, or shown to be false. That is to say, the relationship Lane argues for with respect to a 'textual moment found *denied* in both, yet *shared* by both' can certainly be shown to exist, if only by virtue of the author's rhetorical skill or analytical strategy; however, without the methodological litmus tests of 'empirical corroboration' and 'relevance', can such a statement be falsified?

Let me marshal Popper one last time: 'I regard the comparison of the empirical content of two statements as equivalent to the comparison of their degrees of falsifiability. This makes our methodological rule that those theories should be given preference which can be most severely tested [...] equivalent to a rule favouring theories with the highest possible empirical content.'³⁰ To reformulate this in terms of Beckett studies, I take this to mean that approaching our subject from a position of empirical strength is inherently preferable to not doing so, or of disregarding methodological considerations altogether. Three criteria have been traced out here as potentially helpful to criticism on Beckett's literature; namely, 'falsification' (or refutability), supported by 'empirical corroboration' (or evidentiary basis) and 'relevance' (or utility). Thus, to say that Beckett and Popper somehow suggest each other is wholly subjective and not *falsifiable*; a comparison of Popper's and Beckett's feet may be falsifiable, but is not likely have much *explanatory power*; and finally, barring references or citations linking Beckett to Popper or vice-versa, the *relevance* of any methodology placing the two critically side by side is open to justifiable, prima facie, challenges.

Whatever the post-modern (in the widest sense) evocation of Beckett's (especially later) writing—for example, in *Worstword Ho*: 'Fail again. Fail Better [....] How vast. How if not boundless bounded. Whence the dim. Not now. Know better now. Unknow better now. Know only no out of. No knowing how know only no out of. Into only'³¹—the difference in critical approach in Beckett studies seems remarkably close to the age-old schism between induction and deduction, or what Mauthner called the 'tautologies' of language, as opposed to the empiricism of the senses. Hopefully this text has both underwritten some of the new possibilities and discoveries available through manuscript research, while discussing some fundamental methodological differences within Beckett studies. As we have seen, one of these approaches tends towards verifying Beckettian themes through the works of his contemporaries (who were usually unknown to Beckett during his lifetime) and oftentimes descendants; while another quite distinct approach holds, albeit also too implicitly, that advancing ideas which can be falsified is useful in demonstrably increasing our knowledge of a given subject—even if that knowledge itself concerns ignorance, ineffability, and impossibility. This is especially relevant to Beckett studies given Beckett's notorious literature, so well documented in our discipline over nearly fifty years, and therefore merits restating: methodological falsification attempts to better understand Beckett's work by theorising from a context of empirical strength, *despite the fact that* the subject matter is concerned with how to 'Know better now. Unknow better now.'[32] This should remind us of two things: the paradox that Beckett's literary investigations of wo/man as 'non can-er' was founded on great knowledge (acquired especially between 1929 and 1938); and secondly, that Beckett's interest in what may be called 'arationalism'—what I have called 'non-Euclidean logic'—by no means entails that scholars ought to use the same creative approach.[33] Quite the opposite: Beckett studies, perhaps on account of the very nature of Beckett's writing, mandates a particular clarity of our methodological tools.

In closing, I suppose my own advocacy is also clear; namely, the rather out-of-fashion belief in inter-subjectivity, in promising possibilities of palpably increasing understanding of our shared subject, and in the value of undertaking, oftentimes thankless, academic scholarship to do so. To be sure, this is made problematic by Beckett's literature, and that infamous 'impotence and ignorance' underpinning much of it.[34] The question posed here is, ultimately, how best to approach this within Beckett studies. I have outlined two approaches, one which may be viewed in terms of what Beckett dubbed a 'stink of artifice' in *Mercier and Camier*, and even earlier, 'scaffolding' in *Proust*.[35] In this context, such 'scaffolding' entails applying a methodology to an existing structure (in this case, Beckett's oeuvre), one done in the interest of adding to knowledge about our literary subject (even if, paradoxically, that understanding might take us closer to Beckett's own encounters with ineffability). Contra 'scaffolding', the second technique might be seen as 'interior decorating': a comparison or synthesis of otherwise disconnected subjects in the interest of adding to an understanding of something other than Beckett, exemplified by the philosophers and philosophies detailed in *Beckett and Philosophy*. What is needed is a better appreciation of the academic working methods separating these two techniques, these two approaches, to Beckett's life and work. For it is striking that there is no dearth of theories in Beckett studies—and indeed literary criticism as a whole—but instead, a lack of organising principles to distinguish between *types of theories*. If this modest attempt to do so by standing on the shoulders of Karl Popper is successful, then perhaps further discussion around the proper principles of demarcation is in order. Otherwise let me withdraw, to appropriate an exchange from *Mercier and Camier*—just after the quotation given the in above epigraph—and therefore speak *for myself* rather than *about Beckett*:

> The dogs don't trouble you?
> Why does he not withdraw? said Camier.
> He cannot, said Mercier.
> Why? said Camier.
> One of nature's little gadgets, said Mercier, no doubt to make insemination double sure.
> They begin astraddle, said Camier, and finish arsy-versy.
> What would you? said Mercier. The ecstasy is past, they yearn to part, to go and piss against a post or eat a morsel of shit, but cannot. So they turn their backs on each other. You'd do as much, if you were they.
> Delicacy would restrain me, said Camier.
> And what would you do? said Mercier.
> Feign regret, said Camier, that I could not renew such pleasure incontinent.

NOTES

[1] Karl Popper, 'Truth, Rationality, and the Growth of Scientific Knowledge', in *Conjectures and Refutations* (London: Routledge Classics, 2002), p. 336.
[2] Samuel Beckett, *Mercier and Camier* (London: Calder & Boyers, 1974), pp. 9–10.
[3] Karl Popper, *The Logic of Scientific Discovery* (London: Hutchinson and Co., 1959), p. 121.
[4] Karl Popper, 'Truth, Rationality, and the Growth of Scientific Knowledge', p. 309.
[5] *Ibid.*, pp. 312–3, 327.
[6] *Ibid.*, p. 319.
[7] Bruce Arnold, 'From Proof to Print: Anthony Cronin's *Samuel Beckett: The Last Modernist*', in *Samuel Beckett Today / Ajourd'hui* 8 (2000), p. 209.
[8] James Knowlson, *Damned to Fame: The Life of Samuel Beckett* (London: Bloomsbury, 1996), pp. 1–2.
[9] Richard Begam, 'Beckett and Postfoundationalism: Or How fundamental are those sounds?', in *Beckett and Philosophy*, ed. Richard Lane (Basingstoke: Palgrave, 2002), pp. 13, 17.
[10] Linda Ben-Zvi, 'Fritz Mauthner for Company', in the *Journal of Beckett Studies* 9 (1984), pp. 66, 69–70.
[11] *Ibid.*, pp. 66–7; the full quotation is found in Fritz Mauthner, *Beiträge zu Einer Kritik der Sprache*, 3 vols. (Leipzig: Verlag von Felix Meiner, 1923), 615, vol. III; corresponding to the '*Whoroscope* Notebook', UoR MS 3000, p. 46.
[12] Linda Ben-Zvi, *Samuel Beckett* (Boston: Twayne Publishers, 1986), p. 152.
[13] Linda Ben-Zvi, 'Biographical, Historical and Textual Origins', in *Palgrave Advances in Beckett Studies*, ed. Lois Oppenheim (London: Palgrave, 2004), pp. 137, 150.
[14] Samuel Beckett, *Murphy* (London: Calder, 1993), p. 276.
[15] Dirk Van Hulle, 'Beckett—Mauthner—Zimmer—Joyce', in *The Joyce Studies Annual* 10 (1999), pp. 163–183; and 'Mauthner, Richards, and the Development of Wakese', in *James Joyce: The Study of Languages*, ed. Dirk van Hulle (Brussels, Peter Lang: 2002), pp. 108–116. See also Danis Rose, *James Joyce's The Index Manuscript* (London: A Wake Newsletter Press, 1978).
[16] John Pilling clarifies that volume XI, Cassirer's biography of Kant, constituted the entries before Beckett's transcriptions of Mauthner; see his 'Dates and Difficulties in Beckett's *Whoroscope* Notebook', in the *Journal of Beckett Studies* 13/2 (2004).
[17] For the poem 'ainsi a-t-on beau', see Samuel Beckett *Collected Poems* (London: Calder, 1999), p. 48. Much of this is discussed in Pilling's particularly insightful 'Dates and Difficulties in Beckett's *Whoroscope* Notebook', esp. pp. 43–8; see also note 21.
[18] Beckett to Thomas MacGreevy, 21 November 1931, TCD MSS 10904.
[19] TCD MS 10971/5, Transcriptions of Fritz Mauthner's *Beiträge*, 473–479, vol. II, pp. 2–4; italics added. I am indebted to the late Professor Detlef Mühlberger for this translation from German, in addition to the further assistance provided by Erik Tonning.
[20] I am indebted to John Pilling—who argues for the Beckett-Mauthner encounter likely occurring around late spring or early summer 1938—for repeated discussions on this issue at the University of Reading.
[21] The nominalism often ascribed to Mauthner in Beckett's 'German Letter' of 1937— explicitly, 'to compare Nominalism (in the sense of the Scholastics) with Realism. One the

way to this literature of the unword, which is so desirable to me, some form of Nominalist irony might be a necessary stage.' Beckett, cited in *Disjecta: Miscellaneous Writings and a Dramatic Fragment*, ed. Ruby Cohn (New York: Grove Press, 1984), pp. 51-4, with the English translation provided on pp. 170-3—may well be derived from Beckett's Latin transcription from pp. 96-97 in vol. I of Joseph Gredt's *Elementa Philosophiae Aristotelico-Thomisticae*, 2 vols. (Herder & Co: Freiburg, 1925), possibly obtained or suggested by Brian Coffey in 1936.

[22] Samuel Beckett, 'Rough for Radio II', in *The Complete Dramatic Works* (London: Faber and Faber, 1990), p. 276. For an important account of changes registered in *Watt*, see Gottfried Büttner, *Samuel Beckett's Novel* Watt, trans. Joseph P. Dolan (Philadelphia, University of Pennsylvania Press, 1984); for a rare and recent discussion of Mauthner's work in English, see Elizabeth Bredeck, *Metaphors of Knowledge: Language and Thought in Mauthner's Critique* (Detroit: Wayne State University Press, 1992).

[23] Samuel Beckett, *Murphy* (London: Calder, 1993), p. 7; and Beckett's 'Psychology Notes', TCD MS 10971/7/8, corresponding to Robert S. Woodworth *Contemporary Schools of Psychology* (London: Methuen, 1931), pp. 121-5.

[24] Samuel Beckett, 'Act without Words I', in *The Complete Dramatic Works*, pp. 201, 204.

[25] Cited in Knowlson, *Damned to Fame*, p. 353.

[26] J.D. O'Hara, Review of Anzieu's *Beckett et le Psychanalyste* in the *Journal of Beckett Studies* 4/1 (1994), p. 179.

[27] Didier Anzieu, 'Beckett and the Psychoanalyst', in the *Journal of Beckett Studies* 4/1 (1994), p. 25.

[28] *Ibid.*, pp. 30-1.

[29] Richard Lane, 'Beckett and Nietzsche: The Eternal Headache', in *Beckett and Philosophy*, p.166.

[30] Popper, *The Logic of Scientific Discovery*, p. 121.

[31] Samuel Beckett, *Worstward Ho* (London: Calder, 1983), pp. 7, 11.

[32] *Ibid.*, p. 11.

[33] Matthew Feldman, *Beckett's Books: A Cultural History of Samuel Beckett's Interwar Notes* (London: Continuum, 2006), pp. 1-5.

[34] Knowlson, *Damned to Fame*, p. 55.

[35] Samuel Beckett, *Mercier and Camier* (London: Calder & Boyers, 1974), p. 9; and Beckett, 'Proust', in *Proust and Three Dialogues* (London: Calder & Boyers, 1970), p. 11.

BECKETT AND PHILOSOPHY, 1928–1938:
A Falsifiable Reappraisal

§1

As this chapter revisits Beckett's relationship with philosophy, it is useful to start out by revisiting two quotations that are equally familiar and misleading. Ten years after the Unnamable's savaging of philosophical 'college quips'—'[t]hey must consider me sufficiently stupefied with all their balls about being and existing'[1]—Beckett further effaced his relationship with philosophy by claiming an ignorance many critics have found difficult to square with his art. And indeed, even if the specifics of his remarks are broadly accurate, the strong implication that Beckett was a philosophical novice must be regarded as untenable:

> Have contemporary philosophers had any influence on your thought?
> I never read philosophers.
> Why not?
> I never understand anything they write.
> All the same, people have wondered if the existentialists' problem of being may afford a key to your works.
> There's no key or problem. I wouldn't have had any reason to write my novels if I could have expressed their subject in philosophic terms.[2]
> One cannot speak anymore of being, one must speak only of the mess. When Heidegger and Sartre speak of a contrast between being and existence, they may be right, I don't know, but their language is too philosophical for me. I am not a philosopher. One can only speak of what is in front of him, and that now is simply the mess.[3]

Beckett's evasion over whether or not philosophers have actually influenced his thought is underscored by the ambiguity of 'read', serving both present and past tenses. It will be argued here that, while it may be fairly said that Beckett was not reading philosophers for influence *in the present tense* by 1961, he had certainly read, and derived sizeable influence from, philosophy *in the past tense*. Undertaken over ten years of essentially self-directed study between 1928 and 1938, this was a time in Beckett's life when the contrast between being and existence, for example, was not at all too philosophical to understand or engage. Before substantiating these claims by recounting Beckett's direct relationship with philosophy in the interwar years, however, an aside is necessary at the outset regarding the methodological approach undertaken here, that of 'falsifiability'.

In doing so, an appeal is again made to Karl Popper's deductive approach to evidence—at its most basic, the 'purely logical' possibility of refuting an argument—which he saw as the decisive principle in increasing humanistic knowledge, a self-reflective practice he called, later in life, 'modified essentialism':

> The fundamental difference between my approach and the approach for which I long ago introduced the label "inductivist" is that I lay stress on *negative arguments*, such as negative instances or counter-examples, refutations, and attempted refutations—in short, criticism—while the inductivist lays stress on "*positives instances*", from which he draws "non-demonstrative *inferences*", and which he hopes will guarantee the "*reliability*" of the conclusions of these inferences.[4]

Having gestured at the interpretative approach taken here, to quote from Beckett's unpublished article late August 1938, 'Les Deux Besoins', '[L]et's get on with falsifying'. As 'The Two Needs' is one of the chronological bookends of this chapter, it is worth recalling Beckett's conclusion on that

> holy reasoning, *this slippery and dangerous place*. Nothing less resembles the creative process than these convulsions of enraged vermin, propulsed in spasms of judgment towards a rotting election. For in the enthymemes of art, it's the conclusions which are lacking, not the premises.[5]

By the autumn of 1938, exhausted of external advice, Beckett had come to view reason as inimical to his artistic process. And with this realisation—along with the critical shift to writing in French (evidenced in both the unpublished 'Les Deux Besoins' article and the *Petit Sot* series of poems)—Beckett had returned full-circle to his position of ten years earlier: engaging with philosophy was no longer a necessity for his artistic purposes. However, the key difference between 1928 and 1938 was that Beckett had come to this artistic insight via a position of knowledge instead of philosophical superficiality; or better still, through the embrace of what Fritz Mauthner termed 'learned ignorance'. The falsifiable argument here, in short, is that the influence of philosophy upon Beckett was a short and intense affair, one that both started and ended in interwar Paris. Of course, philosophical themes were to recur across Beckett's oeuvre again and again, right up to his death in 1989. But these were artistic reformulations of the work he had done in the pivotal decade leading to the outbreak of war in Europe. Thereafter, Beckett's philosophical *development* ceased, and only philosophical *reinforcement* is in extant evidence—such as a rereading of Arthur Schopenhauer in the late 1970s/early 1980s 'Sottisier Notebook', or more contentiously, his later reading of Ludwig Wittgenstein.[6]

Yet as John Calder's 2002 *The Philosophy of Samuel Beckett* emphasises, this need not preclude a separate matter; namely lifelong alterations to Beckett's philosophy. Richard Lane's previously-cited volume from the same year makes plain, too, that numerous scholars have employed the fashionable philosophers to highlight elements of a Beckettian contemporary world. I want to place both these influential readings in abeyance by recourse to Calder's insightful (if unfalsifiable) suggestion that 'Beckett was the last of the great stoics'.[7] In terms of outlook, this may well be spot on; certainly many scholars have recognised it as a keystone of Beckett's humanistic temperament. Yet as I have been trying to suggest thus far, this general question of philosophical outlook is a matter separate from 'Beckett and philosophy', strictly speaking. The latter relationship—in terms drawn from Beckett's 1932–3 'Philosophy Notes'—may be better characterised as one of scepticism rather than stoicism.

> Stoicism a return to Socratic position via the cynics. Practical virtue implies a certain positive disposition of the soul. Whereas cynics emphasised negative aspect of Sage's well-being (independence of health, wealth, etc.), Stoics emphasised positive aspect (ultra-joyful & -sorrowful tranquillity). [.... But sceptics] resist the seducements to opinion and action. He knows that nothing can be affirmed as to phenomena, that no opinion may be assented to, and so restrains himself from judgment, and thereby from action. In the suspension of judgment, he finds imperturbability, rest within himself, ataraxy. The sceptics were called "The Suspenders."[8]

By coming to his own sceptical position of 'learned ignorance' with regard to philosophy—precisely *through* a sustained period of philosophical self-education—Beckett had reached what was to become the most profound armistice with Western philosophy in modern literature. To again quote from Beckett's transcriptions from the critical summer months of 1938, one of the inspirations for this 'self-destruction of the metaphorical', Fritz Mauthner, had this to say about what he regarded as the greatest form of epistemological nominalism:

> Whatever the human may dare to do through superhuman strength in order to discover truth, he always finds only himself, a human truth, an anthropomorphic picture of the world. The last word of thought can only be the negative act, the self-destruction of anthropomorphism, the insight into the profound wisdom of Vico: not everything is intelligible to men.[9]

§2

Vico was, of course, one of the very first philosophers the 22-year-old Beckett was to consult upon arriving in France as an English *lecteur* at the École Normale in November 1928. The early celebration of James Joyce, leading to the 1929 'Dante...Bruno.Vico..Joyce', ensured that these Italian demolishers of dialectical contraries (such as speed and rest) were Beckett's first real, if superficial, engagement with philosophy. This point has been made in Deirdre Bair's 1978 biography, where Beckett, in a letter of 24 October 1974, 'stressed he did not study philosophy' prior to leaving Ireland: 'Because he had not taken a philosophy course at Trinity College, which he felt was a serious defect in his education, he set out on what he thought was a systematic schedule of readings.[10]

Eclipsing Beckett's fleeting interest in Descartes evident in the first half of 1930, and indeed returned to all of his life thereafter, was Schopenhauer. This was so much the case that Mark Nixon, for one, already detected an 'aesthetic of unhappiness' in the *Proust* monograph sent to Chatto & Windus at the end of that year. While Beckett, as he wrote to MacGreevy in late July 1930, doubtless found Schopenhauer's 'intellectual justification of unhappiness' of no small personal interest, his engagement went still further intellectually.[11] For one of Schopenhauer's great concerns was to be taken up by Beckett in the ensuing eight years of philosophical study, tirelessly set out, for example, in the opening pages of Volume II of the *World as Will and Representation*:

> Subjective and objective do not form a continuum. That of which we are immediately conscious is bounded by the skin, or rather by the extreme ends of the nerves proceeding from the cerebral system. Beyond this lies a world of which we have no other knowledge than that gained through pictures in our mind. Now the question is whether and to what extent a world existing independently corresponds to these pictures.[12]

More than any other issue, this was the backbone for Beckett's ensuing philosophical thinking to 1938; namely, the relationship between subject and object. Much of this engagement has been impressively covered in Erik Tonning's *Samuel Beckett's Abstract Drama*, and only certain features will be recounted here in turning to that meaty period of Beckett and philosophy: the 1930s. Stirring above this clashing of philosophical dialectics, now taking on real significance, were seemingly superficial changes to the style of what Beckett called, in summer 1931, 'the old demon of note-snatching'.[13] Correspondingly, Beckett's relationship with philosophy may be argued to have gone through three distinct, if overlapping, stages—as registered across his 'Interwar Notes'.

The first phase of Beckett's philosophical development seems to have petered out around the completion of *Dream of Fair to Middling Women* in summer 1932, as Beckett was moving away from James Joyce. Dirk van Hulle has aptly described Beckett's process at this time as intellectual treasure hunting for what he has dubbed 'linguistic oddities'. Emphatically bearing this out is John Pilling's edited *Beckett's Dream Notebook*, composed by Beckett between 1930 and 1931 from a mélange of sources. On the whole, very few philosophical sources are in evidence here, even with a generous definition of 'philosophy' embracing St Augustine's *Confessions* and Robert Burton's *Anatomy of Melancholy*. Other 'philosophical' texts noted from this explicitly Joycean period and recycled for *Dream*—and, as Pilling shows, sometimes for *More Pricks Than Kicks*—include surveys such as W.R. Inge's *Christian Mysticism*, and interestingly, the final text noted (excluding Tennyson/Chaucer poems from which the abortive book's title is derived), the far more philosophically-directed, indeed Nietzschean, 1930 edition of Jules de Gaultier's *From Kant to Nietzsche*, giving especial attention to the 'relation between <u>object</u> & its <u>representation</u>, between the <u>stimulus</u> & <u>molecular disturbance</u>, between <u>percipi</u> and <u>percipere</u>'.[14]

To be sure, the vexing relation between subject and object persisted in Beckett's notes beyond the completion of *Dream* in summer 1932. At this point, a post-Joycean period of systematic summarisation seems to have commenced with a trip to England in July-August 1932, when Beckett first read in the British Library. Again depending on how widely one wishes to contextualise this second phase, Beckett's synoptic readings over the next four years were of more structured note-taking extended to a variety of subjects, revealed by such texts as R. H. Wilenski's *An Introduction to Dutch Art*, John G. Robertson's *A History of German Literature*, and Robert Woodworth's *Contemporary Schools of Psychology*. For present purposes, however, nothing rivals the 267 folios—mostly recto and verso—comprising Beckett's 'Philosophy Notes', likely ranging from summer 1932 to later 1933. Betraying a deep interest in the *formation* of these philosophical dualisms in the Western canon, two of Beckett's three texts specifically covered, in detail, the origins of Western philosophy: the entirety of John Burnet's 1914 *Greek Philosophy, Part I: Thales to Plato*, and Archibald Alexander's 1907 *A Short History of Philosophy*—at least until he tires of Alexander's prosaic account in the second-century A.D. Yet from the era of the Alexandrians (e.g. Justin Martyr and St Ignatius) right up until Nietzsche, Beckett's knowledge of Western philosophy was mediated by one book, perhaps one of a handful of those most significant to Beckett's development, Wilhelm Windelband's revised 1901 *A History of Philosophy*. Unlike Alexander's narrative, Windelband's lively writing recounts something of a philosophical story that is 'a connected and interrelated whole'; meaning that in 'some direction and in every fashion every philosophy has striven to reach, over a more or less extensive field, a formulation in conception of the material given in the world and in life [....] How conceptions and forms have been coined, in which we all, in every-day life as well as in the particular sciences, think and judge the world of our experience.'[15]

Needless to say, this is a locating of subject-object relations at the very core of Western philosophy, one born 'out of the conceptions which the Greek mind wrested from the concrete reality found in Nature and human life', and to which, for Windelband, only Immanuel Kant has rivalled since Greek antiquity. In turn, Beckett devoted thirteen recto and verso sides to Windelband's fourteen pages (537–550) setting out his view of Kant's greatest contribution: '<u>the only object of human knowledge is experience</u>, i.e. phenomenal experience. The distinction prevailing since Plato between <u>noumena</u> and <u>phenomena</u> has no meaning. Knowledge of things in themselves through "sheer reason", extension beyond experience, is a chimera.' Indeed, for Windelband, questions of epistemology and concept formation was the very mark of Kant's genius, providing no less than the

> fundamental antithesis between Kant and Greek theory of knowledge, which had prevailed up till that time in its view of the "objects" as given independently of thought. Kant the first to discover that the objects of thought are themselves the products of thought [....] Kant proceeds from antithesis between activity of the understanding and sensuous perception. Categorical thinking relates the data of perception so that every phenomena is <u>conditioned</u> by other phenomena [....] Thus the relation between sensibility and understanding involving <u>necessary but insoluble problems</u>.[16]

The information gleaned from the absolutely pivotal Windelband also crucially prepared Beckett for the final phase of his 'Interwar Notes'—that of verbatim transcription. Thus, for example, the earliest extant, lengthy transcriptions are taken in January-April 1936 from Arnold Geulincx's complete works—edited by J.P.N. Land between 1891 and 1893 as *Arnold Geulincx Opera Philosophica*—who was previously identified as an unfairly-obscured, if hugely iconoclastic, contributor to the subject-object discussion structuring Western philosophy:

> The ultimate "cause" for causal connection between stimuli and sensations, purpose and action, is God. This is <u>Occasionalism</u>.
> This furthest developed in <u>Ethics</u> of <u>Geulincx</u> [....] Geulincx reduces self-activity to immanent mental activity of man. The "autology" or <u>inspectio sui</u> is not only epistemological starting point, it is also ethical conclusion of his system. Man has nothing to do in outer world. <u>Ubi nihil vales, ibi nihil velis</u>.[17]

This is the first place where this famous formulation occurs in Beckett's hand, later quoted in a letter to Kennedy of 1967 and reprinted in *Disjecta*. This book was of a lifetime's service to Beckett, if indirectly mediated through his 'Philosophy Notes'. For instance, the famous epigraph to Chapter 6 of *Murphy*, describing that eponymous character's mind, is based upon a footnote to Windelband's discussion of post-Cartesianism, forming the 'ethical part of the Spinozistic system as *amor intellectualis quo deus se ipsum amat*'.[18]

Returning to an earlier point, it is worth pausing here to again note that Descartes' progenitors were of far greater philosophical interest—and of far more durable and demonstrable influence—than that of the pastiched protagonist from the 1930 *Whoroscope*. Alongside Geulincx's discussion of humility, for example, Tonning justly locates another 'surprisingly central figure' in Beckett's philosophical development from this period: Gottfried Leibniz.[19] Though described as a 'great cod' to Thomas MacGreevy when first encountered two years earlier, by December 1935 and the midway point in the writing of *Murphy*, it seems, Beckett's Leibniz (or better, Beckett's Leibniz as mediated by the centripetal neo-Kantian, Wilhelm Windelband) appears to have nonetheless help suture philosophy and psychoanalysis around a 'windowless monad' of self-contained, individual consciousness.[20] As Tonning's extensive coverage of this overlooked influence from Beckett's interwar years adjudges, 'monads are thus condemned to endless, unfulfilled striving', in a sort of philosophical shorthand for Beckett's sense of psychological anomie, so heightened during his two years of thrice-weekly psychotherapy with Wilfred Bion at this time.[21] Moreover, citations from the very different post-Cartesians Blaise Pascal and Baruch Spinoza also appear in the '*Whoroscope* Notebook'—Beckett's commonplace book from the 1930s, a key intellectual repository for entries on art and philosophy—with entries for the latter deriving from several different sources.[22] As another letter to MacGreevy (of 19 September 1936) reveals, it was Spinoza and 'his contemporaries' (the Anglophone title of a French text Beckett consulted at this time) greatly piquing Beckett's interest, indeed going so far as to catch 'a glimpse of Spinoza as a solution & a salvation'—itself later personalised as the 'Spinoza formulation—solution congruence' in a 'German Diary' entry from the next year.[23] Many of these entries from the Spinozan milieu, in turn, have little to do with Descartes' famed, if unresolved, philosophical relationship of mind to body. For what appears to have attracted Beckett at this time were the differing and, interestingly, *subsequent*, philosophical struggles with questions over how the mind could adequately represent the world outside it. Whether in the ideas of Nicholas Malebranche, Leibniz, Geulincx or Spinoza, it seems, the post-Cartesians were variously pointing to the interplay of mind and matter, of a perceiving subject, that Beckett was himself struggling with, as he duly copied into his '*Whoroscope* Notebook': 'Whence it is clearly to be seen, that measure, time and number, are merely modes of thinking, or, rather, of imagining'; and again, 'a circle is different from the idea of a circle…nor is the idea of a body that body itself.'[24]

In the months following the completion of *Murphy* in summer 1936, Beckett's jottings were largely confined to his six volumes of 'German Diaries' taken during his travels in Nazi Germany from October 1936 to April 1937. Yet even whilst travelling abroad in the mid-1930s, the subject-object problematic was not far from his mind, whether in terms of recording a conversation about 'the fence between the big and little worlds' in October 1936, or notes on Franz Marc's 'subject, predicate, object relations' in painting in mid-November 1936, and so on.[25] Yet after returning from Germany, it seems, Beckett's '*Whoroscope* Notebook' formed the central notebook of choice for many of these transcriptions—all far shorter than the 15,000 words of elliptical Latin taken, in ascending order, from

Geulincx's *Questions Concerning Disputations*, *Metaphysics*, and of greatest importance, his *Ethics*.

This final stage in Beckett's reading and note taking in philosophy may be said to last from winter 1936 to summer 1938. But importantly and also differently than before, Beckett's verbatim transcriptions not only extend to quotations from canonical philosophers—like the above say, or quotations from Spinoza's *Ethics* and by David Hume and Kant in Ernst Cassirer's biography of the latter, *Kant's Life and Thought*—they also extend to Beckett's philosophical contemporaries. Although he died slightly earlier, in 1923, this assertion can also embrace Beckett's notes on Fritz Mauthner's *Contributions to a Critique of Language*, first encountered around May 1938, as John Pilling has convincingly established. Again the interest in subjectivity and external phenomena is a thread connecting Mauthner to the philosophical readings engaging Beckett over the decade previously. Perhaps because he was, like Geulincx, an abiding philosophical interest of Beckett's, verbatim transcriptions from Mauthner's three-volume *Critique of Language* are actually typed up from a section in Vol. II, *Concerning Linguists*, itself the most important part of the most thumbed of Mauthner's three, extensive volumes (10 of 11 of Beckett's lengthy quotations from Mauthner's work derive from Volume II). This section is especially concerned with Kant's critique of reason, and is tellingly called 'History of Philosophy: The self-destruction of the metaphorical':

> Kant has guided the world up to the present. He knows—admittedly only as far as the critique of language aspects are concerned—that human concepts are always attached to pictorial ideas, that until we get to the recognition of the world of reality, the thing-in-itself, we will never make progress, because our thinking—as we can call it without any constraint—is metaphoric, anthropocentric. Kant does not deserve the smallest credit that through the overwhelming pronouncement of Locke's ideas he showed the way for the new investigation of the human sensory organs. One could on the basis of Kant's works put together an unassailable critical theory of knowledge of 'not knowing,' and even more liberated one as that of the once famous 'docta ignorantia' of Nicolaus Cusanus. In his negative thinking Kant is already the destroyer of everything; we bow before the intellect which in its strongest hours started the gigantic work, which in the form of the de-construction of language or of thought was necessary.
>
> But Kant's last worldview is still nevertheless only that of a period of transition; or perhaps it was especially his recognition of his gigantic power which misled him to permit the negative act to be followed by a positive system. He certainly stands in relation to absolute reason as Count Mirabeau does in relation to absolute monarchy.[26]

Almost certainly overlapping in time—John Pilling has suggested mid-1938[27]—Mauthner's argument is followed by Beckett's returning to Jules de Gaultier in his '*Whoroscope* Notebook'. Interestingly, the translated passage on

Kant below is not of the same character as the *Dream* entry of seven years earlier; this too is a verbatim transcription:

> Now the great work of Kant, accomplished in the fifty pages of the TRANSCENDENTAL AESTHETIC, consists in his having demonstrated that space and time do not on the one hand, have substantial reality and that, on the other hand, they are not properties of the object either; that, on the contrary, they belong to the knowing subject and that they are the forms of this subject's sensibility.[28]

§3

At this time, for Beckett's own aesthetic—roughly halfway between the completion of *Murphy* and the start of *Watt*—the matter seems to have come to a head. In his only published review from these critical months in 1938, 'Intercessions by Denis Devlin', for example, the 'severed' relation of subject and object is mooted as 'the absolute predicament of particular human identity'; moreover, 'the distinction is not idle, for it is from the failure to make it that proceed the common rejection as "obscure" of most that is significant in modern music, painting, and literature'.[29] This is reformulated in the unpublished 'Les Deux Besoins', as I suggested earlier, in much the same way:

> The side and diagonal, two needs, two essences, the being which is the need and the necessity for it being so, the irrational hell from which is raised a cry of blanks, the series of pure questions, the work.
> If its permitted in a similar way to speak of an effective principle, it's not, thanked be God and Poincaré, that which governs the petitions to principle in science and the crossed logos of theology, which feed the storms of affirmative and negative farts whence have come and continue to come those crappy a posteriosis of Spirit and Matter which form despair of Savage peoples. These go forward with blasts of 'yes' and 'no' like a detonating shell, until truth blows up. Another. Irreversible. Dead and wounded bear witness to the fact.[30]

Apparently concluding Beckett's struggle with philosophy in mid-1938 are two of the shortest entries in the '*Whoroscope* Notebook', essentially *aides memoires* taken from Jean-Paul Sartre's MA Dissertation, published as *L'Imagination* by Alcon in 1936. These are *noème* and *noèse*,[31] corresponding to Sartre's rendering: 'The concrete psychic reality is to be called noesis, and the indwelling meaning, noema. For example, "perceived-blossoming tree" is the noema of the perception I now have of it.'[32] *Imagination*, which Beckett likely read in mid-1938—just after finding *Nausea* 'extraordinarily good' in a letter to Thomas MacGreevy of 26 May 1938[33]—builds up a sustained critique, over eight chapters, of the perceptual image in Western philosophy as having 'harboured implicitly a whole metaphysics'. This schism between subjective consciousness and its perceptually-intended object could, however, be countered by a 'an entirely new theory of images', one based on Edmund Husserl's 1913 *Ideas*, for 'the observations he makes there are of the highest order'.[34] As Beckett then read from *Imagination*'s final chapter, 'The Phenomenology of Husserl', from the vantage point offered by Husserlian phenomenology, insists Sartre: 'An image too, is an image of something':

> For having put the world "between parentheses," the phenomenologist does not lose it. The distinction "consciousness / world" loses its meaning, and the line is now drawn differently [....] The problem becomes that of finding motives for forming "matter" into a mental image rather than into a perception [....] Husserl blazed the trail, and no study of images can afford to ignore the wealth of insights he provided. We know now that we must start afresh, setting aside all the prephenomenological literature, and attempting above all to attain an intuitive vision of the intentional structure of the image. It also becomes necessary to raise the novel and subtle question of the relations between mental images and "physical" images (paintings, photographs, etc.).[35]

In fact, both Sartre's philosophical *Imagination* and his literary *Nausea* may be seen as tentative critiques of Edmund Husserl's theory of the phenomenological intentionality (later extended in Sartre's 1940 *L'Imaginare*, recently translated as *The Imaginary*). Seemingly as a personal defence for turning to literature as a way of expressing his philosophical revelation, Sartre concludes his first philosophical study by averring: 'The way is open for a phenomenological psychology.'[36]

And this, in effect, represents the final evidence of Beckett's philosophical struggle with the relation between subject and object, and thereby, of 'Beckett and philosophy'. For Beckett by 1938, it may be argued, Western philosophy had fully served its didactic purpose. Henceforth, while clearly drawing upon material already accumulated over the past decade, in future only those thinkers with whom Beckett feels an affinity seem to be revisited. In terms of Beckett's fiction from the interwar years, his three phases of note taking seem to correspond to changes in his own approach. Thus, Western philosophy is only gaudily marshalled in *Dream of Fair to Middling Women* and its sequels *More Pricks Than Kicks* and the unpublished story 'Echo's Bones', if for no other reason than that Beckett dipped into eclectic texts—seemingly at times, nearly at random—in order to get what he called his quota of 'butin verbal' for his first novel. By the writing of *Murphy*, synoptic texts on the history of philosophy are clearly in structural evidence, as Chris Ackerley has shown in his excellent companion text, *Demented Particulars*. But the writing of *Murphy* had stalled by Christmastime 1935, and it appears that—no longer content with philosophical summarising— Beckett's lengthy transcriptions from Geulincx in early 1936 helped to get his first published novel moving again. By the time Beckett had later encountered

Mauthner, Sartre and Husserl in mid-1938, such philosophical buttressing had been turned into, as it were, interior decorating. Transcriptions of decreasing length show Beckett resolving, or refusing, or reforming, the philosophical lacunae between perceiving subject and the 'Thing-in-Itself' that had been such a hallmark of Western philosophy prior to Husserl.

Here, perhaps, is where the most influential author of the twentieth century met the most influential philosophy of the twentieth century, bringing Beckett's reflections over subject-object relations to an apparent close. For it was at this point Beckett turned to writing in French, composing the *Petit sot* series of poems which, Knowlson reports, show him 'consciously reaching towards a greater simplicity and directness, freeing himself from too much complexity of form and expression [... and] show him already evolving in 1938–39 specifically into a *French* writer'.[37] If these poems may indeed be considered early forays into the writing of direct phenomenological experience, the same may be said of the *Human Wishes* notes and play fragment (reprinted in *Disjecta*), which can be similarly said to foreshadow Beckett evolving into a specifically *dramatic* writer. It would seem that these 'failures' between 1938 and 1941, then, were to be the first, tenuous steps in writing 'post-philosophically'. By returning full circle to *The Unnamable*, only pages after laughing at his earlier 'college quips' the narrator notes, 'I'm the tympanum, on the one hand the mind, on the other the world, I don't belong to either'.[38] Perhaps this image, then, represents Beckett's response to the subject-object dichotomy, and to the philosophy he had earlier studied, if only to later efface, continuing

> perhaps that's what I feel, an outside and an inside and me in the middle, perhaps that's what I am, the thing that divides the world in two, on the one side the outside, on the other the inside, that can be thin as foil, I'm neither one side nor the other, I'm in the middle, I'm the partition, I've two surfaces and no thickness, perhaps that's what I feel [...][39]

NOTES

1. Samuel Beckett, The Unnamable, in *The Beckett Trilogy* [Molloy, Malone Dies and The Unnamable] (London: Picador, 1979), p. 320.
2. Samuel Beckett to Gabriel D'Aubarède, 16 February 1961, cited in Lawrence Graver and Raymond Federman, eds., *Samuel Beckett: The Critical Heritage* (London: Routledge and Kegan Paul, 1979), p. 217.
3. Samuel Beckett to Tom Driver, summer 1961, cited in *ibid.*, p. 219.
4. Karl Popper, *Objective Knowledge: An Evolutionary Approach* (Oxford: Clarendon, 1972), pp. 197, 20; italics in original, which further notes: 'We can sometimes say of two competing theories, A and B, that in the light of the state of the critical discussion at the time t, and the empirical evidence (test statements) available at the discussion, the theory A is preferable to, or better corroborated than, the theory B', p. 19.
5. Samuel Beckett, 'Le Deux Besoins', in *Disjecta: Miscellaneous Writings and a Dramatic Fragment*, ed. Ruby Cohn (New York: Grove Press, 1984), pp. 55–57, private translation; italics in original. For the dating of this text, see John Pilling, *A Samuel Beckett Chronology* (Basingstoke: Palgrave, 2006), p. 81.
6. For references to Schopenhauer in Beckett's 'Sottisier Notebook', see UoR MS 2901, pp. 25–6 (University of Reading, Beckett International Foundation). In respect of Ludwig Wittgenstein, the jury is still out in terms of whether the former had any textual influence on the latter's post-war works. Beckett is known to have had several of Wittgenstein's texts in his library at his death, and he noted in a letter to Barbara Bray of 18 January 1979 that he was reading Wittgenstein 'with interest'.
7. John Calder, *The Philosophy of Samuel Beckett* (London: Calder, 2002), p. 1.
8. TCD MS 10967/114 and TCD MS 10967/123, reproduced in Matthew Feldman, 'Sourcing "Aporetics": An Empirical Study on Philosophical Influences in the Development of Samuel Beckett's Writing' (Unpublished PhD. Thesis: Oxford Brookes University, 2004), pp. 302–3.
9. TCD MS 10971/5/5, cited in *ibid.*, p. 387.
10. Deirdre Bair, *Samuel Beckett: A Biography* (London: Vintage, 1990), pp. 96, 694.
11. Cited in Mark Nixon, 'Beckett and Romanticism in the 1930s', in *Samuel Beckett Today / Aujourd'hui* 18 (2007), p. 69.
12. Arthur Schopenhauer, *The World as Will and Representation*, vol. II, trans. E.F.J. Payne (New York: Dover, 1958), p. 10.
13. See Erik Tonning, *Samuel Beckett's Abstract Drama: Works for Stage and Screen, 1962-1985* (Bern: Peter Lang, 2007), 30ff; and John Pilling, ed., *Beckett's Dream Notebook* (Reading: Beckett International Foundation, 1999), p. xiii.
14. *Ibid.*, p. 165.
15. Wilhelm Windelband, *A History of Philosophy*, 2 vols., trans. James Tufts (New York: Harper, 1958), pp. x, 9–10.
16. Samuel Beckett, 'Philosophy Notes', TCD MS 10967/225v-228r, corresponding to Windelband, *A History of Philosophy*, pp. 543–9.
17. Beckett, TCD MS 10967/189, cited in Feldman, 'Sourcing "Aporetics"', p. 307.
18. Windelband, *A History of Philosophy*, p. 410.
19. See Erik Tonning, *Samuel Beckett's Abstract Drama*, pp. 203ff.

[20] Samuel Beckett, *The Letters of Samuel Beckett, 1929–1940: Volume I*, eds. Martha Dow Fehsenfeld and Lois More Overbeck (Cambridge: Cambridge University Press, 2009), p. 172.

[21] Cited in Tonning, *Samuel Beckett's Abstract Drama*, p. 213.

[22] Beckett's reading of, and about, Spinoza between 1933 and 1938 has yet to receive sustained comment by Beckett scholars. However, Beckett appears to have read selections of, at the very least, 'Treatise on the Correction of the Understanding', noting Spinoza's first rule of life in his 'Whoroscope Notebook': 'To speak in a manner comprehensible to the vulgar', 60v., corresponding to *Spinoza's Ethics and 'De Intellectus Emendatione'*, ed. Ernest Rhys (J.M. Dent & Sons: London, n.d. [1910]), p. 231. Beckett also consulted, at the minimum, parts of the *Ethica* and from Charles Appuhn's edited French-Latin edition of Spinoza's Ethics (Paris: Garnier 1934); as well as Léon Brunschvicg's *Spinoza et ses Contemporains* (Paris: Alcan, 1923).

[23] See Beckett's reference to Baruch Spinoza in his 'German Diary' entry for 18 February 1937 (cited in Tonning, *Samuel Beckett's Abstract Drama*, p. 210); Beckett to Thomas MacGreevy, 19 September 1936, cited in Samuel Beckett, *The Letters of Samuel Beckett, 1929–1940: Volume I*, pp. 370–1; excerpted transcriptions on Spinoza from Beckett's earlier 'Philosophy Notebook' corresponding to TCD 10967/187r-188v (cited in Feldman, 'Sourcing "Aporetics"', pp. 305–6). See also Beckett's reference to Spinoza's natura naturata in ibid., pp. 73–4, corresponding to an earlier letter to MacGreevy equating Spinoza's phrase with 'humanity' on 25 March 1936, cited in Beckett, *The Letters of Samuel Beckett, 1929–1940: Volume I*, pp. 328, 330.

[24] Cited in English from Spinoza, vol. 2, pp. 320, 12; transcribed from Latin in Beckett's 'Whoroscope Notebook', 70r-71v. At least five of the references from these two pages in Beckett's 1930s notebook correspond to Bruncschvicg's *Spinoza et ses Contemporains*, pp. 368, 64, 21, 72, 77 and 482–3.

[25] Samuel Beckett's 'German Diary' entry of 31 October 1936, cited in Matthew Feldman, 'Theorising Misology', in Beckett's Books: *A Cultural History of Samuel Beckett's 'Interwar Notes'* (London: Bloomsbury, 2008), p. 15.

[26] Beckett, TCD MS 10967/5/2–3, cited in Feldman, 'Sourcing "Aporetics"', p. 384.

[27] John Pilling, 'Dates and Difficulties in Beckett's Whoroscope Notebook', in the *Journal of Beckett Studies* 13/2 (2004), pp. 42–4.

[28] Beckett's transcription from the original French corresponds to p. 61 in his 'Whoroscope Notebook': [C'est la grande oeuvre de Kant, accomplie dans les cinquante pages de l'Esthétique Transcendentale, qui consiste a avoir démontré que l'espace et le temps n'ont point, d'une part, une réalité substantielle, que d'autre part, ils ne soient pas non plus des propriétés de l'objet, qu'au contraire ils appartienent au sujet de la connaisance et qu'ils sont les formes de la sensibilité de ce sujet.]. The Anglophone version provided here is taken from Jules de Gaultier, *From Kant to Nietzsche*, trans. G.M. Spring (London: Peter Owen, 1961), p. 66.

[29] Samuel Beckett, 'Intercessions by Denis Devlin', in Beckett, *Disjecta*, p. 91, private translation.

[30] *Ibid.*, pp. 56–7.

[31] Pilling, 'Dates and Difficulties in Beckett's Whoroscope Notebook', p. 46.

[32] Jean-Paul Sartre, *Imagination*, trans. Forrest Williams (Ann Arbor: Michigan University Press, 1962), pp. 138–9.

[33] Beckett, *The Letters of Samuel Beckett*, p. 626.
[34] Sartre, *Imagination*, p. 131.
[35] Sartre, *Imagination*, pp. 138, 141, 143.
[36] *Ibid.*, p. 143.
[37] James Knowlson, *Damned to Fame: The Life of Samuel Beckett* (London: Bloomsbury, 1996), p. 295; italics in original.
[38] Beckett, *The Unnamable*, p. 352.
[39] *Ibid.*, p. 386.

BECKETT AND PHILOSOPHY

§1

Connections between Samuel Beckett and philosophy were varied and lively throughout his life, and are still kicking more than a generation after his death. After the unexpected critical success of *Molloy* and then *Waiting for Godot* in the early 1950s, French *philosophes* were, perhaps unsurprisingly first off the mark in taking a 'broadly philosophical approach' to Beckett's work.[1] Maurice Nadeau in *Combat* and Georges Bataille in *Critique* set the tone in 1951—the latter aptly calling *Molloy* a 'sordid wonder'—with Jean-Paul Sartre, Gabriel Marcel and Claude Mauriac later weighing in on *En Attendant Godot*, with Maurice Blanchot praising *L'Innomable*.[2] This trend quickly became transnational following influential readings like Georg Lukács *The Meaning of Contemporary Realism* in 1957 and, in the next year Theodor Adorno's highly influential essay, 'Trying to Understand Endgame'.[3] Variously seeing in Beckett's works evidence of existentialism, absurdism or nihilism—collectively, for what it's worth, rejected by the author vis-à-vis the interpretation of works—early philosophical readings may now appear somewhat dated; but then again, they are closely bound up with the European zeitgeist, alongside the post-war recognition as major twentieth century European writer. These early views, nonetheless, bear witness to Lance St John Butler's revealing assessment from 1984: 'In spite of all protestations to the contrary, Beckett is working the same ground as the philosophers.'[4]

The authorial 'protestations' to which Butler referred relate to characteristically evasive comments by Beckett regarding the deployment of philosophical themes in his work; to be sure, in keeping with the latter's famed reticence to discuss his work or intellectual influences. For instance, some eight years after his artistic breakthrough with the Parisian staging of *En Attendant Godot*, and some eight years before receiving the 1969 Nobel Prize for his unremitting explorations of 'the degradation of humanity' Samuel Beckett, quite unusually, consented to be interviewed. According to a now-famous exchange with *Nouvelles Littéraires* journalist Gabriel d'Aubarède, Beckett cast seemingly fundamental doubt upon his engagement with philosophy:

> Have contemporary philosophers had any influence on your thought?
> I never read philosophers.
> Why not?
> I never understand anything they write.
> All the same, people have wondered if the existentialists' problem of being may afford a key to your works.
> There's no key or problem. I wouldn't have had any reason to write my novels if I could have expressed their subject in philosophic terms.[5]

Yet the 'novel' published by Editions de Minuit only the month before, *Comment c'est*—tripartite in structure, unpunctuated in presentation, and notoriously difficult to digest—seemed to directly belie Beckett's claims of philosophical ignorance.[6] Thus, some pages after name-checking the famous Presocratic thinker, Heraclitus the Obscure, and some pages before the same treatment is meted out to the obscure Nicholas Malebranche (an occasionalist follower of René Descartes), the following passage occurs:

> mad or worse transformed à la Haeckel born in Potsdam where Klopstock too among others lived[7]

Amongst the madness and mud and misery and tin-can openers, the phrase is but one of many in *How It Is* betraying what must be considered 'philosophic terms'; if not a suspiciously specific philosophical knowledge.

In the Beckettian world, however, whether biographical or literary, oftentimes little is as it seems. For Beckett's interlocutor had not misheard in February 1961, nor is it likely the interviewee misspoken. Indeed, the sentiment was to be repeated that very summer, just as Beckett was commencing the arduous self-translation of *Comment c'est* into English:

> One cannot speak anymore of being, one must speak only of the mess. When Heidegger and Sartre speak of a contrast between being and existence, they may be right, I don't know, but their language is too philosophical for me. I am not a philosopher. One can only speak of what is in front of him, and that now is simply the mess.[8]

And yet, avers the narrator in Part Three of *How It Is*: 'nothing to be done in any case we have our being in justice I have never heard anything to the contrary'.[9] Which is the real Samuel Beckett? The biographical subject who repeatedly disclaimed any familiarity with philosophy—despite referring to both 'philosophical terms' and famous philosophers in doing so—or the avant-garde artist who unmistakeably, if nevertheless opaquely, incorporated philosophical thinking into his writings?

In here suggesting that Beckett may be profitably read as both—as a brilliant critic perceptively noted long ago: 'Samuel Beckett says in interviews that he knows little about philosophy; but his little could easily be another man's abundance'[10]—a final insight from the 1960s bears mentioning at the outset. In 1967, Beckett recommended to Sighle Kennedy, amongst others, that a starting point for his work could be found in two maxims of Arnold Geulincx and Democritus of Abdera, respectively: 'where you are worth nothing you should want nothing', and 'naught is more real than nothing'.[11] This emphasis upon the void, no less than the 'syzygy' of his position on philosophy, offers a fitting reminder of that contradictory, paradoxical and spartan terrain sometimes called Beckett Country:

> Closed place. All needed to be known for say is known. There is nothing but what is said. Beyond what is said there is nothing. What goes on in the arena is not said. Did it need to be known it would be. No interest. Not for imagining. Place consisting of an arena and a ditch. Between the two skirting the latter a track. Closed place. Beyond the ditch there is nothing. This is known because it needs to be said. Arena black vast. Room for millions. Wandering and still. Never seeing never hearing one another. Never touching. No more is known.[12]

§2

There can be little doubt, as Dermot Moran has suggested, that such a 'stark Beckettian world cries out for philosophical interpretation'.[13] Yet at the same time, in anticipating the pitfalls facing any simplistic mapping of Beckett's (or any other modernist's) literature onto philosophical ideas—in no small measure owing to the challenging opacity of Beckett's (especially post-war) literature—critics have tended toward two strategies in elucidating his relationship with philosophy. These two sides of the 'Beckett and Philosophy' coin will be briefly turned over in the remainder of this chapter.

The first may be said to be generally 'empirical'; that is, working *backwards* in order to demonstrate the philosophical influences in Beckett's development and practice as a writer. Without doubt, the *pièce de résistance* here is the recently unearthed 'Philosophy Notes', compiled by Beckett around 1932–1933 and covering the history of Western philosophy from the Ancient Greeks to Friedrich Nietzsche over 267 pages (recto and verso) of typed and handwritten summaries from a mélange of secondary sources. Even the aforementioned Ernst Haekel, briefly appearing in *How it is*—that Potsdam-born theorist of monism—is glossed in Beckett's most important text on Western philosophy, Wilhelm Windelband's revised, 1901 survey text, *The History of Philosophy* (2 vols.); and correspondingly, referred to at the end of the 'Philosophy Notes'.[14]

Broadly speaking, in turn, a second approach may be considered 'interpretative', principally consisting of looking *forward* at Beckett's work through the lens of leading philosophical themes or thinkers. This hermeneutical undertaking is aptly evoked by the title of a recent article penned by Bruno Clément, 'What Philosophers do with Samuel Beckett'. Other titles or monograph chapters in the critical Beckett canon are similarly telling in this regard: 'Samuel Beckett: The 'Search for Self''; 'What is Man? The Search for Reality'; and most recently, 'The Beckett Absolute Universal'.[15] And with similarly fruitful results, philosophers and literary critics have long been energetically suggesting that Beckett's post-1945 fiction could be said to exemplify—in the case of Wolfgang Iser's influential 'Reader Response' theory—or, in the case of post-structuralism, anticipate a particular philosophical doctrine.[16] These and similar enquiries into the unique *mise en scène* of Beckett Country are set to long continue, with critics continuing to trace out philosophical influences, contexts and legacies of Beckett's literature. Amongst the key contributions deriving from this influential discourse, a representative collection titled *Beckett and Philosophy* contains essays on an array of philosophers much-discussed in the twenty-first century—ranging from chapters on thinkers of whom Beckett was, at least passingly, familiar (Nietzsche, Heidegger, Merleau-Ponty, Adorno) to those only coming to international prominence after his death in 1989 (Habermas, Foucault, Deleuze, Badiou, Derrida).[17]

First up, then, Beckett's texts no less than their germination reveal him to be amongst most philosophical of modernists—in both his 'early' and 'mature' (or post-war) work. To but scratch the explicit surface, his first essay from 1929, in praise of Joyce's then-unfinished *Finnegans Wake*, contained Giordano Bruno and Giambattista Vico in the title. Then, in 1930, an award winning 98-lines of verse parodied the life of René Descartes; and in the next year, Beckett's only academic monograph, *Proust*, was so steeped in the philosophy of Arthur Schopenhauer as to distort the eponymous author's *À la recherche du temps perdu* ostensibly under examination.[18] Other philosophers name-checked across Beckett's subsequent work, to name only some of the more notable figures, include Thales of Miletus in the 1932 poem 'Serena I' (later included in Beckett's 1935 poetry collection, *Echo's Bones*); the 'windowlessness' of Leibnizian monads feature in the novel *Murphy* from 1935–36; a long-unpublished dramatic fragment from 1940, *Human Wishes*, is based around the life of Samuel Johnson; Immanuel Kant's 'fruitful bathos of experience' is quoted in the Addenda to *Watt* from 1945; Arnold Geulincx appears in the short story 'The End' and the first novel of *The Beckett Trilogy*, *Molloy*, over the next two years; Aristotle 'who knew everything' makes an appearance in the *Texts for Nothing* from 1951; Zeno's Paradox opens the 1958 play *Endgame*; the occasionalist philosopher Nicolas Malebranche is cited in 'The Image' and *How it Is* over the next two years; and Bishop Berkeley's tag *essi est percipi* prefaces the 1964 art-house (and Beckett's only) film, *Film*; while Fritz Mauthner 'may be it' in the *Rough for Radio II*, first published in 1975.[19] Many more philosophers, and indeed philosophies, are engaged along the way, needless to say, but these are important and suggestive references from a meticulous writer.

An especially telling example in taking the measure of Samuel Beckett's decade-long philosophical auto-didacticism is demonstrated by his earliest engagement with philosophy. In his first published essay, written to support James Joyce's *Work in Progress*, the 1929 'Dante...Bruno.Vico..Joyce', Beckett revealed tendencies that were to resurface again and again in his private study of philosophy across the 1930s. Despite taking a degree in Italian and French at Trinity College, Dublin, Beckett had no philosophical training upon taking up a two-year teaching post in Paris at the start of November 1928. As he recalled decades later for his first biography (which he neither 'helped' nor 'hindered'), Beckett, in a letter of 24 October 1974, 'stressed he did not study philosophy' prior to leaving Ireland: 'Because he had not taken a philosophy course at Trinity College, which he felt was a serious defect in his education, he set out on what he thought was a systematic schedule of readings.'[20]

On closer inspection, however, these readings were to be anything but systematic. For Beckett clearly relied upon friends to recommend philosophical books. In the case of his initial philosophical engagement upon arriving in France as an English *lecteur* at the École Normale Supérieure, Giambattista Vico seems to have acted as Beckett's introduction to philosophy. This was thanks to his relationship, or better, hero-worship, of James Joyce.[21] Joyce's own use of Vico as a 'trellis'[22] for what was to become *Finnegans Wake* was to act as a catalyst for Beckett's engagement with *La Scienza Nuova*; and more specifically, Vico's 'division of the development of human society into three ages: Theocratic, Heroic, Human (civilized), with a corresponding classification of language: Hieroglyphic (sacred), Metaphorical (poetic), Philosophical (capable of abstraction and generalization)' in order to explain 'the ineluctable circular progression of society.'[23] While it may be tempting to see in this tripartite structure the makings of the later tripartite, circular structure of a text like *How It Is*, Beckett—though he could not have known it then, unknown and unpublished as he was at twenty-two years old—himself warned against such inductive identification in the essay's very first, justly famous, sentence: 'The danger is in the neatness of identifications.'[24]

Importantly, Beckett's knowledge of Vico—and other philosophers in this nascent pattern—derived less from Vico's writings than from Joyce's suggestions, and less from both of these than from extant secondary sources; in this case, from Benedetto Croce's 1911 *La Filosofia di Giambattista Vico*. Despite explicitly disagreeing with Croce's definition of Vico as a 'mystic' who was rendered, in R.G. Collingwood's 1913 translation, 'contemptuous of empiricism', Beckett nevertheless mined this source exhaustively; for example, for the definition of 'Providence', or again, for Vico's understanding of myth as a primitive 'historical statement of fact'.[25] In short, these are Croce's views more than Vico's—let alone that of Niccoló da Conti, cited *en passant* by Beckett and in Croce's primer, but omitted in Vico's original, who defines myth as 'history of such a kind as could be constructed by primitive minds, and strictly considered by them as an account of actual fact'.[26] Thus, Beckett's early readings in philosophy are precisely the 'scaffolding' for later key philosophical themes and concerns (such as Arnold Geulincx's influence on Beckettian ethics). This closely corresponds with James Knowlson's important formulation of Beckett's intellectual influences: 'he does not attempt to reach firm conclusions. Concepts provide him rather with contrasting images, both verbal and visual, which he takes pleasure in weaving into intricate dramatic patterns'.[27] And it is, finally, these 'dramatic patterns' that keeps both readers and critics alike returning to the vexed, yet beautifully uncanny, terrain of Beckett and philosophy.

Space permits only two final, if definitive, examples of this persistent pattern of secondary source 'notesnatching'.[28] In the first place, Beckett appears to follow *La Scienza Nuova's* introductory 'Idea of the Work' (§34) and calls Book II, namely 'Poetic Wisdom', 'the master key to the entire work' (Vico, for his part, actually identifies the 'origins both of languages and of letters' in 'poets who spoke in poetic characters' as his 'master key' in *The New Science*). The debt, yet again, is to Benedetto Croce's primer, not Vico's primary text.[29] 'Dante...Bruno.Vico..Joyce', similarly, advances the earliest reference to a well-known Beckettian tag (given in Italian in his essay): 'the human mind does not understand anything of which it has had no previous impression'. Yet Beckett's initial encounter with this phrase—he was later to transcribe it into his central commonplace book of the 1930s, the so-called '*Whoroscope* Notebook', when he encountered it again 1936 in Léon Brunschvicg's 1923 *Spinoza et ses contemporains*—does not come from the expansive Book II in Vico's *New Science*.[30] Had Beckett found the phrase in the latter, he doubtless would have cited the full sentence there: 'What Aristotle said of the individual man is true of the race in general: *Nihil est in intellectu quin prius ferit in sensu.*' But no. This referent is 2,000 years too early. Instead Beckett tells us that, far from being Aristotle's, the phrase is instead a 'Scholastics' axiom': '*niente è nell'intelletto che prima non sia nel senso*'. And this, in turn, derives from the idiosyncratic Croce, who also seems to have played fast and loose with Giambattista Vico:

> Poets and philosophers may be called respectively the senses and the intellect of mankind: and in this sense we may retain as true the scholastic saying "there is nothing in the intellect which was not first in the senses." Without sense, we cannot have intellect: without poetry, we cannot have philosophy, nor indeed any civilisation.[31]

The (non-) scholastic's axiom above, in turn, passage also highlights the way in which Beckett transformed what he read philosophically into his art. Thus, fully a generation later, this phrase, now truncated and defaced, is placed by the narrator of *Malone Dies* into the beak of the 'whoreson' Jackson's 'dumb' parrot, Polly, which the former 'used to try and teach [...] to say, Nihil in intellectu, etc. These first three words the bird managed well enough, but the celebrated restriction was too much for it, all you heard was a series of squawks.' This led to Jackson's nagging, and Polly's retreat to the corner of her imprisoning cage, which 'was even overcrowded, personally I would have felt cramped'. But as so often in Beckett's art, there is an opaque depth to this comical moment. For the cage is not only for Jackson's parrot; it is also surely, a metaphor for Malone's imprisonment in the 'hallucinations' of the mind—the mind of whom, one might reasonably ask—without the material (dis)comforts of the senses:

> And in the skull is it a vacuum? I ask. And if I close my eyes, close them really, as others cannot, but as I can, for there are limits to my impotence, then sometimes my bed is caught up into the air and tossed like a straw by the swirling eddies, and I in it. Fortunately it is not so much an affair of eyelids, but as it were the soul that must be veiled, that soul denied in vain, vigilant, anxious, turning in its cage as in a lantern, in the night without haven or craft or matter or understanding.[32]

§3

Turning now to the second, and quite different, approach to 'Beckett and Philosophy', philosophers themselves have been quick to invoke Beckett's work for a variety of doctrines. As registered in one volume of articles alone, Beckett was subject of texts by Gabriel Marcel (1953, 1957); William Empson (1956); Maurice Blanchot (1959), Northrop Frye (1960); Claude Mauriac (1960), Raymond Williams (1961), Wolfgang Iser (1966), David Lodge (1968) and, as well as a longer essay by Theodor Adorno entitled 'Trying to Understand Endgame'.[33] In the decades since, longer works have appeared by Gilles Deleuze, Slavoj Žižek, Alain Badiou, and most recently Hélène Cixous.[34] Although this list appears decidedly weighted toward the aforementioned French *philosophes*, in many ways Beckett's international reception was defined by leading intellectuals both across and within nations—from the USA to China—(largely) following the surprise success of *Waiting for Godot*.[35] Even the memorable evasion by Jacques Derrida—that Beckett's work was 'too close' for him to write on—suggests that Beckett's work may be seen as co-evolving with, or even anticipating, some of the major themes in contemporary philosophy (such as phenomenology or even Derrida's poststructuralist philosophy).[36]

Right from the start, in keeping with longstanding Francophone influences, Anglophone critics have interpreted Beckett's writings philosophically. In fact, the conventional starting point for Beckett studies, a 1959 Special Issue of the academic journal *Perspective*, contained essays with titles like 'The Cartesian Centaur' (Hugh Kenner) and 'Samuel Beckett's *Murphy*: A Cartesian Novel' (Samuel L. Mintz). Moreover, as David Pattie deftly summarises of this first period of Beckett criticism in English:

> The *Perspective* issue identified Beckett as an important figure in English literature; and moreover, it introduced the notion that the Beckettian universe was governed by rules that were, at bottom, philosophical [....] English criticism in the1960s linked Beckett not only to existentialism, but to Schopenhauer, Kierkegaard, Wittgenstein, and, most decisively of all, to the work of the seventeenth-century French philosopher René Descartes and his philosophical disciples.[37]

Similarly telling titles were to follow over the next decade, from a 1962 chapter by Martin Esslin—later of 'theatre of the absurd' critical fame—in the collection *The Novelist as Philosopher* and Ruby Cohn's 1965 'Philosophical Fragments in the Works of Samuel Beckett', to John Fletcher's 'Beckett and the Philosophers' two years later; all capped by David Hesla's remarkable 'history of ideas' approach, and the first full-length study of Beckett and philosophy in English, his 1971 *The Shape of Chaos: An Interpretation of the Art of Samuel Beckett*:

> His world is a syzygy, and for every laugh there is a tear, or every affirmation a negation. His art is a Democritean art, energized precisely by the dialectical interplay of opposites—body and mind, the self and other, speech and silence, life and death, hope and despair, being and non-being, yes and no.[38]

Readers of Beckett in English, by this time, should they have wished to consult literary criticism to divine meaning from Beckett's texts—would doubtless have been struck by the philosophical consistency in approaching a writer famed for his protestations of 'ignorance' and 'impotence'.[39] The view taken in this early period, despite the many nuances of this first period of Beckett criticism in English, is shorthanded by a chapter entitled 'The Human Condition' in *The Testament of Samuel Beckett*: 'The whole of Beckett's work moves relentlessly towards the answering of one question: What is existence? or, What is man?'[40]

From this initial period of Beckett studies, furthermore two longstanding philosophical readings emerged: the existential and the Cartesian. The first, largely a product of its time, found in Beckett a fictional exponent of existentialism *par excellence*: 'From its inception, existential thought has felt itself at home in fiction. Because of its intense "inwardness" and the "commitment" of its proponents, it has expressed itself more strikingly in imaginative writing than in fictional treatises.'[41] Yet existential thought—for all its very Beckettian emphasis on solitude, alienation and 'intense self-consciousness'[42]—did not seem able to account for Beckett's artistic preoccupation with frailty, constraint and not knowing; or as advanced in conversation with James Knowlson: 'he found the actual limitations on man's freedom of action (his genes, his upbringing, his social circumstances) far more compelling than the theoretical freedom on which Sartre had laid so much stress'.[43] As for existentialism, so too for Cartesianism—at one point, the *de rigueur* philosophical interpretation of Beckett's work[44]—which may well be a red herring. Without doubt *Whoroscope*, Beckett's first published poem in 1930, centred upon the life of René Descartes, and demonstrated some knowledge of Cartesian philosophy. However, this was unjustifiably extrapolated to the whole of Beckett's thereafter, creating the impression that, as both current online sources and the *Encyclopaedia Britannica* have it, Descartes was 'Beckett's favourite philosopher'.[45] This is surely an overstatement; even a misstatement.

§4

While Beckett's philosophical indebtedness has long been recognised—particularly since the 1996 publication of James Knowlson's unrivalled biography, *Damned to Fame: The Life of Samuel Beckett*—a systematic treatment of leading Beckettian philosophers has been heretofore missing.[46] This is all the more surprising when considering, in light of his notoriously opaque post-war literature, there is little agreement as to what Samuel Beckett got out of the varied philosophers in the 1930s, let alone his wider debt to Western philosophy from that point on. However, Beckett's readings—and correspondingly, writings (especially his interwar non-fiction, collected in *Disjecta*)—from philosophy during the interwar years nonetheless reveal some notable themes that echo across Beckett's fiction and drama. This ranges from subject-object relations (self-other, consciousness-world, and so on) to doctrines whereby knowledge is folded upon itself, such as the *docta ignorantia* of mediaeval nominalism; the 'ineffability' of external motion in occasionalist thinking; and the sceptical linguistic philosophy of language found in Mauthner and others. Favourite phrases were reused as 'tags' and one-liners in Beckett's oeuvre, both as (rare) recommendations for the study of his work, as well as 'little phrases that seem so innocuous' but which 'rise up out the pit and know no rest until they drag you down into its dark'; as in this case from *Malone Dies*, Malone is referring to Democritus' maxim—itself already employed the epigraph to the sixth chapter in *Murphy*—'*Nothing is more real than nothing.*'[47]

More generally, and while still debated in Beckett studies, it seems that his philosophical didacticism during the 1930s helped provide tools with which Beckett was to subsequently and so memorably, assault rational, systematic thought. To give but one example, think of the absurd logic involved in disposing of Mr Knott's uneaten food in *Watt*—'Watt's instructions were formal: On those days on which food was left over, the food left over was to be given to the dog, without loss of time'—which sparks several pages of mathematical permutations on 'a suitable large nerdy local family', the Lynches. This 'fortunate family' (despite the name!) would ensure that such a dog would be present when needed, although this necessitated fully 'twenty-eight souls, nine hundred and eighty years' of service to Mr Knott. Or not. For drawing lengthy considerations to a close is a footnote that declares: 'The figures given here are incorrect. The consequent calculations are therefore doubly erroneous.'[48]

Thus, ultimately, when it comes to philosophy in Beckett's works, one hand giveth and the other taketh away. Protestations of ignorance by his narrators, no less than by Beckett himself, are enveloped within a philosophical *docta ignorantia*, linguistic scepticism and metaphysical agnosticism that are, at bottom, deeply learned. For the philosophy both in and behind Beckett's work calls out for critical attention, which may in turn help to remind readers that this most philosophical of authors was neither *sui generis* nor writing in an intellectual vacuum. Right from the start, as this overview has aimed to show, those questions—the bread and butter of great philosophy, no less than of great literature—have made, and will continue to make, Samuel Beckett our intellectual contemporary. His is a 'timeless parenthesis'. Even in the early, tenuous, and apprentice days of 1929, that Western philosophy contributed to Beckett's brilliant asides in our mythic narrative of human 'progress' remains, to date, obscured. In bringing these into focus, one can only make the hopeful assumption that explorations of Beckett and philosophy, in the broadest sense, will help to keep us, his readers, alive to the 'truly delicate' nature of his philosophical engagement:

> It is thence that one fine day, when all nature smiles and shines, the rack lets loose its black unforgettable cohorts and sweeps away the blue for ever. My situation is truly delicate. What fine things, what momentous things, I am going to miss through fear, fear of falling back into the old error, fear of not finishing in time, fear of revelling, for the last time, in a last outpouring of misery, impotence and hate. The forms are many in which the unchanging seeks relief from its formlessness. Ah yes, I was always subject to the deep thought, especially in the spring of the year. That one had been nagging at me for the past five minutes. I venture to hope there will be no more, of that depth.[49]

NOTES

[1] Shane Weller, 'Beckett among the *Philosophes*: the Critical Reception of Samuel Beckett in France', in Mark Nixon and Matthew Feldman, eds., *The International Reception of Samuel Beckett* (London: Continuum, 2009), p. 24.

[2] See, respectively, Nadeau and Bataille, reprinted in Lawrence Graver and Raymond Federman, eds., *Samuel Beckett: The Critical Heritage* (London: Routledge, 1979), pp. 55–69; Jean-Paul Sartre, 'People's Theatre and Bourgeois Theater', in Michael Contat and Michel Rybalka, eds., *Sartre on Theater*, trans. F. Jellinek (Quartet Books, London: 1976), p. 51; Marcel, Mauriac and Blanchot, reprinted in Lance St John Butler, ed., *Critical Essays on Samuel Beckett* (Aldershot: Scholas Press, 1994), pp. 19, 24, 86–92.

[3] For discussion of Theodor Adorno's work on Beckett, including a planned future essay on *L'Innomable* 'at the end of a projected fourth volume' of his *Noten zur Literature*, see Shane Weller, 'The Art of Indifference Adorno's Manuscript Notes on *The Unnamable*', in Daniela Guardamagna and Rossana M. Sebellin, eds., *The Tragic Comedy of Samuel Beckett* (Rome: Laterza, 2009), pp. 223–237.

[4] Lance St John Butler, *Samuel Beckett and the Meaning of Being: A Study in the Ontological Parallel* (London: MacMillan, 1984), p. 2. A similar view is espoused in a more recent study by Beckett's long-time English publisher, John Calder's *The Philosophy of Samuel Beckett* (London: Calder, 2002), which argues that 'Beckett was the last of the great stoics', p. 1.

[5] The announcement of Beckett's 1969 Nobel Prize for Literature is available online at: www.nobelprize.org/nobel_prizes/literature/laureates/1969/press.html (all websites last accessed 12/12/14); Beckett's interview with Gabriel d'Aubarède of 16 Feb. 1961 is available in *Samuel Beckett: The Critical Heritage*, pp. 217ff.

[6] As Ruby Cohn's *A Beckett Canon* (Ann Arbor: University of Michigan Press: 2004) makes clear, a potential source for the setting of *How It Is* can be found in the fifth circle of Dante's *Inferno*. Also in her work in terms of the tripartite structure employed in *How It Is*, consider Beckett's statement to his friend, the BBC Radio producer Donald McWhinnie: 'The work is in three parts, the first a solitary journey in the dark and mud terminating with discovery of a similar creature known as Pim, the second life with Pim both motionless in the dark and mud terminating with departure of Pim, the third solitude motionless in the dark and mud. It is in the third part that occur the so-called voice "quaqua" its interiorisation and murmuring forth when the panting stops.' (pp. 255–6.)

[7] Samuel Beckett, *How It Is* (London: Calder, 1996), p. 47.

[8] Beckett's interview with Tom Driver of summer 1961 is also reprinted in *Samuel Beckett: The Critical Heritage*, pp. 219ff.

[9] Beckett, *How It Is*, p. 135.

[10] Rubin Rabinovitz, '*Watt* from Descartes to Schopenhauer', in Raymond J. Porter and James D. Brophy, eds., *Modern Irish Literature: Essays in Honor of William York Tindall* (New York: Iona College Press, 1972), p. 261.

[11] Beckett's letter to Sighle Kennedy of 14 June 1967 on Arnold Geulincx and Democritus of Abdera– 'already in *Murphy* and neither very rational'—is reprinted in the oft-cited collection of journalism and miscellany *Disjecta: Miscellaneous Writings and a Dramatic Fragment*, ed. Ruby Cohn (New York: Grove Press, 1984), p. 113. A similar view was advanced

five years earlier in an interview with Lawrence Harvey, as recounted in his *Samuel Beckett: Poet and Critic* (Princeton: Princeton University Press, 1970), p. 267.

12 Samuel Beckett, 'Closed Place', in *Texts for Nothing and Other Shorter Prose 1950–1976*, ed. Mark Nixon (London: Faber, 2009d), p. 147.

13 Dermot Moran, 'Beckett and Philosophy', in Christopher Murray, ed., *Samuel Beckett: 100 Years* (Dublin: New Island, 2006), p. 94. Despite merely seeing many philosophical allusions in Beckett's work as simply 'a kind of arbitrary collection or *bricolage* of philosophical ideas', the philosopher nonetheless astutely continues: 'Beckett's relation to philosophy is difficult to complex. He was not a philosopher; if he had been, he would not have needed to engage with art.' (pp. 93–94).

14 Samuel Beckett, 'Philosophy Notes', TCD MS 10967/256v, corresponding to Haeckel's 'so-called Monism' in Wilhelm Windelband, *A History of Philosophy, Volume II: Renaissance, Enlightenment and Modern* (New York: Harper Torchbacks, 1958 [1901]), p. 632.

15 See Bruno Clément, 'What the Philosophers do with Samuel Beckett', trans. Anthony Uhlmann, in *Beckett after Beckett*, ed. S.E. Gontarski (Tallahassee: University of Florida Press, 2006). Also cited above are works by respectively, Martin Esslin, *The Theatre of the Absurd*, ch. 1 (London: Penguin Books, 1968); 'Introduction' to Paul Davies, *The Ideal Real: Beckett's Fiction and Imagination* (London: Associated University Presses, 1994); and 'Conclusion' in Eric P. Levy, *Trapped in Thought: A Study of the Beckettian Mentality* (New York: Syracuse University Press, 2007).

16 See, for example, Wolfgang Iser, *The Implied Reader: Patterns of Communication in Prose from Bunyan to Beckett* (London: The Johns Hopkins University Press, 1987), pp. 164–179, and pp. 257–273; and Anthony Uhlmann, *Beckett and Poststructuralism* (Cambridge: Cambridge University Press, 1999).

17 Richard Lane, ed., *Beckett and Philosophy* (Hampshire: Palgrave, 2002); see also P.J. Murphy, 'Beckett and the Philosophers', in *The Cambridge Companion to Samuel Beckett*, ed. John Pilling (Cambridge: Cambridge University Press, 1994); and Anthony Uhlmann, 'Beckett and Philosophy' in S.E. Gontarski, ed., *A Companion to Samuel Beckett* (Oxford: Wiley-Blackwell, 2010), pp. 84–96. Additional recent works on the subject of Beckett and philosophy include Anthony Uhlmann's *Samuel Beckett and the Philosophical Image* (Cambridge: Cambridge University Press, 2006); Garin Dowd, *Abstract Machines: Beckett and Philosophy after Deleuze and Guattari* (New York: Rodopi, 2007); Shane Weller, *A Taste for the Negative: Beckett and Nihilism* (Oxford: Legenda, 2005); and Simon Critchley, 'Lecture 3: Know Happiness—on Beckett', in his *Very Little ... Almost Nothing* (London: Routledge, 1997).

18 See, respectively, 'Dante...Bruno.Vico..Joyce', in *Disjecta*; 'Whoroscope', in Samuel Beckett, *Selected Poems 1930–1989*, ed. David Wheatley (London: Faber and Faber, 2009c); and *Proust*, widely reprinted; for example, see Samuel Beckett, *Proust and Three Dialogues* (Calder & Boyers, London: 1970).

19 The dates provided above are taken from Ruby Cohn's indispensable *A Beckett Canon;* see also John Pilling's more data-driven *A Beckett Chronology* (Basingstoke: Palgrave, 2006). Philosophical references correspond to the following: Thales in *Selected Poems 1930–1989*, p. 25; Leibniz in Samuel Beckett, *Murphy*, ed. J.C.C Mays (London: Faber and Faber, 2009), p. 114; the 'Human Wishes' fragment is reproduced in *Disjecta*; Kant's 'das fruchtbare Bathos der Erfahrung' comprises entry 31 of the 55 Addenda items at the end of Samuel Beckett, *Watt*, ed. Chris Ackerley (London: Faber and Faber, 2009), p. 222; Geulincx appears in 'The End', in Samuel Beckett, *The Complete Short Prose, 1929–1989*, ed.

S. E. Gontarski (New York: Grove Press, 1995), p. 91, and in Samuel Beckett, *Molloy*, ed. Shane Weller (London: Faber and Faber, 2009), p. 50; Aristotle appears in 'Text for Nothing VIII', in *Texts for Nothing and other shorter prose 1950–1976*, p. 35; Zeno's paradox offers the backdrop to the opening of *Endgame*, in Samuel Beckett, *The Complete Dramatic Works* (London: Faber and Faber, 1990), p. 93; Malebranche 'less the rosy hue the humanities' is cited in 'The Image', in *The Complete Short Prose, 1929–1989*, ed. S.E. Gontarski (New York: Grove Press, 1995), p. 167, and retained in Samuel Beckett, *How It Is* (London: Calder, 1996), p. 33; Berkeley's 'to be is to be perceived' heads the script for *Film*, in *The Complete Dramatic Works*, 323; and Mauthner is mentioned in *Rough for Radio II*, in *ibid.*, p. 276.

[20] Deirdre Bair, *Samuel Beckett: A Biography* (London, Picador: 1978), pp. 96, 694.

[21] With respect to James Joyce, Beckett remarked that his was 'heroic work, heroic being', cited in James Knowlson, *Damned to Fame: The Life of Samuel Beckett* (London: Bloomsbury, 1996), p. 105. Also prior to World War Two, other friends of Beckett who gave philosophical advice included Jean Beaufret, Brian Coffey, and A.J. 'Con' Leventhal.

[22] Cited in H.S. Harris, 'What is Mr. Ear-Vico Supposed to be 'Earing'?', in Donald Phillip Verene, ed., *Vico and Joyce* (New York: SUNY Press, 1987), p. 72. Relevant chapters in this collection bearing on Beckett's first publication also include Peter Hughes, 'From Allusion to Implosion. Vico. Michelet. Joyce, Beckett', and Donald Phillip Verene, 'Vico as Reader of Joyce'. Another angle is provided by Hayden V. White, 'What is Living and What is Dead in Croce's Criticism of Vico', in *Giambattista Vico: An International Symposium*, eds. Giorgio Tagliacozzo and Hayden V. White (Baltimore: Johns Hopkins University Press, 1969).

[23] Samuel Beckett, 'Dante...Bruno.Vico..Joyce', in *Our Exagmination Round His Factification for Incamination of Work in Progress* (Paris: Shakespeare and Co., 1929), reprinted in *Disjecta*, p. 20. To date, the most extensive Anglophone discussions of Vico and Beckett available in print can be found in John Pilling, *Beckett Before Godot* (Cambridge: Cambridge University Press, 1997), pp. 13–25; and, to a lesser extent, Massimo Verdicchio, 'Exagmination Round the Fictification of Vico and Joyce', in *James Joyce Quarterly* 26/4 (1989).

[24] Beckett, 'Dante...Bruno.Vico..Joyce', p. 19.

[25] *Ibid.* R.G. Collingwood's translation of Benedetto Croce's *La Filosofia di Giambattista Vico* (Rome: Bari, 1911) was published as *The Philosophy of Giambattista Vico* (London: H. Latimer, 1913); here cited pp. 78, 118–9, and 62–4.

[26] *Ibid.*, 64.

[27] Cited in James Knowlson, 'Samuel Beckett's Happy Days Revisited', in Rachel Falconer and Andrew Oliver, eds., *Re-reading / La Relecture: Essays in Honour of Graham Falconer* (Cambridge: Cambridge Scholars Publishing, 2012), p. 127.

[28] Beckett, letter of 25 Jan. 1931 to Thomas MacGreevy, in reference to the former's reading of St Augustine, cited in John Pilling, *Beckett's Dream Notebook* (Reading: Beckett International Foundation, 1999), p. xiii. Along with details of many other Western philosophers consulted by Beckett, a similar passage on 'phrase-hunting' in Augustine's *Confessions* can be found in *The Letters of Samuel Beckett, Volume I: 1929–1940*, eds. Martha Dow Fehsenfeld and Lois More Overbeck (Cambridge: Cambridge University Press, 2009), p. 62.

[29] Giambattista Vico, *The New Science of Giambattista Vico*, trans. Thomas Goddard Bergin and Max Harold Fisch (Ithaca: Cornell University Press, 1981), pp. 21–2. Compare Collingwood's translation of *La Filosofia di Giambattista Vico*, p. 62.

30 For coverage of this important phrase from Beckett's 1930s commonplace book, see John Pilling's 'Dates and Difficulties in Beckett's *Whoroscope* Notebook', in the *Journal of Beckett Studies* 13/2 (2005), pp. 39–48. The phrase given in 'Dante…Bruno.Vico..Joyce' is *'niente è nell'inelletto che prima non sia nel senso'*, p. 24. For more on the Italian angle in Beckett's first published text, see Andrea Battestini, 'Beckett e Vico', in *Bolletino del Centro di Studi Vichiani* 5 (1975), pp. 78–86.

31 Croce, *The Philosophy of Giambattista Vico*, pp. 49.

32 Samuel Beckett, *Malone Dies* (London: Faber and Faber, 2010), pp. 44, 48–9.

33 See Theodor Adorno, 'Trying to Understand *Endgame*', in Lance St John Butler, ed., *Critical Essays on Samuel Beckett* (Aldershot: Scholar Press, 1993).

34 See, for example, Gilles Deleuze, 'The Exhausted' in his *Essays Critical and Clinical*, trans. Daniel W. Smith and Michael A. Greco (London: Verso, 1998); Alain Badiou, *On Beckett*, edited and translated by Nina Power and Alberto Toscano (Manchester: Clinamen, 2003); Slavoj Žižek, 'Beckett with Lacan', parts one and two available online at: www.lacan.com/article/?page_id=78 and www.lacan.com/article/?page_id=102; and Hélène Cixous, *Zero's Neighbour: Sam Beckett*, trans. Laurent Milesi (Cambridge: Polity, 2010).

35 See Mark Nixon and Matthew Feldman, eds., *The International Reception of Samuel Beckett*.

36 Derrida, cited in his *Acts of Literature*, ed. Derek Attridge (London: Routledge, 1992), p. 60. For a variety of recent phenomenological approaches to Beckett, see Ulrika Maude and Matthew Feldman, eds., *Beckett and Phenomenology* (London: Continuum, 2009); and for well-known discussions of Beckett's work in light of post-structuralism, see Steven Connor, *Samuel Beckett: Theory, Repetition, Text* (Oxford: Basil Blackwell, 1988); Leslie Hill, *Beckett's Fiction: In Different Words* (Cambridge: Cambridge University Press, 1990); and, most recently, Anthony Uhlmann, *Beckett and Poststructuralism* (Cambridge: Cambridge University Press, 1999).

37 David Pattie, *The Complete Critical Guide to Samuel Beckett* (Abingdon: Routledge, 2000), p. 105.

38 David Hesla, *The Shape of Chaos: An Interpretation of the Art of Samuel Beckett* (Minneapolis, MN: University of Minnesota Press, 1971), pp. 10–11.

39 As Ruby Cohn's thoughtful 'Philosophical Fragments in the Works of Samuel Beckett' puts it: 'Beckett's heroes not only deny that they are philosophers; they flaunt an inviolable ignorance [.... But] they nevertheless continue to examine, propounding the old philosophical questions that have been with us since the pre-Socratics; on the nature of the Self, the World, and God.' Reprinted in Martin Esslin, ed., *Samuel Beckett: A Collection of Critical Essays* (Engelwood Cliffs: Prentice-Hall, 1965), p. 169. See also John Cruickshank, 'Samuel Beckett', in *The Novelist as Philosopher: Studies in French Fiction 1935–1960*, John Cruickshank, ed. (Westport: Greenwood, 1962); and John Fletcher, 'Beckett and the Philosophers', in *Samuel Beckett's Art* (London: Chatto & Windus, 1967), pp. 121–137.

40 Josephine Jacobsen and William R. Mueller, *The Testament of Samuel Beckett* (London: Faber, 1964), p. 109.

41 Edith Kern, *Existential Thought and Fictional Technique* (London: Yale University Press, 1970), p. viii. Comparable existential perspectives underwrite Ramona Cormier and Janis L. Pallister's *Waiting for Death: The Philosophical Significance of Beckett's* En Attendant Godot (Tuscaloosa: University of Alabama Press, 1979); and L.A.C. Dobrez, *The Existential and Its Exits* (London: The Athlone Press, 1986).

[42] Hannah Copeland, *Art and the Artist in the Works of Samuel Beckett* (The Hague: Mouton and Co. 1975), pp. 42–3.

[43] James Knowlson and John Haynes, *Images of Beckett* (Cambridge: Cambridge University Press, 2003), pp. 16ff.

[44] To cite only the major accounts of Beckett and Cartesianism, see Edouard Morot-Sir, 'Samuel Beckett and Cartesian Emblems', in Edouard Morot-Sir, ed., *Samuel Beckett and the Art of Rhetoric* (Chapel Hill: University of North Carolina, 1976); Michael Mooney, '*Molloy*, Part 1: Beckett's *Discourse on Method*', in the *Journal of Beckett Studies* 3 (1978); and Roger Scruton, 'Beckett and the Cartesian Soul', in his *The Aesthetic Understanding: Essays in the Philosophy of Art and Culture* (Manchester: Carcanet Press, 1983).

[45] For some of Beckett's sources in the construction of *Whoroscope*, see Francis Doherty, 'Mahaffy's *Whoroscope*', in the *Journal of Beckett Studies* 2/1 (1992). For an argument that Cartesian influence upon Beckett is largely circumstantial, and better recast in terms of a wider engagement with Western philosophy, see my 'René Descartes and Samuel Beckett', in *Beckett's Books: A Cultural History of Samuel Beckett's 'Interwar Notes'* (London: Bloomsbury, 2008).

[46] For a discussion of Beckett's philosophical readings during the 1930s, see James Knowlson, *Damned to Fame: The Life of Samuel Beckett* (London: Bloomsbury, 1996), especially chs. 6 to 11; and *Beckett's Books*, ch. 2.

[47] See *Malone Dies*, p. 177; and *Murphy*, p. 154.

[48] Beckett, *Watt*, pp. 75–87.

[49] Samuel Beckett, *Malone Dies* in *The Beckett Trilogy* [*Molloy, Malone Dies* and *The Unnamable*] (London: Picador 1979), pp. 181–82.

"AGNOSTIC QUIETISM"
AND SAMUEL BECKETT'S EARLY DEVELOPMENT

§1

'All I ever got from the <u>Imitation</u> [*of Christ*, by Thomas à Kempis] went to confirm and reinforce my own way of living', wrote Samuel Beckett in a confessional letter to his friend, Thomas MacGreevy on 10 March 1935, 'a way of living that tried to be a solution and failed'. Beckett then continued, revealingly:

> What is one to make of "seldom we come home without hurting of conscience" and "the glad going out and sorrowful coming home" and "be ye sorry in your chambers" but quietism of the sparrow alone upon the housetop and the solitary bird under the eaves? An abject self-referring quietism indeed, beside the alert quiet of one who always had Jesus for his darling, but the only kind that I, who seem never to have had the least faculty or disposition for the supernatural, could elicit from the text, and then only by means of a substitution of terms very different from the one you propose. I mean that I replaced the plenitude that he calls "God" not by "goodness", but by a pleroma only to be sought among my own feathers or entrails, a principle of self the possession of which was to provide a rationale and the communion with which a sense of Grace [...] I know that now I would be no more capable of approaching its hypostasies and analogies "meekly, simply and truly", than I was when I first twisted them into a programme of self-sufficiency. I would still find it, so far from being a compendium of Christian behaviour with <u>oeuvres pies</u>, humility, utility, self-effacement, etc., etc., in all probability conceived and composed on the rebound from the fiasco of just such an effort in behaviour, your "long, long experience of unhappiness"; and that if certain forms of contact are commended by the way, it is very much by the way, and incidental and secondary to the fundamental contact—for him, with "God". So that to read "goodness and disinterestedness" every time for "God" would seem the accidental for the essential with a vengeance and a mincing of the text; whereas to allow the sceptical position (which I hope is not complacent in my case, however it may be a tyranny), and replace a principle of faith, absolute and infinite, by one personal and finite of fact, would be to preserve its magnificent basis of distinction between primary and secondary, in the interests of a very baroque solipsism if you like. I cannot see how "goodness" is to be made a foundation or a beginning of anything.[1]

Beyond the aesthetic and self-referential qualities of this particularly insightful passage, the basis for extensively quoting Beckett's letter centres upon the fundamental idea propounded both there and here: quietism. If a lowest common denominator—an agnosticism about how words, experience or reality, in addition to an all-too-familiar mental anguish—may be said to be perceptible in Beckett's work, how does one go about characterising it? Surely by *The Beckett Trilogy* and *Endgame*, agnosticism confronts Beckett's creatures in its baldest form: does God exist and therefore bear responsibility for suffering? Does the question itself matter, or offer any succour? Can truth be truly apprehended, even briefly, in the first place? Indeed, how do 'I'—whatever that means—form the words to express to others and myself such sentiments? And to what end?

This ethical and, for Beckett, aesthetic approach to suffering and failure *as a spiritual purgation for living* provides an appropriate heuristic torch to shine into his wan writings. Preceding this discussion, however, this chapter explores and expands upon Beckett's 'quiestism' and relevance to his art, by recourse to the term 'agnostic quietism'. Important work on this subject has been recently undertaken in Mark Nixon's '"Scraps of German": Samuel Beckett reading German Literature', especially with respect to valuable insights into Beckett's interest in the 'quietistic and pessimistic tradition', as well as the development of 'a self-introspective mode closely tied up with German language and culture' in the 1930s. Nixon's text likewise departs from James Knowlson's incisive approach to Beckett's 'quietistic impulse' in *Damned to Fame: The Life of Samuel Beckett*. A third key text on this subject, and to date the only other text to consider this theme in any depth, is 'Samuel Beckett and Thomas à Kempis: The Roots of Quietism'.[2] As usual, it is hard to contest Chris Ackerley's dating and conclusions, and his understanding of quietism—a seventeenth century quasi-Gnostic doctrine condemned by the Inquisition as mystical—will be taken as definitional here (minus the Christian piety for Beckett, of course).

Ackerley notes that quietism is a 'doctrine of extreme asceticism and contemplative devotion teaching that the chief duty of man is the contemplation of God, or Christ, to become independent of outward circumstances and sensual distraction'.[3] But as Beckett makes clear, his 'agnostic quietism' is not passively sceptical. For the ideals of 'humility, utility, self-effacement', when deprived of its Christian teleology, become a way of suffering life without hope of compensation—everlasting or earthly. Thomas à Kempis' *The Imitation of Christ* offers a fitting segue, then, not only because of Nixon, Ackerley and Knowlson's important insights, nor simply because Beckett's 1931 reading of this text contributed immensely to his letter to MacGreevy on quietism.[4] It is also because this forms part of a larger, important trope in Beckett's formative readings and intellectual development. In short, reading Beckett and his art in terms of the suffering, uncertainty, failure, and stoicism that are so often held to be thematically present in his texts, and viewing a prior accumulation of sources on precisely such matters shows precisely how Beckett *used erudition to explore ineffability*.

In his 1934 tribute to MacGreevy, 'Humanistic Quietism', Beckett's 'mind that has raised itself to the grace of humility' is predicated on the view that (good) poetry approaches prayer.[5] Taking the influence of à Kempis as a given, surveying other texts that helped to hatch this 'solitary bird under the eaves' is in order. And by capturing Beckett's artistic temperament through a discussion of 'agnostic quietism' one especially evident in Beckett's formative artistic development and in the explicit references to quietism in his interwar writings, this reading will also resonate loudly with the 'ruinstrewn land' of Beckett's postwar art. This period has been aptly characterised by Beckett's friend and one-time philosophical mentor, Brian Coffey, in a letter to MacGreevy of 23 March 1964:

> For all his position, Sam is still at heart, a sad little thing, I feel. I have wondered sometimes about the quality of the violence and murderous intention his people express, for it is not easy to keep the source intact while the flood waters are flowing. But on the whole I incline to think he is still the loveable being whose memory has endured in me with a quality so admirable I sometimes get ill looking at some of those I have to work with. That's why it is really up to us to communicate as from the stars to that planet his people live on (and himself too, I fear).[6]

The roots of such a 'sad' outlook predate Beckett's reading of the *Imitation of Christ* in late summer 1931, and extend well beyond his self-analysis to MacGreevy in 1935. Although admirably tracing à Kempis beyond the thirty-plus allusions in *Dream of Fair to Middling Women* and persistent references in *More Pricks Than Kicks*, to residua in *Watt, The Beckett Trilogy* and *How It Is*, Ackerley is less concerned with the development of Beckett's own outlook than with charting the sizeable influence of à Kempis in Beckett's texts. Indeed, Ackerley takes Schopenhauer's quietistic fellow-travelling with à Kempis as read; yet these two paragons may be seen to underpin Beckett's voluminous readings into this subject. Such an investigation must, of necessity, be both genealogical and intuitive—what Johann Goethe termed 'elective affinities'– in exploring the sticky issue of artistic temperament. But only in this way can those disparate features (melancholy, pessimism, scepticism, and so on) be understood to add up to a coherent quietist *Weltanschauung*.

§2

By the time of his aesthetic essay on James Joyce's 'luminaries' in 1929, Beckett had already reached an uneasy truce with existence by way of, for one, *The Divine Comedy*. In a rare interjection of personal views in 'Dante...Bruno.Vico..Joyce' only indirectly related to Joyce's form and genius in the *Work in Progress*, the passé stasis of Heaven and Hell is no longer a viable artistic subject matter: 'On this earth that is Purgatory, Vice and Virtue—which you may take to mean any pair of large contrary human factors—must in turn be purged down to spirits of rebelliousness.'[7] Instead, modernist emphasis upon the ongoing purgatorial processes of daily life becomes worthy of celebration in Joyce, and later Marcel Proust. Nevertheless, the penitential quality Beckett found in Dante Aligheri—especially the image of Belacqua, behind a 'great boulder' in ante-Purgatory, 'clasping his knees and holding his face low down between them'—had already been codified in earlier years, as his 'Dante Notebook' makes clear, not to mention the early anti-hero, Belacqua Shuah, of *Dream of Fair to Middling Women* and *More Pricks Than Kicks*.[8] As Knowlson says of Beckett's interest in *Unanimisme*, especially the poetry of Jules Romains and Pierre-Jean Jouve, during his final year at TCD: 'An outlook that sees the individual as finding some degree of solace in a collective must have held some attraction for a young man who at the time was feeling increasingly his own sense of isolation.'[9]

Should Beckett's other literary interests at this time offer any barometer, these were much less concerned with intellectual community than with what he calls, in connection with John Keats, 'a crouching brooding quality'. Moreover, Keats offers a good example of Beckett's developing quietistic temperament: at school with Geoffrey Thompson Beckett had memorised 'Ode to a Nightingale', later citing a line from its sixth stanza to MacGreevy as fitting evidence of his world-weariness. In an earlier reference to Keats in 1931, the Romantic poet's subdued qualities are precisely what set him above his contemporaries, 'because he doesn't beat his fists on the table'.[10] The importance of this quoted line upon Beckett is evident in the conclusion to 'Dante and the Lobster', which alludes to the ineluctable nature of suffering and death central throughout 'Ode to a Nightingale':

> In the depths of the sea it had crept into the cruel pot. For hours, in the midst of enemies, it had breathed secretly. It had survived the Frenchwoman's cat and his witless clutch. Now it was going alive into scalding water. It had to. *Take into the air my quiet breath* [....]
>
> She lifted the lobster clear of the table. It had about thirty seconds to live.
>
> Well, thought Belacqua, it's a quick death, God help us all.
>
> It is not.[11]

The same understated gloominess pervading Keats' poem was invoked by Beckett, mere weeks before his death, during a visit by his friend, the Irish poet, John Montague, when the pitilessly drawn out *coup de grâce* was recognised: "'I'm done," again, with the same vehemence. "But it takes such a long time."' 'Ode to a Nightingale' thus clearly represented for Beckett a trope of artistic mournfulness:

> The weariness, the fever, and the fret
> Here, where men sit and hear each other groan;
> Where palsy shakes a few, sad, last gray hairs,
> Where youth grows pale, and spectre-thin, and dies;
> Where but to think is to be full of sorrow
> And leaden-eyed despairs[12]

Strangely, the feeling of being 'done' communicated with 'resignation and, perhaps, disappointment' to Montague also elicits shades of Giacomo Leopardi: 'Death is not an evil; for it frees man from all evils and, in taking away joy, also removes desire. Old age is the greatest of evils, for it deprives man of every pleasure, while leaving every appetite, and brings with it all sorrows. Yet men fear death, and desire old age.'[13] Like Keats, who Beckett also encountered at Trinity College, Dublin, Leopardi's temperament runs counter to the positivism of much nineteenth century poetry and prose. Yet clearly Leopardi's 'brooding' is much more overt than Keats', and any understanding of 'agnostic quietism' in Beckett's temperament must be predicated upon neither restraint (or otherwise), belief (or otherwise), nor any other salient characteristics. Instead, as Ackerley's text on quietism rightly indicates, the thread linking these views is strongly rooted in a personal asceticism, one eschewing the distractions and sufferings of the world as both ceaseless and superfluous. And for Beckett, art is both the best palliative and most effective endorsement for just such a wan revelation.

A typed copy of Leopardi's 'A Se Stesso' is therefore unsurprisingly included in Samuel Beckett's 'Interwar Notes'.[14] Its importance to Beckett certainly extends to *Proust*: his simile for the world, below, had evidently included as an epigraph in the original published version, later dropped in the John Calder reprint. Moreover, in the essay itself,[15] Leopardi is marshalled as a 'sage' for 'wisdom that consists not in the satisfaction but in the ablation of desire'. Leopardi's conviction stands as a central buttress to Beckett's quietism, later bequeathed by Schopenhauer: '*in noi di cari inganni / non che la speme, il desiderio e spento* [Not only the dear hope / Of being deluded gone, but the desire]'—a phrase pared down and used in *Molloy*.[16] The vigour, the uncompromising resentment, and especially the rejection of willing in 'A Se Stesso' may together explain why *Proust* favours Leopardi with the direct quotation above, while Dante and Keats are relegated to a merely allusive role. Here is a translated excerpt of Leopardi's 'To Himself', which that Beckett had transcribed from Italian—quite possibly around the time of writing *Proust*:

> Rest still for ever. You
> Have beaten long enough. And to no purpose
> Were all your stirrings; earth not worth your sighs.
> Boredom and bitterness
> Is life; and the rest, nothing; the world is dirt.[17]

The middle third reproduced here again raises similarity of temperament, while also acting as a kind of biographical mantra for calming the heart—'that cracked beater' subjecting Beckett to traumatic panic attacks at this time.[18] The importance of reading 'agnostic quietism' into Beckett's life and works is *precisely because* it is biographically apposite: Beckett felt it himself, strengthened it through his readings in the 1930s, and incorporated a personal shaping of this doctrine into his writings thereafter.

Although little concerned with works of art, as a general receptacle for his reading at this time, *Beckett's Dream Notebook* is indispensable in approaching the development of Beckett's quietist outlook. Not only does John Pilling source the overwhelming majority of nearly 1,200 items scribbled around the writing of *Dream of Fair to Middling Women*, but as one of the first artistic notebooks kept by Beckett, UoR MS 5000 is the earliest extant documentation of his intellectual and artistic endeavours after taking his undergraduate degree. *The Imitation of Christ* and *The Confessions* naturally feature prominently, with roughly three dozen entries from the first, and nearly 150 entries from the second. Besides 'phrase-hunting' in St Augustine, Beckett might also be said to be 'temperament-hunting', as suggested by entries like 'What more miserable than a miserable being who commiserates not himself', 'The audacious soul—turned it hath & turned again, upon back sides & belly—yet all was painful' and 'with a new grief I grieved for my grief and was thus worn by a double sorrow (death of Monica)'.[19]

Entries like those above, ticked and incorporated into *Dream of Fair to Middling Women*, reinforce not only the importance of religious texts in Beckett's eclectic reading but also the forlorn sentiments that he emphasised in transcriptions and artistic transformations *within* such books. Consequently, *Beckett's Dream Notebook* answers important questions raised in Beckett's first sustained piece of writing. The narrator's 'Who said all that?', sandwiched between those Augustinian quotations above, thus helps deepen Belacqua's melancholic view of love, contributing as it does to the mournful conviction that this is a 'Beschissenes Dasein beschissenes Dasein' [shitty existence shitty existence]: 'But right enough all the same what more miserable than the miserable man that commiserates not himself, caesura, with new grief grieves not for his grief, is not worn by a double sorrow, drowns not in the ken of shore? [....] turned he hath and turned again, on back, sides and belly.'[20]

With the title alone, Robert Burton's *Anatomy of Melancholy* similarly qualifies as piece of Beckett's quietism around the same point as other texts in the run-up to *Dream of Fair to Middling Women*. And comprising as it does fully one-quarter of *Beckett's* Dream *Notebook*, this is consequently a vital source too frequently overlooked by scholars. Like Beckett's 20,000 words of typewritten notes on what I have elsewhere called the 'Psychology Notes', an overriding impetus in reading the entirety of the *Anatomy of Melancholy* may have been for self-diagnosis, in this case of melancholy instead of neuroses.[21] I have also previously noted Burton's (and especially Beckett's) championing of Democritus—in his preface, 'Democritus to the Reader', Burton calls himself 'Democritus Junior'—on the basis that Democritus was memorably 'melancholy by nature, averse from company in his latter days, and much given to solitariness'.[22] Though casting himself as a mere shadow of the Abderite, Burton sees himself as carrying on his 'senior's' work—laughing at the world, consigning himself to libraries, and studying 'melancholy and madness [...] so as to better cure it in himself'.[23]

Herein rests the difference. While Burton's three books comprising his *Anatomy of Melancholy* respectively on the causes, cures, and forms (particularly love and religious) of melancholy—generally construes melancholy as a condition to be overcome, Beckett's much more artistic construction of melancholy is closer in spirit to Albrecht Dürer's *Melancholia I*; that is, an outlook revealing signs of genius, imagination and a deeper understanding of the 'true' nature of existence. Artistic melancholy is not a subject of any great interest for Burton, which perhaps explains why the entries in UoR MS 5000 use Burton for 'phrase-hunting' in much the same way as Augustine's *Confessions*: the sad, purgatorial and suffering sentiments exist in both texts, but as an instruction against despair in reaching toward happiness rather than creatively harnessing melancholy. Whereas for Burton, solitary and idle preconditions should be avoided as 'fear and sorrow are the true characters and inseparable companions of most melancholy', artists like Keats, Leopardi and Dürer understand melancholy in terms of corporeal asceticism and visionary insight; in short, a ladder toward the 'baroque solipsism' mentioned to MacGreevy.[24] A much later example from Beckett's 'Fizzles' captures this inspired melancholy as perfectly as Dürer's famous etching, through 'that image, the little heap of hands and head, the trunk horizontal, the jutting elbows, the eyes closed and the face rigid listening, the eyes hidden and the whole face hidden, that image and no more, never changing, ruinstrewn land, night recedes, he is fled, I'm inside, he'll do himself to death, because of me, I'll live it with him, I'll live his death [...]'[25]

Moreover, the distinction between melancholy as condition and melancholy as temperament may well explain why the Burton entries employed in *Dream of Fair to Middling Women* are generally used, in Dirk van Hulle's phrase, in 'the non-syntagmatic way in which Joyce jotted down words in his notebooks', not as lengthy quotations or conceptual borrowings.[26] That Beckett understood Burton's 'causes' of melancholy as actually rather desirable—Beckett told Walter Lowenfels, 'all I want to do is sit on my ass and fart and think of Dante'[27]—his 'cures' as impossible on 'this clonic earth',[28] and his forms of melancholy as doubtless incomplete without that artistic conception of Düreresque melancholy; all give particularly good perspectives on our construction of 'agnostic quietism'. For 'Democritus Junior' is fundamentally a philosophical optimist ('Again & again I request you to be merry'[29]) writing on melancholy, while Beckett; and to a lesser extent, Belacqua, is a poet finding melancholy more a Pyrrhic facilitation than an impairment for viewing Burton's 'sky the fairest part of creation':

> When Belacqua came out [...] no moon was to be seen nor stars of any kind. There was no light in the sky whatsoever. At least he could no discover any [...] though he took off his glasses and wiped them carefully and inspected every available inch of the firmament before giving it up as a bad job. There was some light, of course there was, it being well known that perfect black is simply not to be had. But he was in no state of mind to be concerned with any such punctilio. The heavens, he said to himself, are darkened, absolutely, beyond any possibility of error.[30]

A last example highlighting the importance of *Beckett's Dream Notebook* in the development of 'agnostic quietism' is testified by entries 681 and 683— 'Pleroma (totality of divine attributes)' and 'hypostatized Abstraction'. These are taken from the Lecture 'Christian Platonism and Speculative Mysticism' in W. R. Inge's 1899 *Christian Mysticism*, both used in the 1935 letter to MacGreevy to mark Beckett's distance from Christianity; the former recurring in *Dream of Fair to Middling Women*.[31] But more generally, by verifying that Beckett has read the whole of this book, Pilling records the depth of Beckett's understanding of the term 'quietism' used when speaking of MacGreevy's poetry, and later, himself. Thus, Inge's Lecture VI informed Beckett that Miguel de Molinos (c. 1640—1695) initiated quietism in the interests of self-perfection and knowledge of God, which 'consists in complete resignation to the will of God, annihilation of all self-will, and an unruffled tranquillity or passivity of soul'; and furthermore, 'The best kind of prayer is the prayer of silence; and there are three silences, that of words, that of desires, and that of thought. In the last and highest the mind is a blank

[....] In this state the soul would willingly even go to hell, if it were God's will.'[32] Inge also reveals how Molinos ended his days in a Spanish dungeon for teachings construed as dangerous to Catholicism; this superficial, or at the very least, satirical link to the 'dungeon in Spain' noted in *Murphy*, is curious: 'With these and even less weighty constructions he saved his facts against the pressure of those current in the Mercyseat. Stimulated by all those lives immured in mind, as he insisted on supposing, he laboured more diligently than ever before at his own *little dungeon in Spain*.'[33] Further, as an ex-theology student, Murphy's self-bondage in the chair ironically contrasts with Molinos' imposed fate, given their shared rejection of the world (home of the devil for Molinos, of Celia and ginger biscuits for Murphy)—though one suspects their reasoning might be rather at variance. A quietistic reading of *Murphy*, then, even if strictly along Inge's lines, offers a number of fascinating insights.

§3

Yet coming to rest here would neglect a central plank of quietism, even as first constructed by Molinos: rejection of the will. Whereas Christians of Molinos' stamp saw this as a precondition for best communing with God, for one without a 'disposition for the supernatural' yet nevertheless sharing similar sentiments a different sort of guide was needed, a Virgil of melancholy to chart the possibility of will-lessness as an end in itself. Here the most important quietistic influence comes via the writings of Schopenhauer, probably first encountered by Beckett in the summer of 1930, prior to the writing of *Proust*. The chapter 'On the Doctrine of the Denial of the Will-to Live' in *The World as Will and Representation* concerns Molinos, and the character of Christian quietism as an ascetic faith expressing Christianity's 'deepest truth, its high value, and its sublime character'. This is unusually generous praise for Schopenhauer, who typically sees the *practice* of Christianity as antithetical to his philosophy.[34] Perhaps it is for this reason that Mark Nixon's doctoral thesis views Beckett's engagement with this 'aesthetic of unhappiness' in terms of 'secular quietism'. Yet while the reading here understands Beckett's engagement with quietism in terms of Christian philosophy and developing temperament instead of through German literature and culture—and therefore one effectively more speculative and open-ended (hence 'agnostic' rather than 'secular')—one must certainly agree with Nixon's view of 'Beckett's belief that the solitary state is the irrevocable fate of human beings, particularly pronounced in the artist'.[35] Whether or not Beckett read Schopenhauer independent of that Chatto & Windus commission or was attracted through Proustian criticism is unclear; but what Mark Nixon has clarified is that from the earliest stage of conception even Beckett's friends knew that the attempted equation would be 'Sam. Beckett = Proust + Pessimism'.[36]

That Beckett later admitted to overstating Proust's pessimism seems due in large measure to his own outlook, forged over the previous twenty four years, and the simultaneous reading of Schopenhauer alongside writing *Proust*: 'I am going now to buy his "Aphorisms sur la sagesse dans la vie", that Proust admired so much for its originality and guarantee of wide reading—transformed. His chapter in Will and Representation in Music is amusing and applies to P[roust], who certainly read it.'[37] Beckett is here referring to book 3, sect. 52, which makes its way into *Proust* as one of the three explicit references to Schopenhauer: 'The influence of Schopenhauer on this aspect of the Proustian demonstration is unquestionable. Schopenhauer rejects the Leibnizian view of music as "occult arithmetic" and in his aesthetics separates it from the other arts, which can only produce the Idea with its concomitant phenomena, whereas music is the Idea itself.'[38] And more than just his definition used in *Proust*, Schopenhauer's views of fine art, from approbations and anathemas to artistic definitions and tropes, undoubtedly contributed to Beckett's views in this area as well.[39] Given Schopenhauer's conviction, well captured by Moorjani, that 'art stills temporarily the suffering and terror of existence'—and is thus a kind of talisman against the despair created by those conditions—surprisingly little on the marked influence of Schopenhauer has been said in Beckett studies, in this vein or another.[40] To my knowledge, scholars who have looked closely at the Beckett-Schopenhauer relationship via *Proust* agree that Beckett had a 'sensed affinity' with Schopenhauer and consequently emphasised his pessimism, artistic views and the role of the will; all to the detriment of a more detached, even-handed analysis of Proust's *Remembrance of Things Past*.[41]

Beckett friend and scholar, Gottfried Büttner, finds three Schopenhauerian 'recommendations' for 'enduring the misery of existence', of which the 'aesthetic contemplation' noted above is one. The other two, 'compassion and resignation', will be discussed below, using Büttner as a template. Based on his intimacy with Beckett, Büttner is able to link Schopenhauer's pessimism to Beckett's 'inner mood', the 'melancholic temperament, his inclination to resignation', while simultaneously ensuring such an understanding remains utterly distinct from nihilism.[42] But for present purposes, Büttner's final consideration of Schopenhauer's influence is held here to be most striking for the young Beckett: resignation. Just as Beckett's reification of art necessitated Büttner's first point, and the religious texts—in particular à Kempis—highlighted the importance of compassion, Schopenhauer's unique and profound legacy in Beckett's art is, above all, an acceptance of suffering; a denial of the material world and the desire accompanying it; a jettisoning of hope; or to cite *The Unnamable,* 'lashed to the stake, blindfold, gagged to the gullet'.[43] An excerpt from Schopenhauer beautifully conveys that rejection of the will 'recommended' by Schopenhauer to Beckett, and in turn by Beckett to his creatures:

> The unspeakable pain, the wretchedness and misery of mankind, the triumph of wickedness, the scornful mastery of chance, and the irretrievable fall of the just and the innocent are all here presented to us; and here is to be found a significant hint as to the nature of the world and of existence. It is the antagonism of the will with itself [....] where the phenomenon, the veil of Maya, no longer deceives it. It sees through the form of the phenomenon, the *principium individuationis*; the egoism resting on this expires with it. The *motives* that were previously so powerful now lose their force, and instead of them, the complete knowledge of the real nature of the world, acting as a quieter of the will, produces resignation, the giving up not merely of life, but of the whole will-to-live itself.[44]

Later in this paragraph, Schopenhauer's discussion of tragic literature as the summit of poetical achievement invokes Pedro Calderón's sin of birth, explicitly invoked by Beckett in *Proust*. Already by 1930 an internalisation of Schopenhauer's views on existence are evident in Beckett's writing; unlike 'Dante...Bruno.Vico..Joyce', the demarcation between the start of Beckett's views and the end of those advanced by his Schopenhauerian Proust is obscured—perhaps purposely so:

> Tragedy is not concerned with human justice. Tragedy is the statement of an expiation, but not the miserable expiation of a codified breach of a local arrangement, organised by the knaves for the fools. The tragic figure represents the expiation of original sin, of the original and eternal sin of him and all his "socii malorum", the sin of having been born.
>
> > "Pues el delito mayor
> > Del hombre es haber nacido."[45]

Indeed, strange as it sounds, there is no overstatement in asserting the impact of Schopenhauer upon *Proust* to be comparable to the impact of Proust upon *Proust*. Schopenhauer's stamp is affixed to the nostalgically capitalised Idea, Beckett's take on individual perception of the world as a projection of consciousness (and perhaps, indirectly, Beckett's discussion of Time upon Habit as a succession of perceptions made familiar through Memory); and of course, the application of the will-to-live. It is fitting, then, that the final word in *Proust* is Schopenhauer's.[46]

§4

Yet Schopenhauerian wisdom and ideas do not a twentieth century quietist make; or at least, no more than the nigh-heretical asceticism practised by à Kempis made him a forerunner of Catholic quietism. A conflation of factors is necessary in order to construct such a personal doctrine, and here Beckett is no exception. A rejection of eternal salvation as envisioned by the Christians above is doubtless one factor. Clearly, a view of existence as more desolate and punitive than is acceptable to artistic, theological and philosophical optimism is also a prerequisite. Achievements within the arts—as a vehicle for the reflection necessary to apprehend, redeem and palliate these painful human circumstances—become revelatory, especially for an artist at heart like Beckett. Indeed, art acts as both a melancholic insight into the 'true' human condition and a practical mechanism for ameliorating the suffering inherent in that condition. Nevertheless, a guarding against wilfulness—that 'ablation of desire' commended in *Proust*—is another trope, tying together otherwise divergent figures like Leopardi and Molinos, and finding an ethics in the hopelessness of struggle and the consequent jettisoning of the will. Finally, all of these ideas are restated with great vehemence in Schopenhauer's philosophy, one Beckett admired before he wrote any of his extended fiction. Indeed, despite the unmistakeable contributions by Burton, Augustine, Keats et. al., it is Schopenhauer who appears most influential in giving shape and form to Beckett's construction of 'agnostic quietism'.

Furthermore, Schopenhauer's prime influence upon Beckett, his pessimistic *pièce de résistance*, demands consideration. This, noted in the quotation from Schopenhauer above, is the 'veil of Maya', or the division between individual perception—called by Schopenhauer the *principium individuationis* (or 'principle of individuation', and occasionally 'egoism')—and Reality, the thing-in-itself, or what Beckett dubs 'non-anthropomorphised humanity' in a letter to MacGreevy: in fine, the world independent of subjectivity.[47] Schopenhauer is absolutely clear on the importance of this point and returns to it again and again. 'Maya' is his Hindu word for the paradox of humankind expressed through individual existence: 'precisely this visible world in which we are, a magic effect called into being, an unstable and inconstant illusion without substance, comparable to the optical illusion and the dream, a veil enveloping human consciousness, a something of which it is equally false and equally true to say that it is and that it is not'.[48]

More striking still is the importance given to this screen, Beckett's literary 'caesura', by Schopenhauer. For the 'veil of Maya' is the cause of individual anguish through self-serving pursuits, is the impediment to that 'deliverance from life and suffering [which] cannot even be imagined without complete denial of the will' existing beyond the 'veil of Maya'; and finally and most pivotally, is the doorway to true compassion itself.[49] Therefore, seeing the 'veil of Maya' for what it is—an egoistic delusion, a web of self-interest separating us from other beings—leads both to a rejection of needing to live, an identification with all suffering, and an expression of simultaneous ethical resignation and altruism that Schopenhauer asserts is the summit of human achievement:

> If that veil of Maya, the *prinicipium individuationis*, is lifted from the eyes of a man to such an extent that he no longer makes the egoistical distinction between himself and the person of others, but takes as much interest in the sufferings of other individuals as in his own [...] then it follows automatically that such a man, recognizing in all beings his own true and innermost self, must also regard the endless sufferings of all that lives as his own, and thus take upon himself the pain of the whole world [....] He knows the whole, comprehends its inner nature, and finds it involved in a constant passing away, a vain striving, an inward conflict, and a continual suffering.[50]

We shall see that the applicable value regarding Beckett's writing is twofold: first, his characters become less and less distinct, the setting more and more timeless, even placeless (one thinks of *Company* here, for example), in order to approach 'the endless sufferings of all that lives'; and secondly, Schopenhauer's ocular metaphor for seeing the world as it is resonates across Beckett's work, and addresses many of the same considerations.

This 'unveiling' is exemplified by what is called 'the vision at last' in *Krapp's Last Tape*: a realisation mixing light and dark, alongside a quieting of the will and an acceptance of the human curse of enduring and expressing pain; altogether a worthy and heretofore unexplored artistic seam for Krapp (and Beckett).[51] And for Beckett, the subject of that artistic contemplation may very well be the 'veil of Maya' itself. At least, it surely reflects a reading and artistic interest running from *Proust* and UoR MS 5000, to the journalism of the period and, especially, images cast in *Dream of Fair to Middling Women*: 'At night, to be sure, galavanting and cataracting behind the sweating wall-paper, just behind the wall-paper, slashing the close invisible plane with ghastlily muted slithers and somersaults. He thought of the rank dark room, quiet, *quieted*, when he would enter, then the first stir behind the paper, the first discreet slithers.'[52] Whether Belacqua's wall-paper, Watt's fence with Sam, the curtain in *Ill Seen Ill Said*, or even Murphy's chair, a division between the world and the 'close invisible plane' behind it, a trope of veiled perception, can be profitably construed as the mechanism whereby Beckett's 'agnostic quietism' becomes a subject for literature. Again and again, through all the affirmations and negations, the creative destructions, Beckett's writing approaches and encroaches the boundaries of the possible, knowable, expressive, real: 'I cannot say I am, I can't say anything, I've tried, I'm trying, he knows nothing, knows of nothing, neither what it is to speak, not what it is to hear, to know nothing, to be capable of nothing, and to have to try, you don't try any more, no need to try, it goes on by itself, from word to word [...]'[53]

However, lest we too are caught unawares by the 'veil of Maya', two points bear emphasising. First, even Beckett's obvious indebtedness to Schopenhauer may itself be subsumed into a greater affinity with 'artistic melancholy', to employ Giuseppina Restivo's useful phrase. In rightly linking Beckett to Walther von der Vogelweide and Albrecht Dürer (to which I have added Keats, Leopardi, Goethe, even Burton and Molinos), '*Melencolias* and Scientific Ironies in *Endgame*' reinforces Büttner's Schopenhauerian 'recommendations' for Beckett.[54] Both of these contributions are drawn upon in advancing the term 'agnostic quietism', shorthand for both the angst and philosophical inspiration contributing to Beckett's specific experiences and texts during the 1930s and thereafter. Largely, this interwar decade offered the battleground for Beckett's health, intellectual and artistic development; and derivatively, struggles with the role of subject and object in art—especially literature—through an increasing interest in charting a 'no-man's-land' between the two.

And secondly, like so much of Beckett's reading, what initially appears exhaustive frequently turns out instead to be focussed or synoptic. In keeping with his use of secondary sources, references to Schopenhauer in *Proust* come from sections 51 (Calderón) and 52 (Leibniz) in *The World as Will and Representation*. A dozen sections either way also gives the definition of art 'as *the way of considering things independently of the principle of sufficient reason*' also figuring in *Proust*,[55] and the sustained critique of the Thing-in-Itself undertaken by Schopenhauer in his fourth book, subtitled 'With the Attainment of Self-Knowledge, Affirmation and Denial of the Will to Live'. More specifically, this hundred or so pages offers significant discussion of the partition between subjective experience and objective existence; and furthermore, may well be responsible for Beckett's introduction to Goethe, whom Schopenhauer so venerates that he reproduces the final stanza of 'Prometheus' as evidence of the '*denial of the will-to-live*' and the '*quieter* of the will' found beyond the 'empty mirage and the web of Maya'.[56]

While disputing neither a fascination with Schopenhauer nor Beckett's voracious reading tendencies, that he would have become most familiar with this summative tenth of Schopenhauer's masterpiece, in preparation for writing *Proust*, is consistent with his own 'Habit'. And even these select pages proffer all sorts of provocative material for Schopenhauerian readings of Beckett's work. As a potential inspiration behind the 'tragicomedy' of *Waiting for Godot* as vivid as Caspar David Friedrich's, Schopenhauer's take on poetry as a 'mirror' of existence is particularly intriguing:

> The life of every individual, viewed as a whole and in general, and when only its most significant features are emphasised, is really a tragedy; but gone through in detail it has the character of a comedy [...] Thus, as if fate wished to add mockery to the misery of our existence, our life must contain all the woes of tragedy, and yet we cannot even assert the dignity of tragic characters, but, in the broad detail of life, are inevitably the foolish characters of a comedy.[57]

Despite leaving this final quotation provocatively hanging, both this and the sentiments expressed in *The World as Will and Representation* generally are a lucid reminder of Schopenhauer's presence in Beckett's thinking and, consequently, literature.

§5

Bearing these recollections in mind in terms of an intellectual heritage and burgeoning artistic approach, Beckett's 11 August 1936 entry from the 'Clare Street Notebook' ties together a number of different themes contributing to Beckett's 'agnostic quietism'. And just as surely as it links the so-called 'Victoria Group' in *Faust* to the 'veil of Maya' in the *World as Will and Representation*, the following excerpt also ties Beckett's own progress from the rather naked pessimism of *Proust*, to the more stoic resignation of the will in his post-war writing.

<u>Victoria Group</u>

> There are moments where the veil of hope is finally ripped away and the eyes, suddenly liberated, see <u>their</u> world as it is, as it must be. Alas, it does not last long, the perception quickly passes: the eyes can only bear such a merciless light for a short while, the thin skin of hope re-forms and one returns to the world of phenomena.
>
> Hope is the cataract of the spirit that cannot be pierced until it is ripe for decay. Not every cataract ripens: many a human being spends his whole life enveloped in the mist of hope. And even if the cataract can be pierced for a moment it almost always re-forms immediately; and thus it is with hope. And people never tire of applying to themselves the comforting clichés inspired by hope: hope is the first precondition of life, the instinct that the human race has to thank for not dying out long ago. To thank! Should we really assume as a basic premise that life is so completely unbearable with self-knowledge, that steady, clear self-knowledge whose voice serenely asserts "This is how you are, this is how you will remain. As you have fared until now, so you will continue to fare, till you 'I' decomposes into the parts that are so familiar to you. For you need expect from death nothing either better or worse than this division."[58]

Discussion of the 'veil of hope', in relation to the first paragraph of this incredible entry, is to date only available in Nixon's 'Scraps of German', which he rightly links to Beckett's contemporaneous reading of Goethe, finding that 'this was the zone, the painful but true reality behind the veil, which [Beckett's] writing needed to penetrate'.[59] Moreover, this passage invariably leads to a comparison of related metaphors from the famous 1937 'German letter', such as 'dissolve' and 'porous', and the precise same imagery—in this case 'mist'—is raised in personal terms above much as it is artistically formulated to Axel Kaun a year later: 'more and more my own language appears to me like a veil that must be torn apart in order to get at the things (or the Nothingness) behind it'.[60] In short, should this entry on the 'Victoria Gruppe' be indicative of Beckett's aesthetic and indeed ethical outlook, as I think it most certainly is, even if the creative words dried up after *Murphy* was completed, the creative approach was still being honed along melancholic, sceptical, and nominalist lines.

In Schopenhauer's most critical, and indeed lyrical, passage on the 'veil of Maya', he finds that what Beckett later called an 'unyeilding' light is actually a confusing, 'fearful terror' at the loss of individuality:

> Just as the boatman sits in his small boat, trusting his frail craft in a stormy sea that is boundless in every direction, rising and falling with the howling, mountainous waves, so in the midst of a world full of suffering and misery the individual man calmly sits [.... until] the principle of sufficient reason in one or other of its forms seems to undergo an exception. For example, when it appears that some change has occurred without a cause, or a deceased person exists again; or when in any other way the past or the future is present, or the distant is near.[61]

Schopenhauer's description of the sundered 'veil of Maya' and the 'dread' entailed, exercises both Beckett and Watt: Beckett in his artistic endeavours (for instance, as imparted in his 1937 'German Letter'), and Watt in the difficulties posed by this type of 'fugitive penetration'. Two examples in *Watt* bear mentioning. The first transpires during the piano-tuning undertaken by the Galls, so *resembling* past meaningful experiences despite Watt's inability to contextualise this particular one, contrasting as it does with how he 'had lived, miserably it is true, among face values all his adult life'. In turn, this evokes visions of 'his dead father appeared to him in a wood [...] or the time when alone in a rowing-boat, far from land, he suddenly smelt flowering currant', although Watt is initially untroubled by these (non-) events.[62] Although Watt's experience of causeless change with the Galls forces him to subsequently seek meaning in Mr Knott's house—and from this perspective, touches off his thought experiments in the spirit of 'sufficient reason'—Schopenhauer asserts that a typical person, when confronted with the illusory nature of phenomena, nevertheless 'does everything to maintain them'.[63] Despite (or possibly as a result of) Watt's suspicion that all is not as it should be (or rather, all as it should be is 'not'), the remaining time in Knott's house is marked by the commencement of the exhaustive series that that (as John J. Mood and Ackerley demonstrate) is neither sufficient nor consistently reasonable. Nor is Mood alone: 'even Watt could not hide from himself for long the absurdity of these constructions', which finally crumble at the climax of the novel.[64]

The second illustration of a veil removed from Watt's eyes transpires during Watt's climatic travel to the rail station, where he encounters an unclassifiable figure, which was 'greatly to be deplored': 'For Watt's concern, deep as it appeared, was not after all with what the figure was, in reality, but with what the figure appeared to be, in reality. For since when were Watt's concerns with what things were, in reality?' Once again faced with the Thing-In-Itself, Watt is quite uncharacteristically described with impatience and agitation; that Schopenhauerian 'dread' at seeing the world as it is. Although the figure remains indistinct, 'Watt seemed to regard, for some obscure reason, this particular hallucination as possessing exceptional interest.'[65] But interest is secondary here to changes wrought. Thereafter, Watt experiences Schopenhauer's ablation of the will lying beyond the 'veil of Maya', in stark contrast to the bourgeois characters at the station. In keeping with Beckett's own artistic understatement noted above, the change is muted: Watt 'felt no need, nay, no desire, to pass water'; both Miss Price and the smell in the waiting-room meets with his indifference; and finally, his purchase of a ticket to the end of the line—not caring which end.[66] Watt, it would seem, passed through the hallucinatory doorway of Maya, and embraced the Schopenhauerian denial of the will-to-live, that quieter of the will. Rubin Rabinovitz has touched on this idea of the Schopenhauerian 'screen' explicitly mentioned in this portion of *Watt*: 'This last regular link with the screen [...] he now envisaged its relaxation, and eventual rupture.'[67]

But whereas *Watt*'s 'traditional', if jumbled, narrative structure (at least, when compared to *Texts for Nothing*) concludes with this triumph of 'agnostic quietism' over 'sufficient reason', the phenomenal world and the will-to-live, Beckett's later works cast the 'veil of Maya'—which we recall Schopenhauer defined as 'a something of which it is equally false and equally true to say that it is and that it is not'—as subject matter *per se*. This is a far cry from Belacqua's wall-paper or even Watt's final resignation. Instead of a dividing object in *Dream of Fair to Middling Women*, or a theme of division in *Watt* (evident in Arsene's statement, Watt and Sam's communication via their fence and the two examples noted above), Beckett's later works turn this 'cataract' into both subject and object of literature itself. The division between the knowable and the illusory, in this sense, moves beyond Schopenhauerian tropes to become *the cause of despair itself*. In this regard, perhaps Beckett's pessimism trumps Schopenhauer's: the latter can find solace in seeing the Thing-In-Itself beyond a deceitful existence; but for Beckett, all is *Ill Seen Ill Said*, veiled or otherwise. Yet in this way, Beckett may be said to have solved—insofar as the relationship of form and content is soluble—those problems in the 'no-man's-land' of subject and object so perplexing him in the 1930s.

Ill Seen Ill Said offers a fitting, final perspective upon this change. Right at the start, a black veil separating an old woman's cabin from existence outside is introduced. This curtain, 'trembling imperceptibly without cease', is attached to a hook and hung by a nail covering the window. 'Opened by her to let her see the sky. But even without that she is there. Without the curtain's being opened. Suddenly open. A flash. The suddenness of it all! She still without stopping. On her way without starting. Gone without going. Back without returning.'[68] This passage is immediately followed by the seeming juxtaposition with 'the madhouse of the skull and nowhere else'. Yet conceiving skull and veil separately, as both dividing objective reality and subjective perception, is tempting but hasty:

> On resumption the head is covered. No matter. No matter now. Such the confusion now between real and—how say its contrary? No matter. That old tandem. Such now the confusion between them once so twain. And such the farrago from eye to mind. For it to make what sad sense of it may. No matter now. Such equal liars both. Real and—how ill say its contrary? The counter-poison.[69]

The identification of the two is made explicit toward the end of *Ill Seen Ill Said*—'Black night fallen. But no. In her head too pure wait'—and thereafter becomes a subject upon which all comes to depend: 'But first the partition. It rid they too would be. It less they by as much. It of all the properties doubtless the least obdurate. See the instant see it again when unaided it dissolved.'[70] After the dissolution of the veil, what remains is not so much character, setting, even situation, but the 'uncommon common noun collapsion': 'Then far from the still agonizing eye a gleam of hope. By the grace of these modest beginnings. With in second sight the shack of ruins. To scrute together with the inscrutable face. All curiosity spent.'[71] And with the renunciation of curiosity and desire, what we have here termed 'agnostic quietism' is all that remains, alongside the Schopenhauerian paradox—now extending to both concept ('First last moment') and language ('Know happiness')—used to describe the 'veil of Maya':

> For the last time at last for to end yet again what the wrong word? Than revoked. No but slowly dispelled a little very little like the last wisps of day when the curtain closes. Of itself by slow millimetres or drawn by phantom hand. Farewell to farewell. Then in that perfect dark foreknell darling sound pip for end begun. First last moment. Grant only enough remain to devour all. Moment by glutton moment. Sky earth the whole kit and boodle. Not another crumb of carrion left. Lick chops and basta. No. One moment more. One last. Grace to breathe that void. Know happiness.[72]

Thus far, we have seen a nexus of three especially formative influences upon Beckett's 'agnostic quietism': an artistic trope of melancholic contemplation; an appreciation of human suffering in a nasty world and the stoicism and resignation necessary to go on despite the anguish entailed therein; and finally, the ethical and aesthetic acceptance of a veil separating perception from truth, hope from will-lessness. The third aspect not only becomes the basis for consolation—without hope of Christian salvation, what remains is a shared community of pain mandating compassion for others—but also, I suggest, this Schopenhauerian partition increasingly becomes a literary subject matter itself, situated as 'it' (for lack of an effable term) is between Beckett's concern with the 'no-man's-land' dividing subject and object. In many ways, Schopenhauer's 'recommendations' were paradigmatic in Beckett's emerging worldview, yet these were not exclusive: as Beckett told Israel Shenker his tools were 'impotence' and 'ignorance'. Both should be seen as ancillary concerns in *The World as Will and Representation*, given that a paradoxical strength and knowledge arises from denial of the will-to-live. But not for Beckett. These became the foundation stones of his art. Here a bulk of archival materials support our view that Beckett—already well on the way to developing his own personal and artistic ethos—became interested in that infamous incapacity of deed and word so pervasive in his later works through an intellectual mosaic patched together from the readings and note-taking before the mid-1930s.

NOTES

[1] Beckett to Thomas MacGreevy, 10 March 1935, TCD MS 10904; the English translations of Latin can be found in John Pilling's *Beckett's* Dream *Notebook* [entry 587, 588, 599], pp. 85–6. For the entire letter, *The Letters of Samuel Beckett, 1929-1940: Volume 1*, eds. Martha Dow Fehsenfeld and Lois More Overbeck (Cambridge: Cambridge University Press, 2009), pp. 256–264.

[2] Mark Nixon, '"Scraps of German": Beckett Reading German Literature', in *Samuel Beckett Today / Aujourd'hui* 16 (2006), pp. 264, 278; see also James Knowlson, *Damned to Fame: The Life of Samuel Beckett* (London: Bloomsbury, 1996), p. 353; and Chris Ackerley, 'Samuel Beckett and Thomas á Kempis: The Roots of Quietism', in *Samuel Beckett Today / Aujourd'hui* 9 (2000).

[3] *Ibid.*, p. 88. It is worth noting that á Kempis' fifteenth century text was not intended as mysticism of any kind (though it reads that way now)—one reason it was never placed on the codex of banned books during the Catholic Counter Reformation a century later. In fact, it was intended to be a sort of guidebook for monks and monastic aspirants.

[4] The use of á Kempis in Beckett's letter to MacGreevy is not restricted to the three passages cited above and explicitly quoted from *The Imitation of Christ*: the phrases 'Let Jesu be solely thy darling', 'solitary bird under the eaves', 'a sparrow alone upon the housetop' all appear in Pilling's *Beckett's* Dream *Notebook* many citations from which also appear later in Beckett's *Dream of Fair to Middling Women*; see John Pilling, *Beckett's* Dream *Notebook*, (Beckett International Foundation, Reading: 1999), pp. 84–7.

[5] Samuel Beckett, 'Humanistic Quietism', in *Disjecta*, ed. Ruby Cohn (New York: Grove Press, 1984), p. 68.

[6] 'Ruinstrewn land' is taken from Samuel Beckett, 'Fizzle 3: Afar a Bird', in Beckett, *The Complete Short Prose 1929-1989*, ed. S.E. Gontarski (New York: Grove Press, 1995). I am indebted to John Coffey for Brian Coffey's letter to Thomas MacGreevy, and for his assistance in this matter.

[7] Beckett, 'Dante...Bruno.Vico..Joyce', in *Disjecta*, p. 33.

[8] Dante, *The Divine Comedy of Dante Alighieri; II: Purgatory*, Canto IV, trans. John D. Sinclair (London: John Lane the Bodley Head, 1948), p. 61; TCD MS 10966/1.

[9] Knowlson, *Damned to Fame*, p. 76.

[10] *Ibid.*, pp. 117, 42. The sixth stanza in Keats' 'Ode to a Nightingale' runs:
   Darkling I listen and, for many a time
   I have been half in love with easeful Death,
   Call'd him soft names in many a mused rhyme,
   To take into the air my quiet breath;
   Now more than ever seems it rich to die,
   To cease upon the midnight with no pain,
   While thou art pouring forth thy soul abroad
   In such an ecstasy!
   Still wouldst thou sing, and I have ears in vain—
   To thy high requiem become a sod.

[11] Samuel Beckett, 'Dante and the Lobster' in Beckett, *More Pricks Than Kicks*, (London: Calder, 1998), p. 21; italics added.

12. Cited in John Montague, 'A Few Drinks and a Hymn', in *New York Times Late Edition*, 17 April 1994, see also John Keats, 'Ode to a Nightingale', republished at *The Poetry Foundation*, available at: www.poetryfoundation.org/poem/173744 (all websites last accessed 12/12/14).
13. Giacomo Leopardi, *Selected Prose and Poetry*, trans. I. Origo and J. Heath-Stubbs (London: Oxford University Press, 1966), p. 190.
14. For details of these notebooks, see Matthew Feldman, *Beckett's Books: A Cultural History of Samuel Beckett's 'Interwar Notes'* (London: Bloomsbury, 2008).
15. See Chris Ackerley and S.E. Gontarski, *The Faber Companion to Samuel Beckett* (London: Faber and Faber, 2006), p. 460.
16. *Proust* in Samuel Beckett, *Proust and Three Dialogues* (London: Calder & Boyers, 1970), p. 18; see also *Molloy* in Samuel Beckett, *The Beckett Trilogy* [*Molloy, Malone Dies, The Unnamable*] (London: Picador, 1979), p. 34. J.D. O'Hara asserts that Leopardi's 'e fango e il mondo [The world is dirt]' from 'A Se Stesso' was intended as an epigraph to *Proust*, see his 'Beckett's Schopenhauerian Reading of Proust: the Will as Whirled in Re-Presentation' in Eric van der Luft, ed., *Schopenhauer: New Essays in Honor of his 200th Birthday* (Lewiston: The Edwin Mellen Press, 1988), p. 276.
17. *Ibid.*, p. 281; transcribed in TCD MS 10971/9.
18. The reference is to *Whoroscope*, from Samuel Beckett, *Collected Poems* (London: Calder, 1999), pp. 1–6, and the accompanying reasons for Beckett's wishes that his own 'cracked beater' be stilled can be found in the chapter 'The London Years' in Knowlson's *Damned to Fame*.
19. Pilling, *Beckett's* Dream *Notebook* [entry 80, 122, 177], pp. 12, 17, 25.
20. Samuel Beckett, *Dream of Fair to Middling Women* (Dublin: The Black Cat Press, 1992), pp. 72–4.
21. See Feldman, *Beckett's Books*, chs. 2 and 4.
22. Robert Burton, *Anatomy of Melancholy*, vol. I (London: George Bell and Sons, 1904), p. 16.
23. Burton concludes, 'I write of melancholy, by being busy to avoid melancholy', *ibid.*, p. 20.
24. *Ibid.*, p. 170. For an excellent discussion of artistic melancholy, see Francis Yates' chapter 'Melancholy: Dürer and Agrippa' in *The Occult Philosophy in the Elizabethan Age* (London: Routledge Classics, 1999), pp. 57–70.
25. Beckett, 'Fizzle 3: Afar a Bird', p. 233.
26. Dirk van Hulle, '"Nichtsnichtsundnichts": Beckett's and Joyce's Transtextual Undoings', in *Beckett, Joyce and the Art of the Negative*, *European Joyce Studies* 16 (2005), p. 54. Van Hulle concludes his insightful text on the 'veil' of words by pointing to the distinction between Joyce and Beckett: 'Joyce was looking for words, Beckett tried to find the 'unword'.
27. Deirdre Bair, *Samuel Beckett: A Biography* (London: Picador, 1978), p. 129.
28. Samuel Beckett, 'Serena II' in Beckett, *Collected Poems*, pp. 23–4. This melancholic poem directly invokes á Kempis' 'the sad going out and glad coming home' mentioned in the letter to MacGreevy of 10 March 1935:

>with whatever trust of panic we went out
>with so much shall we return
>there shall be no loss of panic between a man and his dog
>bitch though he be

29 Pilling, *Beckett's* Dream *Notebook* [entry 805], p. 114; used to denote the values of 'mirth' by Burton and Belacqua's mother in *Dream of Fair of Middling Women*.
30 Burton, *Anatomy of Melancholy*, vol. II, p. 46; Beckett, *Dream of Fair to Middling Women*, pp. 240–1.
31 Pilling, *Beckett's* Dream *Notebook* [entries 681–3], pp. 98–9.
32 William Ralph Inge, *Christian Mysticism: The Bampton Lectures (1899)* (London: Metheun & Co, 1921), pp. 232–3.
33 *Murphy*, pp. 100–2, italics added. This, in turn, corresponds to entries on Ernest Jones' *Treatment of the Neuroses*—'Dungeons in Spain. (Mine own.)'—in Beckett's 'Psychology Notes', TCD MS 10971/8/21.
34 Arthur Schopenhauer, *The World as Will and Representation*, vol. II, trans. E. F. J. Payne (New York: Dover Publications, 1969), p. 616.
35 Mark Nixon, '"what a tourist I must have been": The German Dairies of Samuel Beckett', (Unpublished PhD. Thesis, University of Reading: 2005), quoted pp. 59, 40, 57.
36 Entry in George Reavey's diary, 15 July 1930; see 'Scraps of German', pp. 278–9.
37 Letter to MacGreevy of 25 August 1930, TCD MS 10904, I am most grateful to Mark Nixon and John Pilling for their assistance with this letter. Beckett's reflections on *Proust* to John Pilling are contained in John Pilling, 'Beckett's *Proust*', reprinted in S.E. Gontarski, ed., *The Beckett Studies Reader* (Gainesville: University Press of Florida, 1993), p. 22.
38 Beckett, *Proust*, pp. 91–2. The other references to 'an objectivation of the individual's will, Schopenhauer would say' and Schopenhauer's definition of the artistic procedure as "the contemplation of the world independently of the principle of reason"', are found here, pp. 19, 87.
39 Schopenhauer's admiration of the Dutch School in painting, Goethe, his castigation of Christianity and so forth would have doubtlessly appealed to Beckett, as would Schopenhauer's definition of poetry as 'the art of bringing into play the imagination through words', see *The World as Will and Representation*, vol. II, p. 424. Elsewhere Schopenhauer provocatively writes: 'Not merely philosophy but also the fine arts work at bottom towards the solution of the problem of existence.' (vol. I, p. 406.)
40 One exception quoted above is Angela Moorjani's 'Mourning, Schopenhauer, and Beckett's Art of Shadows', in Lois Oppenheim and Marius Buning, eds., *Beckett On and On* (London: Farleigh Dickenson University Press, 1996), p. 85. Perhaps a better exception is found in Rubin Rabinovitz's chapter 'Watt and the Philosophers', which offers an effective survey of Schopenhauer as opponent of Descartes and champion of the will and perception, in addition to offering this intriguing reading of *Watt*: 'Watt's error, in terms of Schopenhauer's philosophy, is to use rational methods (investigations of causality) in trying to understand the effects of a thing-in-itself [....] a person's aspect as a thing in-itself, which is unaffected by causality, is the center of the essential qualities of the self', see *The Development of Samuel Beckett's Fiction* (Chicago: University of Illinois Press, 1984), p. 130.
41 J.D. O'Hara argues Beckett 'made Schopenhauer and Proust serve his own concerns' regarding pessimism', see 'Beckett's Schopenhaurian Reading of Proust: The Will as Whirled in Re-presentation', in Eric van der Luft, ed., *Schopenhauer: New Essays in Honor of his 200th Birthday* (Lewiston: The Edwin Mellen Press, 1988), pp. 275, 285. In like fashion, Steven J. Rosen's chapter 'Beckett, Proust and Schopenhauer', in his *Samuel Beckett and the Pessimistic Tradition* (New Brunswick: Rutgers University Press, 1976)

makes the case (p. 152) that 'Beckett is still more pessimistic than Schopenhauer', and as a result, fails to temper both his and Proust's outlook in terms of any happiness or optimism.

[42] Gottfried Büttner, 'Schopenhauer's Recommendations to Beckett', in *Samuel Beckett's Novel* Watt, trans, Joseph P. Dolan (Philadelphia: University of Pennsylvania Press, 1984), pp. 114, 115. Büttner quotes Beckett's own rejection of the label nihilist: "'I simply cannot understand why some people call me a nihilist. There is not basis for that" [...] And he went on to refer to Hamm's words in *Endgame:* "But beyond the hills? Eh? Perhaps it's still green"', *ibid.*, p. 122.

[43] Beckett, *The Unnamable,* in *The Beckett Trilogy,* p. 360.

[44] Schopenhauer, *The World as Will and Representation,* vol. I, p. 253; italics in original.

[45] Beckett, *Proust,* p. 67. Pilling's 'Beckett's *Proust*' has also shown that quotation of Pedro Calderón's maxim—translated as 'For man's greatest offence / Is that he has been born,' comes via sect. 51 of the *World as Will and Representation,* p. 12.

[46] Beckett's final word on the matter, 'defunctus' is highlighted as 'a beautiful word' in a 1930 letter to MacGreevy, TCD MS 10904.

[47] In the same letter to MacGreevy on 31 January 1938, Beckett also uses the term 'inorganic juxtaposition' to convey his artistic difference of opinion with MacGreevy, and Ireland at large; TCD MS 10904.

[48] Schopenhauer, *World as Will and Representation,* vol. I, Appendix, p. 419.

[49] *Ibid.*, pp. 352, 397.

[50] *Ibid.*, p. 378; italics in original.

[51] Samuel Beckett, *Krapp's Last Tape,* in Beckett, *The Complete Dramatic Works* (London: Faber and Faber, 1990), p. 220; see also Knowlson, *Damned to Fame,* ch. 17.

[52] Beckett, *Dream of Fair to Middling Women,* p. 15.

[53] Beckett, *The Unnamable,* p. 370.

[54] Beckett's notes on Dürer can be found in UoR MS 5001. Beckett's notes on Vogelweide comes from J. G. Robertson's *History of German Literature* which Nixon, in his 'Scraps of German', dates Beckett's reading of to 1934, and may be the source for the poem 'Da Tagte Es', pp. 262-3. Giuseppina Restivo rightly finds a trace of Walther in *Stirrings Still*—'To this end for want of a stone on which to sit like Walther and cross his legs the best he could do'—via Dureresque settings in *Endgame,* concluding that both show significant traces of artistic melancholy; see her '*Melencolias* and Scientific Ironies in *Endgame*: Beckett, Walther, Dürer, Musil', in *Samuel Beckett Today / Aujord'hui,* 11 (2002), p. 105.

[55] Schopenhauer, *The World as Will and Representation,* vol. I, sect. 36, p. 185.

[56] *Ibid.*, pp. 285, 284; italics in original. Beckett also reproduced a typescript copy of Faust's 'Prometheus' in German; TCD MS 10971/1/72.

[57] *The World as Will and Representation,* sect. 58, p. 322. In 1975, Beckett told Ruby Cohn of Friedrich's 1819 painting, *Man and Woman Observing the Moon,* 'This was the source of *Waiting for Godot,* you know'; Beckett first saw the painting in March 1937 during his travels around Germany, although he may well have been thinking of Friedrich's 1824 *Two Men Observing the Moon;* for details, see *Damned to Fame,* pp. 378, 257.

[58] [Es gibt Augenblicke, wo der Hoffnungsschleier endgültig weggerissen wird und die plötzlich befreiten Augen ihre Welt anblicken wie sie ist, wie sie sein muss. Es dauert leider nicht lange, die Wahrnehmung geht schnell vorüber, ein so unerbittliches Licht können die Augen nur auf kurze Zeit ertragen, das Häutchen der Hoffnung bildet sich von neuem, man kehrt in die Welt der Phänomene zurück.

Die Hoffnung ist des Geistes [Star], der nicht zu stechen ist, ehe er ganz [faulreif] wird. Es [reift] nicht jeder Star, es bringt gar mancher Mensch im Dunst der Hoffnung sein ganzes Leben zu. Und wenn der Star auch für den Augenblick geteilt worden sein mag, so bildet er sich fast immer bald von neuem, so auch die Hoffnung. Und man kriegt es niemals satt, die von der Hoffnung eingeblasene Trostformel an sich selbst anzuwenden: -Die Hoffnung ist die erste Lebensbedingung, der Instinkt dem es zu verdanken ist, dass das Menschengeschlecht nicht schon seit langem Zugrunde gegangen ist. Zu verdanken! Soll man denn wirklich als [Ursatz] annehmen, das Leben sei mit der Selbstkenntnis dermassen unverträglich, deren steten klaren Selbstkenntnis deren Stimme gelassen behauptet: - So bist du, so bleibst du. So wie es dir bisher gegangen ist, wo wird es auch [ferner hin] gehen, bis dein Ich in die dir so bekannten Bestandteile zersetzt worden ist. Denn vom Tode brauchst du gar nichts anders als diese Absonderung, weder etwas besseres, noch etwas schlimmeres, zu erwarten], UoR MS 5003, p. 33, 35, 37. For the entire entry, see my 'Sourcing "Aporetics": An Empirical Study on Philosophical Influences in the Development of Samuel Beckett's Writing' (Unpublished PhD. Thesis, Oxford Brookes University: 2004), pp. 394–5. I am especially grateful to Mark Nixon for alerting me to this passage, in addition to our lengthy discussions on this important matter.

[59] Nixon, 'Scraps of German', pp. 273–4.
[60] Beckett, 'German Letter', in *Disjecta*, p. 171.
[61] Schopenhauer, *The World as Will and Representation*, vol. I, sect. 63, pp. 352–3.
[62] Samuel Beckett, *Watt* (London: Calder & Boyars, 1970), pp. 67–71.
[63] Schopenhauer, *The World as Will and Representation*, vol. I, sect. 63, p. 353.
[64] Beckett, *Watt*, p. 131.
[65] *Ibid.*, pp. 226–7.
[66] *Ibid.*, pp. 232–44.
[67] *Ibid.*, p. 232. Rabinovitz, *The Development of Samuel Beckett's Fiction*, ch. 10; see especially p. 138. Dirk van Hulle also mentions Schopenhauer's 'veil of Maya' in his discussion of Beckett in Joyce in 'Nichtsnichtsundnichts'.
[68] Samuel Beckett, *Ill Seen Ill Said* (London: Calder, 1982), pp. 15, 18–9.
[69] *Ibid.*, p. 40.
[70] *Ibid.*, pp. 47, 53.
[71] *Ibid.*, p. 55.
[72] *Ibid.*, p. 59.

BECKETT'S POSS AND THE DOG'S DINNER:
An Empirical Survey of the 1930s "Psychology Notes" and "Philosophy Notes"

> [...] a sufficient quantity of food was prepared and cooked to carry Mr. Knott through the week [...] these things, and many others too numerous to mention, were well mixed together in the famous pot and boiled for four hours, until the consistence of a mess, or *poss*, was obtained, and all the good things to eat, and all the good things to drink, and all the good things to take for the good of the health were inextricably mingled and transformed into a single good thing that was neither food, nor drink, nor physic, but *quite a new good thing*.[1]

§1

Watt's preparations for the sustenance of his obscure master, cited above, clearly involved quite a time-consuming and meticulous process. Yet in the end, all the ingredients 'were inextricably mingled and transformed' in order to serve Mr Knott a 'poss' intended to provide for his immediate future. *Watt* further reveals that the eponymous 'hero' put much of himself into his task: 'tears would fall, tears of mental fatigue, from his face, into the pot, and from his chest, and out from under his arms, beads of moisture, provoked by his exertions, into the pot also'.[2] As an analogy to the exacting process of note-taking embarked upon by Samuel Beckett, our epigraph from the novel written just after that intensive period of study is most appropriate. For Beckett, no less than the conscientious Watt, gathered together a diffuse variety of materials to be subsequently modified and applied to writing projects during the 1930s and after. The present essay will survey some of these materials, specifically those concerned with psychology and philosophy.

The importance of such a survey is attested by other texts in this volume analysing different portions of the 'Interwar Notes' (for brevity), and by the more empirical turn in Beckett studies generally following the publication of James Knowlson's indispensable biography. The main thrust of this shift is succinctly captured by Graley Herren: 'Some of the most interesting research in Beckett studies over the last several decades attempts to trace Beckett's sources and show how he refashioned them to produce original works.'[3] It is precisely this endeavour made possible by the 'Interwar Notes', with methodology acting as a drawbridge in approaching Beckett's readings and self-confessed 'note-snatching' in philosophy and psychology.[4] To be sure, in many other areas the advance guard of Beckett studies has done just as Herren suggests. Worthiest of note here are Knowlson, John Pilling, Chris Ackerley and Frederik Smith. All of these have long contributed to tracing original sources through a common point of departure: materials demonstrably used by Beckett in the construction of his texts. In following their fine examples, the notes discussed below are just such a tangible commodity, especially when seen as a self-education necessarily anticipating the later shedding process seeking to 'eliminate all the poisons and find the right language' in the post-war writing.[5] The readings, transcriptions and, consequently, internalisation, of many of the psychological and especially philosophical texts note-snatched prior to the outbreak of World War II can thus be viewed as a fulcrum around which Beckett conceived his own aims (in the widest sense), and developed the artistic methodology later employed in *The Beckett Trilogy* and thereafter.

Both the primary sources used by Beckett and the method employed in their reformulation take on special relevance with the psychology and philosophy materials. This is due in no small measure to the wealth of critical studies on Beckett's art taking one or the other of these subjects as a point of departure. But here the author's complicity (and arguably anticipation[6]) is evident. Despite claims of never understanding philosophers, Beckett himself rather paradoxically suggested just such an angle of inquiry to Sighle Kennedy in a 1967 letter.[7] And Beckett's well-documented connection to psychoanalysis, borne of his two-year therapeutic sessions under Wilfred Bion in London, have led commentators as diverse as G.C. Barnard and J.D. O'Hara to see psychological theories as fundamental to works such as *Murphy* and *Molloy*. Critical works in these areas ought only to be strengthened by the 'Interwar Notes', which demonstrate a detailed understanding of syntax and ideas from both disciplines.

It will also become clear that the requisite 'straws, flotsam, names, dates, births and deaths' so appealing to Beckett are conspicuously evident throughout.[8] Finally, the subset of 'Philosophy Notes' and 'Psychology Notes' forming the bulk of Beckett's reading annotations and transcriptions (and in rare instances, extrapolation) were scrupulously compiled and as will be indicated, contributed significantly to his artistic approach and construction.

§2

The barest study of Beckettian criticism indicates how central an instrument of siege philosophy has been in attempting to penetrate that notorious literary keep. Yet this should not suggest a monolithic philosophical approach to Beckett's work. Far from it. For this critical trope contains a major interpretative split, made plain by contrasting two quite recent studies: *The Philosophy of Samuel Beckett* and *Beckett and Philosophy*. The former, suffused though it is with John Calder's personal impressions and recollections, firmly locates the influence of particular philosophers *upon* Beckett's thinking and writing. Like Martin Esslin's groundbreaking 1962 text *The Novelist as Philosopher*, Calder's study attempts to locate Beckett within the tradition of the philosopher-poet:

> Voltaire considered himself to be a novelist, a poet, a dramatist and a writer of opera libretti, but we think of him today largely as a philosopher. The same fate may overtake Samuel Beckett, because what future generations can expect to find in his work is above all an ethical and philosophical message; the novels and plays will increasingly be seen as the wrapping for that message.[9]

Conversely, Richard Lane's edited volume represents a more recent paradigm by focussing instead upon the linguistic, conceptual, and impressionistic *affinities* with recent thinkers such as Alain Badiou, Michel Foucault, Jürgen Habermas, Theodor Adorno and others. By raising the spectre of 'meaning on trial' (including criticism itself) in Beckett's art, as well as associated problematics of form and nihilism (or meaninglessness), Lane's introduction, furthermore, approvingly cites one contributor's comment: 'At this moment, the most significant issues in Beckett studies are just beginning to congeal around the question raised by Badiou on one hand, and Adorno and Critchley on the other.'[10] This point is highly contestable.

For what is implied by this particular approach for better understanding Beckett (or for that matter modern literature generally) is clear enough: scholars are best employed as bartenders. They distil Beckett into a decanter (hated by the whisky—as Beckett declared in *Proust*), measuring his ideas with others subjectively perceived to produce a heady mix. While Lane's contributors make some persuasive arguments, it is important to note that this is a sea change in Beckett Studies. Implicitly contained here is an admission by sectors of the Beckett industry to have previously created unpalatable scholarship in previous attempts to link the author to texts he read and how they consequently influenced him. As many philosophers in *Beckett and Philosophy* are themselves of highly recent vintage, it seems far too early to assert that the most significant philosophical readings in Beckett Studies can 'congeal' around those who were undoubtedly more influenced by Beckett than vice-versa (for outside of David Lodge's satirical *Small World*, how could Badiou have bearing on Beckett's thought?). Clearly this is a far cry from Herren's—and in a different manner, Calder's—injunctions to start with Beckett's own development.

In this spirit, the largest source-base is best introduced with Beckett's words; in this case, an exchange of letters with Alan Schneider on the production of *Endgame*. The latter asks 'Have you remembered who that old Greek was?'—a reference contained in one of Hamm's monologues. In a lengthy letter, Beckett responds by stating:

> Old Greek: *I can't find my notes on the pre-Socratics.* The arguments of the Heap and the Bald Head (which hair falling produces baldness) were used by all the Sophists and I think have been variously attributed to one or the other. They disprove the reality of mass in the same way and by means of the same fallacy as the arguments of the Arrow and Achilles and the Tortoise, invented a century earlier by Zeno the Eleatic, disprove the reality of movement. The leading Sophist, against whom Plato wrote his Dialogue, was Protagoras and he is probably the "old Greek" whose name Hamm can't remember. One purpose of the image throughout the play is to suggest the impossibility logically, i.e. eristically, of the 'thing' ever coming to an end. 'The end is in the beginning and yet we go on.' In other words the impossibility of catastrophe. Ended at its inception, and at every subsequent instant, it continues, ergo can never end. Don't mention any of this to your actors![11]

This fascinating letter encapsulates much about Beckett from last to first: his reticence to reveal artistic 'meaning' (to actors, interviewers and so on), his own remarkable knowledge and memory (in this case directed toward philosophical arguments); and most importantly for the present purposes, his reliance on sources accumulated earlier in his life. According to Everett Frost, the notes contained in 'Philosophy Notes' TCD MSS 10967 referred to above cover 267 pages of typed and handwritten folios, recto and verso, on the history of European philosophy, from its Ancient Greek inception to the end of the nineteenth century.[12]

Those Beckett termed 'notes on the pre-Socratics' are unmistakably of greatest importance. As shown above, they were explicitly used in the writing of *Endgame*. More importantly, however, these same Presocratic materials comprised 130 of the 267 total sheets on the history of philosophy. Thus nearly half the entire corpus of 'Philosophy Notes' is taken from the first 300 years of a nearly 3000 year European tradition of thought. Contained in these pages of what Beckett titled '**ANCIENT PHILOSOPHY**' are a wealth of dates, facts, anecdotes, philosophical quotations, as well as a striking hand-drawn colour map of the eastern Mediterranean detailing each Greek philosopher's birthplace (for example, Pythagoras, Melissus and Epicurus are grouped together inside a rectangle connected by a line to Camos). Unlike the corpus of 'Philosophy Notes' as a whole, these were almost certainly compiled from a number of different sources. Some of the notes were typed (probably in one of Beckett's London residences) while the remainder—and by far the most important—were handwritten (probably with different pens or colour of ink, and invariably in a London library). The two principal texts used are Wilhelm Windelband's *A History of Philosophy* and John Burnet's *Greek Philosophy*, both handwritten. That these notes were used intermittently all Beckett's artistic life is incontestable, even if their significance for Beckett was later chiefly allusion and pastiche, as in *All Strange Away*: 'ancient Greek philosophers ejaculated with place of origin when possible suggesting pursuit of knowledge at some period'.[13]

Unfortunately, precedent and hypothesis must be our guide for approximating composition dates, which is crucial not least because the sources Beckett used later appear 'transformed' in his texts in various guises and for various ends. Smith is right to assert that Beckett is an intertextual writer of impressive magnitude and erudition, despite the 'paradoxical' fact that the post-war writings generally reduced allusion and erudition in keeping with the movement toward impoverishment: 'the essayists, poets, and novelists whom he read during this period came increasingly to influence his work *as he reduced his allusions to them*'.[14] This consideration redoubles the importance of precisely dating the notes for two reasons. First, as Smith argues, the things Beckett read—and of course for present purposes, the things he noted down in the 1930s—essentially became aids in his project of impoverishment, a project itself paradoxically advanced by wide reading. Thus, a seemingly inauspicious reference to Hamm's 'old Greek' becomes, as we shall see, an esoteric reference to an entire philosophical movement characterised by extreme scepticism and individual perception. Generally speaking, here is where the 'notes on the pre-Socratics' are surely most important: as Beckett noted, the question 'What is the Weltstuff ?' [*i.e.* What are the fundamental building blocks of existence and the world?] was hotly debated by these ancient philosophers.[15] For Thales this primal matter was water, Anaximenes understood it as air; Heraclitus thought all things were one, while Anaxagoras believed that matter was comprised of infinite simple substances. And for Beckett, previously flirtatious with René Descartes' 'first philosophy' of fundamentals, the debate must have been less important than the obvious fact that these basic disputes about the nature of the world remained insoluble—and to a certain degree merely restated and updated by philosophical descendants—over subsequent millennia.

Before a closer look at the 'Philosophy Notes', however, a second and more specific point is necessary regarding the difficulties with dating. Unlike other sources Beckett kept and employed until his death, none of the 267 folios contain composition dates (like the wide-ranging '*Whoroscope* Notebook' or the fastidious 'German Dairies'), nor is their compilation specifically referred to in any extant correspondence (as with notes on Arnold Geulincx) or parallel facts known about Beckett's life (such as the notes taken as an undergraduate at Trinity College Dublin). Still, the influence of Beckett's wide reading seems to fit a general pattern: the last text he read was typically the first incorporated into his work. This is clear from the use made of, for example, Cartesian readings underpinning the 1930 poem *Whoroscope*, the copious Arnold Geulincx notes taken in 1936 and initially featuring in *Murphy*, and the mid-1938 selections from Fritz Mauthner's *Beiträge zu einer Kritik der Sprache* decisively shaping *Watt*.[16] Therefore, failing corroboration by letters or other biographical material, the earliest reference Beckett made to his sources are held here to be the best guide to the composition date of the material in question.

As such, the 'Philosophy Notes' were most likely compiled at some point between July 1932 and the completion of *Murphy* four years later. As Knowlson relates, Beckett writes in an early August 1932 letter to Thomas MacGreevy: 'I couldn't stand the British Museum any more. Plato and Aristotle and the Gnostics finished me.'[17] As heretofore-unknown documents from the British Museum confirm, Beckett received his reader's ticket on 28 July 1932, eight days before professing his exhaustion. Considering his penchant for reading, these must have been long days of study indeed.[18] Nevertheless, these readings make their way into the poem 'Serena I', a completed version the essential *Beckett Before Godot* places at early October 1932.[19] Here is the earliest extant reference taken from the 'Philosophy Notes':

> without the grand old British Museum
> Thales and Aretino
> on the bosom of the Regent's Park the phlox
> crackles under the thunder
> scarlet beauty in our world dead fish adrift
> all things full of gods[20]

This perfectly corresponds to the first three sentences on Thales in the 'Philosophy Notes':

> His primal substance water. Earth afloat (dead fish) on surface of primal substance.
>
> All things are full of gods.[21]

Additionally, as Chris Ackerley's magnificent scholarship makes plain, *Greek Philosophy*—and by obvious extension the 'Philosophy Notes' as a whole—was essential to the construction of *Murphy*. Given the 23 citations to Burnet's work, *Demented Particulars* can be forgiven for not including Windelband, which was even more instrumental to Beckett. Moreover, Ackerley shows how *Murphy* was a depository of Beckett's vast erudition in a manner much less ostentatious than the earlier fiction, while simultaneously showing him that 'the years of learning' lampooned in 'Gnome' could still be put to creative use.[22] But above all, *Demented Particulars* exemplifies the empirical strand in Beckett studies by making plain a particular—if not demented—intertextual method used by Beckett when composing his 1930s writing. Given such considerations, it is easy to imagine that Beckett's 'Philosophy Notes' were jumbled together with the infamous '*Whoroscope* Notebook' in his rucksack during frequent trips to libraries in Dublin and London.

To this end, the way in which Beckett went about composing these pages is interesting, if a bit neurotic. Given that Windelband and Burnet jump around a fair bit when discussing particular philosophers, much indexing was necessarily done by Beckett, who structured the notes either chronologically by philosopher, or, occasionally, by movement (such as Atomic Theory). Although the typed sections were almost certainly taken first, given that they provide the headings and structure for most of the notes (until finishing with second-century Christian gnosticism), it is the meticulousness of work done on the handwritten entries that is most striking. For example, Windelband's first (and for Beckett, most important) part on cosmology, running to a total of 65 pages, is either closely summarised or transcribed *verbatim* over 68 handwritten pages (using both the recto and verso of each folio), and there are undoubtedly numerous occasions where Beckett returned to and reread the same page a handful of times on account of more than one thinker being discussed.[23] Although Beckett transcribed all subsections in both texts—which for Burnet covers Greek philosophy to Aristotle and for Windelband concludes with Nietzsche in the nineteenth century—only sections prior to early Christian philosophy show three or more sources in evidence. Consequently, the final two millennia or so of philosophical history is heavily condensed from Windelband, often with only a key sentence or two in the body of the text to clarify each subsection.

A parenthetical point about the importance of Windelband demands mention: few authors had equivalent impact upon Beckett; one, dare I say, Joycean in importance. Incredibly, the famous epigraph on Murphy's intellectual love for himself—'*Amor intellectualis quo Murphy se ipsum amat*'—is in fact slightly amended from a footnote in *A History of Philosophy*.[24] Confirming Beckett's notable interest in occasionalist ideas of 'miraculous' mind-body interaction—artistically rendered insofar as 'Murphy was content to accept this partial congruence of the world of his mind with the world of his body as due to some such process of supernatural determination', Windelband's following statement is attributed to Baruch Spinoza: '*Intellectus infinitus (Amor intellectus quo deus se ipsum amat—raison universelle of Malebranche)*'.[25]

In all the archival material previously surveyed, right down to rare Greek words in the 'Philosophy Notes', to my knowledge Beckett never translated from one language to another while note-taking: he merely took them down in the language in which he found them (which for Beckett was a handful). And like Mahaffy's Descartes from *Whoroscope,*—described by Harvey as more 'Beckett than Descartes'– the occasionalism in *Murphy* seems to be as much Windelband's construction as Beckett's.[26]

But as regards the 'Philosophy Notes' as a whole, one inescapable conclusion emerges: Beckett spent the most time and energy on the beginnings of philosophy, consulting texts focussing on epistemology, the progression of Greek thought and its heritage. As made plain by the letter to Schneider—and especially Beckett's recollection of the material above 'my notes on the pre-Socratics'—it is no stretch to assert Beckett knew this material exceedingly well. A representative example is the four typed and handwritten pages on Beckett's 'Old Greek', abridged below.

> PROTAGORAS OF ABDERA (480–410) [Above this, neatly handwritten and scored with a line down the right-hand margin are the following phrases: "Legend that he was originally a porter and attracted attention of Democritus by carrying faggots on his head, poised in correct equilibrium.", and in the margin below name, "or what they are like in figure".]
>
> Exiled. His <u>On the Gods</u> burnt in the market-place. It opens: "Of the Gods, I know not whether they are or are not [or what they are like in figure—added in left margin]. Many things, the obscurity of the subject & the brevity of life, prevent us from knowing.""Man is the measure of all things"
>
> "Man is the measure of all things."
>
> Philosophy is the art of being happy.
>
> Happiness & virtue identified.
>
> All opinions equally true.
>
> The first great individualist, relativist & agnostic.
>
> A product of the Atomistic School.
>
> Intellectual head of Sophists and the only one responsible for any conceptions philosophically fruitful and significant.

His <u>Grounds of Refutation</u> probably his most important writing. Formulated the law of the contradictory opposite.

His effort to explain the idea of the human mind psycho-genetically [....]He declared that the <u>entire psychical life consists only in perceptions. Sensualism.</u>

<u>Perception</u> rests in the last instance upon <u>motion</u>, and not only in the thing to be perceived, but also in percipient organ (Cf. Empedocles). If perception is the product of these two motions directed toward one another, it is <u>obviously something else than the perceiving subject</u>, but <u>just as obviously something else than the object which calls forth the perception</u>. Conditioned by both, it is different from both. This pregnant discovery he called the doctrine of the <u>subjectivity of sense-perception.</u>

From this double motion 2-fold result: <u>perception</u> in the man, <u>content of perception</u> in the thing. Perception is <u>completely adequate knowledge of what is perceived</u> but no knowledge of the thing. This is the meaning of the Protagorean <u>relativism</u>, according to which things are for every individual as they appear to him; and this he expressed in the famous proposition, <u>Man is the measure of all things.</u>

This is <u>phenomenalism</u> in so far as it teaches knowledge of the phenomenon limited to the individual and the moment: it is <u>scepticism</u> in so far as it rejects all knowledge that transcends that.

He legislated for Thourioi 444/3 [....]

He is said to have met Zeno at Athens, when problem of continuity was discussed:

Z [Zeno]:	Tell me, P, does a single grain of millet, or ten thousandth part of one, make a noise in falling?
P:	No.
P:	Yes.
Z:	Et alors.. Is there not a ration of a bushel of millet to 1 grain and ten thousandth of 1 grain [?—sic]
P:	Yes.
Z:	Then will not the sounds leave the same ratio? As the sounding objects to one another, so the sounds. There if the bushel makes a noise, the grain and ten thousandth grain will make a noise.

"Man" should [be—added above] understood [with Plato—added above] as individual rather than, with modern view, as "Man as such". Democritus favoured Plato in this interpretation.[27]

Moreover, this single entry was used at least twice: in the composition of *Endgame* noted above; and, with respect to the dialogue between Protagoras and Zeno, in *Mercier and Camier*: 'And in between all are heard, every millet grain that falls, you look behind and there you are, every day a little closer, all life a little closer.'[28] As with *Murphy*, the intertextual method remains consistent, but a crucial difference anticipating that unique Beckettian ignorance of the post-war writing is visible. Here the allusion is employed to make a vital point, situated as it is between Mercier's vision of a 'wretched' old man and memories of his childhood, not to mention the swinging of heavy chains; '[o]nce in motion they swing on and on, steadily or with serpentine writhing [...] till it seemed they would never come to rest'—recalling Murphy's rocking chair.[29] But whether or not the latter point on the interminability of motion merely restates Beckett's interest in the subject,[30] or in fact explicitly alludes to *Murphy*, the point remains both vital and paradigmatic: Mercier standing alone with thoughts and perceptions in a world of flux. Richard Coe's excellent chapter 'A Little Heap of Millet' invokes Zeno's paradoxes in making much the same point with reference to Beckett's later drama: 'One millionth part of a grain has been added to the heap, and the heap is still unfinished.'[31] As usual, Coe's explication is breathtakingly close to Beckett's own understanding of his work: 'However, I have to go on [...] I am up against a cliff wall yet I have to go forward. Its impossible isn't it? All the same, you can go forward. Advance a few more miserable millimetres.'[32]

§3

As with the 'Interwar Notes' as a whole, the 'Psychology Notes' are a microcosm in the way Beckett acquainted himself with a particular system of thought prior to utilising that tradition in his own writings. Similarly, nowhere is the conflation of a previous tradition and the development of new ideas more apparent than in Beckett's *Three Dialogues* with Georges Duthuit, composed in the months following completion of *En Attendant Godot*. A close reading of these 'dialogues' as a segue into the 'Psychology Notes'—to reaffirm their pivotal nature in the Beckett canon while showing how they draw upon psychological traditions explicitly noted by Beckett—is therefore instructive. A prime example is found in the 'Second Dialogue', where 'D.' suggests André Masson mixes the spirit and technique of the 'classical' painter with the modern problem of 'transparency' or attempting to 'paint the void'. 'What you say certainly throws light on the dramatic predicament of this artist,' grants 'B.':

> Allow me to note his concern with the amenities of ease and freedom. *The stars are undoubtedly superb*, as Freud remarked on reading Kant's cosmological proof of the existence of God. With such preoccupations it seems to me impossible that he should ever do anything different from that which the best, including himself, have done already. It is perhaps an impertinence to suggest that he wishes to [...] So forgive me if I relapse, as when we spoke of the so different Tal Coat, into my dream of an art unre-

sentful of its insuperable indigence and too proud for the farce of giving and receiving.[33]

Something vitally important is happening in this passage. Beckett is using Immanuel Kant's cosmological proof and Sigmund Freud's reading of it to frame his 'dream' of an art beyond Freud or Kant's massive intellectual undertakings, in much the same way Duthuit posits that Masson undertakes a traditional approach to a modern problem. Yet here Beckett uses his own 'extremely intelligent remarks' to conclude that Masson invariably fails to overcome that 'exquisitely logical attitude' necessary to usher in an inexpressive art.[34] In 'B.'s final speaking part on artists 'skewered on the ferocious dilemma of expression' before the crescendo of Bram van Velde's 'art of a new order' in the 'Third Dialogue', then, Beckett offers a classical example—in this case proof of God via psychoanalysis—to demonstrate the inapplicability of such approaches in creating radical art. Yet traditional means (paintbrush and easel, pen and paper, or an understanding of a tradition in painting, writing, philosophy, etc.) are the essential, if disagreeable, 'poisons' to convey this point. In short, a system of thought is employed, while simultaneously demonstrating that system's inapplicability vis-à-vis modern art. Although clearly insufficient in creating inexpressive art themselves (because they are concerned with the 'plane of the feasible' as 'B.' repeatedly stresses), these classical means nevertheless provide valuable material and methods, signposts, toward this unfurling horizon of characterising the void. And as we shall see, the necessity of understanding and drawing upon a heritage—although not working from within its strictures or following its teleology—was as inescapable for Beckett as it was clearly developmental.

With Beckett's critical summation of Masson and Pierre Tal Coat's 'straining to enlarge the statement of a compromise' excerpted above, the explicit knowledge underpinning such an assessment is taken, in part, from typed psychological notes made by Beckett just before the writing of *Murphy*. Knowlson reports that these 20,000 words were 'discovered in a trunk in the cellar after his death', the dusty provenance of which belies the importance of these notes to Beckett.[35] While the date of their (perhaps symbolic) placement in the trunk is unknowable, the composition date of these notes can be fixed with relative certainty to late 1934 and early 1935, thanks to the MacGreevy correspondence: 'I have finished with Adler. Another one trackmind. Only the dogmatist seems able to put it across.'[36]

As Adler's *The Neurotic Constitution* was the penultimate book used for note-taking (just before Otto Rank's *The Trauma of Birth*), a reasonable estimate suggests that Beckett started compiling this source-base toward the end of 1934, possibly from books borrowed from Camden Public Library, at that time specialising in psychological and philosophical texts. The order of the other sources, similarly typed with care and with an emphasis on the history of psychological schools and disorders—particularly neurosis—is as follows: Karin Stephen's *The Wish to Fall Ill*, R. S. Woodworth's *Contemporary Schools of Psychology*, Ernest Jones' *Papers on Psychoanalysis*, Freud's *Treatment of the Neuroses*, Wilhelm Stekel's *Psychoanalysis and Suggestion Therapy*, and *Practice and Theory of Individual Psychology*. As *Demented Particulars* shows, many of the psychological references—to the Külpe School, 'Kohler and the apes', the 'figure and ground' of Gestalt psychology, even concepts such as the 'id'—used in *Murphy* are drawn from Beckett's understanding of psychoanalysis. More concretely, they are drawn directly from his reading of the above books just before the start of *Murphy* (in August 1935) and contemporaneous with his psychotherapy sessions. The personal significance is obvious. Yet so too is the appropriation of these notes in his writings. Recalling Beckett's invocation of Freud and Kant in the *Three Dialogues*, here is an excerpt taken from *The New Introductory Lectures on Psycho-Analysis* (interestingly, from Chapter XXXI on 'The Anatomy of Mental Personality', the only selection Beckett demonstrably read of Freud, in contrast to the extensive transcriptions of disciples Ernest Jones and Karin Stephen):

>   Id, Ego & Superego
>
> The philosopher Kant once declared that nothing proved to him the greatness of God more convincingly that the starry heavens and the moral conscience within us. The stars are unquestioningly superb...
>
> Superego: heir to Oedipus complex. A special function within the ego representing demand for restriction and rejection. Acute case of over-severity of super-ego towards ego appears in the melancholic attack. Cp. delusions of observation of certain psychotics, whose observing function (super-ego) has become sharply separated from the ego and projected into external reality.
>
> The Ego, (including super-ego), not coextensive with the conscious (since patient is frequently unconscious of his resistances), just as the repressed is not coextensive with the unconscious.
>
> Id: Instinctual cathexes seeking discharge—that in our view is all that the id contains.[37]

The employment of these notes, and their association to that anxious period in Beckett's life (when he no doubt felt wide reading in psychology would give him a better perspective on his own psychotherapy), is thus explicitly connected to the construction of *Three Dialogues*. Another selection, this time taken from *The Trauma of Birth*, is highly suggestive of Cooper's attachment to his hat in

Murphy and the conflation of Molloy's mother with the town in the first few pages of *The Beckett Trilogy*:

> Dream of travelling; such details as missing the train, packing & not being ready, losing luggage, etc., so painfully realised in the dream, can be understood only when one interprets the departure as meaning <u>separation from the mother</u>, the luggage as symbolising the womb, which as we know is replaced by all kinds of vehicles. Every forward movement in the dream is to be interpreted as regressive. Cp. disinclination of many persons to travel with their backs to the engine & <u>sortir les pieds en devant.</u>
>
> Spermatozoa dream (Silberer), regression to spermarium.
>
> Town as mother symbol, 7 hills of Rome corresponding to teats of she wolf.
>
> The crown, the noblest of all head coverings, goes back to embryonal caul, as also our modern hat, the loss of which in a dream signifies separation from part of one's Ego. "I'm back in the caul when I don my hat!" In contrast to the "protected" head, which first leaves the womb, the feet, which come out last, are the weak part. Cp. swollen feet of Oedipus & Achilles' heel.[38]

More specifically, both in *Watt* and *Mercier and Camier*, trains play a recurring role. And in both texts Watt and Mercier, respectively, are explicitly noted as having their backs to the engine.[39] Once sourced, this clarifies what appears to be a nice inside joke in *The Unnamable*: 'what emotion can do, given favourable conditions, what love can do, well well, so that's emotion, that's love, and trains, the nature of trains, and the meaning of your back to the engine'.[40] Indeed Watt, who 'preferred to have his back to his destination', is defined on the last page before the Addenda as 'the long wet dream with the hat and bags'.[41] Both explicitly and more opaquely, then, Beckett's 'Psychology Notes' provided numerous initiatives for his writing.

In keeping with Smith's view of the increasingly opaque allusions in the post-*Watt* writings, the references themselves cease to publicise the formative 'years of learning' mentioned in 'Gnome' in favour of a more solipsistic, esoteric construction. Allusions become like revolving stones to be shifted and manipulated, all the while hidden in pockets of age-old trousers. Without the recipe, such a 'poss' of allusions looks (like) fluid; but with the ingredients to hand, it finally becomes possible to appreciate the mixing, boiling, and above all, the transformation into a 'quite a new good thing'.

§4

The consequent question for scholars, formulated first by Beckett's own oeuvre, remains: What are we to do? Shall we look at the poss, deliberately created so as to defy the most basic categorisation? In Beckett studies this can only ever be alchemic. Instead, ponderously, the need is to understand the ingredients, the methods, employed in the mixing of this 'single good thing'. For my part, I cannot advocate highly enough the importance of *theorising from a position of empirical accuracy*. By way of contribution, one prospective recipe is offered below.

That Beckett was particularly drawn to Ancient Greek ideas is independently confirmed by the vitally important '*Whoroscope* Notebook' which 'assumes exceptional importance from a developmental point of view' in Pilling's view, for 'one comes closer than one would ever have believed possible to a mind in the process of defining itself, and to creative impulses later subjected to more severe self-denying ordinances and restraints.' Dubbing it an 'enchiridion'—the Greek term for handbook contained in that handbook—Pilling views this pivotal manuscript as proof 'that Beckett, having abandoned an academic career, had by no means abandoned the academic habits of mind inculcated by it'.[42] While Pilling justly reviews these habits categorically, we shall instead just focus upon the rich material concerning Ancient Greece, covering various subjects: Greek mythology and lexicography; historical figures and events; and a wealth of references like: 'Epicurean taunted a Stoic with numerous conversions from Stoicism to Epicureanism, whereas hardly ever inversely, Stoic: "A man many become a eunuch, but a enuch [sic] can never become a man."'[43] It is not surprising that Beckett's preference for the former philosophical outlook is recorded in the '*Whoroscope* Notebook', for almost all of Beckett's interests in the second half of the 1930s are. Ranging over most erudite subjects from science and languages to religion and noteworthy quotations, though by no means limited to things Greek, this repository acted as Beckett's intellectual piggy bank.

A final withdrawal from this source is appropriate to connect the '*Whoroscope* Notebook' to the larger 'note-snatching' project of the 1930s, as well as to blend the 'Philosophy Notes' and 'Psychology Notes' as critically important ingredients in the preparation of Beckett's larger, potable 'poss'. As the initial pages of the '*Whorocope* Notebook' set out, the specific importance of Presocratic thinking to the structure of *Murphy* is enormous, if simultaneously concealed. Given that Beckett wrote 'Whoroscope' on the cover of UoR MS 3000/1; given his interest in aspects of early Greece at this time and interest in words generally; and given that both are started roughly simultaneously, it is not surprising that Beckett looked to etymology early in writing *Murphy*: 'Greeks trace horoscope from position of stars and planets at hour of birth (or of conception).'⁴⁴ Along with character and setting, the novel's second sentence points up the hero's (losing) struggle with fate and freedom as integral to plot: 'Murphy sat out of it [the sun], as though he were free, in a mew in West Brompton.' In both the opening pages of the novel—Celia's obtaining the horoscope for Murphy elicits the first, fitting, exchange ('"God blast you", he said. "He is doing so," she replied. Celia.')—and in the notebook, then, the fatalistic nature of the horoscope acts as a trigger.⁴⁵ Vitally, this trigger is methodologically tied to Ancient Greek ideas on the very first page of the '*Whoroscope* Notebook', setting out at this initial period of writing how Beckett intended these diffuse strands to eventually structure *Murphy*. Written even before the character is named, the first eleven of the thirty-four numbered sections (comprising the first sixteen pages of UoR MS 3000/1) offer a marvellous glimpse of Beckett's creative process:

1

Impetus given by H.[orosocope] throughout. To X [Murphy] who has no motive, inside or out, available.

2

Dynamist ethic of X. Keep moving the only virtue vicious = [cindled] etc.

3

H. any old oracle to begin with. If corpus of motives after stichomancy had given quietism oder was. But gradually ratified by its own refutation. Till it acquires authority of fatality. No longer a guide to be consulted but a force to be obeyed. Dutiful death of both!

4

X. and H. clarified side by side. Monads in arcanum of circumstance, each apperceiving in the other till no more of the petites perceptions, that are life. So that H, more and more organic, is realised in X. as he [via] it, and they must perish together (fire oder was).

5

Racinian lighting, darkness devoured.

6

Journey through the "layers" like D.[ante] and V.[irgil] along the Purgatorial cornices, except that V. goes back, H goes out. Purgatorial atmosphere sustained throughout, by stress on Anaximander's individual existence as atonement.

7

H. mentor and [squire], principle of knowledge and dissolution and suggests its life of its own by inexplicable dis—and re appearances, changing, bent, etc.

[3000/1v]

8

Choose "layers" carefully on some such principle as that of V.'s, distribution of sins and punishments. But keep whole Dantesque analogy out of sight.

9

Each undertaking, in accordance with a clause of H., breaks down in accordance with clause of H. (This is the sense of H. being ratified by its own [controversion]) Thus H., and thereby X. decrease in scope and transform their potential into actual. Entelechies.

10

Each "cornice" is occupied by the physical failure which is the metaphysical achievement, in so far as it [narrows] the physical field (petites perceptions) and constitutes an increase in the apperceived. Vocation the essence of purgatory, defunction its negation.

11

Important to vary technique in demonstrating the successive defunctions. Thus an elegiac tune for a quasi-vocation where atonement hardly perceptible, debasing X in the virtual and threatening to incarcerate him [....][46]

Without doubt, references to atonement and Anaximander come from that portion of the 'Philosophy Notes' on the Presocratics; and similarly, Beckett's heavily used pages on Democritus assuredly account for the 'fire oder was [or what]' eventually causing Murphy's demise. In drawing up other influences, Dante provides the purgatorial setting, quietism the mood, Racine the lights. But most prominent, unexpectedly, is Gottfried Leibniz, who Beckett described as 'a great cod' after finishing his *Monadology* in early December 1933.[47] Nonetheless, straddling these two sets of notes, Beckett's reading of Leibniz conveyed a much wider understanding of perception as a human totality, which 'should be carefully distinguished from Apperception or Consciousness, as will appear in what follows. In this matter the Cartesians have fallen into a serious error, in that they treat as non-existent those perceptions of which we are not conscious.'[48] But what appears rather tame in the *Monadology* is seized upon by Windelband, affording Leibniz a central place in the history of philosophy, finding 'in Leibniz all threads of the old and the new metaphysics run together'.⁴⁹ In what may well link Beckett's philosophical and psychological readings, Windelband's breathless admiration extends to discussion of Leibnizian 'entelechies', 'monads' and, especially, 'petites perceptions'. Above, the only philosophical phrase used twice in Beckett's outline is 'petites perception', not found in translations of *Monadalogy* but given this strange definition by Windelband in relating these perceptions to 'the representative side of the monads': 'In the language of to-day the *petites perceptions* would be *unconscious mental states*'.⁵⁰ Here Windelband is unmistakable on the indebtedness of later disciplines to Leibniz:

> The soul (as every monad) always has ideas or representations, but not always conscious, not always clear and distinct ideas; its life consists in the development of the unconscious to conscious, of the obscure and confused to clear and distinct ideas; its life consists in the development of the unconscious to conscious, of the obscure and confused to clear and distinct ideas or representations.
>
> In this aspect Leibniz now introduced a significant conception into psychology and epistemology. He distinguished between the states in which the soul merely *has* ideas, and those in which it is *conscious* of them.⁵¹

Earlier Windelband points out that monads 'have no windows' and this 'windowlessness' is to a certain extent the expression of their 'metaphysical impenetrability'—surely the backdrop to Beckett's descriptions of the 'pads' at the Magdalen Merntal Mercyseat: 'No system of ventilation appeared to dispel the illusions of respirable vacuum. The compartment was *windowless, like a monad* [.... Murphy] had never been able to imagine a more creditable *representation* of what he kept on calling, indefatigably, the little world.'⁵²

My supposition is that Beckett takes this understanding one step further, using Leibniz as the methodological fulcrum for the 'Interwar Notes' so occupying Beckett in the years before the start of *Murphy*. Echoing Windelband's view of Leibniz, consider this entry on the unconscious from Ernest Jones—from his *Papers on Psychoanalysis* that comprise wholly one third of Beckett's 'Psychology Notes':

> <u>The Unconscious:</u> Absurdity of equating <u>unconscious</u> with <u>non-mental</u>. Consciousness merely one component of mentality. The "Limbo" conception of the unconscious (Hartmann, Myer and Jung), as an obscure dumping ground of the mind for the processes devoid of inherent initiative or any primary dynamic faculty, processes utterly inert & passive, as well as for another group of nascent processes for which the conscious personality is not yet ripe. Freud's conception of the unconscious is inductive & scientific as opposed to the a priori philosophic view of the Limboists. The unconscious is essentially a function of repressing and consisting of mental material incompatible with the conscious personality. This is its 1st characteristic, 2nd being the in-

dependent and typically conative nature of its processes. The 3rd its close relation to crude & primitive instincts. The 4th its infantile nature & origin. The splitting up of mentality takes place in 1st year of life, as a result of the conflict between congential amoral & primordial impulses are repressed & their energy diverted to social aims, but they continue to exist underground & to manifest themselves circuitously & symbolically. The 5th is indifference to moral & logical considerations, though it has an emotional logic of its own. The 6th its predominantly sexual character, the sexual impulse being subjected to greater intensity of repression than any of the other primary instincts. This last attribute in no way incompatible with the 4th, given the intensity of pregenital sexuality, which is distinguished from the adult form in its being more diffuse, tentative & preliminary, closely associated with excretory functions & highly coloured by child's relations with the parents (incest complex). Jung distorts these incest fantasies into symbols for ethical ideas & denies them any inherent dynamic initiative.

The unconscious, therefore, according to psychoanalysis, may be summed up as a region of the mind the content of which is characterised by being (1) Repressed (2) Conative (3) Instinctive (4) Infantile (5) Unreasoning (6) Predominantly sexual. A typical instance of an unconscious process, illustrating all 6 characteristics, would be a little girl wishing that her mother might die so that she could marry her father.[53]

The trembling veil between conscious thought and unconscious activity has been aptly yoked by Rubin Rabinovitz's phrase 'mental reality'; elsewhere he emphasises that Beckett's 'quests' within this landscape to chart the accumulation of knowledge systematically and thematically invalidated in *Watt* and *The Beckett Trilogy* (where Rabinovitz found 140 instances of the phrase 'I don't know'). As a consequence of the 1930s material now available in archives, Beckett appears to formulate the 'nescience' of both his own 'note-snatching' projects and characters' attempts to understand existence in terms of the following equation: *one must have knowledge of a subject in order to refute it.* And whether or not Leibniz can legitimately be recognised as the nexus between two distinct disciplines—in the widest sense, love of wisdom as against the study of previously unrecognised mental activity—there can be little doubt that the very amount of time spent over four years certifies a continuity, rather than schism, between Beckett's transcriptions in philosophy and psychology. And even if Beckett's notes failed to root knowledge in the manner of James Joyce, already the seeds of a new method were being tilled that invoked knowledge in order to ruthlessly investigate foundational truth claims along the lines, as Beckett noted, of the first sceptics:

> Relativity of knowledge. We can only know phenomena in relation to other phenomena & to our own minds.
>
> Tendency of all scepticism, with its vaunted suspense of judgment, towards dogmatism. Absolute doubt equals absolute certainty. It must assume what it denies. Sceptics affirm reality of phenomena by denying that it can be known.

> The ataraxy of Pyrrho has closer connection than the Epicureans with the Sophists. His scepticism is the negative obverse of the Socratic-Platonic inference. As these, from the premise that right action is not possible without knowledge, that demand had been made that knowledge must be possible, so here the argument is, that because there is no knowledge, right action is impossible
>
> The wise therefore can only resist the seducements to opinion and action. He knows that nothing can be affirmed as to phenomena, that no opinion may be assented to, and so restrains himself from judgment, and thereby from action. In the suspension of judgment, he finds imperturbability, rest within himself, ataraxy. The sceptics were called "The Suspenders".[54]

Indeed, the 'Interwar Notes' only add empirical credence to Rabinovitz's conclusions on Beckett's art: 'Any sense of establishing facts or of mastering language must be countered by the invocation of a formulaic "I don't know." And alas, this bumbling equivocation is the closest we can come to framing significant statements.'[55] Perhaps underpinning Rabinovitz's reading with archival transcriptions is the closest we can come to understanding that veil between Beckett as subject and his literature as object, and come a few millimetres closer to Beckett's artistic approach: 'All that should concern us is the acute and increasing anxiety of the relation itself, as though shadowed more and more darkly by a sense of invalidity, of inadequacy, of existence at the expense of all that it excludes, all that it blinds to.'[56] Of course, the 'Philosophy Notes' and 'Psychology Notes' do not, and cannot, hold the answer to Beckett's unique contribution to European literature, for such a thing must be the antithesis meticulously carved 'fidelity to failure'. But in the end, this corpus provides an overwhelming flotsam of influence vital to Beckett's literary progression and developmental labours during the 1930s, while also demonstrably impacting his later thought and writing. Aporetically speaking, I think, the 'Interwar Notes' must be of inestimable value to scholars for years to come; so long, that is, if scholarship keeps Molloy's words revolving between its collective pockets:

> And truly it matters little what I say, this or that or any other thing. Saying is inventing. Wrong, very rightly wrong. You invent nothing, you think you are inventing, you think you are escaping, and all you do is stammer out your lesson, the remnants of a

pensum one day got by heart and long forgotten, life without tears, as it is wept. To hell with it anyway.[57]

NOTES

[1] Samuel Beckett, *Watt* (London: Calder & Boyers, 1970), p. 84.
[2] *Ibid.*
[3] *Ibid.*, p. 54.
[4] John Pilling, *Beckett Before Godot* (Cambridge: Cambridge University Press, 1997), p. xiii.
[5] Charles Juliet, *Conversations with Samuel Beckett and Bram van Velde* (Leiden: Academic Press, 1995), p. 140.
[6] Already in 'Dante... Bruno. Vico..Joyce' Beckett's burgeoning academic abilities had put him on guard against over-systemisation in the approach to literature; in the first of a long line of scholarly reproaches: 'Must we wring the neck of a certain system in order to stuff it into a contemporary pigeon hole for the satisfaction of the analogymongers? Literary criticism is not book-keeping', reprinted in Samuel Beckett, *Disjecta: Miscellaneous Writings and a Dramatic Fragment*, ed. Ruby Cohn (New York: Grove Press, 1984), p. 19.
[7] See *Disjecta* for Beckett's well-known profession to Sighle Kennedy: 'If I were in the unenviable position of having to study my work my points of departure would be the 'Naught is more real...' and the 'Ubi nihil vales...' both already in Murphy and neither very rational', p. 113.
[8] James Knowlson, *Damned to Fame* (London: Bloomsbury, 1997), p. 244.
[9] John Calder, *The Philosophy of Samuel Beckett* (London: Calder, 2002), p. 1.
[10] Richard Lane, 'Introduction', in Richard Lane, ed., *Beckett and Philosophy* (Basingstoke: Palgrave, 2002), p. 2.
[11] Samuel Beckett to Alan Schneider, 29 December 1957, cited in Maurice Harmon, ed., *No Author Better Served: The Correspondence of Alan Schneider and Samuel Beckett* (London: Harvard University Press, 1998), p. 23; italics in original.
[12] Everett Frost, 'Beckett's Notebooks at Trinity College Dublin', in *The Beckett Circle / Le Cercle de Beckett: Newsletter of the Samuel Beckett Society*, 25/2 (2002), pp. 12–13.
[13] Samuel Beckett, 'All Strange Away', in Beckett, *The Complete Short Works 1929–1989*, ed. S.E. Gontarski (New York: Grove Press, 1995), p. 175.
[14] Frederik Smith, *Beckett's Eighteenth Century* (London: Palgrave, 2002), p. 11.
[15] Samuel Beckett, 'Philosophy Notes', TCD MS 10967/5.
[16] Samuel Beckett's notes from Arnold Geulincx are catalogued as TCD MS 10971/6/1–36; and notes from Fritz Mauthner catalogued as TCD MS 10971/5/1–4.
[17] Knowlson, *Damned to Fame*, p. 734.
[18] Included in this clutch of archival material is Beckett's reader's ticket receipt, a letter of reference by Chatto & Windus, and Beckett's original letter of application, which cites the his 'need of original texts in French and Italian in greater detail than is available in other collections' he has consulted, which he lists as 'the Library of Trinity College Dublin, the National Library, Dublin, the Library of the École Normale Supérieure, Paris, Ste-Geneviève, and the Bibliothèque Nationale'. Importantly, also included in the card register are the three times Beckett renewed his six-month ticket and his listed address: February 1934 at Paulton's Square, September 1934 at Gertrude Street, and October 1937, at Harrington Road.
[19] Pilling, *Beckett Before Godot*, pp. 86–7.
[20] Samuel Beckett, 'Serena I', in Beckett, *Collected Poems* (London: Calder, 1999), p. 21.

21 Beckett, 'Philosophy Notes', TCD MS 10967/5.
22 Samuel Beckett, 'Gnome', in *Collected Poems*, p. 7.
23 Wilhelm Windelband, *A History of Philosophy* (London: Macmillan, 1901), pp. 29–31.
24 Samuel Beckett, *Murphy* (London: Calder, 1993), p. 63.
25 Windelband, *A History of Philosophy*, p. 410.
26 Lawrence Harvey, *Samuel Beckett: Poet and Critic* (Princeton: Princeton University Press, 1970), p. 53. For discussion of the overwhelming importance of J.P. Mahaffy's *Descartes* (Edinburgh: Edinburgh & Co., 1880) to the composition of *Whoroscope*, see Francis Doherty, 'Mahaffy's *Whoroscope*' in the *Journal of Beckett Studies* 2/1 (1992).
27 Beckett, 'Philosophy Notes', TCD MS 10967/44–10967/45.
28 Samuel Beckett, *Mercier and Camier* (London: Calder, 1999), p. 77.
29 *Ibid.*, p. 78.
30 As Chris Ackerley points out, the earliest reference can be found in Beckett's 'Dante...Bruno.Vico..Joyce': 'Maximal speed is a state of rest', *Disjecta*, p. 21. See also Knowlson's *Damned to Fame* for Beckett's brief analysis of *Murphy*, and the circular structure and dialogue of *Rockaby*, written four decades later, p. 247.
31 Richard N. Coe, *Beckett* (London: Oliver and Boyd, 1968), p. 96.
32 Charles Juliet, *Conversations with Samuel Beckett and Bram van Velde*, p. 141.
33 Samuel Beckett, 'Three Dialogues with Georges Duthuit', reprinted in Beckett, *Disjecta*, pp. 140–1; italics in original.
34 *Ibid.*
35 Knowlson, *Damned to Fame*, pp. 176–8.
36 *Ibid.*, 738. n. 48.
37 Beckett, 'Psychology Notes', TCD MS 10971/7/6. Sigmund Freud's invocation of Immanuel Kant was first pointed out in John Pilling's *Samuel Beckett* (London: Routledge & Kegan Paul, 1976), p. 130.
38 Beckett, 'Psychology Notes', TCD MS 10971/8/35.
39 Beckett, *Mercier and Camier*, p. 40; and Beckett, *Watt*, p. 25.
40 Samuel Beckett, *The Unnamable*, in *The Beckett Trilogy* [*Molloy, Malone Dies and The Unnamable*] (London: Picador, 1976), p. 374.
41 Beckett, *Watt*, p. 246.
42 Pilling, *Beckett Before Godot*, pp. 1, 19.
43 Samuel Beckett, '*Whoroscope* Notebook', UoR MS 3000/1, p. 60.
44 *Ibid.*, p. 5.
45 Beckett, *Murphy*, 5–8.
46 Beckett, UoR MS 3000/1, pp. 5, 1–1v. Chris Ackerley's *Demented Particulars* (Tallahassee: Journal of Beckett Studies Books, 1998) has "arcanum"; and John Pilling's 'From a (W)horoscope to *Murphy*', in *The Ideal Core of the Onion*, eds. John Pilling and Mary Bryden (Reading: Beckett International Foundation) has 'stichomancy'. Further uncertain words, as well as my additions, are in brackets from this extremely difficult passage. I am grateful to Mark Nixon and Dirk van Hulle for assistance with this transcription.
47 Ackerley, *Demented Particulars*, p.103.
48 Gottfried Wilhelm Leibniz, *Discourse on Metaphysics, Correspondence with Arnauld, Monadology* (La Salle: Open Court, 1902), p. 253.
49 Windelband, *A History of Philosophy*, p. 425.
50 *Ibid.*, p. 424; italics in original.

[51] *Ibid.*, pp. 462–3; italics in original.
[52] Beckett, *Murphy*, p. 103; italics added. In his discussion of Leibnizian monads Windelband's *A History of Philosophy* footnotes his view that 'Leibniz is here served a very good turn by the ambiguity in the word "*représentation*"', in according with which the words means, on the one hand, to supply the place of or serve as a symbol of, and on the other hand, the function of consciousness [....] The deeper sense and justification of this ambiguity lies in the fact that we cannot form any clear and distinct idea whatever of the unifying of a manifold, except after the patter of that kind of connection which we experience within ourselves in the function of consciousness', pp. 422–23.
[53] Beckett, 'Psychology Notes', TCD MS 10971/8/9.
[54] Beckett, 'Philosophy Notes', TCD MS 10967/123. See Rubin Rabinovitz, 'Style and Quest for Knowledge in *Watt* and the Trilogy', in *Innovation in Samuel Beckett's Fiction* (Chicago: University of Illinois Press, 1992) for further discussion of Beckett's intellection. The phrase 'mental reality' is indebted to Rubin Rabinovitz's 'Beckett and Psychology', in the *Journal of Beckett Studies* 11/12 (1989), p. 72.
[55] Rabinovitz, Rubin, 'Beckett and Psychology', p. 11.
[56] Beckett, 'Three Dialogues', in *Disjecta*, p. 145.
[57] Beckett, *Molloy*, in *The Beckett Trilogy*, p. 31.

BECKETT AND THE BBC RADIO REVISITED

§1

This chapter reconsiders Beckett's relationship with the post-war BBC through recourse to neglected files held at the Written Archives Centre in Caversham. Collectively, these archival materials reveal a far greater engagement with radio broadcasting than has been previously registered by Beckett studies. This includes, but goes substantially beyond, the crucial years between 1956 and 1962, forming Beckett's oft-discussed 'canonical' works for radio (*All that Fall*, *Embers*, *Words and Music*, *Cascando*, *Rough for Radio I* and *Rough for Radio II*, and sometimes his Pinget translation, *The Old Tune*).[1] In fact, BBC productions during Beckett's lifetime extended to adaptations of most of his prose works (including *Watt*, *The Beckett Trilogy*, and many of his shorter texts), as well as many dramatic works—from *Endgame* in French to *Play*; even *Waiting for Godot* with a narrator! Also evident in Beckett's BBC 'WAC' papers are discussions relating to contracting, correspondence, negotiation over content and more. Donald McWhinnie's well-known remark, in an internal BBC memorandum six weeks after the successful broadcast of *All that Fall* on 13 January 1957, thus prophetically captures the importance of this relationship at its start: 'if he is to write at all in the near future it will be for radio, which has captured his imagination'.[2]

No doubt, then, the wider collection of files on Beckett held at Caversham bear re-examination. This sense is redoubled given that perhaps the principle work on the subject, *Beckett and Broadcasting*, to date one of the few texts to have registered the BBC WAC materials, is now almost 40 years old.[3] Although details are sparse on Beckett's 'non-canonical' radio productions, Clas Zilliacus's appendix—covering the years 1957 to 1973—lists the following BBC broadcasts: *Fin de partie* (2 May 1957; in French); *Molloy* (10 December 1957); 'From An Abandoned Work' (14 December 1957); *Malone Dies* (18 June 1957); *The Unnamable* (19 January 1957); *Waiting for Godot* (27 April 1960); *Endgame* (22 May 1962); *Poems I* (9 March 1966); *Play* (11 October 1966); *Poems II* (24 November 1966); 'Imagination Dead Imagine' (18 March 1967); "Lessness" (Radio 3, 25 February 1971); 'The Lost Ones' (Radio 3, 2 January 1973); and 'First Love' (Radio 3, 7 July 1973).[4] Additionally, an excellent if surprisingly little-known article by James Knowlson adds a further decade of adaptations by the Third Programme's successor, Radio 3: *Texts for Nothing* (in four parts, 12 June—3 July 1975); 'MacGowran speaking Beckett' (11 April 1976); 'For To End Yet Again' (4 October 1976); *The Drunken Boat* (translation of Rimbaud, 12 December 1976); 'Beckett at the National' (13 April 1979); *Company* (20 July 1980); *Ill*

Seen Ill Said (31 October 1982); and *Worstward Ho* (4 August 1983).[5] Details of the above, as well as subsequent adaptations including *A Piece of Monologue* (18 April 1986) and 'Stirrings Still' (2 March 1989), are all contained in the illuminating, if nevertheless patchy, BBC WAC holdings on Samuel Beckett. These materials, then, document fully *two-dozen* additional productions of Beckett's texts—above and beyond the six 'radiogenic works' written between 1956 and 1962.

In its unabashedly non-digitised collection, Beckett's holdings at the BBC WAC are listed by index card, and are then effectively split into two separately held categories. The first corresponds to microfiche production details and scripts for virtually all BBC radio productions listed above, contained in the so-called 'Play Library' collection. Also contained on microfiche are various programmes about Beckett from the more general—and much more muddled—'Talks Library, 1922–1970', some of which were also reprinted in the BBC's 'house journal', *The Listener* (such as Ronald Gray's 'A Christian Interpretation of *Waiting for Godot*', broadcast on 9 January 1957, several days the première of *All That Fall*).[6] By way of example, one all-but forgotten programme is a 32'30" broadcast script devoted entirely to the Beckett's works, which endeavours 'to consider how far the reading of Beckett's novels casts a useful light on his plays.' Aired by the Third Programme's 'New Comment' on 11 October 1961, this episode (No. 41) included a lengthy discussion between Martin Esslin, Patrick Magee and Karl Miller, as well as analysis by Ossia Trilling on Beckett's plays and, from Paris, Barbara Bray on his prose. The latter, in surveying the language of Beckett's fiction, paid close attention to *The Beckett Trilogy*:

> As with words, so with things, incidents, feelings, people. A remorselessly assailing doubt, an impulse to laugh, yet an attachment, a need, that will not be eroded. The great and final irreducible is of course the self [....] For such a content, continually self-opposing, what sort of form remains? The only kind still even remotely authentic is one in which the whole work presents itself as a possible but patently invented utterance, a closed system with no external dependence, which even so must still finally turn on itself and rend its own contrived validity. Thus Part Two of MOLLOY ends by recapitulating, and devastating, the beginning [...]'[7]

Yet it is the second category of BBC WAC materials that surely remains of greatest interest. Archived manuscript holdings for Beckett's work for BBC radio (and television[8]) are concentrated in the following files: 'Samuel Beckett: Source File'; 'Samuel Beckett: Copyright File" (1965–1969); 'Samuel Beckett Drama Writer's Files' (1960–1974 and 1975–1979); and finally and most relevantly here, the four-part 'Samuel Beckett: Scriptwriter Files' (divided into the year 1953–1962; 1963–1967; 1968–1972; and 1973–1982). While each of these files are of scholarly interest, particularly to scholars specifically working on radio, disembodiment and/or sound, the 'Samuel Beckett: Scriptwriter 1953–1962' is doubtless most revealing. Running to some 280 pages, the file covers the BBC's ultimately abortive attempts to air *Waiting For Godot* in the mid-1950s, as well as correspondence on *All That Fall*—like the earliest, on 4 July 1956 from Beckett to the BBC's Paris representative, Cecilia Reeves: 'I should like very much to do a radio programme for the Third Programme, but I am very doubtful of my ability to work in this medium. However since our conversation I have, to my surprise, had an idea that may or may not lead to something.'[9] Thereafter, the majority of this file is taken with Beckett's subsequent radiogenic texts, much of which is effectively covered in the most recent volume of Beckett's letters, covering the years 1957 to 1965. The 'Samuel Beckett, Scriptwriter File, 1953–1962' characteristically concludes with a cordial thank you note from the BBC's new Controller of the Third Programme, P.H. Newby, written in response to Beckett's message of 13 November 1962—after listening to a playback of *Words and Music*—praising the BBC's production.

Indeed, the extent to which Beckett was willing to personally engage in these adaptations—and indeed compromise in some unusual respects—suggests that the myth of Beckett's *tout court* refusal to adapt his work from one medium to another is, at the very least, a vastly overstated one. That, alongside of the clear value he placed upon working with the BBC, is something with which Beckett scholars have yet to properly grapple. In doing so here, these neglected manuscripts are placed into twofold relief; firstly, via alignment with Beckett's biographical context—above all in the late 1950s and early 1960s—and secondly, by connecting them with recent debates in Beckett studies. One of these debates, touched upon in conclusion but worth bearing in mind throughout, is the extent to which these new materials may be said to have underwritten, and perhaps even precipitated, Beckett's later poetics.

§2

As has been well established by numerous scholars, the reception of *Waiting for Godot*'s saw Beckett's reputation as an artist take shape.[10] Quick off the mark was Donald McWhinnie—soon to become one of Beckett's most trusted collaborators—who had already received the French play with an eye to inclusion in the BBC's Third Programme on 24 March 1953. Considering running the original French *En Attendant Godot* in French within two months of its Paris première thus clearly underscores Jeff Porter's recent contention that the Third Programme, launched in September 1946 for the BBC's most Reithian output, 'push[ed] for new abstract and experimental works' from the start.[11] Yet this very ambition posed constraints, as the first Controller of the Third Programme, Harman Grisewood, lamented in 1949:

> Our experience to date has shown that we cannot expect a very substantial flow of worthwhile contemporary radio drama at Third Programme level. We will be lucky if during the year we can find say ten pieces that are suitable. For the rest we must decide what to perform from the corpus of dramatic literature which is written for the theatre.[12]

According to Porter, 'this changed with the appointment of Donald McWhinnie as the BBC's assistant head of drama (sound)', who 'would lead the Third Programme in an aggressive search for original material'.[13] Underscoring these experimental productions, the broader results of the Third Programme's 'search' are reflected in the BBC's WAC holdings, which may be the most important and neglected British archive for the study of modernism. For the BBC has adapted most of the canonical works of twentieth century literature, and extensive files on authors from T.S. Eliot and Dylan Thomas to Beckett and Pinter offer a unique insight into the importance placed upon the institution by very different literary modernists. In terms of Beckett this especially concerned the role of music in his productions, but also extended to synthesised animal noises in Beckett's earliest radio play, *All That Fall*. The latter, in fact, in Martin Esslin's words 'led directly' to the establishment of the BBC's Radiophonic Workshop in the next year.[14]

At this time, to be sure, the Third Programme was most unapologetically high-brow and 'made no concessions to popular taste', in the view of the Third's Controller before P.H. Newby, John Morris.[15] Perhaps fittingly, BBC staff saw in *En attendant Godot*—albeit not without internal dissent—a 'basically radiogenic' work suitable for immediately translation and adaptation on radio, since the play would be 'entirely novel to an English audience in nearly every respect'.[16] In fact, the BBC had received Beckett's completed translation at the end of September 1953, though the project took a mortal blow when McWhinnie's line manager, the Head of Drama (Sound), Val Gielgud, adjudged on 20 October 1953 that there was something ultimately 'phoney' about the play. The idea was then shelved in early 1954 until, eighteen months later, the enterprising BBC producer and director, Raymond Raikes, informed Gielgud—upon seeing Peter Hall's production of *Waiting for Godot* '[o]n your instructions'—that it would be 'culpably unenterprising not to undertake this project'. Raikes concluded in no uncertain terms:

May I suggest that we record and broadcast this production as soon as possible lest it be said that the BBC has once again "missed the boat". It seems to me a minor tragedy that on the strength of the report that this play obtained when it was first received from Paris in April 1953 (a report I have only now just read after seeing the play itself) it was not then given on the Third Programme.[17]

In the event, the play needed to complete its London run first—in fact, broadcasting it within 12 months of its West End finale apparently needed Peter Hall's personal permission—even if there is no doubt that, during this time, the BBC continued 'wooing' Beckett. The latter characterisation is taken from Julie Campbell's article, 'Beckett and the Third Programme', the first extended engagement with BBC WAC holdings since Zilliacus's *Beckett and Broadcasting* and Rosemary Pountney's *Theatre of Shadows*.[18] Although parts of *En attendant Godot* were broadcast in France even before it the play opened on 5 January 1953, however, it was not Beckett's celebrated play but his wartime novel that would introduce his work to British radio listeners.[19] For it seems that, on 8 August 1955—that is, immediately following the opening of Sir Peter Hall's *Waiting for Godot* at London's Royal Court Theatre—the dramatic agent Margaret Ramsey suggested a reading of extracts from the Merlin Press's edition of *Watt*, at that time published only in a limited edition in Paris. According to the second volume of his selected letters, Beckett received 25,000 francs for Jack Holmstrom's 7 September 1955 reading from *Watt* as an 'interlude of prose' for the Third Programme.[20]

Beckett's first appearance on the BBC swiftly led to a broadcast rather better detailed, namely *All That Fall*, a 70-minute radio play, in Paul Stewart's recent judgment, 'in which sexual reproduction is replaced by aesthetic regeneration as a means of creating out of nothing'.[21] As Stewart's reading implies, Beckett's turn to radio came at a propitious time. During his recently-concluded 'siege in the room', Beckett had written *Waiting for Godot* and the earlier play *Eleutheria*, as well as seven poems, *Mercier and Camier,* plus the trilogy of novels—*Molloy, Malone Dies* and *The Unnamable*—in addition to 17 short stories, 13 of which were collected as the 'Texts for Nothing'. Despite these post-war masterpieces, by the mid-1950s Beckett had written himself into a creative corner. This is amply testified by his letters across these years; for example, to his old friend Thomas MacGreevy in September 1953: 'I tell me take art easy, but nothing will come any more, all contracted and unhappy about it.' And, nearly a year later, to his American publisher at Grove Press, Barney Rosset: 'I think my writing days are over. L'Innommable finished me or expressed my finishedness.'[22] As usual, Knowlson's *Damned to Fame* remains the surest guide to Beckett's biographical context, and argues that this period led to 'Impasse and Depression, 1956–1968':

> Beckett's depression was very slow to lift, as he began to experience renewed doubt as to whether there was any way out of the impasse into which *The Unnamable* and *Fin de partie* had led him. The medium of radio, with the challenge of its technical constraints, offered one possible escape route.²³

The writing of *All That Fall* in summer 1956, to be sure, had head-locked Beckett's imagination. Although initially needing 'a little more persuasion' from the BBC, 'since he has never written anything for the radio before', the Third Programme's Controller, John Morris, was swiftly dispatched to Paris, where a fortnight later he reported back to Gielgud:

> As arranged, I saw Samuel Beckett in Paris this morning. He is extremely keen to write an original work for the Third Programme and has indeed already done the first few pages of his script [...] we can expect something pretty good.²⁴

All That Fall was swiftly completed and sent to Morris in London just over two months later. As Zilliacus, Campbell and others have noted, this was something of a breakthrough all round. Even the previously nonplussed Val Gielgud was overwhelmed by the production, writing to McWhinnie the day after the 13 January 1957 broadcast:

> My warmest congratulations on your outstanding success with the Beckett play. I am more than aware what a tremendously difficult production job this was. Indeed, in my experience I cannot think of one presenting more difficulties. Your all over grasp of the problems involved, your exceptional casting, your ingenious use of effects, and your extreme sensitivity of approach, combined to do a fascinating script every sort of justice. Well done.²⁵

The effect on Beckett was equally electric. As the traditional account goes, by no means wrongly, he went on to produce another four radio plays in as many years (or five, if one counts *Rough For Radio I*, not broadcast in Beckett's lifetime): *Embers* in 1959, *Words and Music* in 1961, and *Cascando* from 1962, with both of the *Roughs* probably attempted during this time (*Rough for Radio II* was broadcast by Radio 3 on 13 April 1976, in honour of Beckett's 70th birthday). Alongside Beckett's 1960 radio adaptation of Robert Pinget's *La Manivelle* (broadcast as *The Old Tune*), these well-known works were reissued by the British Library in 2006 as *Samuel Beckett: Works for Radio*. 'Throughout his writing for the radio', concludes Maude's recent summary, 'Beckett is concerned with the distinctive nature of sonorous perception':

> In the first two radio plays, *All That Fall* and *Embers*, Beckett's interest is precisely on the phenomenology of sound and the perceptual particularities of hearing and listening. In *Rough for Radio I* and *II*, he turns his attention to sound technologies and the spatial reconfigurations they effect. In *Words and Music* and *Cascando*, finally, Beckett's focus is on music and its role as a non-conceptual signifying system.²⁶

We shall have cause to consider this bigger picture in closing, especially in terms of how interpretations of Beckett's later work may have been effected by this embrace of radio. Yet given the extent of Beckett's radio adaptations (understood as broadcasted works not specifically written for radio) undertaken by BBC during Beckett's lifetime, surveyed below, it is high time to fundamentally re-evaluate the scope and significance of that work.

§3

Turning now to these materials, focus will be trained upon several overarching themes emerging from the BBC WAC's files. The reason for this impressionistic approach is pretty simple, given more than 2,000 extant pages of text and microfilm in all. By way of situating these materials, this thematic introduction will make use of several recent debates Beckett studies. To be sure, each of the following sections merits a chapter itself: censorship and textual variants; collaboration and creativity; contracts and money; concluding with a final glance at Beckett's reception and some of the broader questions raised by these archives.

Without doubt, there are other fascinating elements in the BBC WAC materials. For example, the Third Programme broadcast and 'first publication' in English of 'For to End Yet Again' on 4 October 1976, that is, three weeks before it was available for purchase in Britain. Or again, with respect to discussions over Beckett's bilingualism, there is the insightful Martin Esslin production, six months later, of Arthur Rimbaud's 'The Drunken Boat', based on Beckett's 1930s translation, as explained in James Knowlson's extensive introduction to this broadcast of 12 March 1977. Indeed, the BBC's 'framing' and prefaces to Beckett's work is another subject worthy of critical attention. For example, the aforementioned Text for Nothing' productions commenced with the following existential-humanist introduction:

> The first programme in four where Patrick Magee will read the whole of Beckett's thirteen texts for nothing. These prose poems are meditations on the nature of the self and the burden of being. The voice we hear has reached a state detached from a world which has become unreal. It is from this vantage point that the speaker looks back at existence.[27]

Furthermore, as is well known, Beckett was a meticulous artist, one loath to make concessions to censors, popular morality or editors of any stripe. In the second half of the 1950s alone, for instance, Knowlson reports that Beckett withdrew from the Dublin International Theatre Festival due to the organisers' 'boycott' of Joyce and O'Casey's art, and ceased allowing his work to be performed in Ireland for some years thereafter. Still more famously, several months later the

Lord Chamberlain's office objected to the 'prayer scene' in *Endgame*, ordering 21 lines to be cut or bowdlerised before granting a license to perform at the Royal Court Theatre. Changing the line 'God the bastard! He doesn't exist' was simply a step too far for Beckett, who wrote to his director, George Devine: 'I am afraid I simply cannot accept omission or mediation of the prayer passage which appears to me indispensable as it stands [....] I think this does call for a firm stand.'[28]

In this light, the extent to which Beckett was willing to modify his own published work at the BBC's request is most unusual. Three examples from the WAC files stand out in this respect. First, parts from *The Beckett Trilogy* were aired on the Third Programme in December 1957, June 1958 and January 1959, all involving the selection of long passages from *Molloy* (59'14"), *Malone Dies* (71'38") and *The Unnamable* (60'51"). *Molloy* proved the least problematic, with the end of the first part broadcast almost completely, while substantial textual excerpting across *The Unnamable* were needed to give the work a radio coherence that it may, indeed intentionally, not have had on the page. Yet BBC WAC materials relating to *Malone Dies* are more revealing, with Beckett rejecting parts containing Saposcat, for 'I don't like them'.[29] As this exchange with Donald McWhinnie from early 1958 makes clear, he was persuaded to include Sapo at the behest of his collaborators, including Patrick Magee and his cousin John Beckett—the latter responsible for the score. 'I wanted to keep Sapo out of the Malone reading', Beckett wrote to Barney Rosset on 10 March 1956; 'But McWhinnie, John and Magee all want him in. So I let him in.' 'Out on the other hand', Clas Zilliacus notes, 'went one or two *Molloy* passages deemed not presentable in public.'[30] So too, unusually, did 'three cuts in the body of the text' to *Malone Dies*, unbeknownst to Beckett beforehand. It is hard to imagine Beckett accepting this from virtually anyone other than McWhinnie.[31]

As with the late 1950s rendering of *The Beckett Trilogy*, so with *Waiting for Godot* on 27 April 1960, produced by McWhinnie for a six-part cast that included Magee as Vladimir, Wilfrid Brambell as Estragon, Donal Donelly as Lucky, Felix Felton as Pozzo, Jeremy Ward as 'A Boy' and—far and away most unexpectedly—Denys Hawthorne as 'Narrator'. The latter surprise led Zilliacus to conclude: 'In a 1971 letter to me, Beckett writes that he must have known about and authorized this version with spoken stage directions, but that he would not consent to it today.'[32] Yet as the script makes clear, these were not just stage directions, but included several alterations to the text as published, as well as some quite intrusive interventions; for example, when Lucky is ordered to think at the end of Act 1, one narrative line simply states, ironically enough: '(SILENCE)'.[33] Finally, given the textual minutiae powering 'genetic criticism'—which, generally speaking, analyses manuscript iterations, sources and variants, in tracing out the writing process between draft and publication—even a change of one word merits attention. For instance, only five years after writing to Zilliacus about *Godot*'s surprise narrator, in offering Martin Esslin the long-dormant *Rough for Radio II* in January 1976, Beckett was willing to consider changing 'Animator' to 'Operator' at the BBC's request.[34]

Still more revealingly, in the 1982 Halloween broadcast of *Ill Seen Ill Said*, first published only a year before, the producer, Ronald Mason, cut the text's very first word, the preposition 'From', thus changing the opening sentence to 'Where she lies she sees Venus rise.'[35] Considering the burgeoning interest in this empirical area of Beckett studies, the variations between text or drama on one hand, and the BBC's radio production as broadcast on the other, are equally fascinating and potentially fruitful. Needless to say, with respect to otherwise refused adaptations of his work, Beckett was far more flexible with the BBC than most anyone else, as indicated in a letter from the BBC's Copyright Department to Curtis Brown regarding the radio version of *Play*, which was later broadcast on 11 October 1966 by the Third Programme. Dated 26 February of that year, this opens:

> You will remember refusing us permission last November to broadcast PLAY because Mr. Beckett did not wish his stage works to be performed in any other medium. Now it seems someone has been at work, and managed to persuade Mr. Beckett to change his mind, at any rate to the extent of giving us permission in principle to broadcast PLAY at an appropriate length of thirty minutes.[36]

§4

Throughout his career, as is widely attested, Beckett went to the wall for his friends, whether in reviewing their work—as illustrated by earlier texts in *Disjecta* on MacGreevy, the van Velde brothers and Jack B. Yeats—or in collaboration with others for translations (especially with Patrick Bowles from French and Elmar Tophoven into German). There were exchanges like the 1949 *Three Dialogues*, and many other examples besides—whether Giacometti's famous tree for *Godot*, or in dedicating works to help friends, as with Beckett's dedication of the 1988 *Stirrings Still* to his American publisher, Barney Rosset. *Samuel Beckett and Music*, for example, Mary Bryden's collection with that title from 1998, contains chapters covering collaborative work with the composer Marcel Mihalovici, who provided the radio score for *Cascando* (and produced the opera *Krapp*, broadcast in France on 15 May 1961),[37] as well as Morton Feldman on both the 1976 prose poem 'neither' and, later, *Words and Music* for 'The Beckett Festival of Radio Plays' in Dublin during April 1989. Similarly, his regard for actors such as Jack MacGowran, Ronald Pickup, Patrick Magee and several others meant that they were invariably cast in BBC productions of Beckett's work—sometimes even as a condition for broadcasting rights. In addition to his trust in these actors faithfully rendering his art, moreover, it is a safe bet that Beckett's close relationships at the BBC—with Barbara Bray, Martin Esslin and Donald McWhinnie, above all—were a driving force in the extent of comparative flexibility toward, and frequent participation in adaptations of his work from the mid-1950s on.

Of course, this high regard cut both ways, which also had its traceable effects. A relevant example is the BBC's first broadcast of *Molloy* and 'From An Abandoned Work', both of which were read by Magee on 10 and 14 December 1957, respectively. On these days, Beckett's BBC reception in Paris was poor, and he requested copies from McWhinnie two days before Christmas. In addition to informing him that the lines 'vero, vero' were cut in 'From An Abandoned Work', McWhinnie responded on New Years' Eve 1957 by admitting 'it may be difficult to arrange records' for him to audit in Paris.[38] Yet strings were subsequently pulled—despite the BBC's policy of not allowing recordings to be circulated, which they were careful to note would not pose a 'broken precedent' even in Beckett's case (he had been allowed tapes of *All That Fall* for his personal use the year before)—and he was able to listen to the recorded broadcasts in BBC's Paris office in early February 1958.[39] In turn, this taped session was apparently enough to spark inspiration: during the month that the BBC dithered over whether to allow him a personal copy of *Molloy* and 'From An Abandoned Work', ultimately embargoed, he completed *Krapp's Last Tape*, memorably using a tape recorder as a central prop.

Correspondingly, critics like Ulrika Maude and Yoshiki Tajiri have written compellingly on Beckett's longstanding interest in technology—whether radio, tape recorders or, later, his engagement with television and film.[40] This certainly extends to the dozen BBC television productions of Beckett's work in as many years from 1961. Beckett's television work with the BBC is also covered in some detail in his BBC WAC files and, while my focus here is upon Anglophone radio, Caversham records on TV, French, Spanish and other language broadcasts are likewise worth scholarly attention. In terms of radio, two final examples—again, from amongst many—of creative collaboration underscore the centrality of this medium for Beckett, and the BBC's pivotal role in facilitating it. As noted earlier, as Head of Drama (Sound) in early 1976, Martin Esslin was able to secure 'Sketch for Radio or Rough for Radio' [i.e. *Rough for Radio II*] for the Third Programme. In the intervening months, they exchanged letters about the piece in the run-up to the broadcast, extending to decisions on silence, sound effects and even the suggestion of a concluding 'faint sob from the stenographer' that sheds light upon the play.[41] Again, the play was written during the period of Beckett's most intense collaboration with the BBC in the late 1950s and early 1960s, so it is perhaps fitting that its resurrection was undertaken for his 70th birthday via the successor to the Third Programme from 30 September 1967, BBC Radio 3.

For yet another, earlier anniversary, in this case the BBC's own 40th in 1962, these themes of friendship, collaboration and technology were collectively in evidence for the lavish production of *Words and Music*. It was finished almost exactly a year earlier.[42] Beckett submitting the script to Esslin on 9 December 1961 with a covering note declaring that it was 'written for the BBC and John Beckett. I hear from him today that he would like to take it on. I hope it may be acceptable to the BBC also.'[43] Naturally, it was, for 'this is supposed to be our prestige production in the Fortieth Anniversary Week', as Esslin pointed out to the Organiser of the radio Production Facilities. This was despite the serious challenges *Words and Music* presented: 'This is an extremely difficult operation, as the play (which is not 15' but 30' duration) is one of the most intricate mergers of sound and music we have ever undertaken.'[44]

Amongst others involved in this taxing enterprise, John Beckett's role was crucial as composer—just as it was for all three broadcasts from *The Beckett Trilogy* in the late 1950s. With influential artists like John Beckett or, again, Harold Pinter—who acted in several radio works for the BBC, including one of six voices for the 1971 *Lessness*, and the role of 'Animator' in *Rough for Radio II* five years later—there is clearly a great deal more work to be done in terms of Samuel Beckett's collaborations. Unlike the process of writing, of course, even the most straightforward radio production—say, the reading of Beckett's poems on the Third Programme over two parts, in March and November 1966—there were questions of musical accompaniment, actors' voices, length and, often, selection of texts, all of which was far from solitary work. When it came to radio, to some degree at least, negotiation and even concession were periodically necessary. But by whom, exactly?

§5

This raises another salient feature of Beckett's BBC WAC files, namely that of contracts and money. One might be forgiven for considering this a dry subject, but in Beckett studies it has been far less so than for other canonical modernists. This is especially the case since the 2011 publication of Steven Dilks's *Samuel Beckett and the Literary Marketplace* which, in Seán Kennedy's incisive review, 'seeks to deprive us of our received understanding of Beckett as a writer who was both indifferent to fame and uninterested in money'.[45] For Dilks, this has led to a 'hagiographic myth' in Beckett studies cultivated by photographers, agents, publishers, critics and even Beckett's Estate—to the extent Beckett's alleged 'salivating over his royalty statements.'[46] In the same Special Issue of *Modernism/Modernity*, entitled *Beckett: Out of the Archive*, Mark Nixon paints a very different picture, with 'nearly half' of Beckett's 'grey canon' of drafts and manuscripts 'donated by Beckett himself either to institutions or to friends', in addition to 'actively support[ing] scholarship on his work'.[47] Nixon's point is that it was Beckett's generosity, not his avarice or image cultivation, that is the better measure of the man. Between these interpretative approaches, Beckett's financial transactions held at Caversham tell a more nuanced story.

A fitting example is provided by the above-cited 30-minute production of *Words and Music*, costing the Third Programme in 1962 about £7,500 in today's currency. This included Beckett's copyright permission for 75 guineas, on top of another £308.19 for the 'approximate costs of music'.[48] As this suggests, the BBC had pretty inflexible financial regulations in place, and rights were usually negotiated between their copyright department and Beckett's representatives. Thus, for Beckett's poetry, rights were held by an amenable John Calder, as evidenced by the two programmes of poetry aired in March and November 1966, with payment agreed by line. Curtis Brown handled Beckett's dramatic rights for television, where the BBC's fee was £3 per minute that same year. Sometimes, a straight television fee was negotiated instead, with £50 for *Act Without Words II* agreed in September 1965. But on occasion, as is hardly surprising, Curtis Brown and other agents—not Beckett himself, in extant BBC records at least—drove a harder bargain. That same year, on 1 July 1965 for example, Margaret McLaren balked at the BBC's offer for the television rights to *Eh Joe*:

> I certainly can't put to him your offer of £125. To get a television play from Sam is a miracle in itself. He has been asked for some years to write for television and always refused until he himself felt he would like to do it. Surely the BBC can do better than this for one of the greatest playwrights of our time. The excitement at receiving an original television play by Samuel Beckett is enormous. As you probably know, the only strings to the play are that Donald McWhinnie shall direct and Jack MacGowran play in it. I am perfectly free to sell the play where ever I wish but I felt sure the BBC would want to buy it.[49]

The affronted McLaren initially requested £600, but in the event agreed to twice the BBC's original offer: £250.

Finally, it appears that, following his award of the Nobel Prize for Literature in 1969, the BBC paid an extra sixth over and above 'the usual scale' for use of Beckett's work. By the later 1970s, rights for some of his dramatic pieces were handled by a hard-nosed Sue Freathy from the London-based Spokesmen agency. On 9 August 1978, she requested a compensation fee for 'misuse of Mr. Beckett's work' following unauthorised broadcast extracts from *Waiting for Godot*, for this 'is something Mr. Beckett dislikes intensely and will only authorise for particular occasions at the request of personal friends.'[50] This did not extend to BBC Radio Cymru, who were asked to pay a £15 fee for sending an *ex post facto* contract and were not even allowed 'to repeat this extract'—which prompted a ticking off by BBC Wales Programme executives a week later, via this 'timely reminder that all copyright material should be cleared in advance not only of broadcast but in advance of recording'.[51]

Then, four months later, rather than accept the then £13 per minute Writers' Guild rates for a new production, Freathy pointed out that 'Samuel Beckett was very special'. On 13 December 1979, she thus requested a flat fee of £1,000 for permission to broadcast *All That Fall*, which seems to have terminated negotiations.[52] At the very least, if Beckett was relatively untroubled by money in the last decades of his life, there was nevertheless, already a 'Beckett industry' that had long-blossomed by his 1969 Nobel Laureateship. For those on the 'inside', this typically meant unselfish promotion of his work, with money a peripheral consideration for friends and close colleagues. But as may be expected of human nature, not always; and Steven Dilks does have a point, if an overstated one. Yet it was less a case of Beckett greedily rubbing his hands than others around him— in the case of agents running a capitalist business, quite understandably so— sometimes pushing the envelope financially. While here, as with the preceding themes addressed above, literary interpretation will hopefully long continue in Beckett studies, materials held at the BBC Written Archives Centre holds the promise of helping empirically ground these and other continuing debates.

§6

But in conclusion, so what? New material, to be sure, but how can this be situated in Beckett's wider work? Regarding Beckett's work specifically written for radio—itself considered highly experimental for the BBC, then searching for a way to compete with the irresistible rise of home television—Ulrika Maude has noted that *Embers* 'can be said to thematise hearing', in a broadcast she adjudged to be 'far more audacious and experimental' than the earlier *All That Fall*.[53] To Maude's well-supported view, Robert Wilcher's incisive chapter from 1987 has long agreed, aptly adding it 'seems likely that *Embers*—both in its subject matter and in its use of the medium—grew out of Beckett's experience of hearing excerpts from the novels transferred from print to sound.'[54] As for prose so too for his plays, which Erik Tonning's 2007 study understands as *Samuel Beckett's Abstract Drama*. Following shortly on the heels of *Comment c'est* and *Happy Days*, the 1962 one-act drama, *Play*, initiates what Tonning calls an 'aesthetic of abstraction', meaning that 'what we see and hear involves a fundamentally new kind of formal achievement; one that underlines the transition in this play to an 'abstract' dramatic style'.[55]

Furthermore, it is precisely this period coinciding with an often-noted change in Beckett's writing from the later 1950s and early 1960s. This principally relates to the revolutionary, unpunctuated text *How It Is*—arguably heralding a kind of second creative breakthrough in Beckett's oeuvre following his well-known 'siege in a room' between 1945 and 1950. Might it be possible to read this sonorous, unpunctuated narrative as a kind of radiogenic text? Just at this point—in fact, only four months after the BBC's premiere of *All That Fall*—Beckett famously described his work 'as a matter of fundamental sounds'.[56] Theorising this phrase has long interested critics, particularly regarding Beckett's prose from this period on, which several scholars have discerned as rhythmic or spectral—such as the 'intricate aural patternings of the brief late poems' which, for Steven Matthews, are 'where the late style of Beckett is most clearly revealed'.[57] Simply put, how much of this 'late style', either dramatic or textual, is owed to Beckett's immersion in radio from 1956 and 1962—let alone thereafter?

Still another area of longstanding interest remains Beckett's reception, both 'domestically' (in France, Ireland or Britain) and internationally. Overwhelmingly, these studies have emphasised the literary and dramatic reception of Beckett's art. Accordingly, much space is given over to literary scholars, drama critics, *philosophes* and other public intellectuals in forming what Shane Weller has characterised as a 'broadly philosophical reading' of Beckett's work.[58] Granted, but that was rarely how it was at the time for non-specialists. In fact, in Britain at least, it is quite likely that many more people, in the 1950s and 1960s at least, *heard* Beckett on the radio than ever *read* his texts or *saw* his plays. And for the most part, their voices have been marginalised. I say for the most part, since a final thematic element from the Caversham manuscripts deserves special attention in closing here: audience reports.

Beyond showing that British radio mediated the reception of Beckett's art far more than previously acknowledged, these BBC audience reports also bear out a view long ago advanced by the theatre critic Vivian Mercier. After attending an academic session, he reported on

> a member of the audience who asked the panel the rhetorical question, "Isn't *Waiting for Godot* a sort of living Rorschach [inkblot] test?" He was clapped and cheered by most of those present, who clearly felt as I still do that most interpretations of that play—indeed of Samuel Beckett's work as a whole—reveal more about the psyches of the people who offer them than about the work itself or the psyche of its author.[59]

In addition to the three themes sketched above, then—collectively revealing a flexibility; a willingness to negotiate; and a collaborative approach quite at odds with traditional views of Beckett—the matter of audience reception is equally revealing. For these were everyday British voices, reacting to what came over their radio sets. For instance, the aforementioned 'New Comment' programme dedicated to Beckett's work on 11 October 1961 received an A or A+ (7%) rating from 46% of the 61 questionnaires returned to the BBC, with only 25% rating it a C or, the lowest mark, a C- (5%). Nonetheless, the overall audience appreciation index came in at 56, well below the 'New Comment' series average of 61. Some of the criticism of Beckett was fierce: a Farmer heard 'people trying to make something profound and eternal out of his plays'; a retired Art Mistress found merely proof of 'decadence in literature'; while a Teacher thought that, in keeping with other avant-garde artists, Beckett's work and its supposed elucidation was 'meaningless to normal people'.[60]

An earlier audience survey likewise found opinions 'sharply divided' over Beckett's *Molloy* and 'From An Abandoned Work', both broadcast in December 1957:

> That neither of these two programmes was given as good an overall reception as "All That Fall" was due to some extent to a feeling of satiation on the part of many listeners with variations on the "dustbins of life" theme that Beckett had made his peculiar own [...] More listeners than not though, would have agreed that the works certainly held fascination (unhealthy though it might be) [...] they were all, in company with many others, prepared to give the works a high rating because of the power and compulsion of the writing; the brilliance of thought and execution.[61]

For *Molloy*, responses were advanced by a 'Writer' ('meaningless'); a 'Research Worker' ('poor'); a 'Retired Colonial Administrator'; an 'Insurance Clerk'; a 'Flight-Lieutenant'; a 'Physicist'; two 'Clerks'; a 'Secretary'; a 'Statistician'; a 'Psychotherapist'; and a 'Commercial Artist', the latter concluding: 'I'm sorry I can't be more lucid. It is not so much what Mr. Beckett has to say as the way he says it which so grips one.'[62] Then as now, it was the force of Beckett's work which grabbed the attention of Britons from all walks of life. For many, although it may be largely forgotten this today, this was an experience enhanced, one indeed facilitated, by the Third Programme's unapologetically Arnoldian content. Without the post-war BBC, Beckett's Anglophone reception following the surprise success of *Waiting for Godot* might have advanced more like his narrator in 'From An Abandoned Work': 'one of the fastest runners the world has ever seen, over a short distance', but in the long run, proceeding 'very slowly, little short steps and the feet very slow through the air'.[63] Fortunately in retrospect, the BBC doused its listeners in Beckett, contributing to both his continuing experiments at the limits of artistic expression, no less than attendant public perceptions; and thereby, indirectly, to the on-going reception and interpretation of those 'fundamental sounds'.

NOTES

[1] These works are all contained in Samuel Beckett, *The Complete Dramatic Works* (London: Faber, 1990).

[2] Donald McWhinnie, internal BBC memorandum, 21 February 1951, cited in James Knowlson, *Damned to Fame: The Life of Samuel Beckett* (Bloomsbury: London, 1996), p. 431.

[3] Clas Zilliacus, *Beckett and Broadcasting: A Study of the Works of Samuel Beckett For and In Radio and Television* (Åbo: Åbo Akademi, 1976). Other works on Beckett and radio include Katharine Worth, 'Beckett and the Radio Medium', in *British Radio Drama*, ed. John Drakakis (Cambridge: Cambridge University Press, 1981); Everett Frost, 'Fundamental Sounds: Recording Samuel Beckett's Radio Plays', in *Theatre Journal* 43/3 (1991); Marjorie Perloff, 'The Silence That Is Not Silence: Acoustic Art in Samuel Beckett's *Embers*', and Stanley Richardson and Jane Alison Hale, 'Working Wireless: Beckett's Radio Writing', in *Samuel Beckett and the Arts: Music, Visual Arts, and Non-Print Media*, ed. Lois Oppenheim (New York: Garland Publishing, 1999); Barry McGovern, 'Beckett and the Radio Voice', in *Samuel Beckett: 100 Years: Centenary Essays*, ed. Christopher Murray (Dublin: New Island, 2006); Kevin Branigan *Radio Beckett: Musicality in the Radio Plays of Samuel Beckett* (Oxford: Peter Lang, 2008); and most recently, and Gaby Hartel, 'Emerging out of a Silent Void: Some Reverberations of Rudolf Arnheim's Radio Theory in Beckett's Radio Pieces', in the *Journal of Beckett Studies* 19/2 (2010).

[4] Zilliacus, *Beckett and Broadcasting,* pp. 209ff.

[5] James Knowlson, 'Introduction to the Words of Samuel Beckett: A Discography', *Recorded Sound: Journal of The British Library National Sound Archive* 85 (1984), pp. 26–28.

[6] This transmission is included in Raymond Federman and John Fletcher, eds., *Samuel Beckett: His Work and His Critics* (Berkeley: University of California Press, 1970), pp. 307–9. Additionally listed as broadcast by the BBC between 1957 and 1965, in chronological order, are: J.W. Lambert for the Home Service on *Waiting for Godot* (21 August 1955, 'The Critics'); Lennox Milne, also on *Godot* for the Home Service (1 August 1956, 'Arts Review'); Marie Budberg on *All That Fall* for the Home Service (20 January 1957, 'The Critics'); G.S. Frasier's on *All that Fall* for Third Programme (24 January 1957, 'Comment'); J.J. Whiteman's theatre review of *Fin de Partie* and *Acte sans paroles* (4 April 1957); A.J. 'Con' Leventhal's 'Samuel Beckett: Poet and Pessimist' for the Third Programme (30 April 1957); Patrick Bowles' 'A Master Work of Disillusion' for the Third Programme (15 June 1958); Karl Miller on *Embers* and *All That Fall* for the Third Programme (25 June 1959, 'Comment'); Barbara Bray on *Comment c'est* for the Third Programme (2 February 1961, 'Comment'); Peter Bull's radio documentary on *Waiting for Godot* for the Third Programme (14 April 1961, 'Comment'); Denis Donahoe's 'The Play of Words' for the Third Programme (30 June 1962); Bamber Gascoine on *Happy Days* for the Home Service (18 November 1962, 'The Critics'); Barbara Bray on *Words and Music* for the Home Service (9 December 1962); Laurence Kitchin's general twentieth century drama production for the Third Programme, which includes discussion of Beckett, 'Compressionism: The Cage and the Scream' (8 January 1963); Louis MacNeice and Jack McGowran on 'Beckett's work from the actor's viewpoint' for the Third Programme (11 July 1963, 'New Comment'); Harold Hobson on *Play* for the Home Service (19 April 1964, 'The Critics'); Barbara Bray on

Endgame for the Third Programme (2 June 1964, 'New Comment', including interviews with Jack MacGowrn and Patrick Magee); J.W. Lambert on *Endgame* for the Home Service (19 July 1964, 'The Critics'); Christopher Ricks, 'The Roots of Samuel Beckett' for the Third Programme (18 November 1964), Eric Rhode on *Waiting for Godot* for the Third Programme (6 January 1965, 'New Comment'); J.W. Lambert, also on *Godot*, for the Home Service (10 January 1965, 'The Critics'); and John Fletcher's 'Beckett as Critic' for the Third Programme (2 October 1965).

[7] Barbara Bray, cited in 'New Comment' No. 41, Third Programme, 11 October 1961, held in the BBC's WAC's 'Talks Library 1922–1970'. This broadcast is also cited in Federman and Fletcher, *Samuel Beckett*, p. 308.

[8] Beckett's works for BBC (and other) television outlets at this time are excluded from discussion here; for an overview of these works for television and film, see Jonathan Bignell, *Beckett on Screen: The Television Plays* (Manchester: Manchester University Press, 2009), pp. 10–11, with the wider post-war BBC context surveyed on pp. 88–89.

[9] Beckett to Cecilia Reeves 4 July 1956, contained in the 'Samuel Beckett, Scriptwriter File: 1953–1962', RCONT1, BBC Written Archives Centre, Caversham. This letter is reproduced in *The Letters of Samuel Beckett, 1941-1956: Volume 2*, eds. George Craig, Martha Dow Fehsenfeld, Dan Gunn and Lois More Overbeck (Cambridge: Cambridge University Press, 2011), p. 632, n. 5.

[10] Mark Nixon and Matthew Feldman, eds., *The International Reception of Samuel Beckett* (Continuum: London, 2009).

[11] Jeffrey Lyn Porter, 'Samuel Beckett and the Radiophonic Body: Beckett and the BBC', in *Modern Drama* 53/4 (2010), p. 432.

[12] Harman Grisewood, cited in *ibid.*, p. 433.

[13] *Ibid.*

[14] Martin Esslin, cited in Julie Campbell, 'Beckett and the Third Programme', in *Samuel Beckett Today / Aujourd'hui* 25 (2013), p. 113.

[15] John Morris, cited in *ibid.*, p. 111. The late Julie Campbell's important text is one of the few to employ BBC WAC materials to date.

[16] J. Ormerod Greenwood to McWhinnie, 2 February 1954, in 'Samuel Beckett, Scriptwriter 1953–1962'.

[17] Raymond Raikes to Val Gielgud, 29 September 1955, in *ibid.*

[18] Campbell, 'Beckett and the Third Programme', p. 112; see also Rosemary Pountney, *Theatre of Shadows: Samuel Beckett's Drama, 1956–76: From* All that Fall *to* Footfalls, *with commentaries on the latest plays* (Gerrard's Cross: Colin Smythe, 1988), pp. 196–210.

[19] I am grateful to John Pilling for assistance with this information, and for use of a recording of this rare 1952 production.

[20] See Beckett to Jérôme Lindon, 1 October 1955, in *The Letters of Samuel Beckett, 1941-1956: Volume 2*, pp. 552–3.

[21] Paul Stewart, 'Sterile Reproduction: Beckett's Death of the Species and Fictional Regeneration' in *Beckett and Death*, eds. Steven Barfield, Matthew Feldman and Philip Tew (London: Continuum, 2009), p. 183.

[22] Beckett to Thomas McGreey, 27 September 1953; and Beckett to Barney Rosset, 21 August 1954, cited in *The Letters of Samuel Beckett, 1941-1956: Volume 2*, pp. 407, 497.

[23] Knowlson, *Damned to Fame*, p. 431.

[24] John Morris to Val Gielgud, 18 July 1956, 'Samuel Beckett, Scriptwriter: 1953–1962'.

[25] Gielgud to McWhinnie, 14 January 1957, cited in *ibid.*

26 Ulrika Maude, 'Working on Radio', in *Samuel Beckett in Context*, ed. Anthony Uhlmann (Cambridge: Cambridge University Press, 2013), pp. 189–90.
27 BBC Production Details for Samuel Beckett's 'Texts for Nothing: I-III', produced by Martin Esslin, 12 June 1975, 'Play Library' collection, BBC Written Archives Centre, Caversham.
28 Beckett to George Devine, cited in Knowlson, *Damned to Fame*, pp. 447–8.
29 Beckett to McWhinnie, 26 February 1958, in 'Samuel Beckett, Scriptwriter: 1953–1962'.
30 Zilliacus, *Beckett and Broadcasting*, p. 148.
31 McWhinnie to Beckett, 16 June 1958, Samuel Beckett, Scriptwriter: 1953–1962'.
32 Zilliacus, *Beckett and Broadcasting*, p. 150.
33 BBC Production Details for Samuel Beckett's *Waiting for Godot*, produced by Donald McWhinnie, 27 April 1960, in the 'Play Library' collection, BBC Written Archives Centre, Caversham.
34 Beckett to Esslin, 19 January 1976, in 'Samuel Beckett, Scriptwriter: 1973–1982', BBC Written Archives Centre, Caversham.
35 BBC Production Details for Samuel Beckett's *Ill Seen Ill Said*, directed by Ronald Mason, 31 October 1982, 'Play Library' collection, BBC Written Archives Centre, Caversham.
36 Jack Beale to Margaret McLaren, 26 February 1966, in 'Samuel Beckett, Copyright File I: 1965–1969', RCONT18, BBC Written Archives Centre, Caversham.
37 Edith Fournier, 'Marcel Mihalovici and Samuel Beckett: Musicians of Return', in *Samuel Beckett and Music*, ed. Mary Bryden (Oxford: Oxford University Press, 1998), p. 133.
38 McWhinnie to Beckett, 31 December 1957, in 'Samuel Beckett, Scriptwriter: 1953–1962'.
39 Reeves to McWhinnie, 4 February 1958, in *ibid*.
40 See Ulrika Maude, *Beckett, Technology and the Body* (Cambridge: Cambridge University Press, 2009); and Yoshiki Tajiri, *Samuel Beckett and the Prosthetic Body: The Organs and Senses in Modernism* (Basingstoke, Palgrave: 2007).
41 Beckett to Esslin, 1 Jan. 1976 and *passim*, in 'Samuel Beckett, Scriptwriter: 1973–1982'.
42 John Pilling, *A Samuel Beckett Chronology* (Basingstoke: Palgrave, 2006), p. 157.
43 Beckett to Esslin, 9 December 1961, in 'Samuel Beckett, Scriptwriter: 1953–1962'.
44 Esslin, internal BBC memorandum, 4 September 1962, in 'Samuel Beckett, Scriptwriter: 1953–1962'.
45 Seán Kennedy, review of *Samuel Becket in the Literary Marketplace*, in *Samuel Beckett: Out of the Archive*, Special Issue of Modernism/Modernity 18/4 (2012), p. 919.
46 Steven Dilks, *Samuel Becket in the Literary Marketplace* (Syracuse: Syracuse University Press, 2011), pp. 36–7.
47 Mark Nixon, 'Beckett's Manuscripts in the Marketplace', in *Samuel Beckett: Out of the Archive*, pp. 827, 829.
48 Michael Bakewell, internal BBC memorandum, 19 June 1962, in 'Samuel Beckett, Scriptwriter: 1953–1962'.
49 Margaret McLaren to Edward Caffrey, 1 July 1965, in 'Samuel Beckett, Copyright File I: 1965–1969', RCONT18.
50 Sue Freathy to Alannah Hensler, 9 August 1978, in 'Samuel Beckett, Copyright: 1975–1979, RCONT21', BBC Written Archives Centre, Caversham.
51 Hensler, internal BBC memorandum, 15 August 1978, in *ibid*.
52 Freathy to Kathryn Turner, 13 December 1979, in *ibid*.
53 Ulrika Maude, 'Working on Radio', pp. 185–86.

54 Robert Wilcher, '"Out of the Dark": Beckett's Texts for Radio', in *Beckett's Later Fiction and Drama: Texts for Company*, eds. James Acheson and Arthur Katernyna (Basingstoke: MacMillan, 1987), p. 2.
55 Erik Tonning, *Samuel Beckett's Abstract Drama: Works for Stage and Screen, 1962–1985* (Bern: Peter Lang, 2007), p. 73.
56 Beckett to Alan Schneider, 29 December 1957, cited in *No Author Better Served: The Correspondence of Alan Schneider and Samuel Beckett*, ed. Maurice Harmon (London: Harvard University Press, 1998), p. 23.
57 Steven Matthews, 'Beckett's Late Style', p. 202.
58 Shane Weller, 'Beckett among the *Philosophes*: The Critical Reception of Samuel Beckett France', in *The International Reception of Samuel Beckett*, eds. Mark Nixon and Matthew Feldman (London: Continuum, 2009), p. 24.
59 Vivian Mercier, *Beckett/Beckett* (Oxford: Oxford University Press, 1979), p. vii.
60 British Broadcasting Corporation, Audience Research Report, 'Samuel Beckett', in 'Talks, *New Comment*, June 1961–1964', BBC Written Archives Centre, Caversham.
61 BBC Audience Research Report, *Molloy* and 'From An Abandoned Work', in 'Samuel Beckett, Scriptwriter: 1953–1962'.
62 *Ibid.*
63 Samuel Beckett, 'From An Abandoned Work', in Beckett, *The Complete Short Prose, 1929–1989*, ed. S. E. Gontarski (New York: Grove Press, 1995), pp. 157–8.

BECKETT'S TRILOGY ON THE THIRD PROGRAMME

§1

'My work is a matter of fundamental sounds (no joke intended)', Beckett claimed to Alan Schneider on 29 December 1957.[1] It is a striking remark, one that has long since piqued the interest of scholars working in Beckett studies. More widely, many readers of Beckett will undoubtedly associate this remark with Beckett's 'radiogenic writings', specifically *All That Fall* (first broadcast on the BBC's Third Programme on 13 January 1957), followed by *Embers* (24 June 1959; also winner of the 1959 Italia Prize), *Words and Music* (7 December 1962) and *Cascando* (6 October 1964). Most likely during the late 1950s and early 1960s, Beckett also composed the radiogenic 'Roughs'—*Rough for Radio II* (first broadcast 13 April 1976) and the long unrecorded *Rough for Radio I* (first broadcast by RTE Ireland on 12 April 2006)—alongside translating Robert Pinget's *La Manivelle* for the Third Programme's broadcast on 23 August 1960 (with the Anglophone title *The Old Tune*).[2] Accordingly, several key scholarly works have treated these productions as a complete radio corpus. Thus, Beckett's well-known remark to Schneider might be read via his engagement with the Third Programme at this time. Yet as this chapter emphasises, quite literally, that is not the half of it.

A second and more general context around the mid- to late-1950s witnesses something of a critical consensus in Beckett studies, one shared by all three of his main biographies. Beckett's famous 'siege in the room' between roughly 1945 and 1950—in which he wrote two plays and four novels (the latter, most relevant here, including the trilogy of *Molloy, Malone Dies* and *The Unnamable*), several poems and nearly 20 short stories—led to a kind of 'creative impasse', in Anthony Cronin's words, even if, at this time, he was on the verge of 'new relationships, interests and excitements'.[3] Indeed, one of these newfound interests was radio work, as James Knowlson's biography stresses:

> Beckett's depression was very slow to lift, as he began to experience renewed doubt as to whether there was any way out of the impasse into which *The Unnamable* and *Fin de partie* had led him. The medium of radio, with the challenge of its technical constraints, offered one possible escape route. Donald McWhinnie indeed wrote: "My impression is that if he is to write at all in the near future it will be for radio, which has captured his imagination."[4]

Similarly, Deirdre Bair has extended this 'depression at not being able to write prose' to early 1958; that is, with Beckett struggling to complete the English translation of *The Unnamable*.[5] However, claims Bair, by the next summer Beckett's lull) had dissipated with *Comment c'est* [*How It Is*], 'which almost demands to be spoken, in order to savour the full flavor of the language'.[6] Underscoring this point in a splendid 1987 essay, Robert Wilcher opens his '"Out of the Dark': Beckett's Texts for Radio" by declaring: 'Samuel Beckett's encounter with the medium of radio drama between 1956 and about 1962 has been recognized as an episode of some significance in his development as a writer.'[7]

From the above, very different perspectives—to some extent underwritten by Beckett's December 1957 characterisation of his work as 'fundamental sounds'—a rudimentary picture thus emerges in these pivotal years. It is one of an avant-garde author, having written himself into a creative corner, slowly emerges with a new form of expression by the early 1960s: abstract, aural and disembodied. If broadly accurate, then writing for radio played no small role in the development of Beckett's later works. More specifically, it may be that working with the Third Programme at this time inspired Beckett to write radiogenically—even for works not originally written for radio, like *How It Is*—in the remaining three decades of his creative output. In this light, Beckett's collaboration with the BBC can be seen as little short of transformative. Before turning to some tentative conclusions along these lines, shedding some empirical light upon this engagement is present concern.

To date, almost all of the focus trained upon Beckett's radio work for the BBC has been directed at his original broadcast plays. While these are justly celebrated as innovative work in both the radio medium and Beckett's oeuvre, they actually represent less than a quarter of the productions for the BBC of his work. In turn, virtually nothing has been written on Beckett's prose, poetic and dramatic adaptions for the BBC's Third Programme (and after 1967, its successor, Radio 3). This is despite roughly two thousand pages of scripts, contracts, production details and all manner of correspondence relating to some two-dozen radio adaptations held at the BBC Written Archives Centre in Caversham, UK.[8]

Emphasising the close working relationship Beckett shared with the BBC staff—especially between 1957 and 1962—the middle portion of the 'Samuel Beckett, Scriptwriter: 1953–1962' is revealing of his highly unusual flexibility in adapting *The Beckett Trilogy* for the Third Programme. Apparently an unsatisfactory 'computer print-out' of some material was sent to Claus Zilliacus, who notes of *The Beckett Trilogy*: 'the selections were, on the whole, made by the author. Excerpted were the end of *Molloy*, part one, and the beginning of *Malone Dies*; from *The Unnamable* various passages were extracted.'[9] Also too concisely, *Beckett and Broadcasting* tantalisingly reports:

The trilogy was less than enthusiastically received by its audience. The Panel reaction to *The Unnamable*, in particular, was "definitively unfavourable". The reaction indices for the broadcasts were, in chronological order, 52, 55, and 45, all well below average [which was 64].[10]

These fascinating reception indices, in turn, are discussed in the most authoritative text on this subject written to date, Julie Campbell's 'Beckett and the Third Programme'. In particular, she treats the fascinating—and one of the few extant—Audience Listener Survey on the December 1957 readings of *Molloy* and 'From An Abandoned Work'. Together, these prose adaptations

> signal[led] incontrovertibly what is gained by having a broadcasting channel focused on a minority rather than a mass audience: it provided the opportunity to appreciate radical artwork that would find no place anywhere else in broadcasting, yet it is also clear that Beckett's work was appreciated by a minority of the minority.[11]

Campbell's point is apposite, even if the varied comments from respondents still make for some surprising reading. In the four-page Audience Listener Survey treating *Molloy* and 'From An Abandoned Work', selections from several of the paragraph-long comments, broken down by profession, reveal that, in the BBC's internal estimation, respondents 'were all, in company with many more, prepared to give the works a high rating because of the power and compulsion of the writing, the brilliance of thought and execution'. In then providing selections of specific listener feedback on *Molloy* over the next two pages, this survey notes that a 'Retired Colonial Administrator' complained of 'a crashing bore', while an 'Insurance Clerk' stated 'I thoroughly disliked this thing'. On the other hand, a 'Secretary' found *Molloy* to be '[a]n excellent piece of writing', a 'Statistician' praised the 'extremely interesting broadcast'; a 'Psychoanalyst' found it 'wonderful in its sincerity and expressiveness'; a 'Clerk/Translator' praised the 'very solid and fascinatingly written study'; and finally and most disarmingly amongst these paragraphs, a 'Commercial Artist' claimed: 'How to describe one's reactions? I feel quite incoherent when called upon to do so. This programme was fascinating, impressive, but exactly why, in what manner, is something hard to determine'.[12]

Presumably much the same fiercely ambivalent, if ultimately less enthusiastic, reception attended the Third Programme's broadcast of *Malone Dies* and *The Unnamable*, although there does not seem to be any accompanying Audience Listener Surveys for these in the BBC WAC archives. These audience reports also signal an important context worthy of bearing in mind. Even at an estimated '0.1% of the adult population of the United Kingdom' (just over 50 million in the mid-1950s), that still leaves a potential 50,000 auditors for each broadcast of *Molloy, Malone Dies* and *The Unnamable*.[13] Put another way, for most people in Britain during the late 1950s, knowledge they had of Beckett's work was largely derived from hearing his work on the BBC's Third Programme—rather than seeing his plays or reading his prose. For this reason alone, returning to the tripartite production of *The Beckett Trilogy* remains a useful enterprise in 'historicising'.

Interestingly, in terms of the BBC's adaptation of *The Beckett Trilogy*, the idea for performing *Molloy* seems to have been Beckett's. On 7 May 1957, only five days after the Third Programme's transmission of *Fin de partie*, Beckett wrote to his favourite BBC producer, the Assistant Head of Sound, Donald McWhinnie:

> My cousin was here [...] and he talked of you and the 3rd and the possibilities of doing something together. You are right in thinking there is little chance of me writing anything new for months to come. I suggested to John that he might do some music [...] of Part I of Molloy for example, i.e. from the shore to the ditch. He thought it would be possible (on the lines of Diary of a Madman production) [...]^{14}

From there, the ball started rolling quickly, with McWhinnie replying on 16 May, also as recorded in the BBC WAC files: 'The broadcast of "Fin de Partie" went extremely well and I continue to hear enthusiastic comments about it. I think we ought to look very carefully at your suggestion of doing a section of "Molloy" with special music—I think the result might be extremely interesting.'^{15} Six weeks later came the answer from upstairs, with McWhinnie communicating the BBC's decision to Beckett on 26 June: 'I am delighted to say that the Third Programme have accepted the idea of a solo reading of the last section of Part 1 of "Molloy" with special music by your cousin [...] for the Fourth Quarter of this year. Where exactly in the text did you have in mind as a starting point?'^{16} Their next exchange is more interesting still. In response to McWhinnie's request, Beckett quickly replied on 30 June, recommending the following excerpt in reference to the first English edition of *Malone Dies*: '"And now my progress," to end of Part 1, with a cut, p. 107, line 25, "Perhaps it is less to be thought ...", to p.108, line 5, "Time will tell."' In the event, these twelve lines on the anus as 'the true portal of our being' were indeed cut from the broadcast (all subsequent references correspond to the Faber & Faber edition of *Molloy*; here p. 80, line 32, to p.81, line 7). Beckett then added: 'But I am not at all sure we would not find something more suitable in Malone Dies, Grove Press, N.Y. Unfortunately I have no copy with me here in the country. Another possibility would be an extract from my uncompleted translation of L'Innommable.'^{17}

On 3 July 1957, McWhinnie responded to Beckett's suggestion by cautioning: 'I think we had better stick to "Molloy" in the first instance. If it comes off there is no reason why we should not experiment with the others.'^{18} An internal memorandum from the BBC's Copyright Department on 19 August then established permissions costs: 'For a reading lasting between 45 and 60 minutes the fee for the use of the original work would vary between £30.13s.4d. and £40.13s.4d, and for the translation between £23. and £30.10s., according to the actual transmission timing. The same fee would be payable for each broadcast in the U.K. Service.'[19] Considering that the broadcast was 59 minutes and 14 seconds—and repeated on Friday, 13 December 1957 between 8.15 and 9.15pm—one can assume that permissions ran to c.£150 (this fee naturally excluded the BBC's internal costs as well as that for the musical composition and orchestral accompaniment). With the production contracted, McWhinnie wrote to Beckett on 6 September, in the throes of enthusiastic preparation: 'I think "Molloy" is going to be rather exciting. As I expect you know, I have had talks with John Beckett about it and I think his conception of the music is admirable. We are going to meet again early in October to get down to it in really practical terms'.[20] McWhinnie followed this with another letter to Beckett exactly a week later, adding: 'We must certainly meet to talk about "Molloy" before the broadcast.'[21]

From this early exchange, the closeness in collaboration between the BBC (in this case, Donald McWhinnie) and Beckett in the selection, production and incidental music for *Molloy* is unmistakeable. This proximity was indeed borne out by McWhinnie's subsequent meeting with Beckett in Paris during mid-November 1957 to discuss the adaptation. Upon returning, McWhinnie announced that *Molloy* was 'due to be broadcast on Tuesday, 10th December at 9.45pm [...] to be spoken by Magee. I am rehearsing and recording "Molloy" on 30th, 1st 2nd [of November ...] Spent the day with John Beckett yesterday. We went over the music on piano with Magee. It sounds very exciting.'[22] McWhinnie's reference to Beckett's first cousin, John, raises a second consideration regarding Beckett's Third Programme transmissions of *The Beckett Trilogy*. For the BBC's production was far more than Patrick Magee reading extended passages from *Molloy, Malone Dies* and *The Unnamable*: the original score John Beckett provided for all three radio adaptations was both extensive and, at times, quite integral to the wider production. One example from *Molloy*—detailed in the appendix on the BBC's broadcast script for *The Beckett Trilogy* appended at the end of this chapter—concerns the line 'The heart beats, and what a beat.'[23] In this instance, John Beckett's score bookended this sentence, isolating it as a kind of musical italicisation. As the 'Samuel Beckett: Scriptwriter, 1953–1962' file reveals, then, Beckett's collaboration with the BBC not only extended to producers like McWhinnie and actors like Magee, but also to his cousin as composer, who played a crucial role in the adaptation of *The Beckett Trilogy*.

§2

Quite apart from aforementioned BBC Audience Listener Survey, the fallout from the broadcast of *Molloy* on 10 December 1957 was remarkable. For Beckett in Paris, first and foremost, an inability to properly hear the broadcast of *Molloy* (or, four days later, that of 'From An Abandoned Work') led to a meeting in early 1958 at the office of the BBC's Parisian representative Cecilia Reeves. As partially recounted in Beckett's BBC WAC files as well as Knowlson's biography,[24] Beckett's experience of hearing the reel-to-reel playback of *Molloy* and 'From An Abandoned Work' seemed to immediately spark inspiration for a work initially entitled 'Magee monologue'. By the end of the next month, Beckett had turned this into the completed manuscript of *Krapp's Last Tape*—premièred in London later that year by Patrick Magee under Donald McWhinnie's direction—memorably using a tape recorder as the central prop. Rather more in terms of soliciting creativity than facilitating it, McWhinnie had earlier written to Beckett on New Year's Eve 1957, enclosing reviews of *Molloy* and 'From An Abandoned Work' from *The Manchester Guardian*, *New Statesman* and *The Listener*, alongside a declaration of continued—indeed acute—interest: 'If "Molloy" has stimulated your thoughts of possible radio expression, I need hardly say that nothing would please us more to commission you to do something for us, but the thought may be a terrible bore.'[25]

Just as portentously, Roy Walker's write-up in *The Listener* on 19 December 1957 praised the performance; especially noting that Magee 'spoke with extraordinary skill'. In fact, Walker's sole complaint was that there was not enough *Molloy*:

> The reading was of only the last twenty pages of the first part, less than a fifth of it. Beckett's writing is organic, its effects cumulative and, despite the apparent inconsequence of its stream-of-consciousness technique, carefully patterned. If some listeners pardonably mistook the excerpt for formless meandering they are referred to the full context. I cannot help suspecting that if the Third Programme still had an allocation of broadcasting time even remotely appropriate to the importance of its main subject-matter we might have heard the whole of the first part of *Molloy*, perhaps in four readings in one week.

Walker concluded, as it turned out, quite prophetically: 'The Third must do more Beckett, and persuade him to do more for radio.'[26] Beckett, it seems, needed little persuasion to pursue the adaptation of *Malone Dies* with the Third Programme. On 18 February 1958, in fact, the first mention of this project in the 'Samuel Beckett: Scriptwriter, 1953–1962' file already finds Donald McWhinnie sending an internal memorandum stating, in its entirety: 'I should like to ask John Beckett to write some music for the production of Samuel Beckett's "Malone

Dies". I estimate the total cost at not more than £180 and believe that it would probably be less.'²⁷ This was to cover approximately twelve minutes of 'incidental' music, McWhinnie further clarified in a memo of 26 March, 'for a very small combination, probably three or four instruments'.²⁸

Equally clear was Beckett's willingness to be persuaded over just what to include in the adaptation of *Malone Dies*. Two days after requesting fees for John Beckett's musical score for *Malone Dies*, on 20 February 1958 McWhinnie wrote to Beckett about the potential selection of extracts, regretting the latter's proposed exclusion of passages containing Malone's first creation, Saposcat: 'I don't think we should economise too much on "Malone Dies" and it seems a great pity not to include Saposcat. Might I suggest the following sequence which you can tear to pieces and put together again perhaps.' McWhinnie then proceeded to suggest four long excerpts from the novel, taken from amongst the first 52 pages of the 1956 Grove Press printing of *Malone Dies*. He then added:

> Alternatively, one could run the first 23 pages straight through and then jump to a later passage. I am sure we could stand 75 minutes this time. I have spoken to John Beckett about the music and he is very excited. Magee, of course, can hardly wait to get his teeth into it.²⁹

Yet Beckett took some convincing on including Saposcat passages in his adaptation of *Malone Dies*, putting forward two striking reasons in a letter to McWhinnie on 26 February 1958: 'one I don't like them, two, I think they are less suited to Magee than Malone's monologue proper'. However, Beckett conceded, an 'objection to omitting them if of course that you don't get the set-up of the work and that here and there an allusion by Malone to the story he is trying to tell will lose point. This could be overcome by a few lines of introduction which I could write for you.' Beckett then proceeded to suggest a further six shorter sequences from *Malone Dies*, since '[f]rankly, 75 minutes is a bit on the long side', before suggesting that McWhinnie should 'get the reactions of Pat Magee and John Beckett to this choice of passages and to the excluding of Sapo. If they agree with you that he should be included I'll propose another sequence including him.'³⁰ On 4 March McWhinnie responded unequivocally:

> I have talked to John Beckett about "Malone" and we both very much regret losing the Sapo passages. I do believe that you under-estimate Magee's range and I am completely confident that we could get from him a highly effective interpretation of these passages. An additional factor is that if we do keep them in the programme will contrast more with "Molloy" than if we leave them out, and from the listeners' point of view I think this would be a good thing. There is also, of course, the overriding fact that without them we don't really get a true impression of the feel of the work as a whole. I do hope you can see your way to proposing a sequence including Sapo. I am sure you won't regret it.³¹

'So be it,' Beckett conceded three days later, 'straight through then, from the beginning to page 23 "No, I want nothing."'[32] A *volte-face*: 'I wanted to keep Sapo out of the Malone reading', Beckett correspondingly wrote to Barney Rosset on 10 March 1958, 'but McWhinnie, John and Magee all want him in. So I let him in.'[33] In addition to challenging the view of Beckett's collaborative inflexibility, this exchange of letters further indicates the great importance he attached to Third Programme performances of his work in the late 1950s.

The contrast drawn between *Molloy* and *Malone Dies* by McWhinnie's letter is similarly revealing. Most prosaically, unlike the successful production of the former, for instance, this time Beckett's Copyright Permissions fee was £76 for each 75 minute broadcast (the adaptation of *Malone Dies* was repeated by the Third Programme on 19 June and 15 October 1958). Perhaps less expectedly, three days before the BBC's broadcast of *Malone Dies* on 18 June, the Third Programme ran a lengthy piece on *Molloy* by Beckett's co-translator, Patrick Bowles. This piece was then reprinted in *The Listener* at the end of the week (19 June 1958)—clearly with an eye to attracting interest in the first repeat broadcast of *Malone Dies*—with Bowles describing *Molloy* as a 'masterpiece'; 'a powerful vision of humanity *in extremis*'; and 'a revelation of the power which may reside in simplicity'.[34] Finally, the Third Programme's distinction between the first two novels of *The Beckett Trilogy* was explicitly highlighted by McWhinnie's programme note for *Malone Dies*, roughly half of which is excerpted below, sent only two days before the actual transmission—and thus, presumably, without Beckett's having seen it beforehand:

> In tonight's programme [Magee] interprets a sequence from the novel which directly follows "Molloy" and which is an extension of it, "Malone Dies". There is no action to speak of, simply an old man lying in bed close to death trying in his mind to evolve some sort of pattern from the world he lives in. Music for the programme has been specially composed by John Beckett, a cousin of the author, and is played by an unusual combination consisting of harmonics, two mandolins, tuba, cello, and double bass.
> Although Beckett is in no sense a frivolous writer and is concerned profoundly with matters of life and death, he has undoubtedly a great comic talent, and this is perhaps even more in evidence in "Malone Dies" than in the previous two broadcasts from his prose writings. And, of course, his work cries out to be spoken, indeed it is very often difficult to capture its essence from the printed page.[35]

In the end, 75 minutes (or more specifically, 63 minutes of reading and 12 minutes of musical accompaniment) was not enough to exhaust the first 23 pages from Grove's 1956 edition of *Malone Dies*. Timing problems encountered in the rehearsals (9–11 June 1958) and recording (10 and 11 June) meant that subsequent cuts needed to be made. Writing to Beckett of the impending transmission,

McWhinnie declared: 'The performance, I think, is very good. Even more difficult than the other two [*Molloy* and 'From An Abandoned Work'], but very rewarding. John's music is in advance of his score for "Molloy."' Yet in what must have been a quite rare experience for Beckett—especially considering, for example, the conflict with the Lord Chamberlain's office over cuts to *Endgame* only a year before[36]—McWhinnie added, in his letter of 16 June 1958, that the production of *Malone Dies* 'had to make three cuts in the body of the text, but I trust you will not find these too disruptive. They seem to work quite naturally.'[37] As the microfilmed broadcast script makes clear, there were actually four cuts to the text of *Malone Dies*, not three, totalling 9'45" (these are reproduced in the appendix below). Simply put, it is difficult to think of Beckett trusting many others beyond McWhinnie to take such liberties with his published work.

Finally and most boldly, McWhinnie turned to the prospect of adapting *The Unnamable* for the Third Programme in the second half of 1958. Although Beckett's taxing translation of *L'Innommable* had only appeared with Grove the month before, on 15 October 1958, McWhinnie wrote to Beckett's UK publisher, John Calder, enquiring about a British publication date for Calder & Boyars's edition of *The Unnamable*, 'and whether you would have any objection if by any chance the broadcast were to precede publication'.[38] Calder's office responded on 21 October 1958 by estimating the publication date to be around the end of January 1959, and requesting only that the BBC's transmission of extracts 'did not precede the publication date by more than two weeks'.[39] While the BBC WAC holdings on the adaptation of *The Unnamable* are far more slender than that for *Molloy* and *Malone Dies,* the microfilm production details demonstrate all the same that the programme was broadcast by the Third Programme on 19 January 1959 (8:35–9:35pm; repeated on 10 February 1959 between 9:45 and 10:45pm), following a packed four days of rehearsal and recording. As such, the first British 'publication' of *The Unnamable* was audited rather than read by the public in January 1959, further reinforcing the centrality of the BBC's role in disseminating *The Beckett Trilogy*—and indeed Beckett's work more widely from the later 1950s on.

Unlike the earlier two readings from *The Beckett Trilogy* in late 1957 and mid-1958, moreover, this final instalment was not billed as 'An extract from "MOLLOY"' or 'An extract from "MALONE DIES"', but instead as '"THE UNNAMABLE": Extracts from the novel by Samuel Beckett.'[40] That these were very much *the BBC's extracts* is revealed by Beckett's 17 November 1958 letter to Barbara Bray: 'I have no ideas positive or negative of any kind on the U[nnamable] extracts and leave it entirely to you and Donald [McWhinnie].'[41] This resulted in selections across the whole novel, rather than the block extracts used for *Molloy* and *Malone Dies*. For example, the production script shows that the first and third paragraphs of *The Unnamable* were broadcast, but not the second. After skipping another four pages (in the 2010 Faber edition), the third selection starts from p.7, line 26, and runs to the end of the next page. Picking up again on the 28-line paragraph commencing 'All these Murphys, Molloys and Malones do not fool me',[42] another 23 pages go by before starting mid-paragraph with 'But it's entirely a matter of voices, no other metaphor is appropriate'—a passage again citing the earlier Beckettian avatars Murphy, Watt and Mercier.[43] Likewise continuing with the trope of speech in *The Unnamable*, another music-filled gap in the novel then continues at 'Ah if I could only find a voice of my own, in all this babble', concluding with 'I think Murphy spoke now and then, the others too perhaps, I don't remember, but it was clumsily done, you could see the ventriloquist.'[44] Given the nature of these widely-spaced excerpts, then, it is hardly surprising that the BBC's final sequence for broadcast, concluding with the celebrated end of *The Unnamable's* 'I can't go on, I'll go on', actually begins two pages earlier, with the actual novel's mid-sentence declaration, 'all these stories about travellers, these stories about paralytics, all are mine.'[45]

§3

By way of conclusion, four days after the transmission of *The Unnamable*, Beckett sent McWhinnie his completed draft of *Embers* (originally entitled 'Ebb'), recorded by the BBC only three weeks later and broadcast by the Third Programme on 24 June 1959.[46] Having fittingly come full-circle in thus sketching the period between the 1956 composition of *All That Fall* and the completion of a second radiogenic work, the 1959 *Embers*, the question remains: how does this relate to Beckett's wider artistic project? Did Beckett's short and sharp, 13-month experience of adapting *The Beckett Trilogy* for the BBC have a longer lasting impact upon his writing? As noted at the outset of this essay, Beckett had, to some degree at least, run short on creative steam in the wake of his 'siege in the room'. To this end, reported in his well-known interview with Gabriel d'Aubarède, Beckett was quoted as lamenting: '"Malone" grew out of "Molloy", "The Unnamable" out of "Malone", but afterwards—and for a long time—I wasn't at all sure what I had left to say. I'd hemmed myself in.'[47]

One way out, of course, was returning to composing in English, which Beckett properly recommenced in the later 1950s: translating *The Unnamable* from French, writing *All That Fall* and *Embers* as well as *Krapp's Last Tape*; and of course, working on BBC adaptations of *The Beckett Trilogy*. As suggested above in the case of *Krapp's Last Tape*, that these undertakings overlapped, and even reinforced each other between later 1956 and early 1959, is scarcely coincidental. Even if initially only to leverage himself out of the artistic rut in which he found himself after the *Texts for Nothing* and *Endgame*, this outpouring of collaborative creativity—itself directly leading to the breakthrough works from the early 1960s *Comment c'est* and *Play*—with the BBC seems to have contributed to something of a second 'great spurt of enthusiasm' for Beckett at this time.[48]

Finally, Beckett's embrace of radiogenic writing and adaption likely had a more residual, long-standing effect upon his poetics as well. Whether this residua was significant in his 'mature work' is a matter for future debate. And while such a rethinking is necessarily at an early stage given the extensive, and extensively neglected, Beckett materials held by the BBC Written Archives Centre, it remains intriguing to consider the role played by the Third Programme in Beckett's growing embrace of those 'fundamental sounds' he felt so characterised his work.

Without doubt, the BBC broadcasts of *The Beckett Trilogy* contributed to a more general rethinking in Beckett's experimentalism, whether evidenced in the opening couplet from *How It Is* ('how it is three parts I say it as I hear it'[49]), or indeed the much later, spectral texts like 'For To End Yet Again' in the mid-1970s *Fizzles* ('for to end yet again by degrees or as though switched on dark falls there again that certain dark').[50] Both prose texts, incidentally, were also adapted to radio by the BBC—the latter, according to the 19 August 1976 production details, another 'first publication' of a Beckett text on the radio. In this way, the especially 'sonorous' nature of Beckett's later work owes a debt of as-yet inestimable measure to his extensive collaboration and work with the BBC. At the zenith of this intimate association, during the late 1950s, Beckett's own 'revisiting' of *The Beckett Trilogy* for the Third Programme surely played a part in what Steven Matthews has termed the development of 'Beckett's late style', exemplified by his French *mirlitonnades* poems.[51] Tracing out these connections, especially through empirical approaches to Beckett's engagement with radio, thus holds out the promise of new interpretations of those later, disembodied voices, transmitted 'to one in the dark. Imagine.'[52]

APPENDIX:
THE BECKETT TRILOGY ON THE THIRD:

Amendments and Music

NB: All three programmes produced by Donald McWhinnie and spoken by Patrick Magee, with originally scored music by Samuel Beckett's cousin, John Beckett. The conductor for Molloy *was Bertold Goldschmidt and for* Malone Dies *and* The Unnamable *was Bernard Keeffe.*

An Extract from Molloy *(59'14")*

This reading aired on the Third Programme on Tuesday, 10 December 1957, at 9:45—10:45 pm, and was repeated on Friday, 13 December 1957, at 8:15—9:15 p.m. The text corresponds to pages 77–93 of the 2009 Faber edition.

> Announcer:
> This is the BBC Third Programme. This week we are broadcasting two readings form the work of Samuel Beckett. Tonight's reading is an extract from his novel "Molloy" which has been translated from the French by Patrick Bowles in collaboration with the author. It is spoken by Patrick Magee, with music by John Beckett.
> Musical Introduction
> p.77, line 16: *And now my progress…*
> p.78, line 19: *…I'm lost, no matter.*
> Musical Interlude
> p.78, line 20: *If I could event have bent it…*
> p.78, line 24: *…when it was stiff.*
> Musical Interlude
> p.78, line 24: *I was therefore compelled…*
> p.79, line 1: *…I don't know.*
> Musical Interlude
> p.79, lines 1–2: *In any case the ways…*
> p.79, lines 30–31: *…my leg, my legs.*
> Musical Interlude
> p.79, line 31: *But the thought of suicide…*
> p.80, line 3: *…I could have counted them.*
> Musical Interlude
> p.80, line 3: *Ah yes, my asthma…*
> p.80, lines 11–12: *…leaden above infernal depths.*
> Musical Interlude
> p.80, line 12: *Not a word, not a word…*
> p.81, line 27: *…till I think.*
> Musical Interlude
> p.81, lines 27–28: *But you are right, that wasn't…*
> p.82, line 10: *…a fat lot of good that ever did me.*

Musical Interlude
p.82, line 10–11: *The heart beats, and what a beat.*
Musical Interlude
p.82, line 11: *That my ureters—no, not a word on that…*
p.82, line 13: *…the glans. Santa Maria.*
Musical Interlude
p.82, line 13: *If I give you my word, I cannot piss…*
p.82, line 22: *…if there was any justice in the world.*
Musical Interlude
p.82, line 22: *And this list of my weak points…*
p.83, lines 24–25: *…committing me to nothing.*
Musical Interlude
p.83, line 25: *But I was saying that if my progress…*
p.84, lines 26–27: *…there's something shady about it.*
Musical Interlude
p.84, line 27: *I had a certain number of encounters…*
p.85, line 6: *…total stranger. Sick with solitude probably.*
Musical Interlude
p.85, lines 6–7: *I say charcoal-burner…*
p.85, line 33: *…I can tell you. Take it or leave it.*
Musical Interlude
p.85, line 33: *Or I didn't press them…*
p.86, lines 18–19: *…like all that has a moral.*
Musical Interlude
p.86, line 19: *But I did at least eat…*
p.87, line 21: *…I was there.*
Musical Interlude
p.87, line 21: *And being there I did not have to go…*
p.89, line 5: *…seeking the way to her house.*
Musical Interlude
p.89, line 5: *This is taking a queer…*
p.90, lines 19–20: *…were it but a bower.*
Musical Interlude
p.90, line 20: *It was winter, it must have been winter…*
p.90, line 35: *…my trunk? And my head.*
Musical Interlude
p.90, line 36: *But before I go on…*
p.91, line 16: *…my bicycle. When. I don't know.*
Musical Interlude
p.91, lines 16–17: *And now, let us have done. Flat on my belly…*
p.92, line 2: *…to encourage me I suppose.*
Musical Interlude
p.92, line 2: *I kept losing my hat…*
p.92, lines 12–13: *…day and night, towards my mother.*

> Musical Interlude
> p.92, line 13: *And true enough the day came...*
> p. 93, lines 9–10: *...down to the bottom of the ditch.*
> Musical Interlude
> p.93, lines 10 to end of "*Molloy*, Part I": *It must have been spring...*
> End of extract—musical fade out
>
> Closing Announcement:
> That was an extract from "Molloy", the first of two readings, spoken by Patrick Magee, from the work of Samuel Beckett. "Molloy" was translated from the French by Patrick Bowles in collaboration with the Author. The music was composed by John Beckett and composed by Berthold Goldschmidt. The production was by Donald McWhinnie. This programme can be heard again on Friday at quarter past eight. The second reading, which is of a published meditation, "From An Abandoned Work", will be broadcast Saturday at a quarter to nine.

An Extract from **Malone Dies** *(71'38")*

This reading was aired on the Third Programme on Wednesday, 18 June 1958, at 9:00 pm—10:15 pm, and repeated the next day at 9:30—10:45 pm. The text corresponds to pages 3–24 of the 2009 Faber edition.

> Musical Introduction
> First paragraph of *Malone Dies* (to p. 4, line 12: *Enough for this evening.*)
> Musical Interlude
> p.4, line 12: *This time I know where I am going...*
> p.6, line 30: *...a great mistake. No matter.*
> Musical Interlude
> p.6, line 31: *Present state. This room seems...*
> p.6, line 32: *...left in it. All this time.*
> BBC excision from Samuel Beckett's script: p.6, line 32: *Unless it be...* to p.8, line 1: *...before I am avenged.*
> p.8, line 1: *It is an ordinary room. I have little...*
> p.10, line 7: *...clears my little table.*
> BBC excision from Samuel Beckett's script: p.10, line 7: *I don't know how long I have been here...* to p.10, line 17: *...whole days have flown.*
> p.10, line 17: *Does anything remain to be...*
> p.11, line 4: *...would seem to be my present state.*
> Musical Interlude
> p.11, line 5: *The man's name is Saposcat. Like his...*
> p.14, lines 12–13: *...nothing to signify. I can go on.*
> Musical Interlude
> p. 14, line 14: *Sapo had no friends—no, that won't do.*
> Musical Interlude
> p.14, line 15: *Sapo was on good terms with his little friends...*
> p.14, line 33: *...then suddenly bursts and drowns everything.*

Musical Interlude
p.15, line 1: *I have not been able to find out why Sapo...*
p.15, line 10: *...best I can do.*
Musical Interlude
p.15, line 11: *At the age of fourteen he was a plump...*
p.15, line 26: *...a shade lighter, said Mrs. Saposcat.*
Musical Interlude
p.15, line 27: *Sapo loved nature, took an...*
p.16, lines 12–13: *...of pride, of patience and solitude.*
Musical Interlude
p.16, lines 14–15: *I shall not give up yet. I have finished my soup and sent back the little table to its place by the door.*
BBC excision from Samuel Beckett's script: p.16, line 15: *A light has just gone on...* to p.16, line 24: *...not yet come home. Home.*
p.16, line 24: *I have demanded certain...*
p.17, lines 4–5: *...by clear and endurable ways.*
Musical Interlude
p.17, line 6: *Sapo's phlegm, his silent ways, were not of a nature...*
p.17, line 21: *...a little rest, for safety's sake.*
Musical Interlude
p.17, line 22: *I don't like those gull's eyes. They remind me...*
p. 17, 27–28: *...I am on my guard now.*
Musical Interlude
p.17, line 29: *Then he was sorry he had not learnt the art of thinking...*
p.18, line 20: *...Adrian, you have hurt his feelings!*
Musical Interlude
p.18, line 21: *We are getting on. Nothing is less like me...*
p.19, line 8: *I succeed in being another. Very pretty.*
BBC excision from Samuel Beckett's script: p.19, line 9: *The summer holidays. In the morning...* to p.19, line 20: *...the impending dawn. The impending dawn.*
p.19, line 21: *I fell asleep. But I do not want to...*
p.21, line 5: *...other eyes close. What an end.*
Musical Interlude
p.21, line 6: *The market. He inadequacy of the exchanges...*
p.21, line 10: *...no, I can't do it.*
Musical Interlude
p.21, line 11: *The peasants. His visits...*
p.21, line 18: *...a choice of images.*
Musical Interlude
p.21, line 19: *I have rummaged a little in my things...*
p.24, line 33: *...again. Just once again. No, I want nothing.*
End of extract—musical fade out

Extract not recorded but included in *Malone Dies* script:
p.49, line 3: *What a misfortune, the pencil must have slipped...*
p.52, line 15: *...what my prayer should be nor to whom.*

The Unnamable: *Extracts from the novel by Samuel Beckett (60'51")*

This reading was aired on the Third Programme on Monday, 19 January 1959, at 8:35—9:35 pm, and repeated on Tuesday, 10 February 1959, at 9:45—10:45 pm. The text corresponds to pages 1–134 of the 2010 Faber edition.

> Musical Introduction
> First paragraph of *The Unnamable* (to p. 1, lines 27–28: *...never be silent. Never.*)
> Musical Interlude [?]
> p.1, line 17: *...Malone is there. Of his mortal liveliness...*
> p.5, lines 31–32: *...to be feared, incomprehensible uneasiness.*
> Musical Interlude [?]
> p.7, line 26: *Why did I have myself represented in the midst of men...*
> p.8, lines 35–26: *...dealt me these insignificant wounds.*
> Musical Interlude [?]
> p.14, line 6: *All these Murphys, Molloys and Malones...*
> p.14, line 34: *...no more about them.*
> Musical Interlude [?]
> p.37, line 31: *But it's entirely a matter of voices, no other metaphor...*
> p.41, line 31: *...no other spiritual nourishment.*
> Musical Interlude [?]
> p.62, line 21–22: *Ah if I could only find a voice of my own...*
> p.63, line 3: *...you could see the ventriloquist.*
> Musical Interlude [?]
> p.92, line 33: *As far as I personally am concerned...*
> p.95, line 4: *...depart, with an easy mind.*
> Musical Interlude [?]
> p.114, line 29: *Yes, in my life, since we must call it so...*
> p.117, line 2–3: *...who never made my acquaintance*[.]
> Musical Interlude [?]
> p.119, line 6: *Look at this Tunis pink...*
> p.120, line 27: *...every particle of its dust, it's impossible.*
> Musical Interlude [?]
> p.123, line 5–6: [O]ur *concern is with something, now we're getting it...*
> p.124, line 6–7: *...those gifts that can't be acquired.*
> Musical Interlude [?]
> p.132, line 19: [A]ll *these stories about travellers, these stories...*to end of novel
> Musical fade out [?]

NOTES

1. Samuel Beckett to Alan Schneider, 29 December 1957, cited in Maurice Harmon, ed., *No Author Better Served: The Correspondence of Alan Schneider and Samuel Beckett* (London: Harvard University Press, 1998), p. 24.
2. For chronological details of these productions, see John Pilling, *A Samuel Beckett Chronology* (Basingstoke: Palgrave, 2006), 132ff.
3. Anthony Cronin, *Samuel Beckett: The Last Modernist* (London: Flamingo, 1997), pp. 458, 474.
4. James Knowlson, *Damned to Fame: The Life of Samuel Beckett* (London: Bloomsbury, 1996), p. 431.
5. Deirdre Bair, *Samuel Beckett: A Biography* (London: Vintage, 1978), p. 519.
6. *Ibid.*, p. 555.
7. Robert Wilcher, "'Out of the Dark': Beckett's Texts for Radio'", in *Beckett's Later Fiction and Drama: Texts for Company*, eds. James Acheson and Arthur Katernyna (Basingstoke: MacMillan, 1987), p. 1.
8. For further discussion, see ch. 7.
9. Claus Zilliacus, *Beckett and Broadcasting: A Study of the Works of Samuel Beckett For and In Radio and Television* (Åbo: Åbo Akademi, 1976), pp. 208, 148.
10. *Ibid.*, p. 149.
11. See Julie Campbell, 'Beckett and the Third Programme', in *Samuel Beckett Today / Aujourd'hui* 25 (2013), p. 114.
12. BBC Audience Research Report for *Molloy* and 'From an Abandoned Work', in 'Samuel Beckett, Scriptwriter: 1953–1962', BBC Written Archives Centre, Caversham.
13. *Ibid.*
14. Beckett to Donald McWhinnie, 7 May 1957, in *ibid.*
15. McWhinnie to Beckett, 16 May 1957, in *ibid.*
16. McWhinnie to Beckett, 26 June 1957, in *ibid.*
17. Beckett to McWhinnie, 30 June 1957, in *ibid.*
18. McWhinnie to Beckett, 3 July 1957 1957, in *ibid.*
19. BBC Copyright Department, internal BBC memorandum, 19 August 1957, in *ibid.*
20. McWhinnie to Beckett, 6 September 1957, in *ibid.*
21. McWhinnie to Beckett, 13 September 1957, in *ibid.*
22. McWhinnie to Beckett, 22 November 1957, in *ibid.*
23. Samuel Beckett, *Molloy*, ed. Shane Weller (London: Faber, 2009a), p. 82, lines 10–11.
24. Knowlson, *Damned to Fame*, p. 444.
25. McWhinnie to Beckett, 31 December 1957, in 'Samuel Beckett, Scriptwriter: 1953–1962'.
26. Roy Walker, 'In the Rut', in *The Listener* 58 (1957), p. 1048.
27. Donald McWhinnie, internal BBC memorandum, 18 February 1958, in 'Samuel Beckett, Scriptwriter: 1953–1962'.
28. Donald McWhinnie, internal BBC memorandum, 26 March 1958, in *ibid.*
29. McWhinnie to Beckett, 20 February 1958, in *ibid.*
30. Beckett to McWhinnie, 26 February 1958, in *ibid.*
31. McWhinnie to Beckett, 4 March 1958, in *ibid.*
32. Beckett to McWhinnie, 7 March 1958, in *ibid.*
33. Zilliacus, *Beckett and Broadcasting*, p. 148.

34 Patrick Bowles, 'How Samuel Beckett Sees the Universe: Patrick Bowles on "Molloy"', in *The Listener* 59 (1958), p. 1011.
35 BBC Production Details for extracts from Samuel Beckett's *Malone Dies*, produced by Donald McWhinnie, 18 June 1958 (repeated 19 June 1958), in the 'Play Library' collection, BBC Written Archives Centre, Caversham.
36 Knowlson, *Damned to Fame*, pp. 448–52.
37 McWhinnie to Beckett, 16 June 1958, in *ibid.*
38 McWhinnie to John Calder, 15 October 1958, in *ibid.*
39 Pamela Lyon to McWhinnie, 21 October 1958, in *ibid.*
40 BBC Production Details for extracts from Samuel Beckett's *The Unnamable*, produced by Donald McWhinnie, 19 January (repeated 10 February) 1959, in the 'Play Library' collection, BBC Written Archives Centre, Caversham.
41 Beckett to Barbara Bray, 17 November 1958, *The Letters of Samuel Beckett, 1957-1965: Volume 3,* eds. George Craig, Martha Dow Fehsenfeld, Dann Gunn and Lois More Overbeck (Cambridge: Cambridge University Press, 2014), p. 174.
42 Samuel Beckett, *The Unnamable*, ed. Steven Connor (London: Faber, 2010a), p. 14.
43 *Ibid.*, pp. 37–8.
44 *Ibid.*, pp. 63–4.
45 *Ibid.*, pp. 134, 132.
46 Pilling, *A Samuel Beckett Chronology*, pp. 143–6.
47 Beckett to Gabriel D'Auberede, cited in Lawrence Graver and Raymond Federman, eds., *Samuel Beckett: The Critical Heritage* (London: Routledge, 1997), p. 239.
48 *Ibid.*
49 Samuel Beckett, *How It Is* (London: Calder, 1996), p. 7.
50 Samuel Beckett, 'For To End Yet Again', in Beckett, *The Complete Short Prose, 1929-1989*, ed. S.E. Gontarski (New York: Grove Press, 1995), p. 269
51 Steven Matthews, 'Beckett's Late Style', in *Beckett and Death*, eds. Steven Barfield, Matthew Feldman and Philip Tew (London: Continuum, 2009), p. 202.
52 Samuel Beckett, *Molloy*, p. 3.

SAMUEL BECKETT, WILHELM WINDELBAND AND THE INTERWAR "PHILOSOPHY NOTES"

with David Addyman

§1

Between the years 1932 and 1938 Samuel Beckett went through an extensive process of self-education, taking notes on psychology, art history, the history of German and English literatures, Irish and European history—in addition to notes on specific writers as divergent as Dante and d'Annunzio, Mauthner and Mistral, Augustine and Ariosto. Despite protestations later in his life that he neither read nor understood philosophy, far and away the largest portion of these extant 'Interwar Notes', however, are the 267 folios, mostly handwritten recto and verso notebook pages, comprising Beckett's so-called 'Philosophy Notes.'[1] These roughly five hundred sides of typed and handwritten reading notes derive from 1932 and 1933—likely around the time Beckett was converting his abortive novel, *Dream of Fair to Middling Women*, into the short stories *More Pricks Than Kicks* (published 1934). In turn, Beckett's 'Philosophy Notes' were taken from four main sources: J. Archibald Alexander's 1907 *A Short History of Philosophy*; John Burnet's 1914 *Greek Philosophy, Part I: Thales to Plato*; Friedrich Ueberweg's *A History of Philosophy, from Thales to the Present Time*; and Wilhelm Windelband's *A History of Philosophy*.[2]

Amongst these authors, Beckett's engagement with, and subsequent employment of, Wilhelm Windelband was far and away the most profound. In fact, many of those frequently recognized as 'Beckettian' philosophers—Arnold Geulincx, George Berkeley, and Gottfried Leibniz, amongst others—were actually first encountered by Beckett in the revised, second edition of *A History of Philosophy* from 1901. It is from here, for example, that much of the key imagery in Beckett's first novel from 1935–36 (published 1938), *Murphy*, is drawn, even extending to the oft-cited epigraph on Murphy's mind, heading Chapter 6.[3] Furthermore, while Beckett used all four sources for notes on Ancient Greek philosophy, covering his first 109 folios, *A History of Philosophy* is most frequently in evidence. More significant still, though, is that final 157 folios are derived solely from Windelband; that is, the remaining 1,600 years of Western philosophy in the 'Philosophy Notes' are mediated solely by *A History of Philosophy*. Put another way, this volume accounts for more than three-quarters of the entire 'Philosophy

Notes', which itself may be considered a tale of two halves: one, a mosaic of Ancient Greek thinking, deriving from several secondary texts; and two, Beckett's summary of Windelband's summary of the tenets and systems ostensibly governing Western philosophy thereafter.

That said, this quantitative survey of the 'Philosophy Notes' should not be taken as indicative of Beckett's wholesale and wholehearted acceptance of Windelband's views on the history of Western philosophy. Far from it: in his encounter with this *A History of Philosophy*—in which Windelband's philosophical views are writ large—Beckett's note-taking is shrewdly selective. Since nothing has been written on Windelband in Beckett studies to date (no less than Burnet, Alexander and Ueberweg), however, the nature of Beckett's composition of the notes has never been made apparent. This chapter therefore examines Beckett's approach to these 'Philosophy Notes'—with especial focus on Wilhelm Windelband; a new candidate for 'canonical' status amongst 'Beckettian' philosophers—particularly in terms of precisely what Beckett writes down, and equally importantly, that which he omits.

§2

At first sight the idea that Beckett makes the notes his own—that, crucially (if the 'Philosophy Notes' are to be seen as a Beckettian text at all) he may be said to actually author them—is not apparent. His note-taking is oftentimes quite slavish. On the Ancient Greeks, for example, many of Beckett's reading notes are closely summarized or copied nearly verbatim from his sources; this is not just the case for the notes from Windelband but for those from Burnet too (and to a far lesser extent, for entries from Alexander and Ueberweg). One example from perhaps 120,000 words comprising the 'Philosophy Notes' is the following (elements found in Windelband but not in Beckett's notes are indicated by square brackets):

> In forming a conception of [the] Sophistic doctrine we have to contend with the difficulty that we are made acquainted with them almost exclusively through their victorious opponents[,] Plato and Aristotle. The first has given in the <u>Protagoras</u> a [graceful,] lively delineation of a Sophist congress, [redolent with fine irony,] in the <u>Gorgias</u> a more earnest, in the <u>Theaetetus</u> a sharper criticism, and in the <u>Cratylus</u> and <u>Euthydemus</u> supercilious satire of the Sophists' methods of teaching. In the dialogue the <u>Sophist</u>[,] to which Plato's name is attached, an extremely malicious definition of the theories of the Sophists is attempted, and Aristotle reaches the same result in the book on the fallacies of the Sophists.[4]

While the near-verbatim transcription above becomes less frequent and gives way to greater paraphrasing as Beckett progresses through *A History of Philosophy*, there is very little by way of interpolation throughout. Windelband's brief discussion of Arnold Geulincx—representing Beckett's first introduction to the post-Cartesian occasionalist philosopher—provides a rare example of Beckett's textual intervention:

> This furthest developed in Ethics of Geulincx. Illustration of the 2 Clocks which having once been synchronised by same artificer continue to move in perfect harmony, "absque ulla causalitate qua alterum hoc in altero causat, sed propter meram dependentiam, qua utrumque ab eadem arte et simili industria constitutum est".
> What anthropologism![5]

Rather than providing a running commentary, more characteristic are Beckett's notes on the Sophists and Protagoras. Here, over eleven pages Beckett's only insertion are the words 'Et alors' in the following passage (where the original reads 'What then?'):

> [Protagoras] is said to have met Zeno at Athens, when problem of continuity was discussed:
>
> Z [Zeno]: Tell me, P [Protagoras], does a single grain of millet, or ten thousandth part of one, make a noise in falling?
> P: No.
> Z: Does a bushel of millet make a noise in falling?
> P: Yes.
> Z: Et alors ... Is there not a ration of a bushel of millet to 1 grain and ten thousandth of 1 grain [?]
> P: Yes.
> Z: Then will not the sounds leave the same ratio? As the sounding objects to one another, so the sounds. There if the bushel makes a noise, the grain and ten thousandth grain will make a noise.

Parenthetically, and in keeping with the more veiled allusions to Beckett's earlier process of didacticism in his s post-war work, this image provides the opening line from the 1958 *Endgame*: 'Finished, it's finished, nearly finished, it must be nearly finished. [Pause.] Grain upon grain, one by one, and one day, suddenly, there's a heap, a little heap, the impossible heap.'[6] Similarly, the 1946 *Mercier and Camier* expresses this Sophist paradox as 'every millet grain that falls, you look behind and there you are, every day a little closer, all life a little closer'.[7]

Furthermore, Beckett does not merely copy slavishly from his sources. In fact, he carefully edits them. For instance, Beckett omits many passages where the views of one of his chosen authors are at odds with his. From this vantage point, Beckett's input into the composition of the 'Philosophy Notes' is just as revealing in terms of what he leaves out as what is included. In characteristic fashion, Beckett appears as an absence in the notes. The most repeated prominent example of this concerns Beckett's systematic purging of Windelband's interpretative commentary in *A History of Philosophy*. While, as shown above, it is an exaggeration to claim that the 'Philosophy Notes' contain no Beckett, in terms of philosophical values they certainly contain no Windelband. Indeed, it is perhaps symptomatic that Windelband's name never appears in Beckett's published texts or letters. A very rare reference to the 'Philosophy Notes', made in a letter to Alan Schneider of 21 November 1957, underlines the manner in which Beckett makes the notes his own—quite literally in this case:

> I can't find my notes on the pre-Socratics. The arguments of the Heap and the Bald Head (which hair falling produces baldness) were used by all the Sophists and I think have been variously attributed to one or the other. They disprove the reality of mass in the same way and by means of the same fallacy as the arguments of the Arrow and Achilles and the Tortoise, invented a century earlier by Zeno the Eleatic, disprove the reality of movement. The leading Sophist, against whom Plato wrote his Dialogue, was Protagoras and he is probably the "old Greek" whose name Hamm can't remember. One purpose of the image throughout the play is to suggest the impossibility logically, i.e. eristically, of the "thing" ever coming to an end.[8]

It is telling her that Beckett claims that 'I can't find *my* notes', rather than, say, 'I can't find the notes I took from Windelband'—despite the fact that the imagery is taken from the latter's work. The figures of the Heap and the Bald Head, for example, come *A History of Philosophy*, while the word 'eristically' appears in the noun form on the same page of Windelband's work (but in none of the other sources that Beckett used).[9] Before looking in more detail at how Beckett purges *A History of Philosophy* of Windelband, it is worth looking at what he might have found objectionable in the latter's account of that Western philosophy. To do so, it is necessary to say a little more about the life, work and context of this once-famous German philosopher.

§3

Wilhelm Windelband was born in 1848, at a point when philosophy in Germany was at its lowest ebb—a significant factor, as will be seen, in the composition of *A History of Philosophy*. Nevertheless, he had gained a PhD. in philosophy by the age of 22, though his career was to be interrupted by the Franco-Prussian war, for which he received a commission. After that war he took his *Habilitation* at Leipzig in 1873, and was subsequently appointed lecturer in that city. He also taught at Zurich and Freiburg before moving in 1882 to the then-German University of Strasbourg, where he was appointed Rector in 1892. His final post was at Heidelberg (1903), where Windelband died in 1915. At the last two universities, Windelband made his reputation as a philosopher in his own right, even if he is largely remembered today as the author of *Geschichte der Philosophie*. Frederick

Copleston, for example, in his 1963 synthesis, *A History of Philosophy: Eighteenth- and Nineteenth-Century German Philosophy*, introduces Windelband as 'the well-known historian of philosophy', but devotes less than two pages to his actual thought.[10]

Nonetheless, at the turn of the century, Windelband was a key figure in the neo-Kantian movement then dominating academic philosophy—*Schulphilosophie*—in Germany at the time, with most university chairs being occupied by representatives of the movement. The neo-Kantians were broadly divided into two camps, the Marburg and Baden (also called Southwest German) Schools, and Windelband was long the acknowledged leader of the second. While the Marburg School focused on logical, epistemological and methodological themes, for the latter—and for Windelband in particular—the key question for fin de siècle Western philosophy centred upon the demarcation between the natural and the cultural sciences, most urgently where this related to a philosophy of values.[11]

At this time, academic philosophy was fighting a rearguard action against the seemingly-irresistible rise of the materialist sciences in nineteenth-century Europe (ranging from Darwinian biology to Rankean history), which threatened to obviate the very discipline of philosophy itself. As Windelband had it: 'In the nineteenth century, a certain paralysis of the philosophical impulse set in.'[12] Traditional philosophical debates (such as the relation of body to mind) were increasingly held by to be translatable into technical problems that were pragmatically solved by the empirical sciences. Philosophy, it was argued at this time, had reached its peak with positivism and in doing so, had effectively rendered itself redundant. Where it was studied at all, it was approached from a historical perspective as a catalogue of curiosities; there was no belief in philosophy's ability to offer transcendental norms, because there was no interest in transcendental norms in any of the sciences. Amidst this nadir of Western philosophy, Windelband lamented: 'Philosophy is like King Lear, who has bequeathed all his goods to his children, and who must now resign himself to be thrown into the street like a beggar.'[13]

To rectify this parlous state of affairs—which would ultimately throw academic philosophers onto the street, one assumes—it was vital for Windelband and the other Baden neo-Kantians to redefine the parameters of philosophy, and to defend the discipline as a rightly autonomous one. In his 1894 Rectorial Address—delivered at the University of Strasbourg, and formally entitled 'History and Natural Science'—Windelband outlined his philosophical position as an epistemological inquiry into 'the relationship of the general to the particular'.[14] For him, the proper role of philosophy was to *evaluate* and—above all—*critique* the first principles and knowledge claims made by the newly-independent, materialist disciplines. As Windelband's Rectorial Address was given just as *A History of Philosophy* was being translated by James Tufts, this important lecture offers a good indication of Windelband's thought at the time of composing the work that Beckett read so closely.

Windelband's contribution to the firestorm engulfing philosophy in Germany was to argue that the proper terrain of Western philosophy was knowledge claims. As such, any discipline dealing in the acquisition of knowledge—for him, history and psychology in particular—was necessarily involved in philosophical inquiry; it was thus fair game for philosophical criticism. In this way, Windelband began his address by acknowledging the two fashionable routes of discourse open to him:

> the philosopher might well be tempted to provide nothing more than an historical sketch of some aspect of his discipline. Or he might take refuge in the specialized empirical science which the existing academic customs and dispositions still persist in assigning to him: psychology.

However, rejects both options, claiming 'I shall not employ either of these routes of escape. I do not propose to lend credence to the view that philosophy no longer exists, but only its history.'[15]

In setting out a different stall, Windelband then considers differences between the natural and cultural sciences. The first is concerned with the form that remains constant; and the second, vital to the study of history in particular, was the unique, real event. This distinction is used to introduce the now-familiar separation of 'nomothetic' and 'idiographic' methodologies:

> One kind of science is an inquiry into general laws. The other kind of science is an inquiry into specific historical facts. In the language of formal logic, the objective of the first kind of science is the general, apodictic judgment; the objective of the other kind of science is the singular, assertoric proposition. Thus this distinction connects with the most important and crucial relationship in the human understanding, the relationship which Socrates recognized as the fundamental nexus of all scientific thought: the relationship of the general [nomothetic] to the particular [idiographic].[16]

Windelband goes on to complicate this picture, however, by arguing that the two approaches cannot be so easily separated—either from each other or from philosophy more generally. Both make judgments of value. Windelband argues that, for all its focus on one-off events, history remains intrinsically concerned with value. It is not in the practice of listing *every* fact, but only those considered important within the discipline's (and society's) value-system: The facts selected are a result from a priori, even transcendental, judgments of value. Windelband offers the following example to illustrate his point:

> In the year 1780, Goethe had a door bell and an apartment key made. On February 22 of the same year, he had a letter case made. Of this there is documentary proof in a locksmith's bill. Hence it is completely true and certain to have happened. Nevertheless it is not an historical fact, neither a fact of literary history nor of biography.[17]

Philosophy is thus the ground for the other sciences, insofar as the former critiques the assumptions underlying the latter. As Frederick C. Beiser holds with respect to the issue of this neo-Kantian 'normativity':

> Philosophy could only retain its identity as a distinct discipline, and it could still be a science, Windelband argued, if it only became what Kant had originally conceived it to be: namely, a critical philosophy, i.e. an investigations into the conditions and limits of the fist principles of knowledge. All the special sciences, morality and the arts, presuppose first principles that they cannot investigate; and the defining task of philosophy should be to investigate just such principles. Philosophy thus retains its validity, albeit as a *second-order* science, whose role is precisely to examine the logic of first-order sciences.[18]

Value was to be philosophy's currency, critique its method of exchange. In this way, Windelband tasked philosophy to concern itself with the value-dependent claims of the other sciences. Philosophy could thus remain both independent of (and implicitly superior to), the new forms of knowledge knocking at the door of fin de siècle German *Wissenschaft*. In the final analysis, then, Windelband not only helped to rescue philosophy, he did so by reasserting the transcendental, absolute standards of thought.

Consequently, Windelband viewed norms as the 'central concept of the critical philosophy';[19] in fact, as he claimed elsewhere, philosophy itself was nothing more than 'a system of norms'.[20] And so, Windelband's normative critical philosophy, his neo-Kantianism of the south-western German variety in particular, was to form the bedrock of a 'critical science of universally-valid values'.[21] For Windelband, who understood philosophy to be a 'critical science of values', he meant, in Philip J. Swoboda's words, 'that the philosopher does not invent or promulgate norms; he merely attempts to separate out of the mass of evaluative judgments actually made by individuals and societies over the course of history those which enjoy the sanction of the "normal consciousness."'[22] For the remainder of his life, Windelband went on to investigate the relation between the individual bearer of values on the one hand, and the transcendent sphere in which these values were held to derive on the other.

§4

In this context, *A History of Philosophy* was hardly a neutral account of its subject. Indeed, the book's subtitle gives a clue to its partisanship: *with especial reference to the formation of development of its problems and conceptions*: this will be no mere 'historical sketch of some aspect of [the] discipline', but one which lays its emphasis on philosophy as an organic whole, and one whose conceptions were very much still relevant at the time. There is subtle, supporting evidence of Windelband's interests in the preface to the first edition:

> The choice of material has fallen everywhere on what individual thinkers have produced that was new and fruitful, while purely individual turns of thought, which may indeed be a welcome object for learned research, but afford no philosophical interest, have found at most a brief mention.[23]

As Windelband maintains, this is immediately apparent in the 'external form' of the book, with sections devoted to concepts rather than thinkers; examples here include sections like 'Authority and Revelation', 'The Dualism of Body and Soul', and 'The Problem of Civilisation'. On the preface's next page, he makes a bold statement on the value of philosophy (also not recorded by Beckett): 'To understand this as a connected and interrelated whole has been my chief purpose'; it is out of the development of philosophical thought that 'our theory of the world and life has grown'. Presumably history and psychology, as well as the argument that philosophy is no longer valid—'our theory of the life and world'—are all themselves held to be derived from the achievements of philosophy. Windelband then announces his bias in favour of Ancient Greek thought (albeit only certain brands of it) and the work of Immanuel Kant: 'for a historical understanding of our intellectual existence, the forging out of the conceptions which the Greek mind wrested from the concrete reality found in Nature and human life, is more important than all that has since been thought—the Kantian philosophy excepted'.[24]

Given Windelband's neo-Kantian exposition of values, *A History of Philosophy* may seem an odd choice for Beckett who, in a conversation with Charles Juliet, commented, 'Negation is no more possible than affirmation. It is absurd to say that something is absurd. *That's still a value judgment.* It is impossible to protest, and equally impossible to assent.'[25] Although this conversation took place three decades after the composition of the 'Philosophy Notes', Beckett's comments illustrate an attitude towards 'normative values' that is nonetheless discernible in the notes themselves.

As early as his preface to the first edition of *A History of Philosophy*, Windelband announces: 'The philosopher's own expositions [...] have been referred to in the main, only when they afford a permanently valuable formulation or rationale of thoughts.'[26] This leaves a good degree of interpretation for Windelband's ideas to pervade his philosophical synthesis, right down to the manner in which specific thinkers are treated—as may be expected given his rejection of the positivist historical approach to philosophy. In contrast, a handful of years after finishing his 'Philosophy Notes', Beckett wrote, in a memorable entry in his 'German Diary' of 15 January 1937, that what he wanted was the 'straws, flotsam, etc., names, dates, births and deaths' of specific, individual lives.[27] How were Windelband's 'normativity' and Beckett's 'nominalism' (of which more below), then, to be squared?

First of all, the second edition of *A History of Philosophy* includes far more of what might be considered 'straws, flotsam, etc' than its earlier incarnation. In the author's preface to the second edition, Windelband indicates that some new sections have been included, seemingly reluctantly: 'A desire has been expressed by readers of the book for a more extended notice of the personalities and personal relations of the philosophers.' His apologia for not doing so in the first edition was 'because of the special plan' of his work, this had been rectified a decade later: 'Now I have sought to fulfill this demand so far as it has seemed possible *within the limit of my work*, but giving *brief and precise* characterizations of the most important thinkers.'[28] The concessionary material is included in most chapters in smaller font, between a general overview of each period and a more detailed look at 'its problems and concepts'. There appears to have been little attempt to integrate this 'flotsam' and 'jetsam', however, and it often duplicates content from the preceding or following sections. It sticks out like a proverbial sore thumb.

Yet these are very often the entries which interest Beckett most, and from which he takes the closest notes. One excerpt from the 'Philosophy of the Renaissance' makes this clear:

> Main seat of Platonism was Florentian academy, founded by Cosimo de' Medici' [sic]. Impulse for this given by Georgius Gemistus Pletho (1355–1450) author of numerous commentaries & of a treatise in Greek on the difference between Plato and Aristotle.
> Bessarion (born 1403 Trebizond–d. 1472 Cardinal at Ravenna). Pupil of above. His main treatise: Adversus Calumniatorem Platonis (Rome, 1409).
> Most important members of the Platonic circle: Marsilio Ficino (1433–99). Translator of Plato & Plotinus & author of Theologia Platonica (Flor, 1482), & Francesco Patrizzi (1529–97) author of Nova de Universis Philosophia (Ferrara 1591). Giovanni Pico della Mirandola (1463–94) Neo-Platonism alloyed with Neo-Pythagorean & ancient Pythagorean motives.[29]

Beckett's 'Philosophy Notes' are therefore much less an account of 'the formation and development of [philosophy's] concepts' than a list of the 'straws, flotsam, etc'. Yet if Windelband has reluctantly incorporated this biographical material, Beckett happily imports even more of it, through his weaving of other sources into and between his notes from Windelband. Thus, when Windelband is discussing the implications of Protagoras's aforementioned dictum—'man is the measure'—and specifically discussing them in relation to *value*,[30] Beckett abandons *A History of Philosophy* and switches to Burnet, turning not to the latter's own section on 'Man is the measure', but to the opening of the chapter, where he finds and records biographical facts:

> He legislated for Thourioi 444/3. On this his traditional date is based. Everyone connected with Thourioi is supposed to have "flourished" in year of its foundation, and to "flourish" is to be 40. Thus Empedocles, Herodotus, and Protagoras are all given as born 484/3 B.C.
> Celebrated <u>Suit for the Fee</u> (Diog. Laert.) Euathlos was to pay the fee when he had won his 1st case. When Protagoras demanded it he said: "I have not won a case yet." P[rotagoras] answered that he would sue him, then he would have to pay "If I win, because I have won; if you win because you have won."[31]

Significantly, the idea that to 'flourish' is to be 40 is taken from a footnote in Burnet.[32]

Similar to his gravitation towards Windelband's 'disjecta' is Beckett's favourable treatment of footnotes in *A History of Philosophy*. Time and again, Beckett turns to these, copying them painstakingly. Indeed, the image of the Heap and the Bald Head referred to above come from a footnote. This is the case for many of the key images that Beckett retains from Windelband, like the epigraph to chapter six of *Murphy* noted above. By way of further example, the infamous '*Ubi nihil vales, ibi nihil veils'*, so central to *Murphy*, is found in a footnote on page 417 of *A History of Philosophy*. If Beckett's note taking appears slavish, then it is this slavishness—in its attention to detail—that provides him with a number of the key images he uses in his fiction. Yet Beckett, by including in this errata in the body of his 'Philosophy Notes', and later including many of these in fictional texts, creates of Windelband's work something very different from the stated aims of that work. In doing so, he perverts Windelband's take on the transcendental development of Western philosophy, providing the very catalogue of detail *A History of Philosophy* is so keen to avoid.

§5

Finally, Windelband's mediation of Western philosophy—and Beckett's resistance to it—is also apparent in the treatment (or otherwise) of individual philosophies and philosophers. This is especially evident where *A History of Philosophy* treats two related doctrines: sophism, particularly the doctrines of Protagoras, and nominalism. Windelband's normative position, as set out above, unmistakably placed him on one side of the ancient debate between universals and particulars, or in philosophical parlance, realism and nominalism:

> Whoever proposes to discuss philosophical matters must, above all, have the courage to take a general position. He must also possess a kind of fortitude that is even more difficult to maintain: the boldness to steer his audience onto the high seas of the most abstract reflections, where the solid earth threatens to vanish from the eye and disappear beneath the feet.[33]

By contrast, Beckett's interest in constructing his 'Philosophy Notes' is weighted much more toward what *Murphy* dubbed 'those demented particulars', and in those philosophical schools prioritising this:

> The source of Nominalism is the Aristotelian logic, in particular the De Categoriis. In this individual things of experience were designated as true "first" substances [....] Attached to this—sensualism, since the individual is that given by the world of sensible reality.[34]

As may be expected, the exclusion of universals and the attachment to the individual in this movement would be anathema to Windelband. And, indeed, his generally even-handed treatment of philosophy breaks down here. In yet another footnote—not taken down by Beckett—commenting on the nominalists outlined in passage above, Windelband interjects: 'How inferior such considerations are to the beginnings of Greek thought!'[35]

Windelband's lumping together of the two schools in order to better dismiss them—in this case Aristotelianism and mediaeval nominalism—is also apparent in his levelling of the same charge against Protagoras, namely 'sensualism'. And like nominalism, sophism is a doctrine that Beckett later returns to in his work, in *Molloy* and *Endgame* and elsewhere. Considering that Beckett's notes (albeit taken from Alexander this time, not Windelband) assert that Protagoras was the 'first *great* individualist, relativist & agnostic',[36] a clash with Windelband's reading can be expected. Like his presentation of nominalism, Windelband's equanimity is strained in analysing the sophists; in fact, he is little short of scathing towards them. Nonetheless, he begins his overview by begrudgingly offering them some credit:

> while the Sophists were perfecting the scientific development of the formal art of presentation, verification, and refutation which they had to teach, they indeed created with this rhetoric, on the one hand, the beginnings of an independent *psychology*, and raised this branch of investigation from an inferior position which it had taken in the cosmological systems to the importance of a fundamental science, and developed, on the other hand, the preliminaries for a systematic consideration of the *logical* and *ethical norms*.

But Windelband's mood soon changes; here is the rest of the paragraph:

> But as they considered what they practised and taught—viz. the skill to carry through any proposition whatsoever—the *relativity* of human ideas and purposes presented itself to their consciousness so clearly and with such overwhelming force that they disowned inquiry as to the existence of a universally valid truth in the theoretical, as well as in the practical sphere, and so fell into a scepticism which was at first genuine scientific theory and then became frivolous. With their self-complacent, pettifogging advocacy, the Sophists made themselves the mouth-piece of all the unbridled tendencies which were undermining the order of public life.[37]

Characteristically, Windelband considers the sophists' most important contribution to the development of philosophy to be a preliminaries attempt to delimit transcendental norms. Crucially, by contrast, Beckett's version of this paragraph retains only the following:

> As the Sophists considered what they practised and taught—viz. the skill to carry through any proposition whatsoever—the relativity of human ideas and purposes struck them with such overwhelming force that they disowned inquiry as to the existence of a universally valid [sic] in both theory and practice, and so fell into a scepticism which was at first genuine scientific theory and then became frivolous.[38]

Beckett's omission of the word 'But' in the midpoint of Windelband's paragraph, and indeed his omission of the first half of the paragraph, gives the passage an entirely new orientation and impression—such that it may be read as approving of sophist doctrine (the last three words notwithstanding). A page later, Windelband again devalues the sophists, contrasting their 'pettifogging' with 'the plain, sound sense, and the pure and noble personality' of Socrates; and again, Beckett omits this phrase.

It should be clear, then, that the 'Philosophy Notes' are not merely passive reading notes from Windelband (or indeed Burnet, Alexander or Ueberweg), with little input from Beckett. Yet as this chapter has suggested, Beckett made the 'Philosophy Notes' his own throughout. Beckett's authorship appears often as a change of emphasis, as in the re-weighting of Windelband's and Burnet's footnotes, and often in the form of an absence, like his purging of Windelband's views in *A History of Philosophy*. It should thus come as no surprise that Beckett relied upon his meticulously compiled 'Philosophy Notes' across his writing career, for this was a 'Beckettian' job—long before the adjective existed.

§6

However, even when they do not employ images taken directly from Windelband, Beckett's fiction displays a clear distance from the German's thought, and the remainder of this chapter will look at how it does so. In the short story 'A Wet Night,' part of Beckett's first published work, *More Pricks Than Kicks*, the protagonist, Belacqua, stands unable to move in the centre of Dublin, that city made so famous by Joyce as a place of paralysis. But Belacqua does not suffer from the paralysis that affects Joyce's characters—the unwillingness to do anything about one's fate, so well illustrated by Eveline in the story of the same name[39]—so much as from the sense that nothing can come of anything Belacqua does, or any direction in which he goes:

> he squatted, not that he had too much drink taken but simply that for the moment there were no grounds for his favouring one direction rather than another, against Tommy Moore's plinth. Yet he durst not dally. Was it not from brooding shill I, shall I, dilly, dally, that he had come out? Now the summons to move on was a subpoena. Yet he found he could not, any more than Buridan's ass, move to right or left, backward or forward. Why this was he could not make out at all. Nor was it the moment for self-examination. He had experienced little or no trouble coming back from the Park Gate along the north quay, he had taken the Bridge and Westmoreland Street in his stride, and now he suddenly found himself good for nothing but to loll against the plinth of this bull-necked bard, and wait for a sign.[40]

As with Buridan's ass, famously positioned exactly halfway between hay and water such that it is unable to choose between them, and as a result eventually dies of both hunger and thirst, Belacqua is unable to choose. However, in Belacqua's case it is not, as with the ass, that both choices are equally attractive, or as with Eveline that one choice (doing nothing) is more attractive than the other, but rather that all options are equally unattractive. As Andrew Gibson puts it, 'The range of choices matters little. Belacqua has no foundation for any choice [....] Choice itself implodes'.[41] Many of Beckett's letters written from Dublin at the time he was working on *More Pricks Than Kicks* return to this lack of grounds for choice: 'I long to be away and of course can't bear the idea of going & can't understand why Hamburg, where it won't be warm and where I will probably be frightened.'[42] A little later he speaks of 'the old cowardice of keeping one[']s hand off the future. And I'm too old and too poor in guts or spunk or whatever the stuff is to endow the old corpse with a destination & buy a ticket & pack up here.'[43] The suggestion that there is no system of value that underwrites Belacqua's choices is emphasised further in the manner in which he finally chooses, in 'A Wet Night', a direction in which to go. The impetus is provided not by some higher system of value, but by the random blinkings of the illuminated Bovril sign that used to be attached to one of the buildings in this part of Dublin: 'Belacqua had been proffered a sign, Bovril had made him a sign.'[44] The choice is thereby reduced to one between two public houses, and finally it is the quality of the beer he will find in the respective hostelries that moves him one way rather than another: he will go 'where the porter is well up', and where he can avoid 'poets and peasants and politicians'.[45] These are hardly the kind of choice-informing values that Windelband had in mind.

In Beckett's next work, *Murphy*, the idea of a transcendental system of values is subject to questioning in a different way. On its very first page the novel announces that Murphy inhabits a 'big world' in which things have no value other than that given to them by the 'mercantile gehenna'; this is the arbitrary value of exchange, of '*quid pro quo*' as the cuckoo clock puts it.[46] Murphy's response is to attempt to escape into 'the little world' of the mind, in the manner (in his view) of the patients in the Magdalen Mental Mercyseat, an asylum in which he finds employment in chapter nine. These patients, he feels, have attained the ideal state of world-abnegation expressed in Geulincx's maxim, quoted in the novel: *Ubi nihil vales, ibi nihil velis*: where you are worth nothing there you should want nothing.[47] It should be noted that this phrase, taken down by Beckett in his notes from Windelband, is concerned with value, claiming that this should not be attached either to the subject or to the world. However, before self- or world-abnegation (and from there, Geulincx's philosophy) themselves become things of value, the irony, as in *More Pricks Than Kicks*, is stacked against Murphy. This aspect of the novel has been well noted. Paul Davies points out how 'the ironic poise [...] is so finely maintained that all the statements fall just short of assent,'[48] while Gibson argues that irony is the means by which 'Beckett most clearly tips the balance against Murphy's choices'.[49] Thus the narrator says that the difference which Murphy makes between the big world and the little is 'lovingly simplified and perverted,' while the patients' 'frequent expressions apparently of pain, rage, despair and in fact all the usual' suggested 'a fly somewhere in the ointment of the Microcosmos' (i.e., in Murphy's idealisation of the patients' little worlds) which Murphy 'either disregarded or muted to mean what he wanted'.[50]

If the rejection of transcendental values is one way in which Beckett's fiction is at odds with Windelband's philosophy, then the former's gravitation towards superfluous detail, selected without any regard for value is its corollary. Where history and literary biography must reject the example of Goethe's lock, Beckett, in *Watt*, written between 1941 and 1945, and his first text since the statement in his German Diary, indicates how the 'straws, flotsam' might be incorporated into his fiction, distorting not just the art of literature (by forcing it to include material it normally omits), but also the philosophical system. Where the latter is concerned, Ackerley and Gontarski note the novel's concern with scholastic categories, 'Quis? quid? ubi quibis auxiliis? cur? quomodo quando? (Who? what? when? by what means? why? in what way? when?).'[51] Richard N. Coe has called *Watt* 'a pilgrimage in search of meaning' in a 'jungle of hypotheses',[52] and in the absence of meaning, Watt (and his surrogate narrator, Sam) has no way to choose what to select and what to leave out. Thus the novel (in the loosest possible sense of the term) contains a section entitled 'Addenda', into which material is shunted not because it is less valuable than anything in the novel proper, but because '[o]nly fatigue and disgust prevented its incorporation.'[53] Here we find flotsam that are not dissimilar in their focus on given names, assumed names and traditions to what Beckett copies from page 354 of Windelband (see above): 'Art Con O'Connery, called Black Velvet O'Connery, product of the great Shinnery-Slattery tradition.'[54] The lack of any means of selection, though, is most apparent in the infamous passages which detail every possible permutation of a proposition. The following is but one example of many possible:

> With regard to the so important matter of Mr Knott's physical appearance, Watt had unfortunately little or nothing to say. For one day Mr Knott would be tall, fat, pale and dark, and the next thin, small, flushed and fair, and the next sturdy, middlesized, yellow and ginger, and the next small, fat, pale and fair, and the next middlesized, flushed, thin and ginger, and the next tall, yellow, dark and sturdy, and the next fat, middlesized, ginger and pale, and the next tall, thin, dark and flushed, and the next [...][55]

And so on for another page and a half. However, this is not to suggest a *preference* for value on Beckett's part. He is well aware of the paradox of value: it is all too easy to end up valuing the devaluation of value. The *value* of the 'straws, flotsam' is apparently that they undermine all attempts to establish a system of values. This is reinforced in *Molloy* (written 1947, published 1951). At one point in the novel, at the end of a long digression, the narrator says, 'I apologise for these details, in a moment we'll go faster, much faster'; however, he adds, 'And then perhaps relapse again into a wealth of filthy circumstance'; this in turn will 'give way to vast frescoes, dashed off with loathing'.[56] If details fare no better here than normative values, then it seems highly significant that the next line of the text evokes Protagoras: 'Homo mensura can't do without staffage.' Staffage is a term used in sixteenth- and seventeenth-century landscape painting to denote the human (and sometimes animal) figures which are depicted in the scene, but which are not the main subject matter of the painting; they are included merely to balance the composition or in the interests of decoration. Beckett, who could perhaps be said to have taken the 'staffage' from Windelband's *A History of Philosophy*, here suggests that this (the 'straws, flotsam') are no more valuable than the broad brushstrokes of narrative—whether the narrative of *Molloy* or, presumably, that of *A History of Philosophy*.

NOTES

1. These notes were found in a trunk in Beckett's Parisian flat after his death, and were made available for scholarly consultation in 2001. For an overview of Beckett's 'Interwar Notes', including the 'Philosophy Notes', see Matthew Feldman, *Beckett's Books* (London: Bloomsbury, 2008), pp. 21–38.
2. Samuel Beckett's 'Philosophy Notes' correspond to TCD MS 10967, and are described in *Samuel Beckett Today / Aujord'hui* 16, *Notes diverse holo [sic]: Catalogues of Beckett's reading notes and other manuscripts at Trinity College Dublin, with supporting essays* (2006), pp. 67–89.
3. The epigraph on Murphy's mind—'*Amor intellectualis quo murphy se ipsum amat.*,' in Samuel Beckett, *Murphy*, ed. J.C.C. Mays (London: Faber and Faber, 2009b), p. 69—corresponds to a footnote in Wilhelm Windelband, *A History of Philosophy*, 2 vols., trans. James Tufts (New York: Harper Torchback, 1958 [rev. ed. 1901]), p. 410, n. 2.
4. Beckett, 'Philosophy Notes', TCD 10967/40v to TCD 10967/41; corresponding to Windelband, *A History of Philosophy*, p. 71.
5. TCD 10967/189, corresponding to *ibid.*, p. 415. The term 'anthopologism' likely refers to Beckett's rejection of what he called 'anthropomorphisation'. This is put forward in a letter from Beckett to Thomas MacGreevy of 8 September 1934: 'Perhaps it is the one bright spot in a mechanistic age—the deanthropomophizations of the artist. Even the portrait beginning to be dehumanised as the individual feels himself more & more hermetic & alone & his neighbour a coagulum as alien as a protoplast or God, incapable of loving or hating anyone but himself or of being loved or hated by anyone but himself', Samuel Beckett, *The Letters of Samuel Beckett, 1929-1940: Volume 1,* eds. Martha Dow Fehsenfeld and Lois More Overbeck (Cambridge: Cambridge University Press, 2009), p. 223.
6. Beckett, 'Philosophy Notes', TCD 10967/45–10967/46v; see also Samuel Beckett, *Endgame*, in Beckett, *The Complete Dramatic Works* (London: Faber and Faber, 1990), p. 93.
7. Beckett, 'Philosophy Notes', TCD 10967/45; see also Samuel Beckett, *Mercier and Camier* (London: Calder, 1999), p. 77; and Samuel Beckett, *Molloy*, ed. Shane Weller (London: Faber and Faber, 2009), p. 62.
8. Samuel Beckett to Alan Schneider, in *No Author Better Served: The Correspondence of Samuel Beckett and Alan Schneider*, ed. Maurice Harmon (London: Harvard University Press, 1998), p. 23.
9. Windelband, *A History of Philosophy*, p. 89, n. 4.
10. Frederick Copleston, *A History of Philosophy, Volume 7: Eighteenth- and Nineteenth-Century German Philosophy* (London: Continuum, 2008 [1963]), pp. 364–5. It is ironic, given that so many of Beckett's key images come from footnotes in *A History of Philosophy* work, that Windelband's own life is reduced to three-line footnote in Copleston's study; see p. 364, n. 1.
11. See *ibid.*, pp. 361–2, 364.
12. Wilhelm Windelband, 'Rectorial Address, Strasbourg, 1894', reprinted in *History and Theory* 19/2 (1980), p. 171.
13. Cited in Frederick C. Beiser, 'Normativity in Neo-Kantianism: Its Rise and Fall', in the *International Journal of Philosophical Studies* 17/1 (2009), p. 12.
14. Windelband, 'Rectorial Address', p. 175.

15 *Ibid.*, pp. 169–70.
16 *Ibid.*, p. 175. John Jalbert helpfully describes this methodological distinction: 'according to Windelband's formulation, natural sciences are described as "nomothetic" because they aim at general laws, and historical sciences are "ideographic" because they focus their theoretical interest upon the individual and unique', 'Husserl's Position Between Dilthey and the Windelband-Rickert School of Neo-Kantianism', in the *Journal of the History of Philosophy* 26/2 (1969), p. 282. See also Rudolf A. Makkreel, 'Wilhelm Dilthey and the Neo-Kantians: The Distinction of the Geistewissenschaften and the Kulturwissenschaften', in the *History of Philosophy* 7/4 (1969), p. 426.
17 Windelband, 'Rectorial Address', p. 181.
18 Beiser, 'Normativity in Neo-Kantianism', pp. 12–13; italics in original.
19 Lanier R. Anderson, 'Neo-Kantianism and the Roots of Anti-Psychologism', in the *British Journal for the History of Philosophy* 13/2 (2005), p. 314. See also 'Wilhelm Windelband: Philosophy as the Science of Values', in Thomas E. Willey, *Back to Kant: The Revival of Kantianism in German Social and Historical Thought, 1860–1914* (Detroit: Wayne State University Press, 1978), pp. 134–39.
20 Beiser, 'Normativity in Neo-Kantianism', p. 14.
21 Philip J. Swoboda, 'Windelband's Influence on S.L. Frank', in *Studies in East European Thought* 47/3–4 (1995), p. 264, which later highlights 'the characteristically Windelbandian opposition between the valid and the merely factual. The "factual" exhibits a "blind necessity" which contrasts with the self-evident "validity" of the primordial ground and those aspects of being that the latter "illuminates"', p. 282. See also Rudolf A. Makkreel and Sebastian Luft, 'Who were the neo-Kantians?', in *Neo-Kantianism in Contemporary Philosophy*, eds. Rudolf A. Makkreel and Sebastian Luft (Bloomington: Indiana University Press, 2010), pp. 1–4.
22 Swoboda, 'Windelband's Influence on S.L. Frank', p. 272.
23 Windelband, A *History of Philosophy*, p. ix.
24 *Ibid.*, p. x.
25 Cited in Charles Juliet, *Conversations with Samuel Beckett and Bram van Velde* (Leiden: Academic Press, 1995), p. 165; italics added.
26 Windelband, *A History of Philosophy*, p. ix.
27 Cited in James Knowlson, *Samuel Beckett: Damned to Fame* (London: Bloomsbury, 1996), pp. 244–45.
28 Windelband, *A History of Philosophy*, pp. xi-xii; italics in original.
29 Beckett, 'Philosophy Notes', TCD 10967/172v 10967/173, corresponding to Windelband, *A History of Philosophy*, p. 354.
30 *Ibid.*, p. 93.
31 Beckett, 'Philosophy Notes', TCD 10967/45.
32 Burnet, p. 90, n. 2.
33 Windelband, 'Rectorial Address', p. 176.
34 Beckett, *Murphy*, p. 12; and Beckett, 'Philosophy Notes', TCD 10967/155v-10967/156r, corresponding to Windelband, *A History of Philosophy*, p. 296.
35 *Ibid.*, p. 96, n. 4.
36 Beckett, 'Philosophy Notes', TCD 10967/44, corresponding to J. Archibald Alexander, *A Short History of Philosophy* (Glasgow: Maclehose, Jackson and co., 1922), pp. 49–50; italics added.
37 Windelband, *A History of Philosophy*, p. 69; italics in original.

[38] Beckett, 'Philosophy Notes', TCD 10967/40–10967/40v.
[39] Eveline, famously, rejects the opportunity to leave Dublin and start a new life in 'Buenos Ayres' with the sailor, Frank. The last words of the story, as she stands frozen on the jetty unable to follow Frank, underline her paralysis: 'She set her white face to him, passive, like a helpless animal', James Joyce, *Dubliners* (Oxford: Oxford University Press, 2000), p. 29.
[40] Samuel Beckett, 'A Wet Night', in *More Pricks Than Kicks*, ed. Cassandra Nelson (London: Faber and Faber, 2010), p. 33.
[41] Andrew Gibson, 'The Irish Remainder: *More Pricks Than Kicks*,' keynote lecture, 'Beckett in the Thirties' Conference, Ecole Normale Supérieure, Paris, October 2006 (unpublished).
[42] Beckett to Thomas MacGreevy, 11 March 1931, in *The Letters of Samuel Beckett, 1929-1940: Volume 1*, p. 73.
[43] Beckett to Thomas MacGreevy, 12 September 1931, in *ibid.*, p. 88.
[44] Beckett, 'A Wet Night', in *More Pricks Than Kicks*, p. 44.
[45] *Ibid.*, p. 44.
[46] Beckett, *Murphy*, pp. 27, 3.
[47] *Ibid.*, p. 112.
[48] Paul Davies, *The Ideal Real: Beckett's Fiction and Imagination* (London: Associated University Presses, 1994), p. 32.
[49] Andrew Gibson, *Beckett and Badiou: The Pathos of Intermittency* (Oxford: Oxford University Press, 2006), p. 152.
[50] Beckett, *Murphy*, pp. 112–3.
[51] C.J. Ackerley and S.E. Gontarski, *The Faber Companion to Samuel Beckett* (London: Faber and Faber, 2006), p. 629.
[52] Richard N. Coe, *Beckett* (Edinburgh: Oliver and Boyd, 1968), p. 38.
[53] Samuel Beckett, *Watt*, ed. Chris Ackerley (London: Faber, 2009e), p. 215.
[54] *Ibid.*
[55] *Ibid.*, p. 181.
[56] Beckett, *Molloy*, pp. 62–3.

SAMUEL BECKETT, WILHELM WINDELBAND AND NOMINALIST PHILOSOPHY

> I know of no work that presents so clearly in their succession the main problems of past thought, or brings out so connectedly and concentratedly the preparation that was made by the ancient philosophy for the introduction of Christianity, or that exhibits more justly the relations between it an the Christian thought of the first Christian centuries. It is gratifying to follow a writer so thoroughly imbued with the principles of his own science, and so controlled by them, and who recognizes [...] the progress of philosophy, and who does not claim for the latter more than its just due in the shaping of ecclesiastical dogmas. The book deserves the attention of all who would learn how thought has come to be what it is, and who would themselves "learn to think".
> – 1893 review of A History of Philosophy[1]

§1

While it is not known for certain just what drew Samuel Beckett to Wilhelm Windelband's 681-page summary of Western philosophy, the work was certainly well-known in the English-speaking world after James H. Tufts' translation of July 1893. It was hyperbolically endorsed in the contemporaneous review excerpted in the epigraph above, as a text not only useful to readers 'who would themselves "learn to think"'. In the case of Samuel Beckett, on the contrary, his interest was very nearly the opposite. Rather than knowledge, what he increasingly viewed as 'the loutishness of learning'—already decried in his 1934 poem, 'Gnome'—is more likely to have motivated Beckett's extensive notes on *A History of Philosophy* in the early 1930s.[2]

As he informed Anne Atik some four decades later, 'you have to get back to ignorance'; put another way, Beckett sought to 'unlearn to think'.[3] Given the genocidal disasters brought about by twentieth-century thinking to which he was an engaged and traumatised witness, Beckett's position is a refreshingly heretical one. However, it remains the case that both 'learn[ing] to think' and 'unlearning to think' mandated a systematic, *a priori* knowledge of Western thinking. That is to say, for systematic thought to be turned on its head in famously Beckettian fashion, prior knowledge of systematic thought—in this case, of Western philosophy from the Presocratics to Friedrich Nietzsche—was an essential precursor.

Whether 'learned ignorance' or, 'the progress of philosophy', it is nonetheless clear that Beckett's engagement with, and employment of, Wilhelm Windelband was both extensive and profound. This is so much so, I want to suggest that the latter ought to be included in that 'canon' of philosophers exerting the greatest influence upon Beckett's crucial development before 1945. At the time Beckett first encountered Windelband in (likely) later 1932, nowhere was the 'evolution of the ideas of European philosophy' in terms of *'the history of problems and conceptions* [....] as a connected and interrelated whole' more succinctly and accessibly presented than in *A History of Philosophy*.[4] Furthermore, many of those frequently recognised as 'Beckettian' philosophers—Arnold Geulincx, Bishop Berkeley, Gottfried Leibniz and several others—were first encountered in the revised, second edition of *A History of Philosophy* from 1901. Before going on to explore some of these philosophical debts, however, a moment's pause over the context and corpus of Beckett's note-taking during this period is in order.

During his didactic years of self-education over the decade of the 1930s, Beckett took notes on a striking range of subjects. As James Knowlson's excellent biography makes plain, this was a period of dejection, directionless travel, and uncertainty. On one hand, the death of Beckett's father in June 1933 led him to two years of thrice-weekly analysis with the trainee psychotherapist Wilfred Bion, between Christmas of 1933 and 1935. But there were also panic attacks, psychosomatic illnesses, alongside a growing desire to leave the constraints in Ireland for the continent—or indeed anywhere, as letters to the Soviet filmmaker, Sergei Eisenstein, and applications for a lectureship in South Africa make plain.[5] Adding to Beckett's frustrations, on the other hand, was a lack of critical success for his fiction, ranging from the failure to publish his first novel, *Dream of Fair to Middling Women*, and literally dozens of rejection letters from publishers prior to Routledge's publication of *Murphy* in 1938.[6]

Comparatively more successful at this time were Beckett's poetry (notably the collection 1935 *Echo's Bones*) and non-fiction as a freelance journalist (collected in the 1984 *Disjecta*), but this provided neither enough income to live on, nor enough plaudits to convince him that he was, at that time, what he was to become after 1945: a groundbreaking artist; a literary genius; and for some, the very conscience of the last century—or, to use a phrase from the 1969 Nobel Presentation Speech, 'a miserere from all mankind, its muffled minor key sounding liberation to the oppressed, and comfort to those in need'.[7]

Long before that infamous 'negativism' and 'pessimism' earned Beckett the Nobel Prize for Literature, then, were the far less celebrated, but no less important, 'years of wandering' also announced in the quatrain 'Gnome'. As a number of critics in Beckett studies have established over the last generation, this period of intellectual gestation was vital for the breakthrough achieved in the 'frenzy of writing' between 1945 and 1950. Considering that his authorised biography from 1996, *Damned to Fame*, largely sparked this empirical turn toward Beckett's formative years, it is hard to disagree with the conclusion on Beckett's post-war breakthrough offered there: 'the ground was well prepared'.[8] Nowhere are his provisions for an unsettled present and unknown future—captured by Beckett's reflexive question in his (also indispensable) 'German Diary' entry of 13 December 1936: 'What is to become of me?'[9]—better revealed than in the 'Interwar Notes' compiled between the late 1920s and late 1930s. As outlined by the 2006 catalogue published in *Samuel Beckett Today / Aujourd'hui* 16, these reading notes cover psychology, art history, the history of German and English literature, Irish and European history, as well as notes on specific writers as divergent as Dante and d'Annunzio; Mauthner and Mistral; Augustine and Ariosto.[10]

Far and away the largest corpus portion of these extant notes, more to the point, comprise the 267 pages, mostly recto and verso (with a few blank sides scattered throughout), forming Beckett's 'Philosophy Notes'. These were taken from a variety of sources, including John Burnet's 1914 *Greek Philosophy, Part I: Thales to Plato*, J. Archibald Alexander's 1907 *A Short History of Philosophy* and—as most recently identified by Peter Fifield—some entries from Friedrich Ueberweg's two-volume *History of Philosophy: From Thales to the Present Time* from 1871.[11] Alongside Windelband, these sources—and bits from potentially others, such as the *Encyclopaedia Britannica*, or an as-yet unidentified French text—were used to cover the origins of Western philosophy. These origins were, of course, to be found in the '*Philosophy of the Greeks*—from the beginning of scientific thought to the death of Aristotle (600—322 B.C.).' This first section—numbered '1.', following Windelband's 'General Classification'—was clearly of greatest interest to Beckett. In fact, entries on these three first centuries of Western philosophy form fully 40% of the entire corpus of 'Philosophy Notes'; that is, nearly as much as that contained in Windelband's ensuing six eras.[12]

Although passed over in silence amongst Beckett's published texts or letters from the time, *A History of Philosophy* accounts for more than three-quarters of the entire 'Philosophy Notes'. While Windelband is one of (at least) four sources on Ancient Greek philosophy, and one of the two sources employed in section '2.', Hellenistic-Roman Philosophy—with typed entries steadily decreasing until Beckett apparently tired of Alexander's tiring prose with 'Origen (185–254)'[13]— the final five sections are taken from only one source, namely Windelband. That is to say, the rest of Beckett's 'Philosophy Notes', covering the remaining 1,600 years of Western philosophy, are mediated entirely by Windelband. As such, the 267 folios comprising TCD 10967 may be largely seen as a corpus of two halves: the first is a wide-ranging study of classical Greek thought (and to a much lesser extent, classical Roman); the second part is Windelband's view of everything since. Before turning to the outstanding features of this second portion of Beckett's 'Philosophy Notes', however, a few concluding observations on '*Philosophy of the Greeks*' are relevant for what follows.

Evidence for Beckett's attraction to early Greek philosophy is underscored by the multiple sources used in what he called much later, in a letter to Alan Schneider, 'my notes on the pre-Socratics'. Much care was taken in the construction of these notes, with passages from Alexander typed out, those from Burnet entered in red ink, and notes from Windelband in blue or black ink.[14] Moreover, these 200 or so typed and handwritten sides of 'notes on the pre-Socratics' help to date the composition of Beckett's 'Philosophy Notes', with the earliest explicit reference occurring in 'Serena I', which John Pilling authoritatively dates to 1932:

> scarlet beauty in our world dead fish adrift
> all things full of gods

This corresponds to Beckett's notes on the first recorded Western philosopher, Thales of Miletus: 'Earth afloat (dead fish) on surface of primal substance. All things are full of gods.'[15] The last allusion to these 'notes on the pre-Socratics' in Beckett's art, interestingly, takes place almost exactly a half-century later, in the 1981 *Ill Seen Ill Said*, in relation to another Presocratic philosopher, Empedocles of Agrigentum:

> Slow systole diastole. Tightening and loosening their clasp. Rhythm of a labouring heart. Till when almost despaired of a gently part. Suddenly gently.
>
> In the beginning, the Sphere which Love keeps the "roots" in solution. Strife enters, drives Love to centre, and separates elements (cf. concept of world breathing). Until reverse process begins (systole - diastole), Love expanding and Strife expelled. (E. was the first to formulate theory of flux and reflux of blood to and from heart).[16]

Parenthetically, instead of a Cartesianism all too often asserted rather than shown, Beckett's interest in many familiar philosophical debates—such as mind and body interactions, the role of consciousness, and methodological doubt, to name but three—may thus be cast as perennial issues in Western thought; commencing with the Presocratics rather than, two millennia later, with Rene Descartes. It is thus far less the case that it is a 'Cartesian system that underlies the whole of Beckett's work', let alone that Descartes 'was Beckett's favourite philosopher'.[17] Rather, it was the contours and development of Western philosophy as a whole, starting in Ancient Greece, which were under scrutiny.

The utility of these notes as a whole, especially those on the Ancient Greeks, is thus manifest across very nearly the entirety of Beckett's writing life, evidenced in his plays, poetry, prose and even non-fiction alike. This was a corpus of reading notes to which Beckett seems to have returned, again and again. Beckett's notes on what Windelband characterised as the 'Philosophy of the Greeks' consist of some 50,000 words, extending from folio 1r to 109v. Beckett's use of (at least) four sources for these notes on classical Greek philosophy—of which *A*

History of Philosophy is, here too, most frequently in evidence, followed by Burnet's *Greek Philosophy*, Alexander's *A Short History of Philosophy*, and fragments from Johann Eduard Erdmann's *A History of Philosophy*—conclude with the following handwritten passage on Aristotle:

> Reason develops, partly as rational action, partly as rational thought; as perfection on one hand of character, on the other of the faculty of intelligence. Thus excellence of rational man is compound of the <u>ethical</u> and <u>intellectual</u>, or <u>dianoetic</u> virtues. A. gave up the Socratic intellectualism, which made the determination of the will by rational insight stronger than the desire arising from defective knowledge [....] Knowledge of these, the full unfolding of the "active reason", is a "beholding" and with this beholding of the highest truth man gains participation in that <u>pure thought</u>, the essence of deity, and thereby in the eternal <u>blessedness</u> of the divine self-consciousness. For this beholding, existing only for its own sake without ends of will or deed, this wishless absorption in the perception of the highest path, is the blessedest and best of all. Tra-la-la-la.

Like roughly half of these 200 recto and verso sides, this passage is taken from *A History of Philosophy*.[18] Notwithstanding his seeming rejection of Windelband's view with one of his—exceedingly rare—interpolative comments, the above represents yet another of the many instances of Beckett's subsequent use of material gleaned from the 'Philosophy Notes'. In this case, as Chris Ackerley has indicated, Aristotle's apex of virtue is found in *Watt*.[19] That which brings 'complete happiness' for Aristotle forms Arsene's memorable three laughs, or 'modes of ululation', corresponding to the 'successive excoriations of the understanding'. Yet far from supreme truth, virtue or happiness, Windelband's meaning is wholly inverted in Arsene's 'short speech':

> The hollow laugh laughs at that which is not true, it is the *intellectual* laugh. Not good! Not true! Well well. But the mirthless laugh is the *dianoetic* laugh, down the snout—Haw!—so. It is the laugh of laughs, the *risus purus*, the laugh laughing at the laugh, the *beholding*, the saluting of the highest joke, in a word the laugh that laughs—silence please—at that which is unhappy.[20]

This above entry, finally, raises a number of points relating to the 'Interwar Notes' generally, and to the 'Philosophy Notes' in particular: Beckett's recourse to laconic and lapidary summaries from secondary sources, his repeated transformation of these reading notes into his art, and not least, his undeniable knowledge and use of Western philosophy (not just Cartesianism) across his work. Amongst these extant reading notes, furthermore, *A History of Philosophy* emerges as, by far, the most significant of Beckett's selected texts on Western philosophy. It is from here, for example, that much of the dialogue in *Murphy* is drawn, down to the famous epigraph to Chapter 6 on Murphy's mind.[21] In fact, Beckett's extant notes from Windelband are more extensive than for any other author—more than Dante, St Augustine, or Arnold Geulincx.

For his part, at the time of writing *A History of Philosophy* Windelband had ascended the heights of German academic philosophy as a leading exponent of neo-Kantianism. In fact, Windelband's own motto was to shorthand the essence of a neo-Kantianism championed throughout his 45-year career: 'to understand Kant is to go beyond him'. Insofar as this became something of a working programme, Windelband's *Badische*—or Southwest-German school of philosophy— of which he remained the acknowledged leader from the late nineteenth century to the outbreak of the Great War, emphasised the importance of 'objective norms [...] as an attempt to dispense with Kant's dualism', undertaken by focussing upon epistemology and methodology; upon value theory as against then-fashionable positivism; and finally, upon the 'rational will' over and above philosophical scepticism and relativism.[22] So much is this the case that Windelband identified transcendental norms as the 'central concept of the critical philosophy'.[23] In fact, as he claimed elsewhere, philosophy itself was nothing more than 'a system of norms'.[24]

To use a different terminological register, Windelband championed the philosophy of 'realism', not least as their age old opponents, 'nominalists' remain highly unlikely to write systematic histories of philosophy as an 'interrelated whole'. As will be considered presently, this dialectic stretched back to the very origins of Western philosophy. The question also vexed Plato and his disciple Aristotle, and reached boiling point in the late mediaeval debate over universals; indeed, quite literally for those facing the stake for endorsing a nominalist position on, for example, the doctrine of the Trinity and of transubstantiation. It a word, it is hugely ironic that perhaps Beckett's greatest debt to *A History from Philosophy* was the precisely Windelband's discussion on nominalism, to which this essay will now turn.

§2

> I am not interested in the "unification" of the historical chaos any more than I am in the "clarification" of the individual chaos, & still less in the anthropomorphisation of the inhuman necessities that provoke the chaos. What I want is the straws, flotsam, etc., names, dates, births and deaths, because that is all I can know. Pas l'onde, mais les bouchons [....] Whereas the pure incoherence of times & men & places is at least amusing. Schicksal = Zufall, for all human purposes [e.g. fate equals coincidence ....] the expressions "historical necessity" & "Germanic destiny" start the vomit moving upwards.[25]

Beckett famously and repeatedly claimed that he was not a philosopher. Yet he was also a lifelong reader and intellectual, leading Ruben Rabinovitz to rightly note in response: 'Samuel Beckett says in interviews that he knows little about philosophy; but his little could easily be another man's abundance.'[26] Following this point, I want to suggest Beckett's relative philosophical 'abundance' during his 'years of wandering' was, in large measure, indebted to the doctrine of nominalism. This claim is buttressed by Beckett's fascinating confession to his German Diaries, cited above. It was not only the racist 'norms' of Nazi Germany that Beckett was reacting to on 15 January 1937; he was also putting forward a much broader philosophical preference.[27] This may be shorthanded as a rejection of universals in the wake of the abortive *Dream of Fair to Middling Women*—that 'ideal core of the onion' announced in his academic monograph from 1930, *Proust*[28]—via his initial encounter with *A History of Philosophy*. Instead, what *Murphy* memorably dubbed those 'demented particulars' better represent Beckett's philosophical outlook at this time.[29] In may also merit recalling here a lesser-quoted portion of the 1937 'German Letter' to Axel Kaun: tearing at the 'veil of language' and advocating the literary equivalent of 'Beethoven pauses' was to be achieved for Beckett through a 'nominalist irony'.[30]

As this suggests, a key context here is the backdrop of Beckett's interwar maturation and intellectual development; of his didactic approach to Western philosophy; and of course, the archival turn in Beckett studies sensitive to this material and context—one that has been flowering over the past 15 years in the wake of Knowlson's aforementioned biography. By way of a contribution to these areas, two points shall be pursued in this and the following section. The central point will be concerned with establishing Beckett's interest in nominalism, as both first encountered and as wholly mediated by Windelband's *A History of Philosophy*. Secondly, Beckett's continued pursuit of this philosophical thread may also be seen in other, subsequent notebooks, jottings and sources across the 1930s. Yet before undertaking this triangulation of philosophy, interwar note-taking and Beckett's philosophical—and by implication throughout, literary—developments, a final philosophical pause is needed.

It bears restating that, as a neo-Kantian interested in transcendental norms and supra-factual values, Windelband could hardly be further from nominalist thinking. Quite aside from his normative philosophy, additional circumstantial evidence makes clear that Windelband was no champion of nominalism. In fact, in the only other book of his available in English—Joseph McCabe's 1921 translation of *An Introduction to Philosophy* (published in German a year before his death), Windelband addresses nominalism in roughly one out of 346 pages—or to be more particular, a term that shall be pressed into important service shortly—

using 427 words in a book containing some 128,000 of them. This matters because *An Introduction to Philosophy* is thematic, and treats a variety of contemporaneous philosophical debates around issues like Truth, Value, Morality, Aesthetics, History and Religion. Yet the passage in question treats the mediaeval debate between 'realists' and 'nominalists' as briefly as possible (and is the only reference to 'nominalism' given in the index):

> [...] in antiquity and also in the Scholastic movement, there developed the antithesis of the two points of vie won the theory of knowledge which we call Realism and Nominalism. Realism (*universalia sunt realia*) affirms, in the terms of Plato, that, as our knowledge consists of the concepts and must be a knowledge of reality, the contents of the concepts must be regarded as copies of being. This Realism is maintained wherever our views recognise in reality a dependence of the particular on the general. Hence the knowledge of laws of nature is the chief form of Realism in this sense of the word. But from the time of Plato onward the serious difficulties of Realism arise from the fact that it is impossible to form a satisfactory conception of the sort of reality that ideas can have, or of the way in which they condition the other reality, that of the particular and corporeal. These difficulties have driven thought in the opposite direction, into the arms of Nominalism, which regards the concepts as intermediate and auxiliary constructions in the reflecting mind, not as copies of something independent of the mind and existing in itself. Their importance is still further reduced if they are suppose merely to be common names of similar objects (*universalia sunt nomina*). Nominalism will freely grant that the particular elements of our perceptive knowledge have a direct relation (either as copies or in some other way) to reality, but it declares it inconceivable that the results of conceptual reflection, which is a purely internal process of the mind, should have an analogous truth-value. It must, however, concede that this purely internal reflection is actually determined by the contents which it combines in its entire movement and its outcome, and that, on the other hand, the process of thought which its concepts leads in turn to particular ideas which prove to be in agreement with perception. It therefore finds itself confronting the problem, how the forms of thought are related to those of reality: whether they, as belonging to the same total system of reality, point to each other and are in the end identical, or whether, since they belong to different worlds, nothing can be settled as to their identity or any other relation. We thus see that in the last resort it is metaphysical motives which must pronounce in the controversy about universals. All the forms of world-view which we describe as Henistic or Singularistic are from the logical point of view Realistic; whilst all forms of Individualism must have a Nominalistic complexion.[31]

Yet Windelband was unable to get away from the discussion of mediaeval nominalism in his chronological, two-volume *A History of Philosophy*, for this earlier text was intended to cover 'the evolution of the ideas of European philosophy', from antiquity to the late nineteenth century.[32] Prior to considering Windelband's much more substantial treatment of nominalism in *A History of Philosophy*, a bare sketch of this doctrine is merited. At the most basic nominalism contests 'status of mind independent entities' called 'universals'; this doctrine of 'realism' thus 'posits that we are aware of them [universals] not by sense itself but by reason'. 'Nominalism is nothing more than the thesis that there are no abstract entities' on the other hand; a doctrine which 'does away with so many kinds of putative entities that the ontology it yields may not even be properly described as a desert landscape'. Realist opponents of nominalism, continues Zoltán Szabó, 'suspect that nominalism is indeed much like a desert: an uncomfortable place whose main attraction is that it is hard to be there'. This is because conventional renderings of nominalist doctrine stress 'the extent to which rejection of all abstract entities flies in the fact of common sense'. By this, Szabó means that, both in philosophical debates and everyday interactions, nominalists make use of abstract concepts, such as numbers, colours or, *pace* Windelband, normative values. Such a paradox, of course, reeks of Beckett Country, for such a position seems to be 'self undermining':

> Suppose that a nominalist—call him Nelson—just told you that there are no abstract entities. How should Nelson describe what he did? Did he say something? Certainly not, if saying something amounts to expressing a proposition. Did he utter something Clearly not, if uttering something requires the articulation of a sentence type. Did he try to bring you to share his belief? Obviously not, if sharing a belief requires being in identical mental states [....Yet] there is a nominalistically acceptable way of describing what happened: he produced meaningful noises and thereby attempted to bring you into a mental state relevantly similar to one of his own. There is not mention of propositions, sentences, or shareable beliefs here, and still, in an important sense, we are told precisely what was going on.[33]

It is not for nothing that readers familiar with Beckett's *Watt* might see in this explanation of nominalism the vexed conversation between the eponymous Watt and Sam, the novel's narrator: 'These were sounds that at first, though we walked face to face, were devoid of significance to me', laments Sam, unable to grasp the tale of Knott's house until Watt's linguistic inversions and meaningless sounds were frequent enough for Sam to make sense of them: 'But soon I grew used to these sounds, and then I understood as well as ever, that is to say fully one half of what won its way past my tympan.'[34] It is no surprise, therefore, that Chris Ackerley's authoritative book of annotations to *Watt*, *Obscure Locks, Simple Keys* contains fully a dozen references to nominalism. Ackerley's examples range from the opening pastiche on scholasticism regarding the classification of a rat having eaten a consecrated wafer, to the memorable experiences of 'unintelligible intricacies' with Galls father and son, to the arbitrary naming of a 'famished dog', Kate, to eat Mr Knott's leftovers.[35] Right across the narrative of *Watt*, the failure of language is intertwined wit the failure of naming, as with the example of Mr Knott's pots refusing to conform to the universal Ideal of a 'Pot':

> It was in vain that it answered, with unexceptionable adequacy, all the purposes, and performed all the offices, of a pot, it was not a pot. And it was just this hairbreadth departure from the nature of a true pot that so excruciated Watt. For if the approximation had been less close, then Watt would have been less anguished. For then he would not have said, This is a pot, and yet not a pot, no, but then he would have said, This is something of which I do not know the name [....] a thing of which the true name had ceased, suddenly, or gradually to be the tru name for Watt. For the pot remained a pot, Watt felt sure of that, for everyone but Watt. For Watt alone it was not a pot, any more.[36]

Nominalism assumes the imprecision of language. One can only 'fail better', as it were, when employing language to link different concrete objects or entities through 'analogies', 'semantic paraphrase'; in a word, metaphors. 'The nominalist refuses to construe abstract terms as names of entities distinct from individual things', writes Shottenkirk, for 'so-called universals are terms or signs standing for or referring to individual objects and sets of objects, but they themselves cannot be said to exist as mind-independent entities.'[37] Nominalism rejects the one-to-one correspondence of abstract terms and concrete things as nothing more than a sleight of hand by realism. There is no mileage in the identification of categories like genera and species with language—considerations that reach back to Aristotlean categories, Platonic Ideas and, before them, the Presocratic debates over the nature of reality, which Windelband shorthanded as debates on the 'weltsfuff'.[38]

In turn, Beckett's likely introduction to nominalism via *A History of Philosophy* noted the wide-ranging mediaeval debates over the 'problem of universals'. As emphasised above, by this point Beckett' 'Cliff's Notes' on the history of philosophy—itself remarkably consistent in seeking out that flotsam of 'names, dates, births and deaths' noted in his 'German Diary' entry—was fashioned from but one source; that is, Wilhelm Windelband's rendering of the 16 centuries of Western philosophy between the Romans and Nietzsche. Within this period, the attention Beckett paid to the sections on nominalism is arresting, not least given the cursory treatment of sections on either side. Beckett raced through Chapter 1 of Part III on the 'First Period' of the Mediaeval Philosophy until reaching Section 23, entitled 'The Controversy over Universals'. Importantly, Windelband is at pains to stress there that the mediaeval debate between general and particular 'had influence in the succeeding development of philosophy until long past the Middle Ages'.[39] Yet as Beckett carefully noted, the more important direction of influence was not forward, but backward to the ancient Greeks:

> This possibly the same problem as that at the centre of first Greek period. After Socrates had assigned to science the task of thinking the world in conceptions, the question how the class-concepts, the generic conceptions, are related to reality became, for the first time, a chief motiv of philosophy. It produced the Platonic doctrine of Ideas, Aristotelian logic. The mediaeval dispute worked in Paris schools, has its counterparts only in the debates at Athens.[40]

Given his expansive notes on early Greek conceptions of reality in the preceding 'Philosophy Notes', Beckett's interest seems to have been piqued by the medieval debate between nominalism and realism. A few pages later—in both the 'Philosophy Notes' and *A History of Philosophy*—Beckett prominently entered the word 'Nominalism' in the margins. Quite beyond nominalism's connection to Presocratic individualism and scepticism, Windelband argues that this doctrine was 'repressed and stifled' during this mediaeval period, meaning that little written by the nominalists themselves survives. Windelband reckoned that this had much to do with dogmas of the mediaeval Church, for 'Realism in its theory of universals found an instrument for establishing some of the fundamental dogmas, and therefore rejoiced in the approbation of the Church. The assumption of a substantial reality of the logical genera [...] seemed to make possible a rational exposition of the doctrine of the Trinity', amongst other mediaeval Christian ideals, including 'inherited sin' and 'vicarious satisfaction'.

These features of nominalism appear to have been enough for Beckett to have paid close attention to Windelband's ensuing pages. The following is a summary of Beckett's summary:

> The source of Nominalism is the Aristotelian logic, in particular the De Categoriis. In this individual things of experience were designated as true "first" substances [....] it seemed to follow that universals could not be substances. What then? The comprehension of many particularities in one numen [name] vox [voice ...] defined by Boethius as the "motion of the air produced by the tongue". Here all the elements of extreme nominalism are given: universals are nothing but collective names, sounds (flatus vocis) serving as signs for a multiplicity of substances or their accidents [....] Attached to this—sensualism, since the individual is that given by the world of sensible reality [....] This doctrine became moments thro [sic] its application to theological questions by Berengar of Tours and Roscellinus. Theone contested, in doctrine of Sacrament, the possible of transubstantiation of substance while the former accidents were retained; the second reached the consequence that the three persons of divine divinity Trinity were to be looked on as 3 difference substances.[41]

Beyond being a suppressed and near-heretical doctrine that Beckett first encountered in Windelband, the ideas of extreme nominalism appear to be an ideal stomping ground for a modern artist fascinated by language. For what Szabó calls nominalism's use of 'semantic paraphrase', and Willey terms 'analogies' is little more than the idea that individual things are not properly reflected by general categories of names. This mediaeval turn toward language in eleventh and twelfth century Europe later took on the perfectly Beckettian name 'terminism'—which is found underlined in the margin of this portion of the 'Philosophy Notes', even though Windelband only introduces the subject properly some 40 pages later. It was this linguistic aspect of 'extreme Nominalism' that is best represented by William of Occam—he of Occam's Razor fame—the fourteenth century scholastic and champion of the doctrine that Beckett evokes in his letter to Axel Kaun, whereby the Joycean method is associated with the universalising tendencies of realism, while Beckett's preference is for a 'literature of the unword', one 'taking the form of a Nominalist irony'; that is, 'Nominalism '(in the sense of the Scholastics)'.[42]

Some five years before penning his oft-cited 'German Letter', Beckett had noted that 'Nominalism reappeared as Terminism which regarded concepts (termini) as subjective signs for really existing individual things.'[43] As this suggests, it was not only Fritz Mauthner who raised the spectre of linguistic ineffability for Beckett, for 600 years earlier many of the ideas were advanced by the 'extreme Nominalism' of terminism. This key section of *A History of Philosophy*, headed 'Problem of Individuality', also specifically uses a term Beckett first encountered in Schopenhauer to describe the 'principle of individuation' systematically obscured by the 'veil of Maya': 'with the increase of intellectualism the universalistic tendency increase also, the counter current was necessarily evoked all the more powerfully, and the same antithesis in motives of thought which had led to the dialectic of the controversy over universals now took on a more real and metaphysical form in the question as to the ground of existence in individual beings (*principium individuationis*)'.[44] In this light, it is unsurprising that Schopenhauer's own entry in *A History of Philosophy* is headed as 'Doctrine of Irrationalism', which Beckett concludes with 'Dear Arthur's' view that 'it must be a balls aching world'.[45]

The following is the section on terminism in question from Beckett's 'Philosophy Notes'. This is again taken from Windelband's *A History of Philosophy*, and treats the 'victorious development' experience by nominalism in the second period of mediaeval philosophy:

> The Terminism of Occam proceeds from the logical theory of "supposition"; a class-concept or term (terminus) may, in language and logic, stand for the sum of it species, a species-concept for the sum of individual examples (homo = omnes homines), so that in operations of though a term is a sign of its content. Individual things are represented in thought intuitively, without mediation of species intelligibiles, but those mental representations are only signs for things represented, with which they have as little real similarity as any sign towards the object designation. This relation is

that of "first intention". But as individual ideas stand for (supponunt) individual things, so general ideas supponunt individual ideas. This "second intention", in which general idea refers no longer directly to the thing itself, but primarily to the idea of the thing, is no longer nature, but arbitrary (ad placitum instituta).

Upon this distinction Occam bases that between real and rational science, the former relating immediate or intuitively to things, the latter abstractly to the relations between ideas.

For this Terministic Nominalism, knowledge of the world refers to the inner states excited by phenomena. Nicolas Cusanus, who committed himself absolutely to this idealistic Nominalism, taught that human thought possesses only conjectures, modes of representation corresponding to its own nature. This awareness of relatively of all positive prediction, this knowledge of non-knowledge, is the docta ignorantia.[46]

Beckett thus encountered a philosophical doctrine specifically treating the inadequacy of language before the completion of *More Pricks Than Kicks* in later 1933, and before starting *Murphy* in mid-1935. While these ideas are treated humorously in the more Joycean *Dream of Fair to Middling Women* and *More Pricks Than Kicks*, they are put to a more structural use in *Murphy*, where Celia represents nominalism's 'demented particulars', while her grandfather, Mr Kelly, reflects the universal norms of realism. This philosophical dialectic is reflected in much of their dialogue, with Mr Kelly telling Celia to be 'less beastly circumstantial' in her detailed account of Murphy in Chapter 2, for example. In fact, Celia is herself introduced in dementedly particular terms; terms taken from the specific measurements of the Venus de Milo:[47]

Age	Unimportant
Head	Small and round
Eyes	Green
Complexion	White
Hair	Yellow
Features	Mobile
Neck	13¾"
Upper Arm	11"
Forearm	9½"
Wrist	6"
Bust	34"
Waist	27"
Hips, etc	35"
Thigh	21¾"
Knee	13¾"
Calf	13"
Ankle	8¼"
Instep	Unimportant
Height	5' 4"
Weight	123 lb

In contrast, in the thirteenth and final chapter in *Murphy*, following the eponymous 'hero's' death, Celia and Mr Kelly go kite flying at the Round Pound. Mr Kelly's kite loses its particular features and comes to represent a timeline that 'could measure the distance form the unseen to the seen, now he was in a position to determine the point at which seen and unseen met'. This unseen is described in *Murphy* as 'the historical process of the hardened optimists'. Or, as Beckett confided in his 'German Diary', by the Third Reich's rhetoric of 'historical destiny'. Thus, at the close of the *Murphy*, 'Mr Kelly let out a wild rush of line, say the industrial revolution' with a 'pleasure' that was 'in no way inferior to that conferred (presumably) on Mr Adams by his beautiful deduction of Neptune from Uranus.'[48] Despite the undertones of nominalism in *Murphy*; however, it is only after that novel that Beckett appears to have returned to the doctrine still more extensively—both in his notes and subsequent fiction.

§3

One reason for Beckett's return to nominalism after the completion of *Murphy* may well be through the aegis of the Irish poet Brian Coffey. Coffey, a friend of Beckett's from his Dublin days, had been studying in Paris under the renowned Catholic theologian Jacques Maritain. Although Coffey's doctorate concerned the realist doctrine of the mediaeval philosopher St Thomas Acquinas, it may also have facilitated his recommendations for philosophical sources more generally. Beckett's recently-published letters show that, while preparing for his six-month trip to Germany from late 1936 to early 1937, he spent much time with Brian Coffey in Dublin, who recommended reading the philosopher Benedict de Spinoza. Beckett also read works by the 'self confessed nominalist' Bishop Berkeley at this time.[49] It is quite possible that, through this philosophically-minded friend, Beckett again took up the subject of medieval nominalism in 1936. This could, in fact, help to date the following English translation from vol. 1 of Joseph Gredt's 1926, *Elementa philosophiae Aristotelico-Thomisticae*, which Beckett typed out in the original Latin:

> 2. Nominalists: Heraclitus (+475 BC), Cratylus, Heraclitus' disciple, Antisthenes (+369), the Epicureans like Roscellinus (XI century) who was St Anselmus' adversary. The Empiricists, the Sensualists and the Positivists of the most recent periods: Hobbes (1588–1679), Locke (1632–1704), Hume (1711–1776), Condillac (1715–1780), August Comte (1798–1857), Stuart Mill (1806–1873), Spencer (1820–1903), Wundt (1832–1921). They give to "universality" only a mere denominational meaning. In fact, they deny concepts and preach that the term "universal" does not correspond in one's mind to a universal concept, but to a group of individuals already established.

Conceptualists. (the early Stoics, Conceptualists of XIV and XV centuries: William of Occam, John Buridanus, Petrus de Alliaco, Gabriel Biel and finally, Kant (1724–1804) and the Kantians). They admit universal concepts; however, they teach that concepts are a mere creation of our mind and that nothing in nature correspond to them.

Realists believe that universals have a correspondence with the individuals in the external reality. Nevertheless, once more we have two different positions: one which believes that the universal exists independently as such (exaggerated realism). The other instead, (i.e. Aristotle (384–322), Boethius (480–525), St Anselmus (1033–1109), St Thomas (1225–1274) and most Scholastics) teaches that we must distinguish two elements: the matter and what contains the universal concept, namely, nature and form. In fact, they teach that universality is present not only in the intellect but also in the singular object (moderate realism). From this position, as it has been acknowledged by the exaggerated realism, some thinkers believe that the universal as such can exist outside the intellect and outside the object. Others believe instead that the universal is outside the intellect but within the object. The first position is represented by Plato (428–347) who said that pre-existent ideas or forms of objects nevertheless participate to the matter in the same way as the transcendental, universal, and incorruptible eternal matter does.* Another position is the one of Guillelme de Champeaux (1070–1121), who thought that nature does not multiply herself within the same individual species, but there is one and only nature in everything and that individuals are different only in presence of accidents.

Neo-Platonics. Hegel (1770–1831), Schelling (1775–1854) thought that singulars are nothing more than phenomena of the universal nature.

* This is Plato's position as it has been interpreted by Aristotle and the Scholastics. It must be added though, that some thinkers believe that the platonic ideas are divine ideas or copies of objects. But whatever is the nature of the controversy, it is an established fact that Plato did not consider the forms of objects as immanent to the singulars but transcendental.[50]

This single page from Beckett's notes on philosophy is a strong candidate for the scholastic nominalism advanced as a potential literary method in Beckett's 'German Letter' of 1937. This is despite the fact that Beckett purchased the German edition of Windelband's *A History of Philosophy*—surprising, given that he had summarised most of it during 1932 and 1933—including it in one of his books posted home on December 1936 while travelling in Nazi Germany. Interestingly, Gredt includes the Presocratic 'weeping philosopher', Heraclitus, in his list of nominalist philosophers giving 'to "universality" only a mere denominational meaning', thus denying concepts and genera while holding 'that the term "universal" does not correspond in one's mind to a universal concept, but to a group of individuals already established.'

Beckett's final extant notes on philosophical nominalism are revealed by his commonplace book, kept for most of the 1930s, the *'Whoroscope* Notebook'. Although possibly started as early as 1934 or 1935, the bulk of entries date from the period after Beckett's return from Nazi Germany in April 1937. A year later, Beckett first encountered the Austrian language philosopher Fritz Mauthner, who advocated a form of extreme nominalism that, like William of Occam's scholastic terminism, argued that 'Pure nominalism puts an end to thinking':

> the teaching that all concepts or words of human thought are only exhalations of the human voice, logically consistent nominalism, according to which the recognition of reality is just as much denied to the human brain as the make-up of a surface of stone, this pure nominalism, which despite all of the natural sciences still as easily despairs of understanding a fall or colour or electricity as an understanding of consciousness, this epistemological nominalism is not a provable world-view. It would not be nominalism if it pretended to be more than a feeling, than a disposition of the human individual facing the world.[51]

As Dirk van Hulle's important article in the 2002 edition of *Text* makes clear—perhaps the only work to date in Beckett Studies containing nominalism in the title, it might be added—Mauthner's discussion of nominalism occurs at the end of his third and final volume of his revised, 1923 edition of *Beiträge zu einer Kritik der Sprache [Contributions to a Critique of Language]*. Yet it is also in the second volume that Beckett copies large, verbatim transcriptions from Mauthner's opus, which holds that all language is but a poor metaphor to express empirical sensory experience. What van Hulle usefully calls Mauthner's 'nominalist thesis' holds that, on account of its metaphorical nature, language cannot convey concepts, ideas, and general principles. This position is made strikingly clear toward the end of his second volume, *Concerning Linguistics*, in a section fittingly entitled 'History of Philosophy'. Unlike Beckett's other 10 transcribed passages from Mauthner, however, the following, excepted passage on the 'Self-Destruction of the Metaphorical' are not hand-copied into the '*Whoroscope* Notebook', but stand alone as a four page typescript:

> The coherent history of so-called philosophy starts first, however, with the ancient Greeks, who with enormous, bold, false analogies made—either something impossible to imagine, like xxxx, or one of the four elements—into a world view "determining" principle, the sole "of that which exists". This had therefore to be caused by itself, a senseless concept, even if it has dominated for a full two-thousand years. That was recognised immediately by logical thinkers and made "that which does not exists" the cause for "that which exists", whereby the metaphor really makes the world turn a somersault. The Sophists undermined both concepts and made the human being into the standard of the world; one abused them because of that, and Socrates had to die for it. The reaction announced itself in his poetic pupil Plato, who was responsible for raising the over-estimation of metaphorical language to a highpoint which it has occupied for more than a millennium, yes, indeed to the present. While he had learned from a predecessor the deceptiveness of the "reality picture" (Everything is in a state of flux), he did not thereby—as did Socrates—confess to not knowing, but personified

instead the abstractions of language, made ideas into the mothers of the world. Time is turned upside down, the last is termed the first, the concepts abstracted from "individual things" are called the cause of the singular thing.

Aristotle was able to see through the enormity of this false analogy, which after all only made "that which does not exist" the basis for "that which exists" again. That is why he stated ideas as being immanent. One expressed this in the Middle Ages in the following fashion: that he replaced the Universals *ante rem* with Universals *in re*. It was a destruction of the "ideas metaphor". But with a much more dangerous, less easy to comprehend anthropomorphism he now made on his part the "necessity concept" the causal factor for the world, for the soul, for the "form principle" of matter. To these ideas Christendom brought—along with the epigone schools of Greek philosophy which preceded it—the religious concept of God, and for centuries the scholastics wore their teeth out in chewing through the chain of these entwined metaphors. <u>The nominalism of the Middle Ages is the first attempt at a genuine self-destruction of metaphorical thinking</u>. Nominalism could not, despite all sorts of heresies, liberate itself from theology. In this connection Descartes also appears as a theologian who also wore his teeth out. He solves many minor metaphors, but prays to the highest metaphor, God, who is now assigned a much more difficult role than in religion. [....]

This continuity could be represented in such a schematic fashion that one could start the great division with Plato and Aristotle, and even more so with their one-sided interpreters; both intellectual direction want to make that does not exists the cause of all that exists. The Platonists' conceptual ideas, the Aristotleans' "essential concepts" of Scholasticism, which in its spread reaches down to Kant and Schopenhauer, is in all free thinkers an amazingly astute attempt to undermine Plato's teaching of ideas and to surmount the intellect-murdering "word realism". On the effectiveness of "essential concepts" not one of these series of thinkers really has any doubt, since Kant still constructs his practical philosophy on "essential concepts" and Schopenhauer also teaches the "monster" of an admittedly stupid, but still "purposeful-thinking" will in nature [....] our critique of language has taught us that even the most concrete concept does not provide any experience, but only the appearance of experience, that therefore even the brilliant richness of pictures painted by a poet of thought cannot transcend the boundaries of language. A critique of pure reason cannot help here, but only the critique of reason in general, the critique of language. We only understand the world of reality when we act, only when we ourselves stand actively in the midst of reality, never when we just wish to confront it by thinking about it. Whatever the human may dare to do through superhuman strength in order to discover truth, he always finds only himself, a human truth, an anthropomorphic picture of the world.[52]

The proximity to mediaeval terminism should be clear, even if Mauthner's scepticism of the value of language *tout court* might be considered an even more extreme form of 'extreme Nominalism' than that ventured by mediaeval philosophy. Interestingly, following the last of Beckett's transcriptions from Mauthner's 'epistemological nominalism' into his '*Whoroscope* Notebook'—and therefore dating from 1938, ostensibly one of the last extant notes on philosophy—Windelband crops up yet again.[53] Thanks to his preparations for, and travels in,

Germany during 1936 and 1937, Beckett was able to read difficult German passages in philosophy that he likely could not understand four or five years earlier; that is, at the time of his composing his 'Philosophy Notes' from books written in (or translated into) English. The final excerpted transcription, while also focussing on the relationship of the general to the particular, does not come from *A History of Philosophy*, but from another of Windelband's thematic texts, *The Handbook of Philosophy* co-written by Windelband and Heinz Heimsoeth:

> The crucial exemplar for this philosophy of the human mind, for its idealist standpoint and its methodology (considerably differing in detail) is Kant, as creator of the three critiques. The realistic considerations, as well as the metaphysical backgrounds and ultimate intentions, of Kantian reflexion on reason and consciousness are shed, or rather interpreted away, throughout. "Critique" here becomes an excluding antonym [Gegenbegriff] of "metaphysics". Under the influence of the positivistic-agnostic resignation of the 19th century, Kant, and the task of philosophy to be taken over [or: borrowed] from Kant, are seen strictly in terms of "transcendental logic", which as pure self-reflection of the human mind should take the place of all ontology and metaphysics before and after Kant. The fundamental conviction is the absolutely insurmountable immanence of consciousness. All questions touching on the being beyond (or even this side of) consciousness, are to be rejected as "uncritical". The ground of consciousness—as of a spiritual [ideellen] "consciousness as such" constituting everything representational [alles Gegenständliche] in categories of thought and functions of meaning—is the basis for all preconditionless reasoning [Begründung] and thus for all scientific philosophy. The idealism of consciousness [Bewußtseinsidealismus] overcomes the dogmatism of the "scientific worldview" ["naturwissenschaftlichen Weltanschauung"] and demonstrates [or: proves] the autonomous laws of the mind as [being] preconditions of all apparently "given" reality and all encounterable determinations of being [vorfindbaren Seinsdeterminationen]. Consciousness is free [i.e. uninhibited]; its spontaneity lies ahead of [or: before] all causality [Kausalgebundenheit]; the natural laws themselves are creations of the mind. The system of spiritual forms [ideellen Formen] to be researched philosophically lies ahead of all reality that can be experienced; all "being" is itself dependent on the methods of consciousness [....]
>
> It is the limitation and danger of this modern form of "idealism", that although it puts a stop to naturalism with the demonstration of autonomous laws and the superior significance of the mental (as of the human consciousness with its spiritual-meaningful forms which has to be assumed in all science and scientific worldview), reality, however, the representational realm of experience and the sciences, was split off from the mental-spiritual [vom Geistig-Ideellen]: so that on the one hand conscious and thinking, idea and value had to remain purely in the abstract of a "transcendental consciousness" removed from any question of reality, on the other hand, however, all concrete empirical amount of content [Gehaltsfülle], even for instance that of the psyche, was given over to the representational categories [Gegenstandskategorien] of causal thinking. Two worlds, an abstract spiritual and a concrete real, even though in a relation of encompassing, stand facing each other.[54]

Nominalism thus snakes through the veritable entirety of Beckett's 'Interwar Notes', from his beginning of his 'Philosophy Notes' in later 1932 until his encounter with Mauthner, and return to Windelband, some six years later, in mid-1938. That is was Windelband, decidedly no advocate of nominalism, who had introduced Beckett to the subject is an interesting irony; that the latter continued to work on the concept—especially in relation to mediaeval philosophy—suggests something altogether less coincidental. For Windelband's writings effectively book-ended Beckett's philosophical note-taking in the 1930s, and was responsible for the bulk of Beckett's readings about the history of Western philosophy. Even if Beckett was to turn this kind of systematic knowledge on its head from *Watt*—and more notably, in his 'frenzy of writing' after 1945—to embrace a '<u>docta ignorantia</u>' worthy of Nicolas Cusanus and Fritz Mauthner, a major stepping stone on the way to Beckett's artistically employed linguistic scepticism was nominalism. If originally derived from Windelband's systematic history of philosophy comprising a portion of the 'Philosophy Notes', Beckett took further notes on these ideas after the completion of *Murphy* and before the start of *Watt*. From Watt's inability to name a pot to his general need of 'semantic succor', Beckett's wartime novel may be considered the first to employ nominalist—or better, terminist—ideas woven into the very structure of the novel. And while I have not broached works written after 1945 here, what Enoch Brater has called Beckett's 'minimalism' in his later works for stage and page, again, may be similarly read in the light of philosophical nominalism. For it is not for nothing that *Watt* also points forward to the mature works, concluding in good terministic fashion, 'no symbols where none intended'.[55]

NOTES

1. Egbert C. Smyth, 'Brief Notice of Important Books', in *The Andover Review: A Religious and Theological Monthly* 114 (1893), p. 776.
2. Samuel Beckett, 'Gnome', in *Selected Poems 1930–1989*, ed. David Wheatley (London: Faber and Faber, 2009c), p. 9.
3. Cited in Anne Atik, *How It Was: A Memoir of Samuel Beckett* (London: Faber and Faber, 2001), p. 121.
4. Wilhelm Windelband, *A History of Philosophy*, 2 vols., trans. James H. Tufts (New York: Harper Torchbooks, 1958), pp. ix-x; italics in original.
5. Samuel Beckett, The *Letters of Samuel Beckett, 1929-1940: Volume I*, eds. Martha Dow Fehsenfeld and Lois Overbeck (Cambridge, Cambridge University Press: 2009), pp 317, 523–28.
6. For insightful accounts of both of these publishing fiascos, see Mark Nixon, ed., *Samuel Beckett and Publishing* (London: The British Library, 2011), especially chs. 1 and 3.
7. See 'Nobelprize.org', available online at: http://nobelprize.org/nobel_prizes/literature/laureates/1969/press.html (all websites last accessed 12/12/14).
8. James Knowlson, *Damned To Fame: The Life of Samuel Beckett* (London: Bloomsbury, 1996), p. 353.
9. Cited in Mark Nixon, *Samuel Beckett's German Diaries 1936-1937* (London: Bloomsbury, 2011), p. 125.
10. *Notes diverse holo* [sic]: *Catalogues of Beckett's reading notes and other manuscripts at Trinity College Dublin, with supporting essays*, in *Samuel Beckett Today / Aujourd'hui*, 16 (Amsterdam: Rodopi, 2006), pp. 29–172.
11. For further details of Beckett's engagement with 'early Greek philosophy', see Peter Fifield, '"Of being – or remaining": Beckett and Early Greek Philosophy', in *Beckett/Philosophy*, eds. Matthew Feldman and Karim Mamdani, special issue of the *Sophia Philosophical Review* (Sofia: Sofia University Press, 2011).
12. The subsequent periods identified by Windelband, and transcribed verbatim by Beckett, were 'Hellenistic-Roman Philosophy'; 'Mediaeval Philosophy'; 'Philosophy of the Renaissance'; 'Philosophy of the Enlightenment'; 'The German Philosophy'; and seventh, 'Nineteenth Century Philosophy' (TCD 10967/1v).
13. Beckett, 'Philosophy Notes', TCD 10967/145r.
14. Beckett to Alan Schneider, 21 November 1957, in Maurice Harmon, ed., *No Author Better Served: The Correspondence of Alan Schneider and Samuel Beckett* (London: Harvard University Press, 1998), p. 23. Apparently the only critic to have been given access to the original manuscripts of the 'Philosophy Notes' is Everett Frost. Despite a number of howlers (exemplified by the mis-transcription of the volume's title), Frost's overview of the colour coding of TCD 10967 must be taken on trust; see *Notes diverse holo* [sic], p. 67.
15. See 'Serena I', in Beckett, *Selected Poems 1930–1989*, p. 25, corresponding to Beckett, 'Philosophy Notes', TCD 10967/5r. John Pilling's indispensable *A Samuel Beckett Chronology* (Basingstoke: Palgrave, 2006) dates the commencement of this poem to 12 September 1932, p. 39. As Peter Fifield has shown, this reference is actually taken from volume one of Johann Erdmann's 1866 *History of Philosophy*; see his '"Of being – or remaining": Beckett and Early Greek Philosophy', pp. 111–13.

[16] Samuel Beckett, *Ill Seen Ill Said* (London: Faber and Faber, 2009), p. 60, corresponding to TCD 1096730v.

[17] For these canonical discussions of Beckett and Descartes, see respectively, John Fletcher, *Samuel Beckett's Art* (London: Chatto & Windus, 1967), cited p.129; and Roger Scruton, 'Beckett and the Cartesian Soul', in *The Aesthetic Understanding: Essays in the Philosophy of Art and* Culture (Manchester: Carcanet Press, 1983), p. 230. For a counter-argument positing Beckett's more general indebtedness to Western philosophy, see my *Beckett's Books* (London: Bloomsbury, 2008), ch. 3.

[18] TCD 10967/109r-109v, corresponding to Wilhelm Windelband, *A History of Philosophy*, pp. 151, 154. When placed alongside Windelband's original, Beckett's summary gives a useful and representative insight into Beckett's method of taking summative notes from this source:

> As in the animal soul impulse and perception were to be distinguished as different expressions, so, too, the reason develops itself, partly as rational action, partly as rational thought; as perfection, on the one hand, of the character or disposition, on the other, of the faculty of intelligence. Thus there result, as the excellence or ability of the rational man, the ethical and the intellectual or dianoetic virtues.
>
> The ethical virtues grow out of that training of the will by which it becomes accustomed to act according to right insight. It enables man, in his decisions to follow practical reason, i.e. insight into what is correct or proper. With this doctrine Aristotle transcends the principles of Socrates, - with evident regards to the facts of the ethical life: not that he assigned to the will a psychological independence as over against knowledge; the point, rather, is, that he gave up the opinion that the determination of the will arising from the rational insight must itself be stronger than the desire arising from defective knowledge [(151)....]
>
> But knowledge of these, the full unfolding of the "active reason" in man, is again designated by Aristotle as a "*beholding*"; and with this beholding of the highest truth man gains a participation in that pure thought, in which the essence of the deity consists, and thus, also, in the eternal blessedness of the divine self-consciousness. For this "beholding" which exists only for its own sake and has no ends of will or deed, this wishless absorption in the perception of the highest truth, is the blessedest and best of all (154, all italics in original; Windelband's numbering and use of Greek terminology is excluded both here and in Beckett's "Philosophy Notes").

[19] C.J. Ackerley, *Obscure Locks, Simple Keys: The Annotated* Watt (Tallahassee: Journal of Beckett Studies Books, 2005), pp. 73–74.

[20] Samuel Beckett, *Watt*, ed. Chris Ackerley (London: Faber and Faber, 2009e), pp. 39–40, italics added on 'intellectual', 'dianoetic' and 'beholding'.

[21] The corresponding entry used for the epigraph to ch. 6 of Murphy can be found in a footnote by Windelband on p. 410.

[22] 'Wilhelm Windelband: Philosophy as the Science of Values', in Thomas E. Willey, *Back to Kant: The Revival of Kantianism in German Social and Historical Thought, 1860–1914* (Detroit: Wayne State University Press, 1978), pp. 134–39.

[23] Lanier R. Anderson, 'Neo-Kantianism and the Roots of Anti-Psuychologism', *British Journal for the History of Philosophy* 13/2 (2005), p. 314.

[24] Cited in Frederick C. Beiser, 'Normativity in Neo-Kantianism: Its Rise and Fall', in the *International Journal of Philosophical Studies* 17/1 (2009), p. 14.

²⁵ All English passages from Beckett's 'German Diary' entry of 15 January 1937 are taken from Knowlson, *Damned to Fame*, pp. 244–45.
²⁶ Rubin Rabinovitz, '*Watt* from Descartes to Schopenhauer', in *Modern Irish Literature: Essays in Honor of William York Tindall*, eds. Raymond J. Porter and James D. Brophy, (New York: Iona College Press, 1972), p. 261.
²⁷ For discussion of Beckett's claims to not understand philosophy, see my '"I am not a philosopher'. Beckett and Philosophy: A Methodological and Thematic Introduction", in the *Sofia Philosophical Review* 4/2 (2010).
²⁸ Samuel Beckett, *Proust*, in Beckett, Proust *and* Three Dialogues (London: Calder & Boyers, 1970), p. 29.
²⁹ Samuel Beckett, *Murphy*, ed. J.C.C. Mays (London: Faber and Faber, 2009b), p. 13.
³⁰ Samuel Beckett, 'German Letter' of 1937, cited in Beckett, *Disjecta: Miscellaneous Writings and a Dramatic Fragment*, ed. Ruby Cohn (New York: Grove Press, 1984), pp. 51–55, with the English translation provided on pp. 171–73.
³¹ Wilhelm Windelband, *An Introduction to Philosophy*, trans. Joseph McCabe (London: Unwin, 1921), pp. 186–37; italics in original.
³² Windelband, *A History of Philosophy*, p. ix.
³³ Variously quoted in Zoltán Szabó, 'Nominalism', in *The Oxford Handbook of Metaphysics*, in M.J. Loux and D. Zimmerman, eds. (Oxford: Oxford University Press, 2003).
³⁴ Beckett, *Watt*, p. 144.
³⁵ See Ackerley. *Obscure Locks, Simple Keys*, p. 289, with references corresponding to pages in *Watt* on Scholasticism (22–23); the Galls father and son (60ff, quoted 80); and on the 'famished dog' (75ff, quoted 80).
³⁶ Beckett, *Watt*, pp. 67–68. Ackerley writes the passage 'Pot, pot': 'Beckett in the galleys (G26) was particular about this capitalization, the two "forms" intimating the Idea and the particular, the latter evading by a hairbreadth the nature of a true Pot', contributing to 'Watt's awareness of the pot as pot, as individual and not as a class', *Obscure Locks, Simple Keys*, entry #81.2, p. 99.
³⁷ Dena Shottenkirk, *Nominalism and its aftermath* (London: Springer, 2009), p. 5, which continues: 'to summarise, the first problem with universals for the nominalist is that no sense can be made of what exactly these universals are; their existence can't be accounted for in the way tat something is normally said to exist in space and time. Secondly, the exact way that they come to participate in the separate entity of the participating particular is likewise inexplicable, the account usually remaining on the metaphorical level with the use of words such as "instantiating", "inhering in", "partaking in", etc. None of these terms are description of the mechanism of the relationship between the two different ontological entities; in other words, they are no explanations but merely attempts at analogies.'
³⁸ Regrettably, space does not permit a discussion of these classical Greek debates here, except to note Shottenkirk's insightful point *en passant*: 'While the debate between those who maintained the existence of mind-independent universals and those who argued against such entities presented itself from the earliest of pre-Socratic philosophy – framed as the One and the Many – and while this continued throughout ancient Greek writings in the examples of both Plato and Aristotle, it is in two other separate time periods that this issues comes to dominate much of philosophical writing: in the medieval period and in the mid-twentieth century', p. 5.
³⁹ Windelband, *A History of Philosophy*, p. 285.

[40] Beckett, 'Philosophy Notes', TCD 10967/154v, corresponding to *A History of Philosophy*, p. 288.
[41] Beckett, 'Philosophy Notes', 10967/155v-10967/156r, corresponding to *A History of Philosophy*, pp. 296–98.
[42] Samuel Beckett, 'German Letter' of 1937, in *Disjecta*, p. 173.
[43] Beckett, 'Philosophy Notes', TCD 10967/159v, corresponding to *A History of Philosophy*, p. 342.
[44] *Ibid.*, p. 341. For further discussion of Beckett, Schopenhauer and the 'veil of Maya', see ch. 6.
[45] For discussion of Beckett's entry on Schopenhauer in the 'Philosophy Notes', see *Beckett's Books*, pp. 48–50.
[46] Beckett, 'Philosophy Notes', TCD 10967/170v-10967/171r, corresponding to *A History of Philosophy*, pp. 341–43.
[47] Beckett, *Murphy*, pp. 12, 10.
[48] *Ibid.*, p. 157.
[49] Tom Stoneham, *Berkeley's World: An examination of the Three Dialogues* (Oxford: Oxford University Press: 2002), p. 216. Stoneham adds (pp. 220, 221, 223–224): 'Nominalism is a working assumption of Berkeley's philosophy. There is a strong connection between empiricism and nominalism [....] that we never come across universals in our sense experiences [....] we can summarize Berkeley's reasons for agreeing with the "universally received maxim" that everything which exists is particular: only minds and perceived ideas exists; minds are particulars and all perceived ideas are particulars.'
[50] Beckett, TCD MS 10971/6/37, corresponding to Joseph Gredt, *Elementa philosophiae Aristotelico-Thomisticae*, 2 vols. (Freiburg: Herder, 1926), pp. 96–97; the translation, provided by Anna Castriota, is also available in my 'Sourcing "Aporetics": An Empirical Study on Philosophical Influences on the Development of Samuel Beckett's Writings', (Unpublished PhD. Thesis: Oxford Brookes University, 2004), Appendix E.
[51] This entry in Beckett's '*Whoroscope* Notebook', UoR MS 3000/1, translated from the German by the late Prof. Detlef Mühlberger, is the first of 10 verbatim handwritten quotations taken from the 1923 edition of Fritz Mauthner's *Beiträge zu Einer Kritik der Sprache*, 3 vols. (Leipzig: Verlag von Felix Meiner, 1923), p. 615. Windelband's subject discussed in this section is 'Epistemological Nominalism'. For a complete translation of these transcriptions, see Feldman, 'Sourcing "Aporetics"', Appendix D.
[52] Samuel Beckett, TCD 10971/5/1–10971/5/4, a four-page transcription corresponding to Fritz Mauthner's second volume of *Beiträge zu einer Kritik der Sprache*. Translation provided by the late Prof. Detlef Mühlberger, and available in *ibid.*, Appendix D.
[53] Beckett's transcriptions from Mauthner's *Beiträge zu einer Kritik der Sprache* in his '*Whoroscope* Notebook', UoR MSS 3000/1, conclude at 59r, while that from Windelband/Heimsoeth, under Beckett's headed note 'Philosophy in 20th century stresses problem of cognition', begins on 65r.
[54] *Ibid.*, 65r-66v; I am grateful for to Christian Egners for translation for this passage in Beckett's '*Whoroscope* Notebook', corresponding the section 'Philosophy in the 20th Century', pp. 574–576 in Wilhelm Windelband with Heinz Heimsoeth, *Lehrbuch der Geschichte der Philosophie. Billige Ausgabe. Mit einem Schlusskapitel "Die Philosophie im 20. Jahrhundert" und einer Übersicht über den Stand der philosophiegeschichtlichen Forschung* (Tübingen, J. C. B. Mohr: 1935); italics in original.

[55] See Enoch Brater, *Beckett's Minimalism Beckett's Late Style in the Theatre* (Oxford: Oxford University Press, 1987); and Beckett, *Watt*, cited p. 223.

A "SUITABLE ENGINE OF DESTRUCTION"?:
Samuel Beckett and Arnold Geulincx's *Ethics*

> I remember coming out once, the regulation 20 years ago, being at that time less little than now, with an angry article on modern Irish poets, in which I set up, as criterion of worthwhile modern poetry, awareness of the vanished object. Already! And talking, as the only terrain accessible to the poet, of the no man's land that he projects round himself, rather as a flame projects its zone of evaporation. A dismal kind of dodging, right enough, where the hunt goes on.
> – Samuel Beckett, letter to Georges Duthuit[1]

§1

Languishing in darkness on the operating table, with only the 'last ditch' of his mind for company, Belacqua Shuah—the first in a procession of long-suffering Beckettian characters and, arguably, Beckett's literary alter-egos—suddenly realised he had always 'bragged of how he furnished his mind and lived there', and thus 'ransacked his mind for a suitable engine of destruction'. Thus, at this early stage in his writing career, Beckett was already searching for a way of transcending the pricks of consciousness, of abstracting literature in such a way as to 'bore holes in the silence' or a way to 'let being into art', as two later formulations, in 1937 (to Kaun) and 1961 (to Harvey) respectively, put it. But in the 1933 'Yellow', the penultimate story in *More Pricks Than Kicks*, all that Belacqua, and latterly, Beckett, I shall argue, could latch onto were 'the extremes of wisdom' found in one of John Donne's verbal paradoxes: 'Now among our wise men, I doubt not but many would be found, who would laugh at Heraclitus weeping, none which would weep at Democritus laughing.'[2]

Yet if these opposing philosophical responses to the uncertainty and absurdity of human existence had worked for the moribund Belacqua, they failed spectacularly that year for the author. For the lancing of a boil in May, the death of his father in June, and a increasing sense of despair which sent Beckett to Wilfred Bion's couch at the Tavistock Clinic in December 1933, collectively pointed to the end of one way of going on, understood by the contemporaneous quatrain 'Gnome' as merely 'the loutishness of learning'. From this point on, intellect alone was no calmative. More than just 'a suitable engine of destruction' for the mind, 'a suitable engine' for perseverance for the spirit was missing. In a world ungraspable by logic alone, for Beckett, something else was needed: an ethics capable of mediating the problems encountered by this struggling artist in the 1930s.

Enter Arnold Geulincx (1624–1669), who Beckett initially encountered around 1932–3, as part of his 267-page corpus of 'Philosophy Notes'. Over several sides of once-ringed '[l]oose leaves, 162 x 203mm.' wide,[3] originally taken from Wilhelm Windelband's revised *A History of Philosophy*, Geulincx is initially treated as yet another philosopher at the extremes of thought; in this case, through the ideas with which he is traditionally most associated—'Occasionalism':

> This furthest developed in Ethics of Geulincx. Illustration of the 2 Clocks which having once been synchronised by same artificer continue to move in perfect harmony, "absque ulla causalitate qua alterum hoc in altero causat, sed propter meram dependentiam, qua utrumque ab eadem arte et simili industria constitutum est".
> What anthropologism!
> Leibniz illustrated with same analogy his doctrine of "preestablished harmony", characterised Cartesian conception by immediate and permanent interdependence of 2 clocks, and Occasionalist by constantly renewed regulation of clocks by clock master.[4]

Contained above are the seeds of Beckett's later, ongoing fascination with Geulincx, of which more presently. These handwritten notes also point toward the documentary nature of the Beckett-Geulincx connection and, consequently, of the 'falsifiable'[5] methodology undertaken here. In turn, such a focus means relegating a number of interesting historiographical developments to the periphery. These include or, rather, for reasons of space must exclude, the mysterious story of an a seventeenth century philosopher attempting to marry Cartesian rationalism with a kind of Christian quietism;[6] Geulincx's then long-posthumous role, alongside Leibniz, in a nineteenth century academic debate over 'intellectual property rights' (especially the idea of the synchronous clocks noted by Beckett above), spurring on J.P.N. Land's monumental 3-volume edition over 1891–3, *Arnoldi Geulincx Anverpiensis Opera Philosophica*;[7] the placement of these transcriptions within the larger corpus of Beckett's extant reading notes during the interwar years; and even a recounting of Geulincx's recent fashionability, one itself largely due to Beckett's first Latin encounter with, and then heavily influenced by, the *Ethica* in winter/spring 1936.

Rather than these accounts, indicated in the endnotes below, the significance of the latter event is surely of greatest relevance to *Beckett and Ethics*, namely, as Beckett stated to his great friend and correspondent, Thomas MacGreevy on 16 January 1933:

> I have been reading Geulincx in T.C.D., without knowing why exactly. Perhaps because the text is so hard to come by. But that is rationalisation & my instinct is right & the work worth doing, because of its saturation in the conviction that the *sub specie aeternitatis* [from the perspective of eternity] vision is the only excuse for remaining alive.[8]

In contrast to his earlier notes from Windleband, then, Beckett's later reading of Geulincx finds the latter actually *overcoming* 'anthropologism' through an ultimately ethical vision: 'from the perspective of eternity'. I will presently argue that Geulincx's philosophy was, for Beckett (from 1936, if not from 1933), one answer to a perplexing question facing both philosopher and artist; one aptly formulated in Geulincx's *Ethics:* 'if both body and soul are foolish, what is my intelligence worth?'[9]

But first, a contextualising note on the intervening 'London Years' (c.1934–5) is in order. Although the two years after the writing of 'Yellow' saw Beckett also complete *Murphy* and publish *Echo's Bones and Other Precipitates*, these were, first and foremost, long months of particularly intense self-education and psychological distress. Beyond the loss and solitude Beckett felt over the middle 1930s, however, a decisive change in his outlook was simultaneously taking shape. Two fundamental aspects of this evolving view, one of which I have elsewhere shorthanded as 'agnostic quietism',[10] are relevant to this chapter. And both are, arguably, initially presented in two of Beckett's non-fiction reviews published during the summer of 1934; that is, fully eleven years prior to 'the revelation' in his mother's room, later dramatised in *Krapp's Last Tape*.[11] The foremost of these is reflected in Beckett's praise of his Thomas MacGreevy *Poems* for *Dublin Magazine*. 'All poetry, as discriminated from the various paradigms of prosody, is prayer', Beckett declared in his suggestively titled 'Humanistic Quietism', while 'prayer is no more (no less) than an act of recognition.'[12] Here, my suggestion is that, during these transitional years, poetry was progressively taking over the long-lapsed role of belief in Beckett's life. In other words, Beckett's 'recognition' deliberately substituted Art for God.[13]

A second, related consideration may be witnessed in 'Recent Irish Poetry' as a 'principle of individuation' (a phrase actually borrowed from Arthur Schopenhauer)—or indeed demarcated battle lines—separating modern from traditional art in Ireland. This chasm between 'antiquarians and others', for the young Beckett already centred upon an awareness of 'the breakdown of the object, whether current, historical, mythical or spook'; or alternatively, the 'breakdown of the subject. It comes to the same thing—rupture of the lines of communication.' Though for his part strongly against the antiquarians—close connection with James Joyce and the *Work in Progress* circle in Paris from 1929 had ensured this—Beckett tacitly assigned himself an added task: a reconnaissance of what 'Recent Irish Poetry' dubbed the 'no man's land' *between* subject and object.[14]

Precisely this artistic dilemma and precisely this review are, tellingly, referred to in Beckett's 1949 letter to Duthuit from the epigraph above. But that this becomes something of an artistic crusade actually much earlier is demonstrated by Beckett's writing during the 1930s, by the insightful 'German Diaries' of 1936–7, and in various letters from the time—especially to MacGreevy. Exemplifying the latter, in the words of James Knowlson, Beckett offered 'an exhilarating piece of analysis' on art (ostensibly on the painting of Paul Cézanne) in two letters to MacGreevy in September 1934. In the first of these, Beckett praised the post-impressionist who 'seems to have been the first to see landscape and state it as material of a strictly peculiar order, incommensurable with all human expressions whatsoever'. In turn, this view of Cézanne's landscapes dispassionately presented 'an alien view of man himself'. Fascinatingly, this was umbilically linked to personal experience, as Beckett continued: 'he had the sense of his incommensurability not only with life of such a different order as landscape, but even with life of his own order, even with the life [...] operative in himself'.[15]

As with many of his comments on fellow artists, Beckett's view of Cézanne—and indeed, of the Irish poetry scene of the mid-1930s—was heavily coloured by his own artistic preferences. Beckett may even have been writing principally about himself. 'So you can't talk art with me', Beckett wrote twenty years later to George Duthuit, putative 'D.' in the well-known 'Three Dialogues', 'all I risk expressing when I speak about it are my own obsessions'.[16] In this light, it is not surprising to find that, in a second letter on Cézanne from 8 September 1934, Beckett notes with admiration the latter's rejection of anthropomorphisation, an idea roughly interchangeable with the dreaded 'anthropologism!' above. Moreover, variations on the word 'anthropomorphism' occur four times—the last instance through an insightful comment, with hindsight, anticipating Beckett's postwar literature (that veiled subject of the 1949 *Three Dialogues with Georges Duthuit*):

> Perhaps it is the one bright spot in a mechanistic age - the deanthropomorphisation of the artist. Even the portrait beginning to be dehumanised as the individual feels himself more and more hermetic and alone and his neighbour a coagulum as alien as a protoplast or God, incapable of loving or hating anyone but himself.[17]

As distinct from Belacqua's 'suitable engine of destruction', a search was now underway for a method of writing existence from the outside, as it were, as pure perception; to write about life with detachment, as though it were inanimate, which was to be an artistic 'bright spot' amongst human suffering. It was, therefore, necessary to examine the 'no man's land' between subject and object, while simultaneously returning to Art a sense of numinousness and 'incommensurability'. That this was an ethical challenge no less than an intellectual exercise is made clear in a remarkably self-definitional letter to MacGreevy some six months later:

Am I to set my teeth and be disinterested? When I cannot answer for myself, and do not dispose of myself, how can I serve? [....] Macché! Or is there some way of devoting pain and monstrosity and incapacitation to the service of a deserving cause?[18]

Discussing this letter in his groundbreaking thesis, Mark Nixon notes an important difference between the divinely-oriented Geulincx and Thomas á Kempis (the ostensible subject of the letter) with Beckett's own, secular concerns:

> having no "disposition for the supernatural", as he told M[a]cGreevy in his discussion of *The Imitation*, Beckett removed the origin of the self-effacement, the "contempt for self", as deriving from the human worthlessness before God, in order to arrive at the "self-referring quietism". This removal of the transcendental application of the quietist position did nothing to diminish the value of *The Imitation* or the "guignol world" of the *Ethica*, which nevertheless offered an aesthetic and an ethic by which to exist within a meaningless universe.[19]

Beckett, in life no less than in literature, was searching for a way to eff the ineffable, to artistically mediate inner and outer worlds, to find a 'deserving cause' for suffering—all without recourse to God. Over the next ten months the dilemma became still more acute artistically; the writing of *Murphy* began to stall around Christmas 1935. The problem for the character Murphy, the novel *Murphy*, as well as its writer, was how to 'tolerate, let alone cultivate, the occasions of fiasco'. Linguistic paradoxes alone no longer offered 'a suitable engine of destruction'; and for Murphy, it 'was not enough to *want nothing where he was worth nothing*, nor even to take the further step of renouncing all that lay outside the intellectual love in which he alone could love himself'. Affective attachment to the world plagued both author and character, 'as witness his deplorable susceptibility to Celia, ginger and so on. The means of clinching it were lacking.'[20]

Enter Arnold Geulincx again, this time in January 1936. Only at this point did Beckett take up the study of Geulincx specifically and in earnest. In addition to numerous letters documenting his reading of Geulincx at Trinity College, Dublin between 9 January and 15 April 1936, Beckett transcribed nearly 15,000 words, in arduous Latin, from three of Geulincx's central works. These were taken from Land's compendium, *Opera Philosophica*: about one hundred words from *Quaestiones Quodlibeticae* [*Questions Concerning Disputations*] (vol. I, pp. 67–147), some 2,500 words from the *Metaphysica* [*Metaphysics*] (vol. II, pp. 137–310) and the rest from Geulincx's masterpiece, the *Ethica* [*Ethics*] (vol. III, pp. 1–271). As attested by the relative lengths of transcription, the *Ethics* were of a far greatest interest to Beckett than the rest, also borne out by three surviving handwritten pages and a 'fair copy'—meaning that at some point Beckett likely handwrote, typed, and then re-typed his detailed reading notes from the *Ethica*. Alongside a supporting essay by Anthony Uhlmann, these transcriptions are now reproduced in Martin Wilson's important translation, *Arnold Geulincx Ethics*, one of several studies covering Beckett's extant manuscripts between about 1928 and 1938—covering a variety of subjects from literature and painting to philosophy and history—a corpus of materials I have termed 'Interwar Notes'.[21]

In this approximately four-month encounter with Geulincx, moreover, Beckett was to establish a longstanding influence both usually explicit in his work, and equally surprising in terms of the dearth of scholarship on the subject. For Geulincx, it would seem, remains the 'Third Man' of Beckett studies: everyone knows he's there, but no one really knows how. This makes for rich irony given Geulincx's philosophy. But then again, this is Beckett Country. And it is rather doubtful that Geulincx was known for irony, or for humour (his personal maxim was 'Serious and Candid'). For example, consider the core of his philosophy, encapsulated in this excerpt from the *Metaphysics*: 'But for the time being, it is enough for me to recall that what I do not know how to do is not my action. I am persuaded, then, that my human condition depends not on some natural necessity, but on the operation of a will: not my will, obviously, but on another's, namely, God's will.' Put another way, as Beckett has it in *Texts for Nothing 3*, 'It's enough to will it, I'll will it, will me a body, will me a head, a little strength, a little courage, I'm starting now, a week is soon served, then back here, this inextricable place, far from days, the far days, it's not going to be easy.'[22] As a result, Beckett is known as a literary revolutionary, and Geulincx merely a little-known philosopher amongst the many followers of Descartes' New Science.

§2

This encounter with Geulincx's philosophy was the first of its type for Beckett: *erudition that ultimately asserts human ignorance.* Much like his psychoanalytic notes taken two years previously—which were principally typed up from an introduction to psychology and various psychoanalytic texts mainly taken from disciples of Freud—Beckett's transcriptions of the central tenets of Geulincx's moral philosophy hit Beckett for what they ultimately are: a self-cancelling knowledge, or perhaps better, interacting binaries of thought; namely, the mystical and the rational.

Now, if talking about Beckett's thinking about Geulincx's writing about the idea of ineffability not 'doomed to fail' from the outset, a few words on the idiosyncratic Geulincx are necessary. Idiosyncratic is apt if only on account of the strange circumstances in which Geulincx found himself: an erudite believer anxious to reconcile the rationalism of the so-called New Philosophy with the ineffable power of an interventionist God, leading to Proposition 9 that Beckett recorded from the *Metaphysics*: 'I call that body mine, by whose occasion diverse thoughts arise in my mind that do not depend on me.'[23] For this reason, the divine *occasion* of an internally thinking subject and an external object means that thought and action correspond like two simultaneously running clocks, leading this extreme mix of rationalism and mysticism dubbed 'occasionalism'.

Without doubt, *Murphy* is the work most explicitly concerned with Arnold Geulincx, in keeping with Beckett's general practice of drawing upon his contemporaneous reading in his writings (such as selections of Descartes for *Whoroscope*, Dante's *Divine Comedy* for *Dream of Fair to Middling Women*, or *King Lear* for *Worstword Ho*). And Geulincx was to become the singly figure most explicitly referred to across Beckett's oeuvre. Unsurprisingly then, mere days after encountering Geulincx at TCD, Beckett had already identified his famously favourite Geulingian maxim in an insightful comment to MacGreevy:

> I suddenly see that *Murphy* is break down between his: *Ubi nihil vales ibi nihil velis* (position) [where you are worth nothing, you will wish for nothing] and Malraux's *Il est difficile a celui qui vit hors du monde de ne pas rechercher les siens* (negation) [It is hard for someone who lives outside society not to seek out his own].[24]

As the writing of *Murphy* faltered—'with three, four chapters to write, only about 12,000 words, but I don't think they will be' on 29 January; 'Murphy goes from bad to worse' on 25 March; and 'Murphy won't move for me at all. I get held up over the absurdist difficulties of detail' on 15 April 1936[25]—Geulincx was along for the ride, a companion in misery. Yet over these months, too, Beckett found, I want to suggest, a moral justification of what he was looking for:

> I am obliged to read in Trinity College Library, as Arnoldus Geulincx is not available elsewhere. I recommend him to you most heartily, especially his *Ethica*, and above all the second section of the second chapter of the first tractate, where he disquires on his fourth cardinal virtue, Humility, contempus negativus sui ipsius [to comprise its own contemptible negation].[26]

It is a reasonable assumption that Geulincx was directly inserted into Beckett's last 'three, four chapters' of *Murphy* written over Spring 1936, perhaps facilitating both author and character's answer to the 'lacking' means noted in chapter nine, quoted above, itself practically a hymn to the *Ethics*. 'The issue therefore [...] lay between nothing less fundamental than the big world and the little world', Beckett wrote at the turning point of the novel, where Murphy decides for the 'little world' of consciousness: 'His vote was cast. "I am not of the big world, I am of the little world" was an old refrain with Murphy, and a conviction, two convictions, the negative first [....] In the beautiful Belgo-Latin of Arnold Geulincx: *Ubi nihil vales, ibi nihil veils.*'[27]

Earlier Anglophone scholars, such as Samuel I. Mintz and Rupert Wood,[28] have commented upon the overt use of Geulincx in *Murphy;* although again, it is worth noting that Murphy's first good night 'since nights began so long ago to be bad' comes as he retreats into the Magdalene Mental Mercyseat asylum—paralleling the attempted retreat into his 'little world'—'the reason being not so much that he had his *chair* again as that the self whom he loved had the aspect, even to Ticklepenny's inexpert eye, of a real *alienation*. Or to put it perhaps more nicely: *conferred that aspect on the self whom he hated.*'[29]

This is strictly in accordance with Geulincx's chief virtue and second, negative, application of humility, 'It is a requirement of Humility to comprise its own despicable negation.' ('*Requiritur ad Humilitatem contemptus negativus sui ipsius*'—or as Martin Wilson's translation has it: 'Humility therefore calls for *negative* disregard of itself.')[30] This, in turn, provides both the positive and negative obligations of humility toward both God and His gift to humanity, reason, codified as: '*ubi nihil vales, ibi nihil vales'* ('Wherein you have no power, therein neither should you will.') Even if Beckett did not accept the theological basis to Geulincx's thought, the practical aspect of this ethical injunction was to be of great use, found in exactly the place where the just-cited letter recommends:

> The first axiom of Ethics [...] where nothing has value, there everything else is worthless (note this axiom contains both parts of humility to be investigated, the part where nothing has value... and the part where everything is worthless... contempt of oneself, neglecting oneself, is the summary of all the resignation of the human condition within its power); or what it is in the object, nothing for nothing, nothing must be done in vain. Nothing is more clear than this principle forming practical things; whoever resists cannot be less than a fool, and we are used to call all men fools who believe that attempting to do something in undertaking certain deeds that knowingly cannot succeed; thus being frustrated as a result [...][31]

Geulincx's *Ethics* is invoked still more explicitly invoked by the 1945 short story, 'The End', where the narrator's old tutor, Ward, 'had given me the *Ethics* of Geulincx [....] The *Ethics* had his name (Ward) on the fly-leaf.' Although to 'know I had a being, however faint and false, outside of me, had once had the power to stir my heart', this was not enough to keep the narrator from retreating to a boat, ostensibly committing very un-Geulingian suicide, all the while likening the world—with its 'icy tumultuous streets, the terrifying faces, the noises that slash, pierce claw, bruise'—to human excrement.[32] Here the outlook is similar to Geulincx's, but the ultimate result, like for Belacqua and Murphy, is death. In contrast, the allusion to Geulincx and sailing is made yet more specific in *Molloy*, the last and most famous direct invocation of the *Ethics*:

> I who had loved the image of old Geulincx, dead young, who left me free, on the black boat of Ulysses, to crawl towards the East, along the deck. That is a great measure of freedom, for him who has not the pioneering spirit. And from the poop, poring upon the wave, a sadly rejoicing slave, I follow with my eyes the proud and futile wake. Which, as it bears me from no fatherland away, bears me onward to no shipwreck.[33]

This perfectly corresponds to a sentence in Beckett's transcriptions of the *Ethics*: 'Just as a ship carrying a passenger with all speed towards the east, so the will of God, carrying all things, impelling all things with inexorable force, in no way prevents us from resisting his will (as much as in our power) with complete freedom.'[34]

Revealingly, in an earlier work, Anthony Uhlmann reprinted an excerpt from a letter of 17 February 1954 by Beckett to the German translator of *Molloy*, Dr Erich Franzen, with reference to this passage in *Molloy*:

> This passage is suggested (a) by a passage in the Ethics of Geulincx where he compares human freedom to that of a man, on board a boat carrying him irresistibly westward, free to move eastward within the limits of the boat itself, as far as the stern; and (b) by Ulysses' relation in Dante (Inf. 26) of his second voyage (a medieval tradition) to and beyond the Pillars of Hercules, his shipwreck and death [....] I imagine a member of the crew who does not share the adventurous spirit of Ulysses and is at least at liberty to crawl homewards [...] along the brief deck.[35]

Finally and most famously in terms of direct invocations of Geulincx, in a 1967 letter Beckett advised Sighle Kennedy (and thereafter, given it's republication in *Disjecta: Miscellaneous Writings and a Dramatic Fragment*, readers of Beckett's work generally) on how to understand his art:

> I simply do not feel the presence in my writings as a whole of the Proust & Joyce situations you evoke. If I were in the unenviable position of having to study my work my points of departure would be the "Naught is more real..." and the "Ubil nihil vales..." both already in *Murphy* and neither very rational.[36]

A last, more opaque kind of evidence connecting Beckett with Geulincx concerns literary allusions made to Geulingian philosophy. Two, for instance, can be observed in characteristically-defaced 'traces' in the post-war writing. The first occurs near the conclusion of the 1946 *Mercier and Camier*: 'One shall be born, said Watt, one is born of us, who having nothing will wish for nothing, except to be left the nothing he hath.'[37] Similarly, in the 1959 radio play, *Embers*, a play on the word 'ineffable'—transcribed seventeen times in Beckett's notes on Geulincx—is no longer a reference to God, but to Music:

MUSIC MASTER: [*Violently.*] Eff! Eff!
ADDIE: [*Tearfully.*] Where?
MUSIC MASTER: [*Violently.*] Qua! [*He thumps note.*] Fa!
[*Pause.* ADDIE *begins again,* MUSIC MASTER *beating time lightly with rule. When she comes to bar 5 she makes same mistake. Tremendous blow of rule on piano case.* ADDIE *stops playing, begins to wail.*]
MUSIC MASTER: [*Frenziedly.*] Eff! Eff! [*He hammers note.*] Eff! [*He hammers note.*] Eff!
[*Hammered note, 'Eff!' and* ADDIE'S *wail amplified to paroxysm, then suddenly cut off. Pause.*]
ADA: You are silent today.
HENRY: It was not enough to drag her into the world, now she must play the piano.[38]

In addition to these more 'direct' references and allusions, Uhlmann is surely right in arguing that several recurrent Beckettian 'images' also derive from Geulincx. These function as a kind of shorthand for tropes of impotence and ignorance—including pendulum clocks, rocking-chairs and rocking boats—which testify to Geulincx's role in the evolution of Beckett's writing; that is, in 'a shift from an art of relation to an art of nonrelation [...] an understanding of thought which stresses how our thinking is intimately interinvolved with ignorance [...] following Geulincx, he identifies the *cogito* (the 'I think') with *nescio* (an 'I do not know')'.[39]

Uhlmann also finds Beckett's understanding of the cogito is not Cartesian, but Geuilingian; for the two, even if both based on Cartesian first principles, are very different in logical effect: 'Descartes leads us from obscurity to clarity (knowledge), whereas Geulincx leads us into obscurity (and offers no real hope of our departing from there) so that we might recognise our own ignorance and in turn recognise the omniscience and omnipotence of God.'[40] Deeper than mere references, then, Beckett's writings are also marked by Geulincx's philosophy, particularly the virtue of humility that he so carefully transcribed and heartily recommended. Yet even in Beckett's typescript from Treatise I of the *Ethics*, let alone all six difficult treatises of challenging Latin, so great an overlap between the two exists that it seems difficult to pull them apart. Consider, for example, this excerpt from Beckett's transcription from Geulincx's 'Seventh Obligation', death:

> Yet there is this boundless ocean of miseries, on which I presently toss. I am hurled from one calamity to another, only to sink back as often as not from the latter to the former [....] Thrust into a body as if into a prison, am I paying the penalties that I have deserved, and among other this grave one, that I am oblivious of the offence that I am expiating? Someone who is being beaten can at least take comfort in knowing why he is beating.[41]

Viewed through the prism of Beckett's writing, shades of Molloy, Murphy, Didi and Gogo, in fact, most characters, seem to abound. It would seem clear, then, that Geulincx keys into a number of strands later visible in Beckett's writing. But how, precisely? To be sure, there are a number of unmistakable references to Geulincx in Beckett's letters, literature and drama. Yet aside from the odd phrase or allusion to Geulincx—especially in the notoriously opaque 'mature' post-war writing—what is this connection actually worth?

§3

Ethics may be, in fact, the most important answer. The preceding has offered an overview Beckett's reading and direct employment of Geulincx's *Ethics* from 1936. This has been itself largely situated within formative events of the 1930s, especially in respect of Beckett's search for a way of negotiating his artistic impasse and ongoing personal crises. But after this period, a deeper employment of the Geulincx's *Ethics* can be observed, too, in writings after *Murphy*, in the years when Geulincx's ethical vision had marinated over a period of years in the evolution of Beckett's art. These ethical debts are, I want to lengthily conclude by arguing, centring on Geulincx's ideas about *detachment* and *acceptance*. Before applying these to the later prose texts, *Watt* and 'From An Abandoned Work', however, locating the relevant ethical appropriations within Beckett's transcriptions recalls Geulincx's take on these ethical responsibilities.

The first, *detachment*, involves a quietistic submission to God, thereby 'listening to Reason'. With Geulincx, God is the ultimate arbiter and perpetually acting miracle maker, coordinating our motion with the outside world (of just how we are ignorant), which we only partially grasp through a nevertheless inescapable prison of consciousness. But even if one cannot know how an action actually takes place, for Geulincx, this does not relieve individuals from moral responsibility, or from freedom of will—if only within the skull. Through Cartesian reason, as Beckett transcribed, an ethical turning inward to consciousness becomes one of Geulincx's cardinal virtues, *dilegence*: It 'has two parts: Turning away from external things (for they hinder listening), and turning into oneself [....] an intense and continuous withdrawal of the mind (no matter what its current business) from external things into itself, into its innermost sanctum, in order to consult the sacred oracle of Reason.'[42] 'Autology'—or self-inspection—is thus is manifested as a supreme detachment from the world. A stoical withdrawal into consciousness, an ultimate alienation from, or incommensurability with, the grotesque world outside the mind, then, is a direct consequence of Geulincx's metaphysics; specifically, 'I merely experience the World. I am a spectator of the scene, not an actor.'[43] In other words, a 'deanthropomorphisation' of existence follows the escape into consciousness; offering the 'perspective of eternity'. This 'inorganic' view of humanity and the world—one Beckett was searching for until spring 1936—is ethical insofar as it produces a paradoxical kind of wisdom: knowledge of ignorance.

The latter is intimately connected to Beckett's second ethical debt to Geulincx, namely a submission to human powerlessness. This means ultimately *accepting* that true knowledge is ineffable, as Beckett noted at length, 'I cannot get beyond *I do not know*, there is nothing I can add to this *I do not know*. I do not know how I came to this condition.'[44] Such a realisation leads to Geulincx's supreme virtue—and Beckett's personal favourite—humility, which 'is carelessness of oneself; not in a positive sense, but (as I employ the words) in a negative sense. Hence, humility is better described as carelessness and neglect of oneself than as disregard of oneself.'[45] Humility, submission, acceptance: in Geulincx's philosophy, these become ethical responses to ineffability. Simultaneously, they are a way of proceeding. For Beckett's characters after *Murphy* may be tortured by ignorance, but they endure (even the narrator of 'The End' does not *explicitly* die); they withdraw into consciousness and submit to their own impotence. There is no exit for either Geulincx or Beckett's characters. Indeed, this may be again understood as an essentially ethical process: autological detachment from the world, leading to acceptance of ignorance, capped by a 'neglect of oneself', or humility.

This ethical process heavily pervades Beckett's wartime novel, *Watt*. By withdrawing into the mental universe of Mr Knott's establishment—importantly, 'Watt never knew how he got into Mr. Knott's house'[46]—Watt sets the stage for his self-defeating attempts to understand the world, above all through mathematical logic gone awry.[47] Yet Watt's logical travails are preceded by the most important event in the novel, Arsene's 'short statement'. Leaving in synchronicity with Watt's arrival, Arsene describes his shift from detachment to acceptance; a movement from the 'being of nothing' to 'that presence of what did not exist, that presence without, that presence within, that presence between, though I'll be buggered if I can understand how it could have been anything else'[48]. It was this acceptance leading to an ethical humility for Arsene, which naturally earns 'quite useless wisdom so dearly won': 'what we know partakes in no small measure of the nature of what has so happily been called the unutterable or ineffable, so that any attempt to utter or eff it is doomed to fail, doomed to fail'.[49] Interestingly, Arsene describes this 'change of degree' as 'existence off the ladder'. While much speculation has been advanced about the origin of this 'latter joke' in *Watt*— variously ascribed to Mauthner's *Kritik*, Wittgenstein's *Tractatus*, and an old Irish joke[50]—I would argue it comes from the *Ethics*, specifically from Geulincx's section on humility. Considering the corresponding 'ladder' passage in Beckett's transcriptions, Arsene's analogy would seem to make more sense in the context of Geulingian detachment, or withdrawal into consciousness:

> The virtuous man is always ascending and descending this ladder [of existence]: he seeks ease that he may be fit for work; he wants to be fit for work that he may work; he want to work that he may have something else to eat; he wants to eat that he may live; he wants to live because God has ordered it, not because it pleases him, and not because life (as it has become popular to say) is so sweet.[51]

It therefore appears that Arsene's entire statement is powered by an appropriation of Geulingian ineffability. Moreover, this vital speech foreshadows Watt's own attempts to grasp the world through reason alone whilst in Knott's house, including the 'fugitive penetration' by the piano-tuners, his encounter with a 'pseudo-pot' and 'others of a similar kind, incidents that is to say of great formal brilliance and indeterminable purport'. All of these obscure Watt's own pursuit of a 'being of nothing', as when Watt finds himself wondering about Knott's bedclothes: 'Does he seek to know again, what is cold, what is heat? But this was an anthropomorphic insolence of short duration.' But on the whole, by accepting the ineffability of Knott's universe, Watt is able to yield to Geulingian detachment, for 'Watt suffered neither from the presence of Mr. Knott, nor from his absence. When he was with him, he was content to be with him, and when he was away from him, he was content to be away from him. Never with relief, never with regret, did he leave him at night, or in the morning come to him again.'[52]

Upon his rotation out of Knott's house and back into the world, Watt's detachment is interrupted by Micks ('One moment I was out, and the next I was in'), and Watt's acceptance of ineffability is supplanted by an 'inner lamentation' as he departs. Lacking the humility born of self-disregard now that 'logic was on his side' again, Watt quickly becomes fatigued and irritable—despite the fact that, seeing the train station, 'for an instant his mind turned off from care'. But this was insufficient, for Watt then troublingly encounters 'a figure, human apparently' but, unable to determine its movement, gender or 'dimension', finds himself highly impatient, for 'all he desired was to have his uncertainty removed', although 'it was greatly to be deplored, that he cared what it was, coming along the road, profoundly to be deplored'. Waiting for an answer in an ineffable world, 'staring at this incomprehensible staffage, suffering greatly from impatience', Watt remains unable to assimilate this figure into his consciousness. It is this final ineffability that leads to Watt's paradoxical realisation—and perhaps subsequent institutionalisation with Sam—detachment from the world offers knowledge of ignorance, which thereby provides a humble submission to human impotence. Thus, waiting for his train, 'the darkness gradually deepened. There was no longer a dark part and a less dark part, no, but all now was uniformly dark, and remained so, for some time. This notable change took place by insensible degrees.'[53] By the time he buys his ticket, Watt has reconnected with Geulincx's 'supreme principle of Ethics—that is, '*wherein you have no power, therein you should not will*—and consequently does not care in which direction his train leaves.[54]

In turning to 'From An Abandoned Work', an abortive writing project in English originally called 'The Gloaming', Geulingian ethics seem more difficult to locate, in keeping with the well-recognised opacity of Beckett's post-war art. But around the time this text was written, the mid-1950s, Beckett sent Mary Hutchinson information on Geulincx and Democritus on 7 November 1954; two years later he told the same recipient about Geulincx's 'fascinating guignol world'.[55] Some twenty years after first reading him at TCD, then, Geulincx was still not far Beckett's mind.

The scenes presented in 'From An Abandoned Work' ostensibly centre on an unnamed narrator who 'was very quick as a boy and picked up a lot of hard knowledge', focusing especially on memories of three different days, the first offering the opening, representative sentence: 'Up bright and early that day, I was young then, feeling awful, mother handing out of the window in her nightdress weeping and waving.' Like so many Beckett narrators, this unnamed sufferer has 'never in my life been on my way anywhere, but simply on the way'. Similarly, too, the narrator is flayed by memories of his dead mother and father, chooses days seemingly at random to recollect, before sarcastically conceding powerlessness: 'No there's no accounting for it, there's no accounting for anything, with a mind like the one I always had, always on the alert against itself, I'll come back on this perhaps when I feel less weak. There was a time I tried to get relief by beating my head against something, but I gave it up.'[56] Realising that 'all is mental', the narrator clearly used to pursue knowledge at some past point: 'A fair scholar I was too, no thought, but a great memory.' Although it is unclear whether this text is written or dictated, one thing is clear: 'words have been my only loves, not many'. Having never been in love with anything outside the mind, the best of the narrator's 'only loves' is the word 'over'—sometimes inverted as 'vero, oh vero', for which, along with much else, there shall be no apology: 'No, I regret nothing, all I regret is having been born, dying is such a long tiresome business I always found.'[57] In closing, I want to consider this text from the perspective of Geulincx's philosophy, in two complimentary ways.

The first of these is through Uhlmann's discussion of images cited earlier. To be sure, allusions to Geulincx are important, from mention of 'my two books, the little and the big', the latter so often associated with *Murphy's* gloss on Geulincx;

but also the image of 'life in a big empty echoing room with a big old pendulum clock, just listening and dozing, the case open so that I could watch the swinging, moving my eyes to and fro'. There are numerous betrayals of ignorance in 'From An Abandoned Work' as well, from the narrator's inability to distinguish a boy from 'a small man or woman', to phrases like 'why the curses were pouring out of me I do not know, no that is a foolish thing to say', in addition to the ominous question: 'My father, did I kill him too as well as my mother, perhaps in a way I did, but I can't go into that now, much too old and weak.'[58] Therefore, not only in terms of certain evocative phrases and especially images, but indeed in the entire trope of wallowing in what Uhlmann calls 'nescience'—the opposite of omniscience—the narrator of 'From An Abandoned Work' reveals traces of Geulingian ethics. And it would seem clear that, to agree with Uhlmann, there is a *prima facie* case for Beckett's continuing, direct—if nevertheless defaced and allusive—employment of Geulincx, who he read and transcribed fully a generation earlier. And secondly, there is also a deeper influence of Geulingian ethics, one pervading the form of 'From An Abandoned Work' (and by extension, I would suggest, Beckett's corpus as a whole), much like with the structure of *Watt*. To reformulate this in terms of a final question: is there a mode of 'deanthropomorphised' art—understood here as an secular version of Geulincx's ethics of detachment, acceptance and consequent endurance—that Beckett appropriates from Geulincx?

In approaching this question, we are already honing in on the narrator's own ineffability: 'Where did I get it, from a dream, or a book read in a nook when a boy, or a word overheard as I went along, or in me all along and kept under till it could give me joy, these are the kind of horrid thoughts I have to contend with in the way I have said.' For the narrator of 'From An Abandoned Work' talks but no one listens; is a slow walker, but was one of 'the fastest runners the world has ever seen, over a short distance, five or ten yards, in a second I was there'. Here, paradox is the method, and failure is the result. This characteristic Beckettian narrator is old and weak and uncertain, as indeed is the language of the text itself. For example, consider an excerpt from the closing sentence: 'awful English this, fall and vanish from view, you could lie there for weeks and no one hear you, I often thought of that up in the mountains, no, that is a foolish thing to say, just went on, my body doing its best without me'.[59] The memory is insufficient, the language is insufficient, even the body seems to be divorced from consciousness—and all these are major Beckettian tropes recurring across the post-war writings.

As Geulincx has it, this failure of understanding, this ignorance, yields insight into, and demands worship of, an ineffable God: 'I have learned by inspecting myself that the totality of my human condition, comprising birth, life and death, is a monument to the ineffable wisdom of God [....] *we know that it exists, but we do not know how it exists, and we know only this much, that we cannot know*.'[60] But in contrast, in 'From An Abandoned Work', 'the old half-knowledge of when and where gone, and of what, but kinds of things still, all at once, all going, until nothing, that kind of thing'. For as an artist, flailing in a world bereft of God, Beckett's understanding of Geulingian humility, in effect, is not given the relief of belief, meaning that one consequence of trying to 'eff the ineffable' in 'From An Abandoned Work' is that with 'unhappiness like mine, there's no annihilating that'.[61]

And are these sentiments, then, not all the more frightening in Beckett's world, where even God is cuffed in abeyance, even ignorance is radically doubted, and ineffability and failure become literary as well as personal injunctions? The self-defeating logic of this 'Geulingian cogito' was indeed the source of much Beckettian pastiche from *Murphy* on. But 'this submission, this admission' may also be seen in terms of literary expression—as with Beckett's 'syntax of weakness', or 'intent of undoing'—one perhaps similar to Geulincx's habit of writing propositions in the negative, his assertions of ignorance. Or, finally, via the Geulingian paradox raised earlier: knowledge of ignorance is both empowering and simultaneously implies utter powerlessness.

The deeper connection at work in Beckett's reading of Geulincx, then, is manifested in detachment and acceptance—surely not the commands of divine reason. If Beckett submitted to the dictates of anything during the restless 1930s, let alone in the decades beyond, it was certainly not Geulincx's God. Beckett's ideal artist 'is to fail, as no other dare fail, that failure is his world and the shrink for it desertion', as he famously declared in the *Three Dialogues with Georges Duthuit*: 'this fidelity to failure [creates] a new occasion, a new term of relation, and of the act which, unable to act, obliged to act, he makes, an expressive act, even if only of itself, of its impossibility, of its obligation'.[62] The paradoxical *inevitability* of failure, and of the possibility of failing *better*—toward religious knowledge of God for Geulincx, toward artistically expressing the inexpressible for Beckett—leads from introspective detachment to an ultimately ethical acceptance of ignorance. If this is what Beckett may be said to have learned and applied from the *Ethics*, then Arnold Geulincx survives in through an ultimately ethical suffering manifest the former's 'deanthropologised' characters—and narratives generally—in light of the latter's question: 'what is my intelligence worth?'

NOTES

1. Samuel Beckett to Georges Duthuit, cited in Dan Gunn, 'Until the Gag is Chewed', *Times Literary Supplement*, 21 April 2006, p. 15.
2. Samuel Beckett, 'Yellow', in Beckett, *More Pricks Than Kicks* (London: Calder, 1998), cited pp. 174–5.
3. For further physical details of Beckett's 'Philosophy Notes', see *Samuel Beckett Today Aujourd'hui*, 16 *Notes diverse* [sic] *holo* [sic]: *Catalogues of Beckett's reading notes and other manuscripts at Trinity College Dublin, with supporting essays* (Amsterdam: Rodopi, 2006), cited p. 67.
4. Excerpted from Beckett's 'Philosophy Notes', TCD MS 10967/189, recto and verso. Extensive transcriptions from these notes, alongside a discussion of their relevance to Beckett's writing, can be found in my 'Sourcing "Aporetics": An Empirical Study on Philosophical Influences in the Development of Samuel Beckett's Writing' (Unpublished PhD Thesis: Oxford Brookes University, 2004).
5. For discussion of Popper's term 'falsifiablility' in the context of literary criticism, see the introduction to this volume, and ch. 2.
6. For details of Geulincx's philosophy in English, see Jean-Christophe Bardout, 'Occasionalism: La Forge, Cordemoy, Geulincx', *Companion to Early Modern Philosophy,* ed. Steven Nadler (Oxford: Blackwell Publishing, 2002), pp. 140–151; Gabriël Nuchelmans, *Geulincx' Containment Theory of Logic* (Amsterdam: Koninklijke Nederlandse Akademie, 1988); H.J. De Vleeschauwer, *Three Centuries of Geulincx Research: A Bibliographical Survey* (Pretoria: University of South Africa, 1957); Tad M. Schmaltz, 'Descartes and Malebranche on Mind and Mind-Body Union', in *The Philosophical Review* 101/2 (1992), pp. 281–325; and Steven Nadler, 'Knowledge, Volitional Agency and Causation in Malebranhce and Geulinx', in the *British Journal for the History of Philosophy* 7/2 (1999), pp. 263–74.
7. See J.P.N Land, 'Arnold Geulincx and his works', in *Mind* vol. XVI (1891), pp. 223–42.
8. James Knowlson, *Damned to Fame: The Life of Samuel Beckett* (London: Bloomsbury, 1996), p. 219; italics in Knowlson.
9. Beckett, TCD MS 10971/6/29; corresponding to 'Sourcing "Aporetics"', p. 380.
10. For further discussion of 'agnostic quietism', see ch. 5.
11. For Beckett's account of the revelation in his mother's room, see *Damned to Fame*, p. 352.
12. Samuel Beckett, 'Humanistic Quietism', in Beckett, *Disjecta: Miscellaneous Writings and a Dramatic Fragment*, ed. Ruby Cohn (New York: Grove Press, 1984), p. 68.
13. For this argument in full, see my *Beckett's Books: A Cultural History of Samuel Beckett's 'Interwar Notes'* (London: Bloomsbury, 2008), pp. 8–13. Evidence for the substitution of Art and God suffuses Beckett's writing at this time, as exemplified by a July 1934 review of Rainer Maria Rilke's *Poems*. 'This is the very language of apostasy', Beckett writes, 'where God is the tower and the heart whatever you please to call it [....] Such a turmoil of self-deception and naïf discontent gains nothing in dignity from that prime article of the Rilkean faith, which provides to the interchangeability of Rilke and God:
    mit meinem Reifen
    reift
    dein Reich [In my ripening / ripens / what you are.].'

Rilke's 'All Who Seek You', cited in Samuel Beckett, *'Poems. By Rainer Maria Rilke'*, in *Disjecta*, pp. 66–7.

[14] Samuel Beckett, 'Recent Irish Poetry', in *ibid.*, p. 70.

[15] Beckett to MacGreevy, cited in Knowlson, *Damned to Fame*, p. 197.

[16] Beckett to Georges Duthuit, 2 March 1954, cited in Lois Oppenheim, *The Painted Word: Samuel Beckett's Dialogues with Art* (Ann Arbor: University of Michigan Press, 2000), p. 85.

[17] Samuel Beckett, to Thomas MacGreevy, 8 September 1934, TCD MS 10904. That this letter foreshadows the revolutionary comments on art made in Beckett's 'Three Dialogues with Georges Duthuit' is made most clear in the final exchange between 'B.' and 'D.', ostensibly on the painter Bram van Velde:

> All that should concern us is the increasing anxiety of the relations itself, as though shadowed more and more darkly by a sense of invalidity, of inadequacy, of existence at the expense of all that it excludes, all that it blinds to [....] All that is required now, in order to bring even this horrible matter to an acceptable conclusion, is to make of this submission, this admission, this fidelity to failure, a new occasion, a new term of relation. (Cited in Beckett, *Disjecta*, p. 145)

[18] Samuel Beckett, letter to MacGreevy of 10 March 1935; TCD MS 10904. See chapter 5 for additional citation of this important letter, reproduced in full in *The Letters of Samuel Beckett, 1929-1940: Volume 1*, eds. Martha Fehsenfeld and Lois More Overbeck (Cambridge: Cambridge University Press, 2009), pp. 256–264. For discussion of the concept 'non-Euclidean logic' as it relates to Beckett's work, see *Beckett's Books*, pp. 13–20.

[19] Mark Nixon, '"what a tourist I must have been": Samuel Beckett's German Diaries', (Unpublished PhD. Thesis: University of Reading, 2005). Nixon's footnote to this fascinating passage cites the phrase referring to Geulincx, 'guignol world', in a letter from Samuel Beckett to Mary Hutchinson of 28 November 1956: 'Frightful kitchen latin but fascinating guignol world'.

[20] Samuel Beckett, *Murphy* (London: Calder, 1993), pp. 101–2; italics added.

[21] For further discussion of these archival materials, see the following selection: Anthony Uhlmann 'Introduction to Samuel Beckett's Notes to the *Ethics*', in *Arnold Geulincx Ethics, with Samuel Beckett's notes*, trans. Martin Wilson, eds. Han van Ruler, Anthony Uhlmann, Martin Wilson (Amsterdam: Brill, 2006), pp. 301–9; Mark Nixon, '"Scraps of German": Samuel Beckett Reading German Literature', in *Samuel Beckett Today / Aujourd'hui*, 16, pp. 259–82; Dirk van Hulle, 'Samuel Beckett's *Faust* Notes', *ibid.*, pp. 283–298; Daniela Caselli, 'The Promise of Dante in the Beckett Manuscripts', *ibid*, pp. 237–258; John Pilling, '"For Interpolation": Beckett and English Literature', *ibid*; pp. 203–36. See also several essays contained in Dirk van Hulle, ed. *Beckett the European* (Tallahassee: Journal of Beckett Studies Books, 2005); Chris Ackerley, *Demented Particulars: The Annotated* Murphy; John Pilling, *Beckett's* Dream *Notebook* (Reading: Beckett International Foundation, 1999); and Pilling, *Beckett Before Godot* (Cambridge: Cambridge University Press, 1998).

[22] TCD MS 10971/6/3; corresponding to Arnold Geulincx, *Metaphysics*, trans. Martin Wilson (Wisbech: Christoffel Press, 1999), p. 45; and Samuel Beckett, 'Text for Nothing 3', in Beckett, *The Complete Short Prose, 1929–1989*, ed. S.E. Gontarski (New York: Grove Press, 1995), pp. 109–10.

[23] TCD MS 10971/6/2; corresponding to Geulincx, *Metaphysics*, p. 41.

[24] Beckett to MacGreevy, cited in Knowlson, *Damned to Fame*, p. 219; italics in Knowlson.

[25] Beckett, letters to MacGreevy of 29 January; 25 March and 15 April 1936; TCD MS 10904. I am especially grateful to Mark Nixon for his assistance with these passages.

[26] Samuel Beckett, letter to Arland Ussher of 25 March 1936, cited in *Beckett's Books*, p. 132.

[27] Beckett, *Murphy*, p. 101; italics in original.

[28] Samuel I. Mintz, 'Beckett's *Murphy*: A Cartesian Novel', in *Perspective* (1959), pp. 156–65; and Rupert Wood, 'Murphy, Beckett; Geulincx, God', in the *Journal of Beckett Studies* 2/2 (1993), pp. 27–51.

[29] *Ibid.*, p.108; italics added.

[30] Beckett, TCD MS 10971/6/13; cited in *Arnold Beckett Ethics*, p. 326; and 'Sourcing "Aporetics"', pp. 369–70.

[31] Beckett, TCD MS 10971/6/25; corresponding to 'Sourcing "Aporetics"', p. 375. The full passage in question here highlights the difficulty of translating Geulincx, as my translations from 'Sourcing "Aporetics"' are noticeably different; for example, contrast the above with *Arnold Geulincx Ethics*, p. 341. The latter, more readily available text is employed hereafter.

[32] Samuel Beckett, 'The End', in Beckett, *The Complete Short Prose,* pp. 91 and 97–8; italics in original.

[33] Samuel Beckett, *Molloy*, in Beckett, *The Beckett Trilogy* [*Molloy, Malone Dies* and *The Unnamable*] (London: Calder, 1976), p. 48.

[34] van Ruler et. al., *Arnold Geulincx Ethics*, p. 317.

[35] Samuel Beckett, cited Anthony Uhlmann, *Beckett and Poststructuralism* (Cambridge: Cambridge University Press, 1990), p. 54.

[36] Beckett to Sighle Kennedy, cited in *Disjecta*, p. 113.

[37] Samuel Beckett, *Mercier and Camier* (London: Calder, 1993) p. 114.

[38] Samuel Beckett, *Embers*, in Beckett, *The Complete Dramatic Works* (London: Faber, 1986), p. 259.

[39] Anthony Uhlmann, *Samuel Beckett and the Philosophical Image* (Cambridge: Cambridge University Press, 2006), pp. 89–90; italics in original.

[40] *Ibid.*, pp. 101–2.

[41] van Ruler et. al., *Arnold Geulincx Ethics*, pp. 350–1.

[42] *Ibid.*, p. 320.

[43] *Ibid.*, p. 334.

[44] *Ibid.*, p. 334; italics in original.

[45] *Ibid.*, p. 326.

[46] Samuel Beckett, *Watt* (London: Calder, 1970), p. 35.

[47] For discussion of Watt's maddening mathematics, see John J. Mood, '"The Personal System"—Samuel Beckett's *Watt*', in *PMLA* 86 (1971), pp. 255–65; and Chris Ackerley, *Obscure Locks, Simple Keys: The Annotated* Watt (Tallahassee: Journal of Beckett Studies Books, 2005).

[48] Beckett, *Watt*, pp. 38, 43.

[49] *Ibid.*, p.61.

[50] See, for example, James Acheson, 'A Note on the Ladder Joke in *Watt*', in the *Journal of Beckett Studies* 2/1 (1992), pp. 115–6.

[51] van Ruler et. al., *Arnold Geulincx Ethics*, p. 327.

[52] Beckett, *Watt*, cited pp. 67, 78–80, 71, 202, 207.

[53] *Ibid.*, cited pp. 215, 218, 224–5, 226, 235.

[54] van Ruler et. al., *Arnold Geulincx Ethics*, p. 316; italics in original.

[55] For the former reference, see John Pilling, *A Samuel Beckett Chronology* (Palgrave: Basingstoke: 2006), p. 133; for the latter, see note 19.
[56] Samuel Beckett, 'From An Abandoned Work', in Beckett, *The Complete Short Prose*, pp. 155, 157.
[57] *Ibid.*, pp. 158, 162, 158.
[58] *Ibid.*, pp. 162–3, 156, 163, 159.
[59] *Ibid.*, pp. 158, 164.
[60] van Ruler et. al., *Arnold Geulincx Ethics,* p. 345; italics in van Ruler et. al.
[61] Beckett, 'From An Abandoned Work', pp. 162, 163, 159.
[62] Beckett, 'Three Dialogues with Georges Duthuit', in *Disjecta,* p. 145.

"BUT WHAT WAS THIS PURSUIT OF MEANING, IN THIS INDIFFERENCE TO MEANING?":
Beckett, Husserl, Sartre and "Meaning Creation"

§1

Samuel Beckett's wartime novel, *Watt*, confronts both characters and readers with fundamental dilemmas of meaning and meaning-creation. In this sense, it may be read as quintessentially Beckettian: without doubt, 'it has its place in the series', as Beckett wrote to George Reavey in 1947, 'as will perhaps appear in time'.[1] To some extent, such a 'place' in Beckett studies has been created, thanks in large measure to important scholarship on both the 'final' text of *Watt*, but also to extant manuscripts, composed and doodle-festooned in France between February 1941 and May 1945.[2] Yet *Watt* stands out as unusual all the same, even by the standards of Beckett's revolutionary art. Situated between the semi-obscure fiction, poetry and journalism of the interwar years on one side; and the post-war 'frenzy of writing' broadly lasting until 1950, so facilitating his international acclaim on the other, *Watt* may be seen as *the* pivotal novel in Beckett's oeuvre. Simply put, *Watt* is Beckett's artistic fulcrum, linking early and 'mature' writings. For *Watt* marks the abandonment of writing in English for more than a decade; of the progressive abandonment of third-person narration; of the elimination of conventional literary structures like plot and setting; and even more contentiously, of *solving* the problem of writing *about* something which had been of keen interest to Beckett since, at least, his 1929 homage to Joyce's *Work in Progress*:

> Here form *is* content, content *is* form. You complain that this stuff is not written in English. It is not written at all. It is not to be read—or rather it is not only to be read. It is to be looked at and listened to.[3]

As such, this chapter will argue that the breakthrough heralded in *Watt* was achieved by starting to write phenomenologically. To do so, an empirically-bounded methodology is undertaken to explore Beckett's interwar engagements with phenomenological ideas; this is book-ended by an interpretation of *Watt* as representing Beckett's 'phenomenological turn' in literature.

'Hymeneal still it lay, the thing so soon to be changed, between me and all the forgotten horrors of joy', recounts Arsene, attempting to explain 'existence off the ladder' to the eponymous newcomer, despite his 'recent costiveness and want of stomach. But in what did the change *consist*?'[4] Grappling with this question over his twenty page 'short speech', Arsene sets out his own struggle with (non-) meaning in Mr Knott's sanctuary, thereby also summarising Watt's ensuing struggle with meaning-creation, or 'intellection':[5]

> The change. In what did it consist? It is hard to say. Something slipped. There I was, warm and bright, smoking my tobacco-pipe, watching the warm bright wall, when suddenly somewhere some little thing slipped [....] To conclude from this that the incident was internal would, I think, be rash. For my—how shall I say?—my personal system was so distended at the period of which I speak that the distinction between what was inside it and what was outside it was not at all easy to draw. Everything that happened happened inside it, and at the same time everything that happened happened outside it [....] It was not an illusion, as long as it lasted, that presence of what did not exist, that presence without, that presence within, that presence between, though I'll be buggered if I can understand how it could have been anything else.[6]

Yet Arsene's 'radical change of appearance' so distending his 'personal system' owes much to another novel also exploring 'abstract change without object', Jean-Paul Sartre's near-contemporaneous *La Nauseé*.[7] First published in April 1937, *Nausea* presents Antonin Roquentin's battle with a very similar phenomenological crisis: 'Nothing has changed and yet everything is different. I can't describe it; it's like the Nausea and yet it's just the opposite: at last an adventure happens to me and when I question myself I see that it happens *that I am myself and that I am here*; I am the one who splits the night, I am as happy as a hero in a novel.'[8] Upon reaching the end of this 'anti-hero's' enquiry into consciousness, Beckett enthused to Thomas MacGreevy on 26 May 1938: 'I have read Sartre's Nausée and find it extraordinarily good.'[9] The basis for this praise, as will become clear, was over the treatment of the subject-object relation, rendered as a 'no-man's-land' in the 1934 'Recent Irish Poetry'[10]—one also central to Edmund Husserl's construction of phenomenology—that Beckett had been engaging with from the very outset of his writing career.

Additional parallels in the novels are overwhelming, from structural affinities—such as *Watt's* climactic '(MS. Illegible)' and '(Hiatus in MS.)'[11] with *Nausea's* introductory 'Word left out' and 'Word [...] is illegible'[12]—to concluding scenes at a railway station, and explicit 'editorial' interventions across both works.[13] Indeed, the two texts complement each other in the most intimate of ways, especially if extending to psychological readings of 'madness', notably schizophrenia.[14] Roquentin laments to his diary—in a manner immediately redolent of Watt's finding himself 'in the midst of things which, if they consented to be named, did so as it were with reluctance'[15]—'Things are divorced from their names [...] I am in the midst of things, nameless things. Alone, without words, defenceless, they surround me, are beneath me, behind me, above me.'[16] In one of a series of distinctly phenomenological passages on this experiential change, Roquentin, like Arsene, is outdoors, and

> then all of a sudden, there it was, clear as day: existence had suddenly unveiled itself. It had lost the harmless look of an abstract category: it was the every past of things, this root was kneaded into existence. Or rather the [tree] root, the park gates, the bench, the sparse grass, all that had vanished: the diversity of things, their individuality, were only an appearance, a veneer. This veneer had melted, leaving soft, monstrous masses, all in disorder—naked, in a frightful, obscene nakedness.[17]

In passing judgement on this perceptual change, although 'I was not even conscious of the transformation', Roquentin notes his 'atrocious joy': 'This moment was extraordinary. I was there, motionless and icy, plunged in a horrible ecstasy.'[18] When Roquentin is in this state of Husserlian 'bracketing', even uttering words is 'a little like an exorcism'.[19] But in *Watt*'s overlapping case, this failure is even more general, and indeed pessimistic: 'For to explain had always been to exorcise, for Watt'.[20]

Edith Kern[21] is one of very few Anglophone critics to have appreciated this philosophical congruence, noting 'Sartre and Beckett evoke in this respect analogous situations and even use similar terms to describe them. Like the Roquentin of *Nausea*, Watt feels closing in on him a world that has lost its human meaning and can no longer be put into human categories or safely expressed in ordinary language.'[22] Whereas Jacqueline Hoefer was ready to see in *Watt* a pastiche on logical positivism and Wittgenstein's early attempt at an 'ideal language' in the *Tractatus Logico-Philosophicus* as the 'empirical and rational system' Watt lives by,[23] Kern was far happier to cast Watt's linguistic instabilities in existential terms in 1970: 'Explaining and naming are man's weapons to exorcise an otherwise demonic universe that is threatening in its purposelessness.'[24] Despite this early and impressive critical linking of Beckett and Sartre, however, this chapter will demonstrate that it was the 'phenomenological' Sartre of the later 1930s of interest to Beckett, and far less the 'existentialist' Sartre made famous by the wartime *No Exit* (1942) and *Being and Nothingness* (1943). This sense is captured by Beckett's response, discussing Sartrian philosophy, to Knowlson's 'arguing that, from my own perspective, we were too firmly *en situation* (too limited by our situation) for the existentialist's emphasis on human freedom to have a lot of meaning', constraints largely glossed over by existentialist philosophy. 'Beckett agreed enthusiastically with this objection', Knowlson reports, 'saying that he found the actual limitations on man's freedom of action (his genes, his upbringing, his social circumstances) far more compelling than the theoretical freedom on which Sartre had laid so much stress.'[25] This corresponds with letters linking Sartre's *Nausea* to Camus *The Stranger* in the mid-1950s; and more importantly, a letter of October 1945, some six months after the completion of *Watt*, where Beckett comments on Morris Sinclair's request for academic advice regarding a PhD on Sartre: 'His German adhesions would be into your barrow. Husserl—? (*Das Schloss, Der Prozess*). Kierkegaard comes in also. I should be very glad to help you and could introduce you to Sartre & his world.'[26]

However, if struggles with intellection ultimately lead to Watt's institutionalisation—and however much *Watt* was largely written in wartime hiding 'to stay sane'—the manuscript's 1945 completion immediately preceded Beckett's 'revelation': '*Molloy* and the others came to me the day I became aware of my own folly. Only then did I begin to write down what I feel.'[27] As emphatically set out by Knowlson's authorised biography, even though the 'vision at last', so famously dramatised in *Krapp's Last Tape*, initiated the breakthrough writings of the postwar years—whereby 'outside reality would be refracted through the filter of his own imagination'—a far longer process of stocking Beckett's fertile imaginings, of drawing upon experiences and erudition from the interwar period, nevertheless meant 'the ground had been well-prepared'.[28]

But in terms of Beckett's artistic development, 'in what did the change *consist*?' Although there are several fruitful responses to this question (psychology, material conditions, wartime experiences, the shift to French, and so on), one largely overlooked by Beckett studies is the phenomenological rendering of intellection; translated into artistic terms, of representing the vexed relation for a conscious subject depicting objects as they are perceived. Just as existential and poststructuralist accounts in Beckett studies might be aided by, as it were, moving backward to their shared heritage in Husserlian phenomenology, so too will moving backward here assist in illuminating the path leading to Beckett's engagement with phenomenology.

§2

First of all, what is 'phenomenology' anyway? A useful working definition is offered in a recent philosophical biography of Edmund Husserl, undisputed founder of phenomenological philosophy, who 'envisaged *phenomenology* as the descriptive, non-reductive science of whatever appears, in the manner of its appearing, in the *subjective* and *intersubjective* life of consciousness'. Extending his initial idea for phenomenology in the 1900–1901 *Logical Investigations* from Franz Brentano's sketch of intentionality gave Husserl the *epoché*, or phenomenological reduction, in order to get at the essences of *consciousness directed toward objects* (whether 'real' or 'imaginary'). 'He explicitly characterizes phenomenology as the systematic study of the essential correlation of subjectivity with objectivity',

Dermot Moran continues, leading to a philosophical methodology which is 'essentially "correlation-research".'[29]

Indeed, with his phenomenological motto 'back to the things themselves!', late in life Husserl sometimes saw phenomenology's bracketing, the reduction of objects to individual consciousness to examine their underlying essence, as 'his paramount achievement', as 'the point of bracketing is to turn our attention away from the objects that normally concern us to our consciousness of these objects, and to the meanings through which we experience them'.[30] Vitally, phenomenology may therefore be considered as much a process and a method as an epistemology and a modern(ist) philosophical system. Phenomenology as established by Husserl is furthermore guided by self-reflexive strictures of method, always revisiting certainties, always 'bound by its essential nature to make the claim of being "first" philosophy and to provide the means for all the rational criticism that needs to be performed; that it therefore demands the completest freedom from all assumptions and absolute reflexive insight in relation to itself'.[31] In short, every Husserlian phenomenological statement has 'perhaps' lingering somewhere in its formulation. Apropos Watt and Roquentin, the very act of 'bracketing' the ubiquitous natural standpoint—namely, through the refraction of the 'objective' world through individual consciousness—is the greatest *a priori* (in Husserl's terminology, 'eidetic') form of doubt possible; for Husserl, this is an uncertainty for more radical than Descartes' method (which never seriously doubted either God or Euclidean logic).[32] Husserl's breakthrough was effected by extending Immanuel Kant's 'transcendental idealism' beyond the essence of objects (the Kantian 'Thing-in-Itself') to the essential processes of consciousness; a *'transcendental-phenomenological Idealism* in opposition to every form of psychologistic Idealism'. A final excerpt from Husserl's English preface to his celebrated exposition, *Ideas*—a work of critical importance to Beckett in 1938, if only indirectly—clarifies the intended role for phenomenological philosophy, one far more foundational than the Cartesianism preceding it:

> I obtain an original and pure descriptive knowledge of the psychical life as it is in itself, the most original information being obtained from myself, because here alone is perception the medium [...] This transformation of meaning concerns myself, above all, the "I" of the psychological and subsequently transcendental inquirer for the time being [...] It leads eventually to the point that I, who am here reflecting upon myself, become conscious that under a consistent and exclusive focusing of experience upon that which is purely inward, upon what is "phenomenologically" accessible to me, I possess in myself an essential individuality, self-contained, and holding well together in itself, to which all real and objectively possible experience and knowledge belongs, through whose agency the objective world is there fore me with all its empirically confirmed facts [...] The absolute positing means that the world is no longer "given"

to me in advance, its validity that of a simple existent, but that henceforth it is exclusively my Ego that is given.[33]

Yet that said, in terms of a corresponding 'phenomenological school' Moran's earlier, magisterial *Introduction to Phenomenology* complicates the picture. Similar to Karl Marx's rejection of 'Marxism' later in life—evocative of another Marx's (this one admired by Beckett: Groucho) refusal to join any group that would have him as a member—Husserl, following his retirement, 'declared himself the greatest enemy of the so-called "phenomenological movement"'. (Surely due in no small measure to Martin Heidegger's defection toward a 'Being' fully realised, for him, in a Nazism persecuting Husserl in the last five years of his life.[34]) This self-distancing from his phenomenological progeny means that, in part, as Paul Ricouer has noted, 'phenomenology is the story of the deviations from Husserl; the history of phenomenology is the history of Husserlian heresies'.[35] The religious terminology is surely apt when considering that Husserl's final work, *The Crisis of European Sciences*, viewed phenomenological approaches to the world as akin to a Damascene conversion: 'Perhaps it will even become manifest that the total phenomenological attitude and the epoché belonging to it are destined in essence to effect, at first, a complete personal transformation, comparable in the beginning to a religious conversion.'[36]

Shades of Beckett's 'personal system' abound, not least in his corresponding deification of art.[37] Yet Beckett was as much a revolutionary artist as Husserl was a positivistic scientist, a vital distinction between the two needing to be borne in mind. Despite these vocational poles—Husserl's 'foundational philosophy' as against Beckett's 'non-Euclidean logic'—for both men, the role of consciousness in meaning-creation was as central for the early Beckett as it was for the later Husserl.[38] For instance, in 1931:

> Husserl also spoke in the deeper sense in which the world is infinite: not only is the world as already "there" unlimited, but through our new experiences, and our new insights, our decisions, our activity, new reality is constantly and forever created.[39]

This sentiment is, in and of itself, heuristically comparable to Beckett's remarks at the outset of *Proust*, published in March of that year:

> [T]he world being a projection of the individual's consciousness (an objectivation of the individual's will, Schopenhauer would say) the pact must be continually renewed [...] The creation of the world did not take place once and for all time, but takes place every day.[40]

Considering the existentialist and poststructuralist 'heresies' overtaking phenomenology in post-war Europe (for example, Derrida's 1954 dissertation was entitled *The Problem of Genesis in Husserl's Philosophy*, while his first book in

1962 introduced and translated Husserl's *Origin of Geometry*), perhaps another idiosyncratic phenomenological approach may be added: art. How else can Sartre's decision to write *La Nauseé* be explained, alongside the 'four years' of intensive study it took Sartre 'to exhaust Husserl'?[41] Upon being introduced to Husserl's ideas by Raymond Aron, just back from Berlin in 1933—'this glass, this table [...] phenomenologists spoke of them philosophically'—'Sartre discovered in Husserl's phenomenology an intellectual process whose every stage and every theme referred him back to his own'.[42] As this serendipitous introduction decisively shaped the 1937 *Nausea*, it thus seems perfectly reasonable (at least for the purposes of this literary essay) to employ David Woodruff-Smith's, the leading Anglophone Husserlian, more maximal definition of phenomenology as a self-reinforcing 'theory of the study of consciousness as lived or experienced from the first person perspective; especially, focussing on pure consciousness and its characteristic intentionality, its structure in the stream of consciousness'.[43]

With these last three words, in particular, Beckett returns to view. Or does he? For all their similarities, Husserl and Beckett have, to date, made unusual bedfellows. This is, itself, all the more unusual given that both existential humanism and post-structuralism—the two dominant readings of Beckett's oeuvre—are themselves the children of Husserlian phenomenology. Moving backward critically, as it were, therefore offers a paradoxical opening for phenomenology as mode of literary criticism; this is especially relevant to Samuel Beckett's art, even if it has largely been left to phenomenologists, rather than literary critics, to make this case.[44] Broadly, arguments that phenomenology might be ideally expressed through literature are left to philosophical, not literary, commentaries, such as Valdes' hermeneutical aside on how *The Unnamable*

> brings to the surface of the reader's consciousness those presuppositions from which spring all operations of comprehension [....] Once the reader becomes conscious of the necessary presuppositions of comprehension, he or she will find that the foundations of all unassailable knowledge begins to shift.[45]

Another rare sally across disciplinary boundaries is provided by Maurice Natanson's *The Erotic Bird*, containing a chapter on the way in which the 'transcendental in *Waiting for Godot* lies in the bracketing of the axioms of existence which everyday life otherwise takes for granted as "real"', thus 'forfeiting the world of reality for a perspective on what composes the world in surreptitious ways'.[46] Still, these are exceptions amongst phenomenological literary criticism. A still lonelier monograph using a 'structural phenomenology' approach to Beckett is, in effect, only a New Critical analysis of Beckett's principal works, not a consistent phenomenological enquiry into the nature of the Nobel Laureate's phenomenological representation of an 'unhappy consciousness'.[47]

Such a neglect of Husserl and Beckett has been rivalled by Beckett studies, despite numerous studies on the role of consciousness in the latter's art.[48] And this is despite existential humanist and post-structuralist critics intimating that precisely such an exploration would be profitable. In respect of the latter, Locatelli's otherwise excellent *Unwording the World* fails to cash in the tantalising promissory note advanced in her introduction:

> [M]ethodologically, Beckett could thus be compared to Husserl, whose 'reductions' constitute a process, a dynamic, investigative device, well known to the analyses of descriptive Phenomenology. Obviously, Beckett's investigation develops on and through literature, and in a non-transcendental direction. Unlike Husserl, he is not looking for an irrefutable foundation of knowledge, a discovery which in itself is charged with an important cognitive significance.[49]

In turn, Butler's impressive *Samuel Beckett and the Meaning of Being* posited that '[i]n spite of all protestations to the contrary, Beckett is working the same ground as the philosophers'.[50] But Butler's existential phenomenology takes its point of departure from Hegel not Husserl, giving him a skewed perspective on Heidegger and Sartre's phenomenological 'heresies'. In like manner, if one could just substitute 'Husserlian phenomenology' for references to existentialism in the preface to Edith Kern's aforementioned *Existential Thought and Fictional Technique*:

> From its inception, existential thought has felt itself at home in fiction. Because of its intense "inwardness" and the "commitment" of its proponents, it has expressed itself more strikingly in imaginative writing than in non-fictional treatises. According to modern existentialist thinkers, the paradox and absurdity of life can be more readily deduced from fundamental human situations portrayed in fiction than described in the logical language of philosophy which is our heritage. Existentialism's abhorrence of rigid thought systems as being alien to life and existence has equally pointed toward a preference for poetry and fiction.[51]

If the criticism above may be considered suggestive 'near-misses' in connecting Beckett with Husserl, it is nevertheless clear that appropriating a phenomenological methodology to analyse the rendering of intellection in Beckett's work is a viable heuristic foundation for literary interpretation—even without any evidence of direct correlations between the two. And even if Beckett studies has remained virtually silent on Husserlian phenomenology, archival deposits have not. As shall become clear, Beckett's foundering on the rocks of the subject-object distinction was decisively aided by Husserlian philosophy in spring 1938. Noting in his uniquely insightful notebook from the later 1930s, the *'Whorosocope* Notebook', that 'Philosophy in the 20th c. stresses problem of cognition', Beckett took this lengthy German excerpt on Husserl, translated and reproduced here:

> This philosophy, oriented towards a critique of knowledge and a philosophy of science, has found its most significant form in the "transcendental idealist's" way of thinking, represented in Germany above all in the neo-Kantian movements and schools (above all in the "Marburg School": H. Cohen, P. Natorp, E. Cassirer and the "Baden" or "Southwest German School": W. Windelband and H. Rickert, E. Lask, Br. Bauch), under whose systems of thought one must count the "immanence philosophy" (Schuppe) as well as the theory of consciousness [Bewußtseinslehre] and "transcendental idealism" of E. Husserl. In France philosophers of science such as Hamelin, or Milhaud, even Hannequin stand close to such a form of thinking.
>
> From the neo-Kantian movement the Marburg School has forcefully moved the focus of attention of the transcendental question to the categories of ideas of the mathematical natural sciences and from there pursued the systematic discovery of the formal laws of knowledge even for such areas as ethics, aesthetics, and the philosophy of religion. The special merit of the fully developed form of thinking of the Baden School, pioneered by W. Windelband, and reflected today in H. Rickert's system, has been the transition to the use of logic and methodology in the discipline of history.
>
> Cf. Kants [sic] definition of "transcendental" [written in English]: I call transcendental all cognition that deals not so much with objects as rather with our way of cognizing objects in general insofar as that way of cognizing is to be possible a priori [(Kant 66)....]
>
> Critique of Knowledge:
> After preparatory work in the 19th century (in Germany for instance [by] Helmholtz, H. Hertz, Kirchhoff, in Austria E. Mach) this critique of knowledge has seen a great development above all in France (H. Poincaré, P. Duhem, Milhaud, Meyerson, Le Roy, Rougier, Hannequin). The questions raised here, equally significant for both our views on nature [Naturanschauung] and the theory of epistemology, with the further progressing "foundational crisis" [Grundlagenkrisis] of the sciences, continuously gain new fuel and topicality. In England Whitehead, Russell, Eddington for instance have provided important contributions to the critical reflection on the foundations of mathematics and the natural sciences. New advances and questions have also been brought up by Hugo Dingler, and E. Mach (d. 1916), which are yet to be clarified.[52]

Just as the above quotation ties Edmund Husserl's 'transcendental idealism' (via Kant) to Beckett's readings, it also represents the end of the latter's nearly ten-year struggle with philosophy. That is to say, Beckett's engagement with phenomenology around mid-1938 marked the conclusion of Beckett's search for philosophical answers, particularly regarding the subject-object relation in art. Philosophical thought (particularly that of Schopenhauer and Dr Johnson) would henceforth be consulted to reinforce or extend Beckett's literary endeavours. In short, in finding the phenomenological ideas in contemporaneous philosophy first put forward by Edmund Husserl, Beckett solves—or at least to his satisfaction, resolves—the matter of how individual perception makes meaning out of objects. Critically, these need not be objects of the world, but can be those of individual consciousness too. Yet at the same time, Beckett's break was a progressive one.

For haggling over the subject-object relation is part and parcel of Beckett's artistic co-evolution in the 1930s.

§3

An account of Beckett's engagement of subject-object relations, leading to its resolution in 1938, must be here of a necessarily brief and biographical sketch. Rather than looking at the recently covered fictional works of the period—the early poems, *Dream of Fair to Middling Women*, and *Murphy*—an overview will be taken through Beckett's manuscripts, letters and non-fiction at this time.[53] Interestingly, grappling with the elusive subject-object relation was commenced by two opposing forces, canonical philosophy and contemporary art –both only truly introduced to Beckett in 'The Paris Years.'[54] By the end of nearly two years (early November 1928 to mid-September 1930) at the École Normale Supérieure, Beckett had already employed Vico's theory (via Bruno) on the identification of opposites and 'rejection of the transcendental' in praising James Joyce's 'High Modernist' style: 'His writing is not *about* something; *it is that something itself.*[55] And while the 98-line poem *Whoroscope*—replete with Eliotesque footnotes, supplied at Richard Aldington's request on 16 June 1930—may be philosophically downplayed as part of a short flirtation with Descartes, two recurrent features stand out. First is the yoking of European philosophy to radically modernistic aims, (even if these early works were rather tame compared with the post-war fictions); and second, Beckett here starts to specifically enquire into those dialectics that are the bread and butter of Western philosophy, exemplified by the tradition of mind-body dualism.[56] With more of his own views advanced, perhaps, than in either of the two previous publications (*Whoroscope* and 'Dante...Bruno.Vico..Joyce') before *Proust*, submitted to Chatto & Windus upon Beckett's return to Dublin in September 1930, takes these twin features even further. Like Joyce, Marcel Proust 'makes no attempt to dissociate form from content. The one is a concretion of the other, the revelation of a world.' Over 16 volumes of *Remembrance of Things Past*, argues a highly reflexive Beckett, Proust achieves this feat through effecting the breakdown of Habit through 'artistic experience': 'When the subject is exempt from the will the object is exempt from causality (Time and Space taken together) and this human vegetation is purified in the transcendental apperception that can capture the Model, the Idea, the Thing in itself.' As this excerpt suggests, in saluting Proust's literary impressionism, 'his non-logical statement of phenomena in the order of their perception, before they have been distorted into intelligibility', Beckett again seeks philosophical support, this time from Schopenhauer's first volume of the *World and Will and Representation*.[57]

While the influence of Schopenhauer on *Proust* has long been noted in Anglophone scholarship, Beckett's gravitation toward the former's 'veil of Maya'—or 'what Kant calls the phenomenon as opposed to the thing-in-itself', even if 'Kant did not arrive at the knowledge that the phenomenon is the world as representation and that the thing-in-itself is the will'—is, without doubt, a major influence on both Beckett's artistic temperament and philosophical outlook during the interwar period.[58] Moreover, by rationalising away the fact that phenomena were representations of reality, and that these representations were illusions created by individual egoism (what Schopenhauer calls the principle of individuation), Kant is admonished in *The World as Will and Representation* for failing to consider moments when the 'veil of Maya' stops deceiving the mind, leaving existence to be perceived directly in its essence; one beyond 'this visible world in which we are, a magic effect called into being, an unstable and inconstant illusion without substance, comparable to the optical illusion and the dream, a veil enveloping human consciousness, a something of which it is equally false and equally true to say that it is and that it is not'. Schopenhauer's 'Criticism of the Kantian Philosophy', 'that we never know the essential nature of the world, namely the thing-in-itself'—the first of many 'neo-Kantian' attempts to overcome the master's 'idealism' regarding individual subjectivity grasping at external objects—thus becomes connected to the artist's unique ability to counter the *principium individuationis*.[59] Sounding more like Schopenhauerian rendering of Brahmanism, Beckett's essay ascribes this artistic overcoming to Proust's use of 'involuntary memory':

> it abstracts the useful, the opportune, the accidental, because in its flame it has consumed Habit and all its works, and in its brightness revealed what the mock reality of experience never can and ever will reveal—the real. But involuntary memory is an unruly magician and will not be importuned. It chooses its own time and place for the performances of its miracle.[60]

Beckett then developed this interest 'on relation between <u>object</u> & its <u>representation</u>, between the <u>stimulus</u> & <u>molecular disturbance</u>, between <u>percipi</u> and <u>percipere</u>' through 'the old demon of notesnatching', as demonstrated by jottings from the introduction of Jules de Gaultier's *De Kant à Nietzsche* near the end of the 1931–1932 '*Dream* Notebook'.[61] As is typical of the Joycean style undertaken in *Dream of Fair to Middling Women*, Gaultier's reference is recycled for a section of *Dream* parodying Beckett's tutor, Rudmose-Brown (the Polar Bear), 'if we could only learn to school ourselves to nurture that divine and fragile Fünkelein of curiosity struck from the desire to bind for ever in imperishable relation the object to its representation, the stimulus to the molecular agitation that it sets up, percipi to percipere'.⁶² As Erik Tonning recounts, Gaultier 'seems to go even further' than Schopenhauer's Mayan illusion: 'Within the phenomenal world, subjects are confronted with nothing but a "representation" or "screen", never with objects themselves.'⁶³ Like his venerated Schopenhauer a century earlier, Gaultier is at pains to castigate the 'disloyal breach that Kant himself made in order to escape on the wing of the old dogmas'; namely, the separation of subject and object, or of phenomena and Thing-In-Itself, without attention to the truly critical matter at hand: 'the phenomenal screen of the shadows, in which it is represented and strives to apprehend itself.'⁶⁴ In this way, Kant's variously supposed limitations thus become the starting point for Western philosophy thereafter; this no less true of Husserl's phenomenology than Schopenhauer's: 'Kant's mental gaze rested on this [phenomenological] field, although he was not yet able to appropriate it and recognize it as the centre from which to work up on his own line a rigorous science of Essential Being.' Here again, the phenomenological reduction—or Schopenhauer's 'veil of Maya' and Gaultier's 'screen'—is explicitly set out as a way of overcoming the challenge of Kantian idealism.⁶⁵

Yet Beckett had neither read Kant nor about Husserl by spring 1932; that challenge was still six years away. Over the next four years, in fact, Beckett's knowledge of philosophy, psychology and literature were overwhelmingly mediated by overviews like Gaultier's. Nowhere is this clearer than Beckett's 'Philosophy Notes' of 1932–1933—containing just under 100 sides of handwritten summaries on the period 'from Kant to Nietzsche' in Wilhelm Windelband's *A History of Philosophy*, with fully a quarter of these dedicated to Kant.⁶⁶ In turn, fully thirteen sides are devoted to 'The Object of Knowledge' in Kantian philosophy (covering fourteen pages in Windelband, 537–550), hinging on the question: 'the relation of knowledge to its object, in what does it consist, and what does it rest?'⁶⁷ Similarly formulated a decade later by Beckett, *Watt* asks, 'what was this pursuit of meaning, in this indifference to meaning. And to what did it tend? These are delicate questions.'⁶⁸ But precisely such haste led Peter Murphy to claim that '*Watt* is a Kantian novel': 'Kant's philosophy offers the difficult and paradoxical situation of man as phenomenally determined but noumenally free, as determined and free at the same time.'⁶⁹

Despite valuable insights, Kant goes too far for Beckett, just as Murphy goes too far in linking the two in *Watt*. For it is precisely the connection of subject and object, of free mind and fixed world—as with Beckett's comments to Knowlson on Sartre above—that Windelband's rendering of Kant points *beyond*:

> Human knowledge is limited to objects of experience, because the perception required for use by categories is in our case only the receptive sensuous perception in space and time. If one could suppose a <u>perception of a non-reflective kind</u>, producing synthetically not only its Forms, but also its contents—a truly 'productive imagination'—its object would no longer be phenomena, but things-in-themselves. Such a faculty would be <u>intellectual perception</u> (intuition) or <u>intuitive intellect</u>, the unity of the two knowing faculties of sensibility and understanding, which in man appear separated, though their constant inter-reference indicates a hidden common root. Thus Noumena, things-in-themselves, are <u>thinkable negatively as objects of a non-sensuous perception</u>, of which unknowable can predicate matter. They are thinkable as <u>limiting conceptions</u> of experience.[70]

By way of further contrast, in terms of 'the Kantian distinction between the beautiful and sublime' highlighted by Murphy,[71] Beckett here reverts back to his standard note-taking style, summarising Windelband's 'Natural Purposiveness' on Kant's aesthetic, moral and artistic theories in just over a page.[72] Instead, it was the interaction of '<u>phenomenal appearance</u>, behind which the thing-in-itself remains unknown', the nature of 'intellection', sought in Windelband's account of Kant's epistemology, one doubtless contributing to Beckett's evolving view of the vicissitudes and instabilities of individual consciousness.[73]

Kant's views on art, it also seems, were about 200 years out of date for an artist claiming only a year later, in opening 'Recent Irish Poetry': 'I propose, as rough principle of individuation in this essay, the degree in which the younger Irish poets evince awareness of the new thing that has happened, or the old thing that has happened again, namely the breakdown of the object.' In Beckett's view, this 'no-man's-land, this 'rupture of the lines of communication', offers nothing like a stable, Kantian basis for the categorisation of phenomena; for the 'artist who is aware of this may state the space that intervenes between him and the world of objects'. Thus, even if he is reading about 'antiquarians' in philosophy, Beckett's heart was with those modernist 'others' refusing the artistic 'flight from self-awareness': Jack B. Yeats, Eliot, Denis Devlin and Brian Coffey.[74] Recalling that review for its early awareness of the 'vanished object' to his friend, the art critic Georges Duthuit, Beckett explicitly linked the 'no man's land' of subject-object relations to Proust's own 'zone of evaporation':

> I remember coming out once, the regulation 20 years ago, being at that time less little than now, with an angry article on modern Irish poets, in which I set up, as criterion of worthwhile modern poetry, awareness of the vanished object. Already! And talking, as the only terrain accessible to the poet, of the no man's land that he projects round himself, rather as a flame projects its zone of evaporation.[75]

In the mid-1930s however, it was painting, not poetry, best communicating the complexities of the subject-object relation to Beckett. Without doubt, this provides much of the interior landscape for Beckett's trip through Nazi Germany, following the completion of *Murphy*, between October 1936 and April 1937. In one of the few accounts of daily life in the Third Reich by a non-German, Beckett's encounter with a young Nazi enthusiast, Claudia Asher, prompted him to claim that 'the fence between the big and little worlds is Zwei Herren dienen [serving two masters]. I talk bilge (Kimwasser? Schlagwasser?) about relation of subject and object.' Four days later, in viewing a portrait by one of the 'degenerate' Expressionists, Karl Schmidt-Rottluff, Beckett discussed the matter with Dr Rosa Shapire, as recorded in his highly revealing 'German Diaries':

> Launch into mixed dissertation, twin object-subject round stem of art as prayer. New figure occurs as I speak. The art (picture), that is a prayer sets up prayer, releases prayer, in onlooker, i.e. Priest: Lord have mercy upon us. People: Christ have mercy upon us. What is the name of this art. [....] Leave about 12¼. Went to be mocked, stayed to pray.[76]

Also in mid-November 1936, Beckett came across yet another German Expressionist, Franz Marc's, aphorisms and letters on 'subject, predicate, object relations in painting', commenting in the 'German Dairies': 'The object particularises, banalises the "thought". Which gives me: Musik is Satz ohne Objekt. Lied is music nur insofar als die Noten bloss Laute sind.' But if Beckett's notes on Marc 'alogical' painting methods explicitly 'affirm the ability of the artist to intuitively grasp the true form of things being appearance'—the same phenomenological peering behind the veil of objects to glimpse the thing-in-itself, Husserl's 'essence of beings'—they simultaneously imply something else. Modernist painting, and to a lesser degree, music, were better able to render this 'inner artistic logic' than were mere words; and not least, philosophical words.[77] Even if, after Descartes and especially Kant, Western philosophy could analyse the nature of subject-object antimonies, its logical and descriptive method meant that, for Beckett, it could not adequately address a dilemma 'ineffable' in nature.[78]

A week later, Beckett visited Karl Ballmer's studio, viewing several paintings, including *Kopf in Rot* [Head in Red], prompting Beckett to remark:

> Would not occur to me to call this painting abstract. A metaphysical concrete. Nor Nature convention, but its source, fountain of Erscheinung. Fully a posteriori painting. Object not exploited to illustrate an idea, as in say Léger or Baumeister, but primary. The communication exhausted by the optical experience that is its motive and content. Anything further is by the way.[79]

Alongside radical art, Ballmer dabbled in contemporary philosophy, some of which Beckett read months later, including a 1933 pamphlet employing Rudolf Steiner 'on the cognitive process' to 'elucidate the painting of Ballmer'. In addition to offering Beckett deeper perspectives on Ballmer's art, the text in question,

Aber Herr Heidegger!, is important for two further reasons. This provides early evidence of a deep synthesis of contemporary philosophy with modernist art, setting Ballmer's thought against 'Aristotle, Descartes, Spinoza, Leibniz, Kant critic of reason Heidegger? It is the old Plato-Aristotle Realist-Nominalist Idealist-Materialist Antithesis?' As Beckett later noted in his 'German Diaries' on 20 March 1937, Ballmer '[r]epresents Heidegger as mere thinker to the end of motifs [...] With not an original contribution except perhaps the doctrine of the Greek qualitative criterion of truth, whereby "truth" (a-<u>letheia</u>) is nothing more than the Uncovering of objective being.' And secondly, in investigating these questions, Beckett was specifically introduced to two contemporary philosophers: Martin Heidegger and Fritz Mauthner. Given his distaste for the 'NS gospel' registered across the 'German Diaries', it is perhaps unsurprising that Beckett shied away from Heidegger's ideas, not least considering that *Aber Herr Heidegger!* is, in part, an account of the latter's first act as a National Socialist: his inaugural rectoral address at Freiburg in May 1933.[80]

On the other hand, Fritz Mauthner's 'negative' approach to logic—'he made fun of all logic and of all philosophical claims of thinking because all thinking was, after all, only speaking'—showed Beckett a potential way out of the post-Kantian subject-object antimonies. That is to say, Mauthner's 'learned ignorance', his identification of language and thought behind a metaphorical 'screen' of inchoate perceptions; and indeed, his view that both made language suitable for poetic rather than epistemological thought—all of these suggested what might be termed a 'linguistically phenomenological' way out of the subject-object dualism. As Beckett read in *Aber Herr Heidegger!*:

> Mauthner did not consider that the logical laws of thought— which do not correspond to, in Aristotelian fashion, a spoon-feeding limited by an externally-imposed nature of thought, but which might even seize the true nature through of its own propulsion - must in any case be different ones than the time-honoured "Laws of Thought" that Mauthner recognised as mere grammar.[81]

This method of using language against itself, of course, finds its most familiar artistic expression in Beckett's oft-cited 'German Letter' of 1937:

> To bore one hole in another in it [language], until what lurks behind it—be it something or nothing—begins to seep through; I cannot imagine a higher goal for a writer today [...] In this dissonance between the means and their use it will perhaps become possible to feel a whisper of that final music or that silence that underlies All.'[82]

However, the above excerpt to Axel Kaun was not written with Mauthner in mind, for those readings—and Beckett's additional readings in phenomenology—were still a year away. Only then, fully a year after the 'German Letter' of 1937, did the three intersecting threads from the interwar period, discussed above, come together. These derived from, first, a revolutionary artistic programme, one drawing upon modernist art and criticism; second, a background in Western philosophy stressing fundamental dualisms, especially regarding the relation between subject and object; and finally, a struggle with post-Kantian attempts to account for the 'screen' dividing the two. A concluding look at how Beckett synthesised these ideas in 1938 now turns to that great intellectual repository of the later 1930s, the '*Whoroscope* Notebook'.

§4

The conclusion to Beckett's own struggles with 'intellection' through Western philosophy, it seems, occurred in the months following his nearly fatal stabbing in January 1938. Assuming that the '*Whoroscope* Notebook' runs in a roughly chronological order, more than half the material was added after this date, as John Pilling has impressively demonstrated.[83] At this point, and once again helping Joyce with the interminable *Work in Progress*, Beckett transcribed eleven excerpts from *Beiträge zu einer Kritik der Sprache*, focussing on Mauthner's 'Self destruction of the metaphorical'. Here again, Kant is the straw man; in this case, for a radical critique of language:

> This insight into the nature of experience and thinking, which at this level no longer present themselves as opposites, but as two ways in which memory views things, we owe to a continuation of Kant's critique, and we would owe it to Kant himself, if Kant had undertaken, instead of his critique of pure reason, a critique of reason in general, if he, the most astute and hopefully last of all the "word realists", had not taken abstractions for reality, words for definable judgments, worthless currency as real money [...] Kant's reasons for the sole dominance of experience, that is against all materialism, do not need to be repeated. It has become for us a platitude that the world, the "thing-in-itself", can only develop from our consciousness, from our subjective thought and not the other way around. If even the most banal experience, a comparison of two perceptions, requires thought, so every higher experience, every science with its so-called laws, is an addition of thought to experience. Conformity to a natural law is regular causality; and understanding causality has never yet uncovered a simple perception in the world. That is what Kant taught, after all, and added to it Hume's critique of the concept of causality, so that even the projection of a perception into the External world, that is the simplest objective perception, which, e.g. traces back the sensation of green of the tree before my window, hypothesises an uncontrollable unverifiable cause of the perception of consciousness.[84]

Interspersed with the Mauthner entries are jottings from the 'antediluvian edition' of Kant's works, which Peter Murphy notes Beckett obtained in early 1938.[85] Interestingly, virtually all are from the last of eleven volumes, Ernst Cassirer's biography, *Kant's Life and Thought*, with two passages working their way into

Watt.⁸⁶ This train of thought is followed by a return to Jules de Gaultier, with Beckett transcribing a further passage on Kant's 'antinomial' distinction between perceptual phenomena and thought:

> Now the great work of Kant, accomplished in the fifty pages of the TRANSCENDENTAL AESTHETIC, consists in his having demonstrated that space and time do not on the one hand, have substantial reality and that, on the other hand, they are not properties of the object either; that, on the contrary, they belong to the knowing subject and that they are the forms of this subject's sensibility.⁸⁷

For Beckett's own aesthetic, the matter had come to a head. In his only published review from these critical months, 'Intercessions by Denis Devlin', for example, this 'severed' relation is mooted as 'the absolute predicament of particular human identity'; moreover, 'the distinction is not idle, for it is from the failure to make it that proceed the common rejection as "obscure" of most that is significant in modern music, painting, and literature'.⁸⁸

Enter the 'extraordinarily good' *Nausea* in late May 1938, where Beckett encountered Sartre's alter-ego (a far cry from Beckett's Belacqua), Roquentin's, overcoming of this subject-object distinction: 'suddenly, the veil is torn away, I have understood. I have *seen*.'⁸⁹ Quite possibly in order to chase up this philosophical-artistic rendering of subject-object synthesis, Beckett then read Sartre's *L'Imagination*, making three entries short entries into his '*Whoroscope* Notebook'.⁹⁰ A few pages (presumably close in time to reading Sartre) later, Beckett transcribed portions of Windelband and Heinz Heimsoeth's sketch of Husserl, translated above—tellingly given the same subtitle as Mauthner used in his self-appointed enterprise, *Wissenschaftkritik*. And this, in effect, represents the final evidence of Beckett's philosophical struggle with the relation between subject and object. For Beckett in mid-1938, it may be argued, Western philosophy had fully served its didactic purpose. Henceforth, while clearly drawing upon material already accumulated over the past decade, in future only those thinkers with whom Beckett felt a personal affinity seem to be revisited. Yet philosophy is by no means abandoned, as Rabinovitz observed in analysing *Watt*: 'It is not that he is reluctant to use philosophical themes, rather, he is unwilling to permit them to undermine the aesthetic integrity of his works.'⁹¹ In aesthetic terms, in fact, Beckett may be writing in the 'no-man's-land' between subject and object, *writing the veil*, the experience of self-reflexive consciousness itself. In this light, a final question can be raised: did Beckett see Watt in Sartre's imagination; or rather, what did Beckett see in Sartre's *Imagination*?

The short answer is Husserl. Or rather, Sartre's Husserl, first introduced in his École dissertation, published in 1936, as opposing Henri Bergson, who 'was not of the opinion that consciousness must have a correlate, or, to speak like Husserl, that a consciousness is always consciousness *of* something'.⁹² Sartre's view of Husserlian phenomenology, moreover, envisages it dissolving nearly everything to have come before. Over several preceding chapters that criticise Western philosophy's tradition of smuggling in metaphysical assumptions about the perceptual image, Sartre concludes his study with 'The Phenomenology of Husserl', specifically the 'great event of pre-World-War-I philosophy', Husserl's 1913 *Ideas*, 'destined to revolutionize psychology no less than philosophy'.⁹³ Mired in Husserl and his as-yet unpublished *Nausea*, for Sartre of the mid-1930s it was Husserlian 'bracketing'—the phenomenological reduction of Kantian intellection to the experience of consciousness—that answered all the big problems. This, for Sartre, was like a secular revelation: 'The notion of *intentionality* gives a new conception of images', considering that an 'image, too, is an image *of* something.'⁹⁴ In a critical passage, he argues:

> By becoming an intentional structure the image has passed from the condition of an inert content of consciousness to that of a unitary and synthetic consciousness in relation with a transcendent object [...] At a stroke vanish, along with the immanentist metaphysics of images, all the difficulties adduced [...] concerning the relationship of the simulacrum to the real object, and of pure thought to the simulacrum. [...] Husserl freed the psychic world of a weighty burden and eliminated almost all the difficulties that clouded the classical problem of the relations of images to thoughts. Husserl did not stop there with his suggestions, however. In effect, if an image is but a name for a certain way in which consciousness takes aim on its object, nothing prevents us from aligning physical images (paintings, drawings, photographs) with images termed "psychic".⁹⁵

Sartre illustrates this by describing, at length, Husserl's analysis of a painting by Albrecht Dürer. Symbolically, at least, the tables had turned: Beckett was now reading modernist philosophy critiquing 'classical' art. With subject and object unified around an intending consciousness, Sartre's essay concludes by leaving it to others—modernist artists and writers in particular—to address a new fissure arising from Husserlian phenomenology, not between subject and object but between images and perceptions; what Sartre respectively called 'memory-images' and 'fiction-images'. In what might read as a programme for *Watt* and Beckett's post-war fictions, Sartre concluded his twenty-page paean to Husserl with a call to arms:

> We know that we must start afresh, setting aside all the prephenomenological literature, and attempting above all to attain an intuitive vision of the intentional structure of the image. It also becomes necessary to raise the novel and subtle question of the relations between mental images and "physical" images (paintings, photographs, etc.) [...] The way is open for a phenomenological psychology.⁹⁶

Where *Imagination* ends, it seems, *Watt* begins. 'The ambiguous and maddening ineffability that will infuse not only *Watt* but all of Beckett's later work is already present and half-formulated', David Hayman persuasively argues, especially evident in 'the development of the opening sequence' of the novel.[97] Focussing on the first two pages of the third notebook toward *Watt*—dating from May 1942, some four years after Beckett's engagement with Husserlian phenomenology—Hayman reproduces these 'mediations', strikingly evocative of the conclusion to Sartre's *Imagination*:

> The creative consciousness is driven & obscure. Obscure and obscene when it acts, terrible and driven when it receives.
> Its action is a receiving, its receiving an acting.
> When it acts it receives its own act, when it receives it acts on the act of another.[98]

> There are not, and never could be, images in consciousness. Rather, an image is *a certain type of consciousness*. An image is an act, not some thing. An image is a consciousness *of* some thing.[99]

As this chapter has shown, Beckett had travelled a long way in tracing out his own philosophical-artistic relation between subject and object, arriving, after a decade, at what might be a described as a phenomenological perspective on the 'creative consciousness'. As Sartre imparted to him in mid-1938, the difference between 'real' and 'fictional' images need not be seen as an unbridgeable chasm, but as a void to be fruitfully explored. Finally, if *Watt* can be considered the workbook for Beckett's later fictions, of a last, stumbling exercise in writing direct experience prior to the post-war 'frenzy of writing', then it was in this novel that subject and object first ceased to be viewed as 'two holes [that] had been independently burst' in the 'fence' separating image and world. Instead, through the synthesis of subject and object offered especially to Beckett by Sartre's rendering of Husserl in both fiction and non-fiction, an alternative conclusion first comes into view in *Watt*: 'was it not after all just possible [...] the two fences were but one?'[100]

NOTES

1. Cited in John Pilling, *Beckett Before Godot* (Cambridge: Cambridge University Press, 1997), p. 185.
2. For an overview of the *Watt* manuscripts, held at the Harry Ransom Center in Austin, Texas, see David Hayman, 'Getting where? Beckett's opening gambit for *Watt*', in *Contemporary Literature* XLIII/1 (2002). Some of the hallmarks of scholarship on the published novel include Jacqueline Hoefer, '*Watt*', reprinted in *Samuel Beckett: A Collection of Critical Essays*, ed. Martin Esslin (Englewood Cliffs: Prentice Hall, 1965); John J. Mood, '"The Personal Sytstem" – Samuel Beckett's *Watt*', in *PMLA* 86/2 (1971); and Rubin Rabinovitz, *The Development of Samuel Beckett's Fiction* (Chicago: University of Illinois Press, 1984), pp. 124–150. The perspective taken here, if less psychologically driven, is generally in line with Hugh Culik's view of *Watt*'s 'nonlogical mental processes': 'Because these [artistic] concerns receive an inadequately "direct expression" in *Watt* – that is, because content and form are fused only on a highly rationalized allusive level – the work only suggests the elements more perfectly fused in the trilogy'; see Hugh Culik, 'The Place of *Watt* in Beckett's Development', in *Modern Fiction Studies* 29/1 (1983), pp. 69, 58.
3. Samuel Beckett, 'Dante…Bruno.Vico..Joyce', in Beckett, *Disjecta: Miscellaneous Writings and a Dramatic Fragment*, ed. Ruby Cohn (New York: Grove Press, 1984), p. 27.
4. Samuel Beckett, *Watt* (London: Calder & Boyers, 1970), pp. 41–2; italics in original.
5. The useful concept of 'intellection' is applied by Adrien Van der Weer and Ruud Hisgen's 'Intellection in the Work of Samuel Beckett' as 'the natural way for rational, human beings to try to imagine the unimaginable [limits of expression] via language'; see Adrien Van der Weer and Ruud Hisgen, 'Intellection in the Work of Samuel Beckett', in *Samuel Beckett Today / Aujourd'hui* 1 (1992), p. 91.
6. Beckett, *Watt*, pp. 41–3.
7. Jean-Paul Sartre, *Nausea*, trans. Lloyd Alexander (New York: New Directions Books, 1969), p. 4.
8. *Ibid.*, p. 54; italics in original.
9. Beckett to Thomas MacGreevy, 26 May 1938, TCD MS 10904.
10. Samuel Beckett, 'Recent Irish Poetry', in *Disjecta*, p. 70.
11. Beckett, *Watt*, pp. 238–240.
12. Sartre, *Nausea*, p. 125.
13. Regarding textual interventions, both novels ostensibly use footnotes for the guidance of the attentive reader, as with *Watt*'s 'editorial' warning on the numbers given for the Lynch family: 'The figures given here are incorrect. The consequent calculations are therefore doubly erroneous.' (Beckett, *Watt*, pp. 101, 211); or *Nausea*'s 'the text of the undated pages ends here' (Sartre, *Nausea*, p. 3).
14. The only Anglophone work to treat this intimacy in any detail is found in the impressive theoretical treatment provided in Louis Sass' *Madness and Modernism: Insanity in the light of modern art, literature, and thought* (New York: Basic Books, 1992), developed by Damien Love's doctoral thesis (Unpublished PhD. Thesis: Oxford University, 2004), ch. 2.
15. Beckett, *Watt*, p. 78.
16. Sartre, *Nausea*, p. 125.

[17] *Ibid.*, p. 127.
[18] *Ibid.*, p. 131.
[19] *Ibid.*, p. 125.
[20] Beckett, *Watt*, pp. 74–5.
[21] Edith Kern, *Existential Thought and Fictional Technique* (London: Yale University Press, 1970), p. 190.
[22] In a work published the year previously, Michael Robinson also notes *Watt*'s 'refusal of things to assume their time-honoured names is a modern dilemma which has occupied writers since it was first acknowledged by Hofmannsthal, Rilke and Proust [...] Although he is more coherent Roquentin is in a very similar position to Watt. In the midst of the nameless he too sets to trying names on things'; see Michael Robinson, *The Long Sonata of the Dead: A Study of Samuel Beckett* (London: Rupert Hart-Davis Ltd., 1969), pp. 125–126.
[23] Hoefer, '*Watt*', pp. 74–5.
[24] Kern, *Existential Thought and Fictional Technique*, pp. 190–1.
[25] James Knowlson and John Haynes, *Images of Beckett* (Cambridge: Cambridge University Press, 2003), pp. 16–18; italics in original.
[26] Cited in Dan Gunn, 'Until the gag is chewed: Samuel Beckett's letters: eloquence and "near speechlessness"', in the *Times Literary Supplement*, 21 April (2006), p. 14.
[27] James Knowlson, *Damned to Fame: The Life of Samuel Beckett* (London: Bloomsbury, 1996), pp. 333, 351–2; 772 n. 55.
[28] *Ibid.*, pp. 352–353.
[29] Dermot Moran, *Edmund Husserl: Founder of Phenomenology* (Cambridge: Polity, 2005), pp. 2, 7.
[30] David Woodruff-Smith, *Husserl* (Abingdon: Routledge, 2007), pp. 45, 29.
[31] Edmund Husserl, *Ideas: General Introduction to Pure Phenomenology*, trans. W.R. Boyce Gibson (London: Collier Books, 1962), p. 172.
[32] Paul S. MacDonald, *Descartes and Husserl: The Philosophical Project of Radical Beginnings* (Albany, NY: State University of New York Press, 2000), pp. 1–17.
[33] Husserl, *Ideas*, pp. 7–8, 11.
[34] For a discussion of Heidegger's embrace of German fascism, see my 'Between Geist and Zeitgeist: Martin Heidegger as Ideologue of Metapolitical fascism', in *Totalitarian Movements and Political Religions* 6/2 (2005). Regarding Heidegger's progressive distancing from his onetime mentor's philosophy, Husserl commented in 1931 that 'a careful reading of Heidegger showed him how far Heidegger was from him. He laid this to Heidegger never having freed himself completely from his theological prejudices, and to the weight of the war on him. The war and ensuing difficulties drive men into mysticisms. This too accounts for Heidegger's popular success. But [is not] Heidegger by far the most important of the non-Husserlian philosophers today? His work bears the mark of genius'; see Dorian Cairns, ed., *Conversations with Husserl and Fink* (The Hague: Martinus Nijhoff, 1976), p. 9.
[35] Paul Ricouer, cited in Moran, *Edmund Husserl*, pp. 2–3.
[36] MacDonald, *Descartes and Husserl*, p. 15.
[37] For further discussion of Beckett's early development, see ch. 5.
[38] See MacDonald, *Descartes and Husserl*, p. 93, which locates a critical difference between Descartes and Husserl on the matter of mathematics: 'The touchstone for cognition which is immune to doubt in these early stages, against which both Descartes and Husserl evaluate other epistemic claims, is that of the intuition of mathematical truths.' (p. 6.) For Beckett's

artistic evolution in the 1930s described as 'non-Euclidean logic', see Feldman, *Beckett's Books: A Cultural History of Samuel Beckett's 'Interwar Notes'* (London: Bloomsbury, 2008), pp. 13–20.

[39] Cairns, *Conversations with Husserl and Fink*, p. 47.

[40] Samuel Beckett, *Proust*, in Beckett, *The Grove Centenary Edition, Vol. IV: Poems, Short Fiction, Criticism*, ed. J. M. Coetzee (New York: Grove Press, 2006), pp. 515–6.

[41] Jean-Paul Sartre, *War Diaries: Notebooks from a Phoney War, November 1939–March 1940*, trans. Quintin Hoare (London: Verso, 1984), p. 184.

[42] Annie Cohen-Solal, *Sartre: A Life* (London: William Heinemann Ltd, 1987), p. 91.

[43] Woodruff-Smith, *Husserl*, p. 441.

[44] For further discussion of phenomenological approaches to Beckett's work, see ch. 1.

[45] Mario J. Valdés, *World-Making: the Literary Truth-Claim and the Interpretation of Texts* (London: University of Toronto Press, 1996), p. 36.

[46] Maurice Natanson, *The Erotic Bird: Phenomenology and Literature* (Princeton: Princeton University Press, 1998), pp. 72, xv.

[47] Eugene F. Kaelin, *The Unhappy Consciousness: The Poetic Plight of Samuel Beckett: An Inquiry at the Intersection of Phenomenology and Literature* (Dordrecht: Kluwer, 1987), p. 7.

[48] For example, two important works in English on the role of consciousness in Beckett's work make either passing reference to Husserl; see *ibid.*, 1–12; and Daniel Katz, *Saying 'I' No More: Subjectivity and Consciousness in the Prose of Samuel Beckett* (Evanston: Northwestern University Press, 1999), p. 87), or no reference at all, as in Lance St John Butler, *Samuel Beckett and the Meaning of Being: A Study in the Ontological Parable* (London: Macmillan, 1984). One exception here, however, is the discussion of Husserl found in Livio A.C. Dobrez, *The Existential and its Exits: Literary and Philosophical Perspectives on the Works of Beckett, Ionesco, Genet, & Pinter* (London: Athlone Press, 1986), pp. 53–62.

[49] Carla, Locatelli, *Unwording the World: Samuel Beckett's Prose Works after the Nobel Prize* (Philadelphia: University of Pennsylvania Press, 1990), pp. 2–3.

[50] Lance St John Butler, *Samuel Beckett and the Meaning of Being*, p. 2.

[51] Kern, *Existential Thought*, p. viii.

[52] [Ihre bedeutsamste Ausprägung hat diese erkenntniskritische u. wissenschaftstheoretisch gerichtete Philosophie gefunden in der Denkweise des tranzendentalen Idealismus,- vertreten in Deutschland vor allem durch die Richtungen u. Schulen des Neu Kantianismus (vor allem die "Marburger Schule": H Cohen, P. Natorp, E. Cassirer u. die "badische" oder "südwestdeutsche Marburg Schule": W. Windelband u. H. Rickert, E. Lask, Br. Bauchs), denen Gedankenbildungen wie die "Immanenzphilosophie" (Schuppe) oder die "Grundwissenschaft" Relankes sowie auch der "tranzendentale Idealismus" E. Husserls beizuordnen sind. In Frankreich stehen bedeutende Wissenschaftsphilosophen wie Hamelin oder Milhaud, auch Hannequin solcher Denkweise nahe –
Cf Kants definition von "transcendental":
Ich nenne alle Erkenntnis transzendental, die sich nicht sowohl mit Gegenständen, sondern mit unserer Erkenntnisart von Gegenständen, sofern diese a priori möglich sein soll, überhaupt beschäftigt.
(Kritik der reinen Vernunft, Einleitung VII; III, 49) [....] Von den neukantischen Richtungen hat die Marburger Schule mit besonderer Energie die Gedankenkategorien der mathe-

matischen Naturwissenschaft in den Mittelpunkt der transzendentalen Fragestellung gerückt u. von da die systematische Erforschung der formalen Bewusstseinsgesetzlichkeiten auch für die Gebiete der Ethik, Äesthetik, Religionsphilosophie betrieben. Das besondere Verdienst der durch W. Windelband begründeten, in H. Rickerts System dann zur vollen Ausgestaltung gelangten Denkweise der <u>badischen Schule</u>, ist der Überschritt zur Logik u. Methodenlehre der Geschichtswissenschaft gewesen.] (Samuel Beckett, '*Whoroscope* Notebook', UoR Ms. 3000/1, Beckett International Foundation, Reading, pp. 65–6, corresponding to Wilhelm Windelband and Heinz Heimsoeth, *Lehrbuch der Geschichte der Philosophie, Mit einem Schlusskapitel 'Die Philosophie im 20. Jahrhundert' und einer Übersicht über den Stand der philosophiegeschichtlichen Forschung* (Tübingen: Mohr, 1935), pp. 574–575.

[53] For detailed analyses of *Murphy*, see Chris Ackerley, *Demented Particulars* (Tallahassee: Journal of Beckett Studies Books, 1998); for *Dream of Fair to Middling Women*, see John Pilling, ed., *Beckett's* Dream *Notebook* (Reading: Beckett International Foundation, 1999); and for an outstanding discussion of Beckett's interwar poetry, see the late Seán Lawlor's '"Making a noise to drown an echo": Allusion and quotation in the early poems of Samuel Beckett, 1929–1935' (Unpublished PhD. Thesis: University of Reading, 2008).

[54] Knowlson, *Damned to Fame*, pp. 87–119.

[55] Beckett, 'Dante…Bruno.Vico..Joyce', in *Disjecta*, pp. 26–7.

[56] For further discussion of Beckett's understanding of philosophical dualism, see my *Beckett's Books*, pp. 41–57.

[57] Beckett, *Poems, Short Fiction, Criticism*, pp. 550–2.

[58] Arthur Schopenhauer, *The World as Will and Representation*, vol. I., trans. E.F.J. Payne (New York: Dover Publications, Inc., 1969), pp. 419, 421. For discussions of Schopenhauer's influence on Proust, see J.D. O'Hara, "Beckett's Schopenhaurian Reading of Proust: The Will as Whirled in Re-presentation" in *Schopenhauer: New Essays in Honor of his 200th Birthday*, ed. Eric van der Luft (Lewiston: The Edwin Mellen Press, 1988); and John Pilling, "Beckett's Proust", reprinted in *The Becket Studies Reader*, ed. S.E. Gontarski (Gainesville: University Press of Florida, 1993). For discussion of Schopenhauer's 'veil of Maya', see Erik Tonning, *Samuel Beckett's Abstract Drama: Works for Stage and Screen, 1962–1985* (Bern: Peter Lang, 2007), pp. 30–48; and ch. 2 in this volume.

[59] Schopenhauer, *The World as Will and Representation*, pp. 417–22.

[60] Beckett, *Poems, Short Fiction, Criticism*, p. 523.

[61] John Pilling, ed., *Beckett's* Dream *Notebook* (Reading: Beckett International Foundation, 1999), pp. 165, xiii.

[62] Samuel Beckett, *Dream of Fair to Middling Women* (Dublin: The Black Cat Press, 1992), p. 160.

[63] Tonning, *Samuel Beckett's Abstract Drama*, p. 40.

[64] Jules de Gaultier, *From Kant to Nietzsche*, trans. G. M. Spring (London: Peter Owen, 1961), pp. xi, 5.

[65] Husserl, *Ideas*, p. 160.

[66] See Wilhelm Windelband, *A History of Philosophy*, 2 vols., trans. J.H. Tufts (New York: Harper & Brothers, 1958 [1901]), pp. 529–682; general discussion of Kant occurring at pp. 532–567; for analysis of Beckett's 'Philosophy Notes' see *Beckett's Books*, pp. 39–77.

[67] Samuel Beckett, 'Philosophy Notes', TCD MS 10967/223.

[68] Beckett, *Watt*, p. 72.

[69] Peter J. Murphy, 'Beckett and the philosophers', in *The Cambridge Companion to Beckett*, ed. John Pilling (Cambridge: Cambridge University Press, 1994), pp. 229–30.

[70] Beckett, 'Philosophy Notes', TCD MS 10967/227–227v; corresponding to Windelband, *A History of Philosophy*, p. 547.

[71] Murphy, 'Beckett and the philosophers', p. 231.

[72] Windelband, *A History of Philosophy*, pp. 559–67; corresponding to Beckett, 'Philosophy Notes', TCD MS 10967/232–232v.

[73] Beckett, 'Philosophy Notes', TCD MS 10967/224v.

[74] Beckett, 'Recent Irish Poetry', in *Disjecta*, pp. 70–1.

[75] Gunn 'Until the gag is chewed: Samuel Beckett's letters: eloquence and "near speechlessness"', p. 15. For the connection between this letter and Beckett's *Proust*, see Lawlor, '"Making a noise to drown an echo"', pp. 1–2.

[76] 'German Diary' entry for 15 November 1936, cited in *Das Raubauge in der Stadt: Beckett liest Hamburg*, eds. Michaela Giesing, Gabby Hartel and Carola Veit (Goettingen: Wallstein Verlag, 2007), p. 133. For a general discussion of Beckett's 'German Diaries', see Knowlson, *Damned to Fame*, pp. 230–261; portions are also provided on the 'Beckett and Hamburg' website, available at: http://schaukasten.sub.uni-hamburg.de/beckett/beckett_e/ (last accessed 12/12/14). See also Mark Nixon, '"what a tourist I must have been': The German Diaries of Samuel Beckett" (Unpublished PhD. Thesis: University of Reading, 2005); and most recently, Mark Nixon, *Samuel Beckett's German Diaries* (London: Continuum, 2011).

[77] Tonning, *Samuel Beckett's Abstract Drama*, pp. 126–7; and Feldman, *Beckett's Books*, p. 15.

[78] The term, used by Arsene in Watt, belongs to Arnold Geulincx; for details on Beckett's reading of his Metaphysics and Ethics in early 1936, see Feldman, *Beckett's Books*, pp. 131–137.

[79] James Knowlson, 'Beckett's first encounters with modern German (and Irish) art', in *Samuel Beckett: A Passion for Paintings*, ed. Fionnuala Croke (Dublin: National Gallery of Ireland, 2006), pp. 70–1.

[80] 'German Diary' entry of 20 March 1937, Beckett International Foundation, Reading. I am particularly grateful to Mark Nixon for his assistance with this passage. For a discussion of Heidegger's rectoral address, see Feldman, 'Between Geist and Zeitgeist'.

[81] [Mauthner zog nicht in Erwägung dass die logischen Gesetze eines Denkens, das nicht aristotelisch am Gängelbande der dem Denken von außen gegebenen Natur einhergeht, sondern sich der wirklichen Natur möglicherweise aus seiner Eigenkraft bemächtigt, jedenfalls andere sein müssten als die hergebrachten 'Denkgesetze', in denen Mauthner nur lauter Grammatik erkennt...]; see Karl Ballmer, *Aber Herr Heidegger! Zur Freiburger Rektoratsrede Martin Heideggers* (Basel: Verlag von Rudolf Geering, 1933), pp. 19–20; translation by Christian Egners.

[82] Beckett, 'German letter' of 1937, in *Disjecta*, p. 172.

[83] John Pilling, 'Beckett and Mauthner Revisited', in *Beckett after Beckett*, eds., S.E. Gontarski and Anthony Uhlmann (Gainesville: University of Florida Press, 2006).

[84] [Diese Einsicht in das Wesen von Erfahrung u. Denken, welche sich auf dieser Stufe nicht mehr als Gegensätze, sondern als zwei Betrachtungsweisen des Gedächtnisses darstellen, verdanken wir einer Fortführung der Kantschen Kritik, und wir würden sie Kant selbst verdanken, wenn Kant anstatt einer Kritik der reinen Vernunft eine Kritik der Vernunft

überhaupt unternommen hätte, wenn er nicht als der scharfsinnigste u. hoffentlich letzte aller Wortrealisten Abstraktionen für Wirklichkeit, Worte für definierbare Urteile, uneinlösbare Scheine für bare Münze genommen hätte [....] Kants Gründe gegen die alleinige Herrschaft der Erfahrung, also gegen allen Materialismus, brauchen nicht wiederholt zu werden. Es ist für uns ein Gemeinplatz geworden, dass man die Welt, das Ding-an-sich, nur aus unserem Bewusstsein, aus unserem subjektiven Denken erschliessen dürfe u. nicht umgekehrt. Ist schon zur banalsten Erfahrung eine Vergleichung zweier Wahrnehmungen, also Denken notwendig, so ist jede höhere Erfahrung, jede Wissenschaft mit ihren sogenannten Gesetzen, ein Hinzukommen des Denkens zur Erfahrung. Gesetzmässigkeit ist regelmässige Ursächlichkeit; u. den Begriff der Ursache hat noch niemals eine blosse Wahrnehmung in der Welt gefunden. Das hat ja Kant eben gelehrt u. es Humes Kritik des Ursachbegriffs hinzugefügt, dass schon das Projizieren einer Wahrnehmung in die Aussenwelt, also schon die einfachste Wahrnehmung, die z.B. die Grünempfindung auf den Baum vor meinem Fenster zurückführt, unkontrollierbar eine Ursache der Sinnesempfindung hypostasiert.] Beckett, 'Whoroscope Notebook', pp.56-8; corresponding to Fritz Mauthner, *Beitrage zu einer Kritik der Sprache*, vol. II (Leipzig, Verlag von Felix Meiner, 1923), pp. 699-701.

[85] Murphy, 'Beckett and the philosophers', p. 229.

[86] John Pilling, 'Dates and Difficulties in Beckett's *Whoroscope* Notebook', in *Journal of Beckett Studies*, 13/2 (2004), p. 45.

[87] de Gaultier, *From Kant to Nietzsche*, p. 66; for the full quotation, see ch. 3, n. 28. Beckett's transcription from the original French corresponds to p. 61 in the '*Whoroscope* Notebook': [C'est la grande oeuvre de Kant, accomplie dans les cinquante pages de l'Esthétique Transcendentale, qui consiste a avoir démontré que l'espace et le temps n'ont point, d'une part, une réalité substantielle, que d'autre part, ils ne soient pas non plus des propriétés de l'objet, qu'au contraire ils appartenient au sujet de la connaisance et qu'ils sont les formes de la sensibilité de ce sujet.]

[88] Samuel Beckett, 'Intercessions by Denis Devlin', in *Disjecta*, p. 91.

[89] Sartre, *Nausea*, p. 126.

[90] Pilling, 'Dates and Difficulties in Beckett's *Whoroscope* Notebook', p. 46.

[91] Rabinovitz, *The Development of Samuel Beckett's Fiction*, p. 140.

[92] Jean-Paul Sartre, *Imagination: A Psychological Critique*, trans. Forrest Williams (Ann Arbor: University of Michigan Press, 1962), p. 39; italics in original.

[93] *Ibid.*, p. 127.

[94] *Ibid.*, pp. 131–3; italics in original.

[95] *Ibid.*, pp. 134–5.

[96] *Ibid.*, p. 143.

[97] David Hayman, 'Getting where? Beckett's opening gambit for Watt', in *Contemporary Literature*, XLIII/1 (2002), pp. 33, 35.

[98] *Ibid.*, p. 33.

[99] Sartre, *Imagination*, p. 146; italics in original.

[100] Beckett, *Watt*, pp. 159–60.

BIBLIOGRAPHY

Unpublished and Archival Materials:

Beckett International Foundation, University of Reading:

UoR MSS 1519/1–6, Beckett's 'German Diaries'

UoR MS 2901, Beckett's 'Sottisier Notebook'

UoR MS 3000/1, Beckett's '*Whoroscope* Notebook'

UoR MS 5000, 'Beckett's *Dream* Notebook'

UoR MS 5001, Beckett's notes on European painting

UoR MS 5002, Beckett's 'German Workbook'

UoR MS 5003, Beckett's 'Clare Street Notebook'

UoR MS 5004 and 5005, Beckett's *Faust* Notes

UoR MS 5006, Beckett's German Phrasebook

Beckett Collection, Trinity College, Dublin:

TCD MS 10904, Samuel Beckett-Thomas MacGreevy Correspondence

TCD MS 10948/1, Samuel Beckett-Barbary Bray Correspondence

TCD MS 10966/1, Beckett's notes on Dante

TCD MS 10967, Beckett's 'Philosophy Notes'

TCD MS 10971/5, Transcriptions from Fritz Mauthner's *Beiträge zu Einer Kritik der Sprache*, vol. 2, 473–479

TCD MS 10971/6, Transcripts of Joseph Gredt's *Elementa Philosophiae Aristotelico-Thomisticae*, vol. 1, pp. 96–7

TCD MS 10971/7 and 10971/8, Beckett's 'Psychology Notes'

BBC Written Archives Centre, Caversham:

British Broadcasting Corporation, 'Samuel Beckett: Scriptwriter, 1953–1962', RCONT1

– 'Samuel Beckett, Copyright File I: 1965–1969', RCONT18

– 'Samuel Beckett, Copyright: 1975–1979', RCONT21

– *Molloy*, prod. Donald McWhinnie (1957), microfiche

– *Malone Dies*, prod. Donald McWhinnie (1958), microfiche

– *The Unnamable*, prod. Donald McWhinnie (1959), microfiche

– *Waiting for Godot*, prod. Donald McWhinnie (1960), microfiche

Audience Research Report, 'Samuel Beckett', in 'Talks, *New Comment*, June 1961–1964', (1961)

– 'Texts for Nothing: I-III', prod. Martin Esslin (1975), microfiche

– 'For to End Yet Again', prod. Martin Esslin (1976), microfiche

– *Ill Seen Ill Said*, prod. Ronald Mason, (1982), microfiche

Works by Beckett:

Beckett, Samuel, *Beckett's Dream Notebook*, ed. John Pilling (Reading: Beckett International Foundation, 1999)

– *The Beckett Trilogy* [*Molloy, Malone Dies* and *The Unnamable*] (London: Calder, 1959)

– *Collected Poems* (London: Calder, 1999)

– *The Collected Poems of Samuel Beckett*, eds. Seán Lawlor and John Pilling (London: Faber and Faber, 2012)

– *Company* (London: Calder, 1996)

– *Company, Ill See Ill Said, Worstward Ho, Stirrings Still*, ed. Dirk van Hulle (London: Faber, 2009)

– *The Complete Dramatic Works* (London: Faber and Faber, 1990)

– *The Complete Short Prose 1929–1989*, ed. S.E. Gontarski (New York: Grove Press, 1995)

– *Dream of Fair to Middling Women* (London: Calder, 1993)

– *Disjecta: Miscellaneous Writings and a Dramatic Fragment*, ed. Ruby Cohn (New York: Grove Press, 1984 [1983])

– 'Echo's Bones', ed. Mark Nixon (London: Faber, 2014)

– *Eleuthéria: A Play in Three Acts*, trans. Michael Brodsky (New York: Foxrock, 1995)

– *The Grove Centenary Edition, Vol. IV: Poems, Short Fiction, Criticism*, ed. J.M. Coetzee (New York: Grove Press, 2006)

– *How It Is* (London: Calder, 1996 [1982])

- *The Letters of Samuel Beckett, 1929–1940*: vol. 1, eds. Martha Dow Fehsenfeld and Lois More Overbeck (Cambridge: Cambridge University Press, 2009)
- *1941–1956:* vol. 2, eds. George Craig, Martha Dow Fehsenfeld, Dann Gunn and Lois More Overbeck (Cambridge: Cambridge University Press, 2011)
- *1957–1965*: vol. 3, eds. George Craig, Martha Dow Fehsenfeld, Dan Gunn, and Lois More Overbeck (Cambridge: Cambridge University Press, 2014)
- *Malone Dies*, ed. Peter Boxall (London: Faber, 2010)
- *Mercier and Camier* (London: Calder & Boyers, 1974)
- *Molloy*, ed. Shane Weller (London: Faber, 2009a)
- *More Pricks Than Kicks* (London: Calder & Boyers, 1970a)
- *Murphy* (London: Calder & Boyers, 1969 [1993])
- *Murphy*, ed. J.C.C. Mays (London: Faber and Faber, 2009b)
- *Nohow On: Company, Ill Seen Ill Said, Worstword Ho* (London: Calder, 1989)
- *Proust and Three Dialogues* (London: Calder & Boyers, 1970b)
- *Das Raubauge in der Stadt: Beckett liest Hamburg*, eds. Giesing, Michaela, Hartel, Gabby and Veit, Carola (Goettingen: Wallstein Verlag, 2007)
- *Selected Poems 1930–1989*, ed. David Wheatley (London: Faber and Faber, 2009c)
- *Texts for Nothing and Other Shorter Prose 1950–1976*, ed. Mark Nixon (London: Faber, 2009d)
- *The Theatrical Notebooks of Samuel Beckett* [*Happy Days*; *Waiting for Godot*; *Krapp's Last Tape*; *Endgame*; and *The Shorter Plays: With Revised Texts for* Footfalls, Come and Go *and* What Where, ed. James Knowlson (London: Faber, 1985–1999)
- *The Unnamable*, ed. Steven Connor (London: Faber, 2010a)
- *Watt* (London: Calder & Boyers, 1971)
- *Watt*, ed. Chris Ackerley (London: Faber, 2009e)

Other Published Works:

Ackerley, Chris, 'Fatigue and disgust: the addenda to *Watt*', in *Samuel Beckett Today / Aujourd'hui* 2 (1993)

– *Demented Particulars* (Tallahassee: Journal of Beckett Studies Books, 1998)

– 'Samuel Beckett and Thomas á Kempis: The Roots of Quietism', in *Samuel Beckett Today / Aujourd'hui* 9 (2000)

– *Obscure Locks, Simple Keys: The Annotated Watt* (Tallahassee: Journal of Beckett Studies Books, 2006)

– 'The "Distinct Context of Relevant Knowledge": Beckett's "Yellow" and the Phenomenology of Annotation', in *Beckett and Phenomenology*, eds. Ulrika Maude and Matthew Feldman (London: Continuum, 2009)

Ackerley, C.J., and S.E. Gontarski, *The Faber Companion to Samuel Beckett* (London: Faber and Faber, 2006)

Admussen, Richard, *The Samuel Beckett Manuscripts: A Study* (Boston: G.K. Hall, 1979)

Alexander, J. Archibald, *A Short History of Philosophy* (Glasgow: Maclehose, Jackson and Co., 1922)

Amiran, Eyal, *Wandering and Home* (University Park: Penn State University Press, 1993)

Amsterdamski, Stefan, ed., *The Significance of Popper's Thought: Proceedings of the Conference Karl Popper 1902–1994: March 10–12, 1995, Graduate School for Social Research Warsaw* (Amsterdam: Rodopi, 1996)

Anderson, Lanier R., 'Neo-Kantianism and the Roots of Anti-Psychologism', in the *British Journal for the History of Philosophy* 13/2 (2005)

Andersson, Gunnar, 'Naïve and Critical Falsification', in *In Pursuit of Truth: Essays on the Philosophy of Karl Popper on the Occasion of his 80th Birthday*, ed. Paul Levinson (Brighton: Harvester, 1982)

Anzieu, Didier, 'Beckett and Bion', in the *International Review of Psycho-Analysis* 16/2 (1989)

– 'Beckett and the Psychoanalyst', in the *Journal of Beckett Studies* 4/1 (1994)

Arnold, Bruce, 'From Proof to Print: Anthony Cronin's *Samuel Beckett: The Last Modernist*', in *Samuel Beckett Today / Auhourd'hui* 8 (2000)

Atik, Anne, *How It Was: A Memoir of Samuel Beckett* (London: Faber and Faber, 2001)

Badiou, Alain, *On Beckett* trans. by Nina Power and Alberto Toscano (Manchester: Clinamen, 2003)

Bailey, Iain, *Samuel Beckett and the Bible* (London: Bloomsbury, 2014)

Bair, Deirdre, *Samuel Beckett: A Biography* (London: Picador, 1978 [1990])

Ballmer, Karl, *Aber Herr Heidegger! Zur Freiburger Rektoratsrede Martin Heideggers* (Basel: Verlag von Rudolf Geering, 1933)

Bangert, Sharon, *The Samuel Beckett collection at Washington University Libraries: A Guide* (St Louis: The Washington University Libraries, 1986)

Bardout, Jean-Christophe, 'Occasionalism: La Forge, Cordemoy, Geulincx', *Companion to Early Modern Philosophy,* ed. Steven Nadler (Oxford: Blackwell Publishing, 2002)

Barnard, G.C., *Samuel Beckett: A New Approach* (London: Dent, 1970)

Barnes, Johnathan, ed., *Early Greek Philosophy* (London: Penguin, 1987)

Barry, Peter, *Beginning Theory: An Introduction to Literary and Cultural Theory* (Manchester: Manchester University Press, 2002)

Battestini, Andrea, 'Beckett e Vico', in *Bolletino del Centro di Studi Vichiani* 5 (1975)

Beckett International Foundation, *The Samuel Beckett Collection: A Catalogue* (Reading: University of Reading, 1978)

Bignell, Jonathan *Beckett on Screen: The Television Plays* (Manchester: Manchester University Press, 2009)

Begam, Richard, 'Beckett and Postfoundationalism: Or How fundamental are those sounds?, in Richard Lane, ed., *Beckett and Philosophy* (Basingstoke: Palgrave, 2002)

Beiser, Frederick C., 'Normativity in Neo-Kantianism: Its Rise and Fall', in the *International Journal of Philosophical Studies* 17/1 (2009)

Ben-Zvi, Linda, 'Samuel Beckett, Fritz Mauthner, and the Limits of Language', in *PMLA* 95 (1980)

– 'Fritz Mauthner for Company', in the *Journal of Beckett Studies* 9 (1984)

– *Samuel Beckett* (Boston: Twayne Publishers, 1986)

– 'Biographical, Textual, and Historical Origins', in *Palgrave Advances in Samuel Beckett Studies*, ed. Lois Oppenheim (London: Palgrave, 2004)

Bouchard, and *Céline, Gadda, Beckett: Experimental Writing of the 1930s* (Gainsville: University Press of Florida, 2000)

Bowles, Patrick, 'How Samuel Beckett Sees the Universe: Patrick Bowles on *Molloy'*, in *The Listener* 59 (19 June 1958)

Boxall, Peter, *Samuel Beckett: A Reader's Guide to Essential Criticism* (Cambridge: Icon Books, 2000)

Branigan, Kevin, *Radio Beckett: Musicality in the Radio Plays of Samuel Beckett* (Oxford: Peter Lang, 2008)

Brannigan, John, *New Historicism and Cultural Materialism* (Basingstoke: Palgrave Macmillan, 1998)

Brater, Enoch, *Beckett's Minimalism Beckett's Late Style in the Theatre* (Oxford: Oxford University Press, 1987)

Bredeck, Elizabeth, *Metaphors of Knowledge: Language and Thought in Mauthner's Critique* (Detroit: Wayne State University Press, 1992)

Burnet, John, *Greek Philosophy: Part I Thales to Plato* (London: Macmillan and Co., 1914)

Burton, Robert, *Anatomy of Melancholy* (London: George Bell and Sons, 1904)

Büttner, Gottfried, *Samuel Beckett's Novel Watt*, trans. Joseph P. Dolan (Philadelphia, University of Pennsylvania Press, 1984)

Butler, Lance St John, *Samuel Beckett and the Meaning of Being* (London: Macmillan, 1984)

Cairns, Dorian, ed., *Conversations with Husserl and Fink* (Hague: Martinus Nijhoff, 1976)

Calder, John, *The Philosophy of Samuel Beckett* (London: Calder, 2002)

Calder Publications, *Beckett at 60: A Festschrift* (London: Calder & Boyars, 1967)

– *As No Other Dare Fail: For Samuel Beckett on his 80th birthday* (London: Calder, 1986)

Campbell, Julie, '"A Voice Comes to One in the Dark. Imagine": Radio, the Listener, and the Dark Comedy of All That Fall', in *Beckett and Death*, eds. Steven Barfield, Matthew Feldman and Philip Tew (London: Continuum, 2009)

– 'Beckett and the Third Programme', in *Samuel Beckett Today / Auhourd'hui* 25 (2013)

Cassirer, Ernst, *Kant's Life and Thought*, trans. James Haden (Ann Arbor: Yale University Press, 1981)

Cixous, Hélène, *Zero's Neighbour: Sam Beckett*, trans. Laurent Milesi (Cambridge: Polity, 2010)

Clément, Bruno, 'What the Philosophers do with Samuel Beckett', trans. Anthony Uhlmann, in *Beckett after Beckett*, ed. S.E. Gontarski (Tallahassee: University of Florida Press, 2006)

Coe, Richard N., *Beckett* (London: Oliver and Boyd, 1968)

Cohen-Solal, Annie, *Sartre: A Life* (London: William Heinemann Ltd, 1987)

Connor, Steven, *Samuel Beckett: Theory, Repetition, Text* (Oxford: Basil Blackwell, 1998)

Copeland, Hannah, *Art and the Artist in the Works of Samuel Beckett* (Mouton: The Hague, 1975)

Copleston, Frederick, *A History of Philosophy, Volume 7: Eighteenth– and Nineteenth-Century German Philosophy* (London: Continuum, 2008 [1963])

Cormier, Ramona, and Janis L. Pallister's *Waiting for Death: The Philosophical Significance of Beckett's* En Attendant Godot (Tuscaloosa: University of Alabama Press, 1979)

Cronin, Anthony, *Samuel Beckett: The Last Modernist* (London: Harper Collins, 1996)

Croce, Benedetto, *La Filosofia di Giambattista Vico* (Rome: Bari, 1911)

– *The Philosophy of Giambattista Vico*, trans. R.G. Collingwood (London: H. Latimer, 1913)

Critchley, Simon, *Very Little ... Almost Nothing* (London: Routledge, 1997)

Culik, Hugh, 'The Place of *Watt* in Beckett's Development', in *Modern Fiction Studies* 29/1 (1983)

Dante, *The Divine Comedy of Dante Alighieri; II: Purgatory*, trans. John D. Sinclair (London: John Lane The Bodley Head, 1948)

Davies, Paul, *The Ideal Real: Beckett's Fiction and Imagination* (London: Associated University Presses, 1994)

Davis, Robin J., *Samuel Beckett: Checklist and Index of his Published Works, 1967–1976* (Stirling: The Compiler, 1979)

Deleuze, Gilles, 'The Exhausted' in *Essays Critical and Clinical*, trans. Daniel W. Smith and Michael A. Greco (London: Verso, 1998)

Derrida, Jacques, *Acts of Literature*, ed. Derek Attridge (London: Routledge, 1992)

Dilks, Steven, *Samuel Becket in the Literary Marketplace* (Syracuse: Syracuse University Press, 2011)

Dobrez, L.A.C., *The Existential and Its Exits: Literary and Philosophical Perspectives on the Works of Beckett, Ionesco, Genet, and Pinter* (London: Athlone Press, 1986)

Doherty, Francis, 'Mahaffy's Whoroscope', in the *Journal of Beckett Studies* 2/1 (1992)

Dowd, *Abstract Machines: Beckett and Philosophy after Deleuze and Guattari* (New York: Rodopi, 2007)

– 'Prolegomena to a Critique of Excavatory Reason: Reply to Matthew Feldman', in *Samuel Beckett Today / Aujourd'hui* 20 (2008)

Ellmann, Richard, *James Joyce* (London: Oxford University Press, 1965)

Erdmann, Johann Eduard, *History of Philosophy*, 2 vols. trans. W.S. Hough (London: Swan Sonnenschein, 1890)

Esslin, Martin, 'Samuel Beckett and the Philosophers', in *The Novelist as Philosopher*, ed. John Cruickshank (London: Oxford University Press, 1962)

– *Samuel Beckett: A Collection of Critical Essays* (Englewood Cliffs: Prentice-Hall, 1965)

Farrow, Anthony, *Early Beckett: Art and Illusion in* More Pricks Than Kicks *and* Murphy (Troy: Whitson, 1991)

Federman, Raymond, *Journey to Chaos* (Berkeley: University of California Press, 1965)

Federman, Raymond, and John Fletcher, *Samuel Beckett: His Work and His Critics* (Berkeley: University of California Press, 1970)

Feldman, Matthew, 'Sourcing "Aporetics": An Empirical Study on Philosophical Influences in the Development of Samuel Beckett's Writings' (Unpublished PhD Thesis: Oxford Brookes University, 2004)

– 'Between Geist and Zeitgeist: Martin Heidegger as Ideologue of Metapolitical fascism', in *Totalitarian Movements and Political Religions* 6/2 (2005)

- *Beckett's Books: A Cultural History of Samuel Beckett's Interwar Notes* (London: Bloomsbury, 2008 [2006])
- 'In Defence of Empirical Knowledge: Rejoinder to "A Critique of Excavatory Reason"', in *Samuel Beckett Today / Auhourd'hui* 20 (2008)
- '"I am not a philosopher'. Beckett and Philosophy: A Methodological and Thematic Introduction", in the *Sofia Philosophical Review* 4/2 (2010)

Fifeld, Peter, '"Of being—or remaining": Beckett and Early Greek Philosophy', in *Beckett/Philosophy*, special issue of the *Sofia Philosophical Review*, eds. Matthew Feldman and Karim Mamdani (Sofia: Sofia University Press, 2011)

Fletcher, John, *Samuel Beckett's Art* (London: Chatto & Windus, 1967)

Fordham, Finn, 'The Modernist Archive', in *The Oxford Handbook of Modernisms*, eds. Peter Brooker, Andrzej Gąsiorek, Deborah Longworth, and Andrew Thacker (Oxford: Oxford University Press, 2010)

Frost, Everett, 'Fundamental Sounds: Recording Samuel Beckett's Radio Plays', in *Theatre Journal* 43/3 (1991)

- 'Beckett's Notebooks at Trinity College Dublin', in *The Beckett Circle/Le Cercle de Beckett: Newsletter of the Samuel Beckett Society* 25/2 (2002)

Gaultier, Jules de, *From Kant to Nietzsche*, trans. G.M. Spring (London: Peter Owen, 1961)

Geulincx, Arnold, *Arnoldi Geulincx Antverpiensis Opera Philosophica*, 3 vols., ed. J.P.N. Land (The Hague: Martinum Nijoff, 1891–1893)

- *Metaphysics,* trans. Martin Wilson (Wisbech: Christoffel Press, 1999)
- *Arnold Geulincx Ethics, with Samuel Beckett's notes*, trans. Martin Wilson, eds. Han van Ruler, Anthony Uhlmann, Martin Wilson (Amsterdam: Brill, 2006)

Gibson, Andrew, 'The Irish Remainder: *More Pricks Than Kicks*,' unpublished keynote lecture, 'Beckett in the Thirties' Conference, Ecole Normale Supérieure, Paris, October 2006

- *Beckett and Badiou: The Pathos of Intermittency* (Oxford: Oxford University Press, 2006)
- *Samuel Beckett* (London: Reaktion, 2010)

Gontarski, S.E., *The Intent of Undoing in Samuel Beckett's Dramatic Texts* (Bloomington: Indiana University Press, 1985)

– ed., *Samuel Beckett and the Arts* (Edinburgh: Edinburgh University Press, 2014)

Gonzalez, J.W., 'The Many Faces of Popper's Methodological Approach to Prediction', in *Karl Popper: Critical Appraisals*, eds. Philip Catton and Graham MacDonald (London: Routledge, 2004)

Gordon, Lois, *The World of Samuel Beckett 1906–1946* (London: Yale University Press, 1996)

Gorton, William, *Karl Popper and the Social Sciences* (Albany: State University of New York Press, 2006)

Graver, Lawrence, and Federman, Raymond, eds., *Samuel Beckett: The Critical Heritage* (London: Routledge & Kegan Paul, 1979)

Gredt, Joseph, *Elementa Philosophiae Aristotelico-Thomisticae*, 2 vols. (Freiburg: Herder & Co., 1926)

Gunn, Dan, 'Until the gag is chewed: Samuel Beckett's letters: eloquence and "near speechlessness"', in *Times Literary Supplement* 21 (2006)

Gussow, Mel, *Conversations with (and about) Samuel Beckett* (London: Nick Hern, 1996)

Harmon, Maurice, ed., *No Author Better Served: The Correspondence of Samuel Beckett and Alan Schneider* (London: Harvard University Press, 1998)

Harris, H.S., 'What is Mr. Ear-Vico Supposed to be 'Earing'?', in *Vico and Joyce*, ed. Donald Phillip Verene (New York: SUNY Press, 1987)

Hartel, Gaby, 'Emerging out of a Silent Void: Some Reverberations of Rudolf Arnheim's Radio Theory in Beckett's Radio Pieces', in the *Journal of Beckett Studies* 19/2 (2010)

Hayman, David, 'Getting where? Beckett's opening gambit for *Watt*', in *Contemporary Literature* XLIII/1 (2002)

Harvey, Lawrence, *Samuel Beckett: Poet and Critic* (Princeton: Princeton University Press, 1970)

Herren, Graley, 'Nacht und Träume as Beckett's Agony in the Garden', in the *Journal of Beckett Studies* 11/1 (2001)

Hesla, David, *The Shape of Chaos: An Interpretation of the Art of Samuel Beckett* (Minneapolis, MN: University of Minnesota Press, 1971)

Hill, Leslie, *Samuel Beckett's Fiction in Different Worlds* (Cambridge: Cambridge University Press, 1990)

Hoefer, Jacqueline, '*Watt*', reprinted in *Samuel Beckett: A Collection of Critical Essays*, ed. Martin Esslin (Prentice Hall, Englewood Cliffs, 1965)

Husserl, Edmund, *Ideas: General Introduction to Pure Phenomenology*, trans. W.R. Boyce Gibson (London: Collier Books, 1962)

– *Cartesian Meditations: An Introduction to Phenomenology* (London: Kluwer, 1988)

Inge, William Ralph, *Christian Mysticism: The Bampton Lectures (1899)* (London: Metheun & Co., 1921)

Iser, Wolfgang, *The Implied Reader: Patterns of Communication in Prose from Bunyan to Beckett* (London: Johns Hopkins University Press, 1974)

Jacobsen, Josephine, and William R. Mueller, *The Testament of Samuel Beckett* (London: Faber, 1964)

Jalbert, John, 'Husserl's Position Between Dilthey and the Windeband-Rickert School of Neo-Kantianism', in the *Journal of the History of Philosophy* 26/2 (1969)

Jewinski, Ed, '*Company*, Post-structuralism, and Mimetalogique', in *Rethinking Beckett,* eds. Lance St John Butler and Robin J. Davis (London: Macmillan Press, 1990)

Jones, Ernest, *Treatment of the Neuroses* (London: Ballière, Tindall and Cox, 1920)

Joyce, James, *Dubliners* (Oxford: Oxford University Press, 2000)

Juliet, Charles, *Conversations with Samuel Beckett and Bram van Velde* (Leiden: Academic Press, 1995)

Kant, Immanuel, *Critique of Pure Reason: Unified Edition*, trans. W.S. Pluhar (Cambridge: Hackett Publishing Co., 1996)

à Kempis, Thomas, *The Imitation of Christ*, trans. Bernard Bangley (Guildford: Highland Books, 1983)

Katz, Dan, *Saying I No More: Subjectivity and Consciousness in the Prose of Samuel Beckett* (Evanston: Northwestern University Press, 1999)

Kavanagh, Jacquie, 'BBC Archives at Caversham', in *Contemporary British History* 6/2 (1992)

Kaelin, Eugene, *The Unhappy Consciousness: The Poetic Plight of Samuel Beckett* (Boston: Kluwer, 1981)

Kenner, Hugh, *A Reader's Guide to Samuel Beckett* (London: Thames & Hudson, 1973)

Kern, Edith, *Existential Thought and Fictional Technique* (London: Yale University Press, 1970)

Keuth, Herbert, *The Philosophy of Karl Popper* (Cambridge: Cambridge University Press, 2005)

Kiernan, Ryan, ed., *New Historicism and Cultural Materialism: A Reader* (London: Bloomsbury, 1996)

Knowlson, James, *Samuel Beckett: An Exhibition held at Reading University Library, May to July 1971* (London: Turret Books, 1971)

– ed., *Samuel Beckett,* Krapp's Last Tape: *A Theatre Workbook* (London: Brutus Books, 1980)

– 'Introduction to the Words of Samuel Beckett: A Discography', in *Recorded Sound: Journal of The British Library National Sound Archive* 85 (1984)

– *Damned to Fame: The Life of Samuel Beckett* (London: Bloomsbury, 1996)

– 'Beckett's first encounters with modern German (and Irish) art', in *Samuel Beckett: A Passion for Paintings*, ed. Fionnuala Croke (Dublin: National Gallery of Ireland, 2006)

– 'Samuel Beckett's Happy Days Revisited', in *Re-reading / La Relecture: Essays in Honour of Graham Falconer,* eds. Rachel Falconer and Andrew Oliver (Cambridge: Cambridge Scholars Publishing, 2012)

Knowlson, James, and Elizabeth Knowlson, eds., *Beckett Remembering / Remembering Beckett: Uncollected Interviews with Samuel Beckett and Memories of those who Knew him* (London: Bloomsbury, 2007)

Knowlson, James, and John Haynes, *Images of Beckett* (Cambridge: Cambridge University Press, 2003)

Knowlson, James, and John Pilling, *Frescos of the Scull: The Later Prose and Drama of Samuel Beckett* (New York: Grove Press, 1979)

Lake, Carlton, *No Symbols Where None Intended: A Catalogue of Books, Manuscripts, and other Material relating to Samuel Beckett in the Collection of the Humanities Research Center* (Austin, University of Texas, 1984)

Land, J.P.N., 'Arnold Geulincx and his works', in *Mind* vol. XVI (1891)

Lane, Richard, 'Beckett and Nietzsche: The Eternal Headache', in *Beckett and Philosophy*, ed. Richard Lane (Basingstoke: Palgrave, 2002)

Leibniz, Gottfried Wilhelm, *Discourse on Metaphysics, Correspondence with Arnauld, Monadology* (La Salle: Open Court, 1902)

Leopardi, Giacomo, *Selected Prose and Poetry*, trans. I. Origo and J. Heath-Stubbs (London: Oxford University Press, 1966)

Levy, Eric P., *Trapped in Thought: A Study of the Beckettian Mentality* (New York: Syracuse University Press, 2007)

Locatelli, Carla, *Unwording the World: Samuel Beckett's Prose Works after the Nobel Prize* (Philadelphia: University of Pennsylvania Press, 1990)

Losee, John, *Theories on the Scrap Heap: Scientists and Philosophers on the Falsification, Rejection, and Replacement of Theories* (Pittsburgh: University of Pittsburgh Press, 2005)

MacDonald, Paul S., *Descartes and Husserl: The Philosophical Project of Radical Beginnings* (Albany: State University of New York Press, 2000)

Makkreel, Rudolf A., 'Wilhelm Dilthey and the Neo-Kantians: The Distinction of the Geistewissenschaften and the Kulturwissenschaften', in the *History of Philosophy* 7/4 (1969)

Makkreel, Rudolf A., and Sebastian Luft, 'Who were the neo-Kantians?', in *Neo-Kantianism in Contemporary Philosophy*, eds. Rudolf A. Makkreel and Sebastian Luft (Bloomington: Indiana University Press, 2010)

Matthews, Steven, 'Beckett's Late Style', in *Beckett and Death*, eds. Steven Barfield, Matthew Feldman and Philip Tew (London: Continuum, 2009)

Mauthner, Fritz, *Beiträge zu Einer Kritik der Sprache*, 3 vols. (Leipzig: Verlag von Felix Meiner, 1923)

Maude, Ulrika, *Beckett, Technology and the Body* (Cambridge: Cambridge University Press, 2009)

– 'Working on Radio', in *Samuel Beckett in Context*, ed. Anthony Uhlmann (Cambridge: Cambridge University Press, 2013)

McGovern, Barry, 'Beckett and the Radio Voice', in *Samuel Beckett: 100 Years: Centenary Essays*, ed. Christopher Murray (Dublin: New Island, 2006)

Mercier, Vivian *Beckett/Beckett* (Oxford: Oxford University Press, 1979)

Mintz, Samuel I., 'Beckett's *Murphy*: A Cartesian Novel', in *Perspective* 2/3 (1959)

Misak, C.J., *Verificationism: Its History and Prospects* (London: Routledge, 1995)

Montague, John, 'A Few Drinks and a Hymn: My Farewell to Samuel Beckett', in *The New York Times*, Sunday Late Edition, 17 April 1994

Mood, John J., '"The personal system": Samuel Beckett's *Watt*', in *PMLA* 86/2 (1971)

Mooney, Michael, '*Molloy*, Part 1: Beckett's *Discourse on Method*', in the *Journal of Beckett Studies* 3 (1978)

Moorjani, Angela, 'Mourning, Schopenhauer, and Beckett's Art of Shadows', in *Beckett On and On*, eds. Lois Oppenheim and Marius Buning (London: Farleigh Dickenson University Press, 1996)

Moran, Dermot, *Introduction to Phenomenology* (London: Routledge, 2000)

– *Edmund Husserl: Founder of Phenomenology* (Cambridge: Polity, 2005)

– 'Beckett and Philosophy', in *Samuel Beckett: 100 Years,* ed. Christopher Murray (Dublin: New Island, 2006)

Morot-Sir, Edouard, 'Samuel Beckett and Cartesian Emblems', in *Samuel Beckett and the Art of Rhetoric*, ed. Edouard Morot-Sir (Chapel Hill: University of North Carolina, 1976)

Murphy, Peter J., *Reconstructing Beckett: Language for Being in Samuel Beckett's Fiction* (London: University of Toronto Press, 1990)

– 'Beckett and the philosophers', in *The Cambridge Companion to Beckett*, ed. John Pilling (Cambridge: Cambridge University Press, 1994)

Nadler, Steven, 'Knowledge, Volitional Agency and Causation in Malebranhce and Geulinx', in the *British Journal for the History of Philosophy* 7/2 (1999):

Natanson, Maurice, *The Erotic Bird: Phenomenology and Literature* (Princeton: Princeton University Press, 1998)

Nixon, Mark, '"what a tourist I must have been': The German Diaries of Samuel Beckett' (Unpublished PhD. Thesis: University of Reading, 2005)

– '"Scraps of German": Samuel Beckett reading German Literature', in *Samuel Beckett Today / Aujourd'hui* 16 (2006)

– 'Beckett and Romanticism in the 1930s', in *Samuel Beckett Today / Auhourd'hui* 18 (2007)

– 'Solitudes and Creative Fidgets: Beckett Reading Rainer Maria Rilke', in *Litteraria Pragensia* 17/33 (2007)

- 'Beckett's Manuscripts in the Marketplace', in "Samuel Beckett: Out of the Archive" special issue, *Modernism/Modernity* 18/4 (2012)

- *Samuel Beckett's German Diaries. 1936–1937* (London: Bloomsbury, 2011)

- ed., *Samuel Beckett and Publishing* (London: The British Library, 2011)

Nuchelmans, Gabriel, *Geulincx' Containment Theory of Logic* (Amsterdam: Koninklijke Nederlandse Akademie, 1988)

O'Hara, J.D., 'Beckett's Schopenhaurian Reading of Proust: The Will as Whirled in Re-Presentation', in *Schopenhauer: New Essays in Honor of his 200th Birthday*, ed. Eric van der Luft (Lewiston: The Edwin Mellen Press, 1988)

- Review of Didier Anzieu's *Beckett et le Psychanalyste*, in the *Journal of Beckett Studies* 4/1 (1994)

- *Samuel Beckett's Hidden Drives: Structural Uses of Depth Psychology* (Gainesville: University Press of Florida, 1997)

Oppenheim, Lois, *The Painted Word: Samuel Beckett's Dialogues with Art* (Ann Arbor: University of Michigan Press, 2000)

Pattie, David, *The Complete Critical Guide to Samuel Beckett* (Abingdon: Routledge, 2000)

Perloff, Marjorie, 'The Silence That Is Not Silence: Acoustic Art in Samuel Beckett's Embers', in *Samuel Beckett and the Arts: Music, Visual Arts, and Non-Print Media*, ed. Lois Oppenheim (Garland Publishing, New York: 1999)

Pilling, John, *Samuel Beckett* (London: Routledge & Kegan Paul, 1976)

- 'From a (W)horoscope to Murphy', in *The Ideal Core of the Onion*, eds. John Pilling and Mary Bryden (Reading: Beckett International Foundation, 1992)

- 'Beckett's Proust', in S.E. Gontarski, ed., *The Beckett Studies Reader* (Gainesville: University Press of Florida, 1993)

- *Beckett Before Godot* (Cambridge: Cambridge University Press, 1997)

- *A Companion to* Dream of Fair to Middling Women (Gainesville: University of Florida Press, 2004a)

- 'Dates and Difficulties in Beckett's *Whoroscope* Notebook' in the *Journal of Beckett Studies* 13/2 (2004)

- *A Samuel Beckett Chronology* (Basingstoke, Palgrave, 2006)

- 'Beckett and Mauthner Revisited', in *Beckett after Beckett*, eds. S.E. Gontarski and Anthony Uhlmann (Gainesville, FL: University of Florida Press, 2006b)
- *Samuel Beckett's 'More Pricks Than Kicks': In a Strait of Two Wills* (London: Bloomsbury, 2013)

Popper, Karl, *The Logic of Scientific Discovery* (London: Hutchinson and Co., 1959)
- *Objective Knowledge: An Evolutionary Approach* (Oxford: Clarendon, 1972)
- *Realism and the Aims of Science*, ed. W.W. Bartley, III (London: Hutchinson, 1985)
- *Conjectures and Refutations* (London: Routledge Classics, 2002)

Porter, Jeffrey Lyn, 'Samuel Beckett and the Radiophonic Body: Beckett and the BBC', in *Modern Drama* 53/4 (2010)

Pothast, Ulrich, *The Metaphysical Vision: Arthur Schopenhauer's Philosophy of Art and Life and Samuel Beckett's own way to make use of it* (New York: Peter Lang, 2008)

Pountney Rosemary, *Theatre of Shadows: Samuel Beckett's Drama, 1956–1976, From* All That Fall *to* Footfalls *with commentaries on the latest plays* (Gerard's Cross: Colin Smythe, 1988)

Rabinovitz, Rubin, 'Watt from Descartes to Schopenhauer', in *Modern Irish Literature: Essays in Honor of William York Tindall*, eds. Raymond J. Porter and James D. Brophy (New York: Iona College Press, 1972)
- *The Development of Samuel Beckett's Fiction* (Chicago: University of Illinois Press, 1984)
- 'Beckett and Psychology', in the *Journal of Beckett Studies* 11/12 (1989)
- *Innovation in Samuel Beckett's Fiction* (Chicago: University of Illinois Press, 1992)

Restivo, Giuseppina, 'Melencolias and Scientific Ironies in *Endgame*: Beckett, Walther, Dürer, Musil', in *Samuel Beckett Today / Auhourd'hui* 11 (2002)

Richardson, Stanley, and Jane Alison Hale, 'Working Wireless: Beckett's Radio Writing', in *Samuel Beckett and the Arts: Music, Visual Arts, and Non-Print Media*, ed. Lois Oppenheim (Garland Publishing, New York: 1999)

Robinson, Michael, *The Long Sonata of the Dead: A Study of Samuel Beckett* (London: Rupert Hart-Davis Ltd., 1969)

Rose, Danis, *James Joyce's The Index Manuscript* (London: A Wake Newslitter Press, 1978)

– ed., *The Textual Diaries of James Joyce* (Dublin: Lilliput Press, 1995)

Rosen, Steven J., *Samuel Beckett and the Pessimistic Tradition* (New Brunswick: Rutgers University Press, 1976)

Sass, Louis, *Madness and Modernism: Insanity in the Light of Modern Art, Literature, and Thought* (New York: Basic Books, 1992)

Sartre, Jean-Paul, *Imagination*, trans. Forrest Williams (Ann Arbor: Michigan University Press, 1962)

– *Nausea*, trans. L. Alexander (New York: New Directions Books, 1969)

– *War Diaries: Notebooks from a Phoney War, November 1939–March 1940*, trans. Q. Hoare (London: Verso, 1984)

Schmaltz, Tad, 'Descartes and Malebranche on Mind and Mind-Body Union', in *The Philosophical Review* 101/2 (1992)

Schopenhauer, Arthur, *The World as Will and Representation*, 2 vols., trans. E.F.J. Payne (New York: Dover, 1958)

Schur, David, *The Way of Oblivion: Heraclitus and Kafka* (London: Harvard University Press, 1998)

Scruton, Roger, *The Aesthetic Understanding: Essays in the Philosophy of Art and Culture* (Manchester: Carcanet Press, 1983)

Shottenkirk, Dena, *Nominalism and its Aftermath* (London: Springer, 2009)

Skerl, Jennie, 'Fritz Mauthner's "Critique of Language" in Samuel Beckett's *Watt*', in *Contemporary Literature* 15/4 (1974)

Smith, Frederik, *Beckett's Eighteenth Century* (London: Palgrave, 2002)

Smyth, Egbert C., 'Brief Notice of Important Books', in *The Andover Review: A Religious and Theological Monthly* 114 (1893)

Spinoza, Baruch, Ethics *and 'De Intellectus Emendatione'*, ed. Ernest Rhys (J.M. Dent & Sons: London, n.d. [1910])

– *Ethics*, ed. Charles Appuhn (Paris: Garnier 1934)

– *The Chief Works of Benedict de Spinoza*, 2 vols., ed. R.H.M Elwes (New York: Dover, 1955)

Stewart, Paul, 'Sterile Reproduction: Beckett's Death of the Species and Fictional Regeneration', in *Beckett and Death*, eds. Steven Barfield, Matthew Feldman and Philip Tew (London: Continuum, 2009)

Stokes, Geoffrey, *Popper: Philosophy, Politics and Scientific Method* (Cambridge: Polity, 1998)

Stoneham, Tom, *Berkeley's World: An examination of the Three Dialogues* (Oxford, Oxford University Press, 2002)

Swoboda, Philip J., 'Windelband's Influence on S.L. Frank', in *Studies in East European Thought* 47/3–4 (1995)

Szabó, Zoltán, 'Nominalism', in *The Oxford Handbook of Metaphysics*, eds M.J. Loux and D. Zimmerman (Oxford: Oxford University Press, 2003)

Tajiri, Yoshiki, *Samuel Beckett and the Prosthetic Body: The Organs and Senses in Modernism* (Basingstoke: Palgrave, 2007)

Tanner, James, and Don Vann, *Samuel Beckett: A Checklist of Criticism* (Kent: Kent State University Press, 1969)

Tonning, Erik, *Samuel Beckett's Abstract Drama: Works for Stage and Screen, 1962–1985* (Bern: Peter Lang, 2007)

Tucker, David, *Samuel Beckett and Arnold Geulincx: Tracing 'a literary fantasia'* (London: Bloomsbury, 2013)

Uhlmann, Anthony, *Beckett and Poststructuralism* (Cambridge: Cambridge University Press, 1999)

– *Samuel Beckett and the Philosophical Image* (Cambridge: Cambridge University Press, 2006)

– 'Beckett and Philosophy', in *A Companion to Samuel Beckett*, ed. S.E. Gontarski (Oxford: Wiley-Blackwell, 2010)

Valdés, Mario J., *World-Making: the Literary Truth-Claim and the Interpretation of Texts* (London: University of Toronto Press, 1992)

Van der Weer, Adrien, and Ruud Higgen, 'Intellection in the Work of Samuel Beckett', in *Samuel Beckett Today / Aujourd'hui* 1 (1992)

van Hulle, Dirk, 'Beckett—Mauthner—Zimmer—Joyce', in *The Joyce Studies Annual* 10 (1999)

– 'Mauthner, Richards, and the Development of Wakese', in *James Joyce: The Study of Languages*, ed. Dirk van Hulle (Brussels: Peter Lang, 2002)

- '"Nichtsnichtsundnichts": Beckett's and Joyce's Transtextual Undoings', in *European Joyce Studies* 16 (2005)
- 'Samuel Beckett's *Faust* Notes', in *Samuel Beckett Today / Aujourd'hui* 16 (2006)
- *Manuscript Genetics, Joyce's Know–How, Beckett's Nohow* (Tallahassee: University of Florida Press, 2008)
- *The Making of Samuel Beckett's* Stirrings Still/Soubresauts *and* Comment dire/what is the word (Antwerp: University Press Antwerp, 2011)

'Notebooks and Other Manuscripts', in *Beckett in Context*, ed. Anthony Uhlmann (Cambridge: Cambridge University Press, 2013)
- *Modern Manuscripts: The Extended Mind and Creative Undoing from Darwin to Beckett and beyond* (London: Bloomsbury, 2014)

van Hulle, Dirk, and Mark Nixon, *Samuel Beckett's Library* (Cambridge: Cambridge University Press, 2013)

van Hulle, Dirk, and Shane Weller, *The Making of Samuel Beckett's* The Unnamable / L'Innomable (London: Bloomsbury, 2014)

Verdicchio, Massimo, 'Exagmination Round the Fictification of Vico and Joyce', in *James Joyce Quarterly* 26/4 (1989)

Verhulst, Pim, *The Making of Samuel Beckett's Radio Plays: Interpretative Implications of Reading and Writing Traces* (Unpublished PhD. Thesis: University of Antwerp, 2014)

Vico, Giambattista, *The New Science of Giambattista Vico*, trans. Thomas Goddard Bergin and Max Harold Fisch (Ithaca: Cornell University Press, 1981)

Vleeschauwer, H.J., *Three Centuries of Geulincx Research: A Bibliographical Survey* (Pretoria: University of South Africa, 1957)

Walker, Roy, 'In the Rut', in *The Listener* 58 (1957)

Weller, Shane, *A Taste for the Negative: Beckett and Nihilism* (Oxford: Legenda, 2005)
- 'The Art of Indifference Adorno's Manuscript Notes on *The Unnamable*', in *The Tragic Comedy of Samuel Beckett*, eds. Daniela Guardamagna and Rossana M. Sebellin (Rome: Laterza, 2009)
- 'Beckett among the *Philosophes*: the Critical Reception of Samuel Beckett in France', in *The International Reception of Samuel Beckett*, eds. Mark Nixon and Matthew Feldman (London: Continuum, 2009)

White, Hayden V., 'What is Living and What is Dead in Croce's Criticism of Vico', in *Giambattista Vico: An International Symposium*, eds. Giorgio Tagliacozzo and Hayden V. White (Baltimore: Johns Hopkins University Press, 1969)

Wilcher, Robert, '"Out of the Dark": Beckett's Texts for Radio', in *Beckett's Later Fiction and Drama: Texts for Company*, eds. James Acheson and Arthur Kateryna (Basingstoke: MacMillan, 1987)

Willey, Thomas E., *Back to Kant: The Revival of Kantianism in German Social and Historical Thought, 1860–1914* (Detroit: Wayne State University Press, 1978)

Windelband, Wilhelm, *A History of Philosophy*, 2 vols., trans. James Tufts (New York: Harper, 1958 [1901])

– *An Introduction to Philosophy*, trans. Joseph McCabe (London: Unwin, 1921)

Windelband, Wilhelm, and Heinz Heimsoeth, *Lehrbuch der Geschichte der Philosophie. Mit einem Schlusskapitel 'Die Philosophie im 20. Jahrhundert' und einer Übersicht über den Stand der philosophiegeschichtlichen Forschung* (Tübingen: Mohr, 1935)

– 'Rectorial Address, Strasbourg, 1894', trans. and reprinted in *History and Theory* 19/2 (1980)

Wood, Rupert, 'Murphy, Beckett; Geulincx, God', in the *Journal of Beckett Studies* 2/2 (1993)

Woodruff-Smith, David, 'Mind and Body', in *The Cambridge Companion to Husserl*, eds. Barry Smith and David Woodruff Smith (Cambridge: Cambridge University Press, 1995)

– *Husserl* (Abingdon: Routledge, 2007)

Worth, Katherine, 'Beckett and the Radio Medium', in *British Radio Drama*, ed. John Drakakis (Cambridge: Cambridge University Press, 1981)

Woodworth, Robert S., *Contemporary Schools of Psychology* (London: Methuen, 1931)

Zilliacus, Claus, *Beckett and Broadcasting: A Study of the Works of Samuel Beckett For and In Radio and Television* (Åbo: Åbo Akademi, 1976)

Websites Consulted (all websites last accessed 12/12/14)

"Beckett on Film", at: www.beckettonfilm.com

'Beckett in Hamburg 1936', at: http://schaukasten.sub.uni-hamburg.de/beckett/beckett_e/index.php?okt02.php

BBC Written Archives Centre, Caversham, at: www.bbc.co.uk/archive/written.shtml [archived]

- http://apps.nationalarchives.gov.uk/archon/searches/locresult_details.asp?LR=898

International Dada Archive, at: www.lib.uiowa.edu/dada/

Internet Archive, at: www.archive.org

John Keats, 'Ode to a Nightingale', at *The Poetry Foundation*: www.poetryfoundation.org/poem/173744

The Modernist Journals Project, at: http://modjourn.org

Modernist Magazines Project, at: www.modernistmagazines.com

'Samuel Beckett Digital Manuscript Project', at: www.beckettarchive.org

'Samuel Beckett On-Line Resources and Links Pages', at: www.samuel-beckett.net

'Samuel Beckett: Works for Radio', at: http://shop.bl.uk/mall/productpage.cfm/BritishLibrary/_ISBN_9780712305303/87294/Samuel-Beckett-Works-for-Radio-(audio-CD)

UbuWeb Sound: 'Samuel Beckett', at: www.ubu.com/sound/beckett.html

Yale University Library, Beinecke Rare Book and Manuscript Library, at: http://beinecke.library.yale.edu

Žižek, Slavoj, 'Beckett with Lacan', parts one and two, at: www.lacan.com/article/?page_id=78; and www.lacan.com/article/?page_id=102

Index

absurdism, 39, 89, 96, 98, 100 n. 15, 198, 262

Adorno, Theodor, 89, 92, 95, 99 n. 3, 102 n. 3, 131

Ackerley, Chris, 9, 24, 35 n. 32, 36 n. 35, 84, 100 n. 19, 106, 107, 109, 121, 124 n. 2, 125 n. 15, 130, 134, 150 n. 30, n. 46, n. 47, 205, 209 n. 51, n. 53, 219, 231 n. 19, n. 20, 232 n. 35, n. 36, 252 n. 21, 253 n. 47, 277 n. 53

Adler, Alfred, 139

The Neurotic Constitution, 139

à Kempis, Thomas, 105, 106, 107, 114, 116, 124 n. 2, n.3, n. 4, 125 n. 28, 239

The Imitation of Christ, 106, 107, 110, 124 n. 4

Atik, Anne, 33 n. 8, 211, 230 n. 3, 278 n. 81

Aldington, Richard, 264

Alexander, J. Archibald, 79, 191, 192, 201, 202, 208 n. 36, 213, 214, 215

A Short History of Philosophy, 79, 191, 208 n. 36, 213, 215

Aron, Raymond, 261

Aristotle, 9, 92, 94, 101 n. 19, 134, 135, 192, 199, 213, 215, 216, 220, 225, 227, 231, 232, 269

Bair, Deirdre, 34 n. 22, 63, 77, 86 n. 10, 101 n. 20, 125 n. 27, 173, 189 n. 5

BBC Radio, 11, 30, 99 n. 6, 153, 154, 163, 165

Ballmer, Karl, 268, 269, 278 n. 81

Aber Herr Heidegger!, 269, 278 n. 81

Beckett Country, 91, 92, 219, 240

Beckett, John, 30, 160, 163, 177, 178, 179, 180, 184, 186

Beckett, Samuel, 9, 11–17, 19, 20, 22–31, 33 n. 1–n. 3, n. 5, n. 7, n. 8, 34 n. 13–n. 23, 35 n. 24–n. 26, n. 28–n. 34, 36 n. 35, n. 43–n. 45, n. 47, 37 n. 48–n. 56, 39–54, 55 n. 1, n. 2, n. 4, n. 5, n. 7, n. 12, n. 13, n. 15, n. 16–n. 20, 56 n. 21–n. 26, n. 28–n. 30, n. 32–n. 36, 57 n. 40–45, n. 47, n. 48, n. 50, n. 51, n. 57, 59–72, 73 n. 2, n. 7–n. 10, n. 12–n. 18, n. 20, n. 21, 74 n. 22–n. 24, n. 26, n. 27, n. 29, n. 31, n. 33, n. 35, 75–85, 86 n. 1–n. 3, n. 5–n. 8, n. 10, n. 11, n. 13, n. 16, n. 17, n. 19, 87 n. 20–n. 29, n. 31, 88 n. 33, n. 37, n. 38, 89–98, 99 n. 1–n. 9, n. 11, 100 n. 12–n. 19, 101 n. 20–n. 24, n. 27, n. 28, 102 n. 30, n. 32–n. 41, 103 n. 42–n. 46, n. 48, n. 49, 105–123, 124 n. 1, n. 2, n. 4–n. 7, n. 11, 125 n. 14–n. 16, n. 18–n. 21, n. 25–n. 28, 126 n. 29–n. 31, n. 33, n. 35, n. 37–n. 41, 127 n. 42, n. 43, n. 45–n. 47, n. 51–n. 54, n. 56–n. 58, 128 n. 60, n. 62, n. 64, n. 67, n. 68, 129–136, 138–147, 149 n. 1, n. 4–n. 7, n. 9–n. 16, n. 18–n. 20, 150 n. 21, n. 22, n. 24, n. 26–n. 28, n. 30–n. 33, n. 37–n. 43, n. 45, n. 46, 151 n. 52–n. 57, 153–167, 169 n. 1–n. 6, 170 n. 7–n. 11, n. 14, n. 16, n. 18, n. 20–n. 22, n. 24, 171 n. 26–n. 38, n. 40–n. 45, n. 47–n. 50, 172 n. 54–n. 61, n. 63, 173–184, 186–188, 189 n. 1–n. 5, n. 7, n. 9, n. 11, n. 12, n. 14–n. 18, n. 20–n. 23, n. 25, n. 27, n. 29–n. 33, 190 n. 34, n. 35, n. 37, n. 40–n. 42, n. 46, n. 47, n. 49–n. 52, 191–194, 196, 198–205, 207 n. 1–n. 8, n. 10, 208 n. 25, n. 27, n. 29, n. 31, n. 34, n. 36, n. 38, n. 40–n. 44, n. 46, n. 48–n. 53, n. 56, 211–217, 219–229, 230 n. 2, n. 3, n. 5, n. 6, n. 8–n. 15, 231 n. 16–n. 20, 232 n. 25, n. 27–n. 30, n. 34, n. 36, 233 n. 40–n. 47, n. 50–n. 54, 234 n. 55, 235–250, 251 n. 1–n. 4, n. 8, n. 9, n. 10–n. 13, 252 n. 14–n. 22, n. 24, 253 n. 25–n. 28, n. 30–n. 33, n. 35–n. 39, n. 46–n. 48, n. 50, n. 52, 254 n. 55, n. 56, n. 61, n. 62, 255–273, 274 n. 1–n. 6, n. 9–n. 11, n. 13, n. 15, 275 n. 20, n. 22, n. 25–n. 27, n. 37, n. 38, 276 n. 40, n. 44, n. 47, n. 48–n. 50, n. 52, 277 n. 53, n. 55–n. 58, n. 60–n. 63, n. 66–n. 68, 278 n. 69–n. 80, n. 82–n. 84, 279 n. 85–n. 88, n. 90, n. 91, n. 97, n. 100

and 'agnostic quietism', 11, 14, 16, 29, 37 n. 50, 105–107, 109, 110, 112, 116–119, 121–123, 237, 251 n. 10

and broadcasting, 153, 157, 162, 169 n. 3, n. 4, 171 n. 30, n. 32, 172 n. 60, 174, 175, 178, 184, 189 n. 9, n. 33

and censorship, 159

and financial transactions, 164

and freelance journalism, 212

and the 'German Dairies', 126 n. 35, 134, 268

and the 'German Letter' of 1937, 30, 51, 66, 73 n. 21, 120, 128 n. 60, 217, 222, 225, 232 n. 30, 233 n. 42, 269, 278 n. 82

and his international reception, 95, 99 n. 1, 102 n. 35, 170 n. 10, 172 n. 58

and the Nobel Prize for Literature, 22, 41, 89, 99 n. 5, 164, 212, 276 n. 49

and interwar notebooks, 11, 13, 19, 22, 27, 29, 30, 33 n. 7, 65, 66, 74 n. 33, 75, 76, 78, 80, 81, 84, 87 n. 25, 97, 103 n. 45, 107, 109, 118, 125 n. 14, 129, 130, 138, 145, 147, 191, 207 n. 1, 213, 215, 217, 229, 236, 240, 251 n. 13, 255, 258, 265, 269, 275 n. 38, 277

and the 'Philosophy Notes', 11, 29, 30, 77, 79, 80, 86 n. 16, 91, 100 n. 14, 129, 130, 132–136, 142, 144, 147, 149 n. 15, 150 n. 21, n. 27, 151 n. 54, 191–194, 198–202, 207 n. 1, n. 2, n. 4, n. 6, n. 7, 208 n. 29, n. 31, n. 34, n. 36, 209 n. 38, 213–216, 221, 222, 228, 229, 230 n. 13–n. 15, 231 n. 18, 233 n. 40, n. 41, n. 43, n. 45, n. 46, 236, 251 n. 3, n. 4, 266, 277 n. 66, n. 67, n. 69, n. 72, n. 73

and the 'Psychology Notes', 11, 19, 29, 67, 74 n. 23, 111, 126 n. 33, 129, 130, 138, 141, 142, 145, 147, 150 n. 37, n. 38, 151 n. 53

and his theatre productions, 34 n. 16, n. 21, 156, 157, 159, 160, 166, 169 n. 3, n. 6, 170 n. 18, 234 n. 55

and the '*Whorsocope* Notebook', 61, 63, 65, 66, 73 n. 11, n. 16, n. 17, 81–83, 87 n. 22, n. 24, n. 27, n. 28, n. 31, 94, 102 n. 30, 133, 135, 142, 143, 150 n. 43, 225, 226, 227, 233 n. 51, n. 53, n. 54, 270, 271, 276 n. 52, 278 n. 84, 279 n. 86, n. 87, n. 90

Works:

'All Strange Away', 133, 149 n. 13

All that Fall, 30, 34 n. 21, 153–158, 162, 165–167, 169 n. 6, 170 n. 18, 173, 182

The Beckett Trilogy, 15, 30, 52, 55 n. 12, 56 n. 34, 86 n. 1, 92, 103 n. 49, 106, 107, 125 n. 16, 127 n. 43, 130, 141, 146, 150 n. 40, 151 n. 57, 153, 154, 160, 163, 174, 176, 177, 180–184, 253 n. 33,

Cascando, 30, 153, 158, 161, 173

Company, 33 n. 1, 45, 46, 56 n. 32, n. 35, n. 36, 63, 73 n. 10, 117, 153, 172 n. 54, 189 n. 7

'Dante and the Lobster', 108, 124 n. 11

'Dante…Bruno.Vico..Joyce', 41, 50, 55 n. 17, 64, 77, 93, 94, 100 n. 18, 101 n. 23, n. 24, 102 n. 30, 108, 115, 124 n. 7, 149 n. 6, 150 n. 30, 264, 274 n. 3, 277 n. 55

Disjecta, 33 n. 3, 34 n. 20, 43, 55 n. 15, n. 17, n. 20, 56 n. 29, 57 n. 50, 73 n. 21, 80, 85, 86 n. 5, 87 n. 29, 97, 99 n. 11, 100 n. 18, n. 19, 101 n. 23, 124 n. 5, n. 7, 128 n. 60, 149 n. 6, n. 7, 150 n. 30, n. 33, 151 n. 56, 161, 212, 232 n. 30, 233 n. 42, 243, 251 n. 12, 251 n. 13, 252 n. 17, 253 n. 36, 254 n. 62, 274 n. 3, n. 10, 277 n. 55, 278 n. 74, n. 82, 279 n. 88

Dream of Fair to Middling Women, 34 n. 23, 55 n. 2, 56 n. 24, 63, 78, 84, 107, 108, 110–112, 117, 121, 124 n. 4, 125 n. 20, 126 n. 30, 127 n. 52, 191, 212, 217, 223, 241, 264, 265, 277 n. 53, n. 62

Index 305

Echo's Bones and Other Precipitates, 237

Eleutheria, 34 n. 23, 157

Embers, 30, 36 n. 44, 153, 158, 165, 169 n. 3, n. 6, 173, 182, 243, 253 n. 38

Endgame, 16, 30, 34 n. 23, 89, 92, 95, 100 n. 19, 102 n. 33, 106, 118, 127 n. 42, n. 54, 132, 137, 153, 160, 169 n. 6, 181, 183, 193, 201, 207 n. 6

Film, 92, 100 n. 19

Fizzles, 111, 183

'For to End Yet Again', 123, 153, 159, 183, 190 n. 50

'From An Abandoned Work', 153, 162, 167, 172 n. 61, n. 63, 175, 178, 181, 186, 189 n. 12, 245, 248–250, 254 n. 56, n. 61

'Gnome', 135, 141, 150 n. 22, 211, 212, 230 n. 2, 235

How It Is/Comment c'est, 15, 30, 90, 93, 99 n. 6, n. 7, n. 9, 100 n. 19, 107, 166, 174, 183, 190 n. 49

Human Wishes, 85, 92, 100 n. 19

'Humanistic Quietism', 107, 124 n. 5, 237, 251 n. 12

Ill Seen Ill Said, 56 n. 32, 117, 122, 128 n. 68, 161, 171 n. 35, 214, 231 n. 16

'Imagination Dead Imagine', 153

Krapp's Last Tape, 22, 34 n. 16, n. 23, 117, 127 n. 51, 162, 178, 182, 237, 258

'The Two Needs' / *'Les Deux Besoins'*, 33 n. 3, 76

'Lessness', 47, 48, 57 n. 40, n. 43, 153, 163

Malone Dies, 15, 55 n. 12, 86 n. 1, 95, 97, 102 n. 32, 103 n. 47, n. 49, 125 n. 16, 150 n. 40, 153, 157, 160, 173–182, 184, 186, 187, 190, 253 n. 33

Mercier and Camier, 59, 71, 72, 73 n. 2, 74 n. 35, 137, 141, 150 n. 28, n. 39, 157, 193, 207 n. 7, 243, 253 n. 37

Molloy, 15, 40, 55 n. 12, 56 n. 30, 86 n. 1, 89, 92, 100 n. 19, 103 n. 44, n. 49, 109, 125 n. 16, 130, 141, 147, 150 n. 40, 151 n. 57, 153, 157, 160, 162, 167, 172 n. 61, 173–182, 184, 186, 188, 189 n. 12, n. 23, 190 n. 34, n. 52, 201, 205, 206, 207 n. 7, 209 n. 56, 242, 243, 245, 253 n. 33, 258

More Pricks Than Kicks, 23, 24, 29, 35 n. 29, 37 n. 51, 50, 55 n. 2, n. 4, n. 19, 57 n. 48, 78, 84, 107, 108, 124 n. 11, 191, 203, 204, 209 n. 40, n. 41, n. 44, 223, 235, 251 n. 2

Murphy, 14, 24, 35 n. 32, 39–41, 43, 49, 50, 52, 55 n. 1, n. 4, n. 7, n. 13, n. 19, 56 n. 24, 57 n. 45, 66–68, 73 n. 14, 74 n. 23, 80, 81, 83, 84, 92, 96, 97, 99 n. 11, 100 n. 17, n. 19, 103 n. 47, 113, 117, 120, 126 n. 33, 130, 134–136, 138–145, 149 n. 7, 150 n. 24, n. 30, n. 45, n. 46, 151 n. 52, 182, 188, 191, 200, 201, 204, 207 n. 3, 208 n. 34, 209 n. 46, n. 50, 212, 215, 217, 223, 224, 229, 231 n. 21, 232 n. 29, 233 n. 47, 237, 239, 241–243, 245, 246, 248, 250, 252 n. 20, n. 21, 253 n. 27, n. 28, 264, 266–268, 270, 277 n. 53, 278 n. 69, n. 71, 279 n. 85

'Ping', 42, 43

Play, 30, 153, 161, 165, 169 n. 6, 183

Proust, 43, 56 n. 28, 57 n. 44, 71, 74 n. 35, 78, 92, 100 n. 18, 109, 110, 113–119, 125 n. 16, 126 n. 37, n. 38, 127 n. 45, 131, 217, 232 n. 28, 260, 264, 265, 276 n. 40, 277 n. 58, 278 n. 75

'Serena I', 92, 125 n. 28, 134, 149 n. 20, 214, 230 n. 15

'Recent Irish Poetry', 237, 252 n. 14, 256, 267, 274 n. 10, 278 n. 74

Rough for Radio I, 30, 153, 158, 162, 173

Rough for Radio II, 30, 64, 67, 74 n. 22, 92, 100 n. 19, 153, 158, 161–163, 173

Texts for Nothing, 45, 92, 99 n. 11, 100 n. 19, 121, 153, 157, 171 n. 27, 183, 240

'The End', 92, 100 n. 19, 242, 246, 253 n. 32

The Old Tune, 30, 153, 158, 173

Three Dialogues with Georges Duthuit, 138, 150 n. 33, 238, 250, 252 n. 17, 254 n. 62

The Unnamable, 15, 36 n. 43, 55 n. 12, 56 n. 34, 85, 86 n. 1, 88 n. 38, 99 n. 3, 103 n. 49, 115, 125 n. 16, 127 n. 43, n. 53, 141, 150 n. 40, 153, 157, 158, 160, 173–175, 177, 181, 182, 184, 188, 190 n. 40, n. 42, 253 n. 33, 261

Watt, 14, 15, 20, 24, 29, 31, 35 n. 32, 37 n. 56, 46, 48, 51, 52, 57 n. 51, 61, 66, 67, 74 n. 22, 83, 92, 98, 99 n. 10, 100 n. 19, 103 n. 48, 107, 117, 120, 121, 126 n. 40, 127 n. 42, 128 n. 62, n. 64, 129, 134, 141, 146, 149 n. 1, n. 39, n. 41, 151 n. 54, 153, 157, 182, 204, 205, 209 n. 53, 215, 219, 220, 229, 231 n. 19, n. 20, 232 n. 26, n. 34–n. 36, 234 n. 55, 243, 245–249, 253 n. 46, n. 47, n. 50, n. 52, 255, 256–259, 266, 271–273, 274 n. 2, n. 4, n. 6, n. 11, n. 13, n. 15, 275 n. 20, n. 22, n. 23, 277 n. 68, 278 n. 78, 279 n. 97, n. 100

Whoroscope, 29, 80, 97, 100 n. 18, 103 n. 45, 125 n. 18, 134, 136, 142, 150 n. 26, 241, 264

Words and Music, 30, 153, 155, 158, 161, 163, 164, 169 n. 6, 173

Worstword Ho, 19, 33 n. 1, 56 n. 32, 70, 241

'Yellow', 36 n. 35, 50, 235, 237, 251 n. 2

Ben-Zvi, Linda, 62–67, 73 n. 10, n. 12, n. 13

Berkeley, George, 191

Badiou, Alain, 92, 95, 102 n. 34, 131, 132, 209 n. 49

Beiser, Frederick C., 197, 207 n. 13, 208 n. 18, n. 20, 231 n. 24

Bignell, Jonathan, 170 n. 8

Bion, Wilfred, 67, 69, 81, 130, 212, 235

Blanchot, Maurice, 89, 95, 99 n. 2

Bowles, Patrick, 161, 169 n. 6, 180, 184, 186, 190 n. 34

Brater, Enoch, 9, 229, 234 n. 55

Bruno, Giordano, 92, 264

Bray, Barbara, 86 n. 6, 154, 162, 169 n. 6, 170 n. 7, 181, 190 n. 41

Bryden, Mary, 9, 150 n. 46, 161, 171 n. 37

Burnet, John, 79, 133–135, 191, 192, 200, 202, 208 n. 32, 213–215

    Greek Philosophy, 79, 133, 134, 191, 213, 215

Burton, Robert, 78, 111, 112, 116, 118, 125 n. 22, n. 23, 126 n. 29, n. 30

    Anatomy of Melancholy, 78, 111, 125 n. 22, 126 n. 30

Büttner, Gottfried, 74 n. 22, 114, 118, 127 n. 42

Calder, John, 34 n. 20, 55 n. 12, 56 n. 24, 56 n. 32, n. 36, 73 n. 14, n. 17, 74 n. 23, n. 31, 76, 77, 86 n. 7, 99 n. 4, n. 7, 100 n. 19, 109, 124 n. 11, 125 n. 18, 128 n. 68, 131, 132, 149 n. 9, n. 20, 150 n. 24, n. 28, 164, 181, 190 n. 38, n. 49, 207 n. 7, 251 n. 2, 252 n. 20, 253 n. 33, n. 37, n. 46

Campbell, Julie, 9, 157, 158, 170 n. 14, n. 15, n. 18, 175, 189 n. 11

Camus, Albert, 257

Cartesian philosophy, 97

Index 307

Cassirer, Ernst, 65, 73 n. 16, 82, 263, 270, 276

    Kant's Life and Thought, 82, 270

Cézanne, Paul, 238

Cixous, Hélène, 95, 102 n. 34

Coffey, Brian, 73 n. 21, 101 n. 21, 107, 124 n. 6, 224, 267

Cohn, Ruby, 33 n. 3, 34 n. 20, 55 n. 15, 73 n. 21, 86 n. 5, 96, 99 n. 6, n. 11, 100 n. 19, 102 n. 39, 124 n. 5, 127 n. 57, 149 n. 7, 232 n. 30, 251 n. 12, 274 n. 3

cosmology, 135

Croce, Benedetto, 93, 94, 101 n. 22, n. 25, 102 n. 31

    La Filosofia di Giambattista Vico, 93, 101 n. 25, n. 29

d'Aubarède, Gabriel, 55 n. 18, 56 n. 30, 86 n. 2, 89, 99 n. 5, 182

D'Annunzio, Gabriele, 191, 213

Dante Alighieri, 22, 108, 109, 112, 124 n. 8, 144, 191, 213, 216, 241, 243, 252 n. 21

    The Divine Comedy, 108, 124 n. 8, 241

de Gaultier, Jules, 79, 82, 87 n. 28, 265, 271, 277 n. 64, 279 n- 87,

    From Kant to Nietzsche, 79, 87 n. 28, 265, 266, 277 n. 64, 279 n. 87

Deleuze, Gilles, 92, 95, 100 n. 17, 102 n. 34

de Molinos, Miguel, 112

Democritus, 50, 91, 97, 99 n. 11, 111, 112, 136, 137, 144, 235, 248

Derrida, Jacques, 45, 92, 95, 102 n. 36, 260

Descartes, René, 15, 29, 55 n. 19, 78, 80, 81, 90, 92, 96, 97, 99 n. 10, 103 n. 45, 126 n. 40, 133, 136, 150 n. 26, 214, 227, 231 n. 17, 232 n. 26, 240, 241, 244, 251 n. 6, 259, 264, 268, 269, 275 n. 32, n. 36, n. 38

Dilks, Steven, 163, 165, 171 n. 46

Dürer, Albrecht, 111, 112, 118, 125 n. 24, 127 n. 54, 272

Duthuit, Georges, 48, 49, 138, 139, 150 n. 33, 235, 237, 238, 250, 251 n. 1, 252 n. 16, n. 17, 254 n. 62, 267

    Three Dialogues with Georges Duthuit, 138, 150 n. 33, 238, 250, 252 n. 17, 254

Eisenstein, Sergei, 212

Epicurus, 132

Erdmann, Johann Eduard, 215, 230 n. 15

Empson, William, 95

Esslin, Martin, 41, 42, 56 n. 21, n. 23, 96, 100 n. 15, 102 n. 39, 131, 154, 156, 159, 161–163, 170 n. 14, 171 n. 27, n. 34, n. 41, n. 43, n. 44, 274 n. 2

existentialism, 17, 52, 89, 96, 97, 262

Feldman, Morton, 161

Fifield, Peter, 10, 11, 35 n. 31, 213, 230 n. 11, n. 15

Fletcher, John, 34 n. 17, 96, 102 n. 39, 169 n. 6, 169 n. 6, 170 n. 7, 231 n. 17

Foucault, Michel, 92, 131

Freud, Sigmund, 40, 138–140, 145, 150 n. 37, 240

    The New Introductory Lectures on Psycho-Analysis, 140

Frye, Northrop, 95

Geulincx, Arnold, 12, 14, 16, 31, 37 n. 55, 80–82, 84, 91, 92, 94, 99 n. 11, 100 n. 19, 134, 149 n. 16, 191, 193, 204, 212, 216, 235–237, 239–250, 251 n. 6, n. 7, 252 n. 19, n. 21–n. 23, 253 n. 28, n. 31, n. 34, n. 41, n. 54, 254 n. 60, 278 n. 78

    Ethics, 12, 31, 80, 82, 87 n. 22, 193, 235–237, 239–245, 247, 248, 250, 252 n. 21, 253 n. 30, n. 31, n. 34, n. 41, n. 51, n 54, n. 60, 278 n. 78

    ineffability, 63, 71, 97, 107, 222, 240, 246, 247, 249, 250, 273

    Metaphysics, 82, 239–241, 252 n. 22, n. 23, 278 n. 78

    Questions Concerning Disputations, 82, 239

gnosticism, 135

Habermas, Jürgen, 92, 131

Heimsoeth, Heinz, 228, 233 n. 53, n. 54, 271, 276 n. 52

Herren, Graley, 129, 130, 132, 268

Hesla, David, 96, 102 n. 38

Hill, Leslie, 44, 56 n. 33, 102 n. 36, 103 n. 44

Hoefer, Jacqueline, 257, 274 n. 2, 275 n. 23

Husserl, Edmund, 12, 14, 16, 17, 27, 31, 52–54, 57 n. 58, n. 59, 84, 85, 208 n. 16, 255–263, 266, 268, 271–273, 275 n. 29–n. 36, n. 38, 276 n. 39, n. 43, n. 48, n. 52, 277 n. 65

    phenomenology, 27, 31, 52–54, 57 n. 57, 84, 95, 158, 256, 258–263, 266, 269, 272, 273

Inge, W.R., 78, 112, 113, 126 n. 32

    Christian Mysticism, 78, 112, 126 n. 32

Iser, Wolfgang, 55 n. 6, 92, 95, 100 n. 16

Jewinski, Ed, 44–46, 56 n. 35

Johnson, Samuel, 92

Jones, Ernest, 126 n. 33, 140, 145

    Papers on Psychoanalysis, 140, 145

Jouve, Pierre-Jean, 108

Joyce, James, 25, 29, 31, 33 n. 2, 43, 50, 62, 64–66, 73 n. 15, 77–79, 92, 93, 101 n. 21–n. 23, 108, 112, 125 n. 26, 128 n. 67, 135, 146, 159, 203, 209 n. 39, 222, 223, 237, 243, 255, 264, 265, 270

Kant, Immanuel, 29, 30, 65, 66, 73 n. 16, 79–83, 87 n. 28, 92, 100 n. 19, 138–140, 150 n. 37, 195, 197, 198, 207 n. 13, 208 n. 16, n. 18–n. 21, 216, 217, 225, 227, 228, 231 n. 22–n. 24, 259, 263, 265–272, 276 n. 52, 277 n. 64, n. 66, 278 n. 84, 279 n. 87

Keats, John, 108, 109, 111, 116, 118, 124 n. 10, 125 n. 12

Kenner, Hugh, 52, 55 n. 5, 96

Kern, Edith, 102 n. 41, 257, 262, 275 n. 21, n. 24, 276 n. 51

Knowlson, James, 10, 13, 22, 24, 34 n. 13, n. 16, n. 23, 35 n. 24, n. 25, n. 27, n. 28, n. 31, 55 n. 16, 62, 63, 73 n. 8, 74 n. 25, n. 34, 85, 88 n. 37, 94, 97, 101 n. 21, n. 27, 103 n. 43, n. 46, 106, 108, 124 n. 2, n. 9, 125 n. 18, 127 n. 51, 129, 130, 134, 139, 149 n. 8, n. 17, 150 n. 30, n. 35, 153, 157, 159, 169 n. 2, n. 5, 170 n. 23, 171 n. 28, 173, 178, 189 n. 4, n. 24, 190 n. 36, 208 n. 27,

Index 309

212, 217, 230 n. 8, 232 n. 25, 238, 251 n. 8, 252 n. 15, n. 24, 257, 258, 266, 275 n. 25, n. 27, 277 n. 54, 278 n. 76, n. 79

Land, J.P.N., 80, 236, 239, 251 n. 7

   Arnoldi Geulincx Anverpiensis Opera Philosophica, 236

Lane, Richard, 69, 70, 73 n. 9, 74 n. 29, 76, 100 n. 17, 124 n. 8, 131, 149 n. 10

   Beckett and Philosophy, 69–71, 73 n. 9, 74 n. 29, 92, 100 n. 17, 131, 149 n. 10

Leibniz, Gottfried W., 80, 81, 92, 100 n. 19, 114, 118, 144–146, 150 n. 48, 151 n. 52, 191, 212, 236, 269

   Monadology, 144, 150 n. 48

Leopardi, Giacomo, 109–111, 116, 118, 125 n. 13, n. 16

Locatelli, Carla, 44, 52, 57 n. 55, 262, 276 n. 49

Lodge, David, 42, 43, 56 n. 26, 95, 132

Lukács, Georg, 89

MacGowran, Jack, 153, 161, 164

Magee, Patrick, 154, 159–162, 169 n. 6, 177–180, 184, 186

Marcel, Gabriel, 89, 95

Mauriac, Claude, 89, 95, 99 n. 2

Mauthner, Fritz, 16, 30, 31, 62–67, 71, 73 n. 10, n. 11, n. 15, n. 16, n. 19–n. 21, 74 n. 22, 76, 77, 82, 85, 92, 97, 100 n. 19, 134, 149 n. 16, 191, 213, 222, 226, 227, 229, 233 n. 51–n. 53, 246, 269–271, 278 n. 81, n. 83, n. 84

   Beiträge zu einer Kritik der Sprache, 62, 134, 226, 233 n. 52, n. 53, 270, 278 n. 84

MacGreevy, Thomas, 65, 73 n. 18, 78, 80, 81, 83, 87 n. 23, 101 n. 28, 105–108, 111, 112, 116, 124 n. 1, n. 4, n. 6, 125 n. 28, 126 n. 37, 127 n. 46, n. 47, 134, 139, 157, 161, 207 n. 5, 209 n. 42, n. 43, 236–238, 241, 252 n. 15, n. 17, n. 18, n. 24, 253 n. 25, 256, 274 n. 9

Marc, Franz, 268

Maude, Ulrika, 12, 36 n. 35, 37 n. 48, 102 n. 36, 158, 162, 165, 171 n. 26, n. 40, n. 53

McWhinnie, Donald, 99 n. 6, 153, 155, 156, 158, 160, 162, 164, 169 n. 2, 170 n. 16, n. 25, 171 n. 29, n. 31, n. 33, n. 38, n. 39, 173, 176–182, 184, 186, 189 n. 14–n. 18, n. 20–n. 22, n. 25, n. 27–n. 32, 190 n. 35, n. 37–n. 40

mediaeval philosophy, 220, 222, 227, 229, 230 n. 12

Melissus, 132

Mercier, Vivian, 166, 172 n. 59

Mihalovici, Marcel, 171 n. 37, 161

Montague, John, 109, 125 n. 12

Murphy, P.J., 10, 49, 50, 52, 57 n. 45, 100 n. 17

Nadeau, Maurice, 89, 99 n. 2

Natanson, Maurice, 261, 276 n. 46

neo-Kantianism, 197, 207 n. 13, 208 n. 16, n. 18–n. 21, 216, 231 n. 23, n. 24

nihilism, 50, 89, 100 n. 17, 114, 131

nominalism, 9, 16, 30, 63, 73 n. 21, 77, 97, 199, 201, 216–227, 229, 232 n. 33, n. 37, 233 n. 49, n. 51

O'Hara, J.D., 68, 74 n. 26, 125 n. 16, 126 n. 41, 130, 277 n. 58

occasionalism, 80, 136, 236, 241, 251 n. 6

phenomenology, 11, 12, 14, 16, 27, 28, 31, 36 n. 35, 37 n. 48, 39, 52–54, 57 n. 57, n. 58, 84, 95, 102 n. 36, 158, 256, 258–263, 266, 269, 272, 273, 275 n. 29, n. 31, 276 n. 46, n. 47

Pickup, Ronald, 161

Pilling, John, 10, 11, 23, 34 n. 23, 35 n. 28–n. 30, 37 n. 51, 63–66, 73 n. 16, n. 17, n. 20, 78, 82, 86 n. 5, n. 13, 87 n. 27, n. 31, 100 n. 17, n. 19, 101 n. 23, n. 28, 102 n. 30, 110, 112, 124 n. 1, n. 4, 125 n. 19, 126 n. 29, n. 31, n. 37, 127 n. 45, 130, 142, 149 n. 4, n. 19, 150 n. 37, n. 42, n. 46, 170 n. 19, 171 n. 42, 189 n. 2, 190 n. 46, 214, 230 n. 15, 252 n. 21, 254 n. 55, 270, 274 n. 1, 277 n. 53, n. 58, n. 61, 278 n. 69, n. 83, 279 n. 86, n. 90

  Beckett's Dream Notebook, 34 n. 23, 78, 86 n. 13, 101 n. 28, 110–112, 124 n. 1, n. 4, 125 n. 19, 126 n. 29, n. 31, 252 n. 21, 277 n. 53, n. 61

Pinget, Robert, 30, 153, 173

  La Manivelle, 158, 173

Pinter, Harold, 156, 163, 276 n. 48

Popper, Karl, 11, 13, 19–21, 23, 26, 28, 31, 33 n. 1, n. 4–n. 6, n. 9, 59–62, 64, 66, 67, 69, 70, 72, 73 n. 1, n. 3, n. 4, n. 30, 75, 86 n. 4, 251 n. 5

  Conjectures and Refutations, 20, 33 n. 1, n. 3, n. 4, n. 6, n. 9, 61, 73 n. 1

  The Logic of Scientific Discovery, 60, 61, 73 n. 3, 74 n. 30

  falsification, 11, 15, 16, 19–22, 24–29, 31, 32, 33 n. 6, 59, 61, 62, 69–71, 75, 76

post-structuralism, 17, 27, 47, 49, 52, 60, 92, 102 n. 36, 261

Presocratics, 144, 211, 214

Proust, Marcel, 108, 114, 264

  Remembrance of Things Past, 114, 264

Protagoras, 132, 137, 192–194, 200, 201, 205

psychology, 13, 19, 23, 67, 68, 84, 129, 130, 140, 145, 146, 191, 196, 198, 201, 213, 240, 258, 266, 272

psychoanalysis, 20, 67, 81, 130, 139, 140, 146

Pythagoras, 39, 132

quietism, 14, 16, 37 n. 50, 105–107, 109–113, 116–119, 121–123, 143, 144, 236, 237, 239, 251 n. 10

Robertson, John G., 79, 127 n. 54

  A History of German Literature, 79

Romains, Jules, 108

Rank, Otto, 139, 195

  The Trauma of Birth, 139, 140

Ricouer, Paul, 260, 275 n. 35

Rosset, Barney, 157, 160, 161, 170 n. 22, 180

Sartre, Jean-Paul, 12, 14–16, 28, 31, 75, 83–85, 87 n. 32, 88 n. 34, n. 35, 89, 90, 97, 99 n. 2, 255–258, 261, 262, 266, 271–273, 274 n. 7, n. 12, n. 13, n. 16, 276 n. 41, n. 42, 279 n. 89, n. 92, n. 99

  La Nauseé, 14, 256, 261

Schopenhauer, Arthur, 13, 29, 37 n. 50, 76, 78, 86 n. 6, n. 12, 92, 96, 99 n. 10, 107, 109, 113–123, 125 n. 16, 126 n. 34, n. 38–n. 41, 127 n. 42, n. 44, n. 48, n. 55, 128 n. 61, n. 63, n. 67, 222, 227, 232 n. 26, 233 n. 44, n. 45, 237, 260, 263, 265, 266, 277 n. 58, n. 59

    Pessimism, 114, 119, 122, 126 n. 41

    on quietism, 113, 116, 118, 119, 121

    'veil of Maya', 29, 115–122, 128 n. 67, 222, 233 n. 44, 265, 266, 277 n. 58

    The World as Will and Representation, 78, 86 n. 12, 113, 118, 119, 123, 126 n. 34, n. 39, 127 n. 44, n. 45, n. 55, n. 57, 128 n. 61, n. 63, 265, 277 n. 58, n. 59

Schneider, Alan, 16, 34 n. 23, 55 n. 20, 132, 136, 149 n. 11, 172 n. 56, 173, 189 n. 1, 194, 207 n. 8, 214, 230 n. 14,

Smith, Frederik, 128, 149 n. 14

Sophists, 132, 136, 147, 192–194, 201, 202, 226

Spinoza, Baruch, 16, 81, 82, 87 n. 22–n. 24, 94, 136, 224, 269

St Augustine, 22, 78, 101 n. 28, 110, 216

Stekel, Wilhelm, 140

    Psychoanalysis and Suggestion Therapy, 140

    Practice and Theory of Individual Psychology, 140

Stephen, Karin, 140

    The Wish to Fall Ill, 140

Stewart, Paul, 10, 157, 170 n. 21

Szabó, Zoltán, 219, 221, 232 n. 33

Tajiri, Yoshiki, 10, 162, 171 n. 40

terminism, 222, 226, 227

Thales of Miletus, 92, 214

Thomas, Dylan, 40, 156

Tonning, Erik, 9, 11, 13, 73 n. 19, 78, 80, 81, 86 n. 13, n. 19, 87 n. 21, n. 23, 165, 172 n. 55, 266, 277 n. 58, n. 63, n. 77

    Samuel Beckett's Abstract Drama, 78, 86 n. 13, n. 19, 87 n. 21, n. 23, 165, 172 n. 55, 277 n. 58, n. 63, 278 n. 77

Tophoven, Elmar, 161

Ueberweg, Friedrich, 191, 192, 202, 213

    History of Philosophy: From Thales to the Present Time, 213

Uhlmann, Anthony, 10, 35 n. 24, 100 n. 15–n. 17, 102 n. 36, 171 n. 26, 239, 243, 244, 248, 249, 252 n. 21, 253 n. 35, n. 39, 278 n. 83

van Hulle, Dirk, 10, 11, 26, 33 n. 1, n. 2, 35 n. 24, 36 n. 43, 37 n. 54, 64–66, 73 n. 15, 78, 112, 125 n. 26, 128 n. 67, 150 n. 46, 226, 252 n. 21

Vico, Giambattista, 50, 77, 92–94, 101 n. 22, n. 23, n. 25, n. 29, 102 n. 30, n. 31, 264

    The New Science, 94, 101 n. 29

Walker, Roy, 178, 189 n. 26

Wilcher, Robert, 165, 172 n. 54, 174, 189 n. 7,

Wilenski, R.H., 79

   An Introduction to Dutch Art, 79

William of Occam, 222, 225, 226

Williams, Raymond, 95

Wilson, Martin, 10, 240, 242, 252 n. 21, n. 22

   Arnold Geulincx Ethics, 240, 252 n. 21, 253 n. 31, n. 34, n. 41, n. 54, 254 n. 60

Windelband, Wilhelm, 9, 11, 12, 15, 16, 30, 79, 80, 81, 86 n. 15, n. 16, n. 18, 91, 100 n. 14, 133, 134–136, 144, 145, 150 n. 23, n. 25, n. 49, 151 n. 52, 191–205, 207 n. 3, n. 4, n. 9, n. 10, n. 12, n. 14, 208 n. 16, n. 17, n. 19, n. 21–n. 23, n. 26, n. 28, n. 29, n. 33, n. 34, n. 37, 211–222, 225, 227–229, 230 n. 4, n. 12, n. 18, n. 21, n. 22, 232 n. 31, n. 32, n. 39, 233 n. 51, n. 53, n. 54, 236, 263, 266, 267, 271, 276 n. 52, 277 n. 66, 278 n. 70, n. 72

   A History of Philosophy, 30, 79, 86 n. 15, n. 16, n. 18, 100 n. 14, 133, 135, 150 n. 23, n. 25, n. 49, 151 n. 52, 191, 192, 194–196, 198–200, 202, 205, 206, 207 n. 3, n. 4, n. 9, n. 10, 208 n. 23, n. 26, n. 28, n. 29, n. 34, n. 37, 211–213, 215–218, 220–222, 225, 228, 230 n. 4, 231 n. 18, 232 n. 32, n. 39, 233 n. 40, n. 41, n. 43, n. 46, 236, 266, 277 n. 66, 278 n. 70, n. 72

Woodworth, Robert S., 67, 74 n. 23, 79, 140

   Contemporary Schools of Psychology, 67, 74 n. 23, 79, 140

Zilliacus, Clas, 153, 157, 158, 160, 161, 169 n. 3, n. 4, 171 n. 30, n. 32, 174, 189 n. 9, n. 33

   Beckett and Broadcasting, 153, 157, 169 n. 3, n. 4, 171 n. 30, n. 32, 174, 189 n. 9, n. 33

Žižek, Slavoj, 95, 102 n. 34

Zeno, 92, 100 n. 19, 132, 137, 138, 193, 194

***ibidem*-**Verlag

Melchiorstr. 15

D-70439 Stuttgart

info@ibidem-verlag.de

www.ibidem-verlag.de
www.ibidem.eu
www.edition-noema.de
www.autorenbetreuung.de